PROMISE

PROMISE

A Novel

RACHEL
ELIZA
GRIFFITHS

RANDOM HOUSE
NEW YORK

Published in the United States by Random House, an imprint and division of Penguin Random House LLC, New York.

RANDOM HOUSE and the HOUSE colophon are registered trademarks of Penguin Random House LLC.

LIBRARY OF CONGRESS CATALOGING-IN-PUBLICATION DATA
Names: Griffiths, Rachel Eliza, author.
Title: Promise: a novel / Rachel Eliza Griffiths.
Description: New York: Random House, [2023]
Identifiers: LCCN 2022032273 (print) | LCCN 2022032274 (ebook) |
ISBN 9780593241929 (hardback; acid-free paper) |
ISBN 9780593241936 (ebook)
Subjects: LCGFT: Novels.
Classification: LCC PS3607.R5494 P76 2023 (print) |
LCC PS3607.R5494 (ebook) | DDC 813/.6—dc23/eng/20220707
LC record available at https://lccn.loc.gov/2022032273
LC ebook record available at https://lccn.loc.gov/2022032274

Printed in Canada on acid-free paper

randomhousebooks.com

2 4 6 8 9 7 5 3 1

First Edition

Frontispiece art: Adobe Stock/konoplizkaya

Book design by Susan Turner

For my parents

Michele Antoinette Pray-Griffiths

Norman Dwight Griffiths

"How, then, could I not answer her life
with mine, she who saved me with hers?"
—Natasha Trethewey

"Real gods require blood."
—Zora Neale Hurston

ONE

I

THE DAY BEFORE OUR FIRST DAY OF SCHOOL ALWAYS SIGNALED THE END of the time Ezra and I loved most. Not time like the clocks that ticked and rang their alarms every morning; we knew *that* time didn't really begin or end. What we meant by time was happiness, a careless joy that sprawled its warm, sun-stained arms through our days and dreams for eight glorious weeks until our teachers arrived back in our lives, and our parents remembered their rules about shoes, bathing, vocabulary quizzes, and home training.

More than anything, we prayed that the air would remain mild for as long as possible, mid-October even, so that we could retain some of our summer independence, free to roam the land we knew and loved. We weren't yet grown, but even the adults could pinpoint when time would tell us we would no longer be young.

We mourned summertime's ending and made predictions about autumn and ourselves. Mostly we repeated all the different ways that summer was more honest than the rest of the year. It was the only time we could wear shorts and cropped tops with little comment from our mother. Ezra and I were allowed to walk nearly anywhere we wanted—in the other seasons, we needed permission even to walk to the village docks. And the eating! How we could eat! Mama loosened her apron strings about salt and sugar. Each day, it felt like we were eating from the menu of our dreams—fresh corn, ice cream, sliced tomatoes with coarse salt and pepper, chilled lobster, root beer floats, watermelon, oysters, crab and shrimp salads, fried chicken, homemade lemon or raspberry sorbet, grilled peaches, potato salad, and red ice pops.

In the summer, the wildflowers returned, even in the village square. Some dead local official once believed the square, arranged around a small pond with a handful of benches, was a civil idea. Indeed, it would have been charming except there was the sea. Steps away from the square, down the narrow central passage of our village, the main street opened into a slender, shining pier where everything happened.

God faced the water.

A lone church, St. Mary Star of the Sea, stood high enough to tempt staffs of lightning that flashed during wonderful summer heat storms. Its coarse doors were carved with fishes, dolphins, angels, pilgrims, and afflicted saints. The sea mocked the salt-stained bells that rang each hour, while villagers prayed against the clapping of waves.

The church kept a well-tended public garden with flecked benches and a stone statue of the Virgin that was painted each year after winter ended. Winters pulled the paint away from the Madonna's profile, leaving a flaked heap of aging stone that resembled something primitive. The villagers never thought to cover the statue when the ice and snow began. Instead, they seemed to feel an odd pride at what the elements had done to the mother of God.

Our mother and father had little faith when it came to the village. We'd never prayed or celebrated holidays at St. Mary Star of the Sea. For years, Mama and Daddy had repeated that they'd only settled in Salt Point, Maine, because of my father's good job. He was a teacher. Our parents had been able to purchase a few acres that nobody else wanted, set farther inland, away from the sea.

But I knew there were other reasons too. After my older sister

Ezra's birth, my parents wanted to leave Damascus for a place that knew nothing of the Kindred tragedy.

In Salt Point, no one would remind my father of his grandparents' ambitions. They would not bother to question the loss of Daddy's left arm, because there were fishermen in the village who were also missing legs, arms, faith, and eyes. My father's headstrong youth somewhere in the South would be of no interest to anyone in New England, nor would they connect it to his lack of capacity for rage or trouble of any kind.

My father believed that grace and dignity must be earned by the life a man lived. He scorned the idea of an unknown father whose face he had never glimpsed except in fire and brimstone. Perhaps my father didn't know how to look for such a father since he'd never met his own. Daddy had to recognize his own face. Still, he couldn't make up his mind about heaven or resurrections. We lived in a place where our faces wouldn't have been welcomed by the villagers at Mass on Sunday mornings.

There were whole years when my father refused to kneel to a god who'd taken his arm and the life of his young brother, whom he refused to speak about. We'd only heard our uncle's name spoken when my father shouted himself awake from his nightmares. Our mother said Daddy blamed himself, even though anyone would've chalked up the tragedy to foolishness. The only place my father was not fearful was inside the pages of the books he loved and taught.

Beyond the church, the village consisted of incomplete, asymmetric rows of houses, most of which shared small yards filled with wild chickens, iridescent cocks, goats tied to posts, sagging clotheslines, and stingy vegetable patches.

At the farthest end of the main street, away from St. Mary Star of the Sea, was another cluster of essential buildings—the bar, the beauty parlor, and a small plaza of rented offices. These blanched buildings faced a lot that was transformed into a fresh air market on Saturdays. During the summers, the lot was sometimes used for carnivals, antiques fairs, and a traveling circus that featured a marvelous freak show. When the lot wasn't being rented, it was a place where teenagers raced cars and scowled, aware that more than likely they'd all eventually marry one another.

Beyond the empty lot, the land curved like a bony finger towards the sea. This wild ground was ash and gravel. Away from the main street and church, it was where villagers yielded their true selves to the raw air. It was the ideal place for picnics, lovers, children's games, arguments, and solitary hours of determined fishing and drinking. At the very end of the point was a squat, cement lighthouse that no longer functioned. Rheumatic trees, blown backwards by sea winds, marked the length of the bluffs. The physical meanness of the land gave no warning of its steep cliffs, which was something my parents were always nervous about.

We lived where the land was only slightly softer but more abandoned. Nestled in the woods that led up towards the highest bluffs, our home on Clove Road was nearly an anomaly with its pond and sloping curves. Beyond our house, higher still, was the stingy campus of our school, where my father taught and where Ezra and I went, which was founded by a man named Benedict Hobart.

Previous incarnations of this property included an opulent private residence, a monastery, a convent, an asylum, an orphanage, and a soldiers' hospital. All of the village children who could be spared from domestic work attended for free.

. . .

WHEN MY FATHER WAS HIRED at Hobart, many of the villagers had objected. They disliked the idea of a Negro man living amongst their families and teaching their children. When the townspeople finally understood that my father would keep to himself, and that he would not force any integration beyond a curt nod from the wheel of his car, they let us be.

By 1957, our family was one of the only two Black families that lived on the outskirts of the village. The other Black family, the Junketts, were our only true neighbors and friends.

Caesar and Irene Junkett, and their four children, Ernest, Lindy, and the twins Rosemary and Empire, had arrived in Salt Point when I was nine years old. Our families befriended each other with a southern and warm familiarity. My parents were born in Damascus, a barely incorporated community buried inside Sussex County, Delaware. The Junketts hailed from a place called Royal, nestled in deep rural Virginia. Each of these towns boasted a soulfulness that we children only understood from what was and was not said about what it meant to leave those lush, hand-carved cradles. Mr. Junkett, whom we called Mr. Caesar, had taken a job at Hobart as the chief custodian of the school. Mr. Caesar spoke often about his decision to relocate far north, explaining that it would've been unlikely for him to earn as much if he had remained, as his father had, in the South. The other issue, Mr. Caesar said, was that the northern white men he'd encountered were mostly far more agreeable than southern white men when it came to leaving him and his family to themselves.

Some villagers speculated that the hiring of my father and Mr. Junkett was related to Mr. Benedict Hobart's well-known reputation for crookedness and his shunning of unions. Because we lived in the most northern part of the country, there were no nearby organizations for Negroes to resolve issues regarding wages or labor. Had those spaces even existed, it was unlikely that my father would have joined. He tended to avoid anything that endangered his need for silence, logic, and order. It was ironic to me that he'd believed that Salt Point was a home that could provide these things for us.

As it was, my father and Mr. Caesar took care to stay away from anything that could attract attention. When he was angry, Mr. Caesar called Salt Point a sundown town, and though I never asked any of the adults what that was, I knew that it wasn't good. The tendency for individuals to enforce their own sense of justice menaced the

most innocent misunderstandings, helped along by the visible am-
munition that was part of ordinary life. Mr. Caesar laughed a boom-
ing laugh about the way the fishermen in our village carried a fishing
rod in one hand and a shotgun in the other. And Miss Irene, Mr.
Caesar's wife, rolled her eyes at the village women who carried their
grandmothers' guns to the bakery; then she spoke to us kids of how
white people needed to constantly perceive themselves to be under
threat in order to value their lives. *Ain't nothing but birds and bears
and rocks up here to harm them,* she once said, sucking her teeth.
*They never got to think of what the trees must feel like down home
when our bodies be swinging from their branches.*

The people of Salt Point could indeed be fearsome about the
world beyond themselves; most of them would be born and die without ever having gone more than twenty or thirty miles from houses
that were crammed with generations of their families.

This is how things had been for a very long time in Salt Point.
But something was shifting at the end of summer 1957. As news
from other corners of America began to cover conflicts over freedom,
equality, and justice for Negroes, our presence started to agitate the
villagers more and more. At the same time, grown men began pausing silently to take in the sight of Ezra, barely fifteen, and me, thirteen, in our cutoffs. At nightfall, both Mr. Caesar and my father
made sure our families were locked inside our homes.

· · ·

SCHOOL WOULD BEGIN THE NEXT day, and my sister and I savored our
last lunch of freedom. Between bites, I noticed Ezra's eyes darting to
the clock on our kitchen wall. I knew that her secrecy had something
to do with our neighbor Ruby, her best and only friend, as it always
did. Ruby was white, but because she was poor, she was viewed on a
level not too far above our own position.

I followed Ezra into her bedroom upstairs, begging her to let me come, having no last-day-before-the-first-day-of-school adventure of my own. The plight of baby sisters all over the world.

Sighing, Ezra took my hand while leading me through the bathroom we shared back into my own bedroom.

"We're doing *some*thing," said Ez.

"Something what?"

"Come on then, Cinthy. Put a dress on and hurry up. Don't take all day to do it either." She made my name sound like a snake on her tongue, instead of how she usually said it, softly, the way Mama always said it because she'd named me after her favorite kind of flower—Hyacinth.

"It's hot. I want to wear shorts."

"Dress," said Ezra in a flat, nonnegotiable voice as she fixed her eyes at me, her fingers working through tangles to tame her hair into a single braid that twisted between the blades of her shoulders.

Sighing, Ezra plopped herself down on a faded cushion arranged on the sill in the large window of my bedroom. "Put on that dress or stay here and read one of those gigantic books you love. Don't make no difference to me."

"*Any*," I said. "*Any difference.*"

Looking out the window, I could see the shining green leaves of my beloved oak, which made my room glimmer as though we were in an underwater room with flowered wallpaper.

Across from us, there was a charred house set back from the road, its black face nestled like a rotting skull in wild grass. Growing up, we'd never had a tree house, but I thought we were luckier because we had a haunted house.

From my window, I could see white-green wings hovering above the butterfly bush that nearly obstructed the original entrance to the ruined house. The porch and front door were sooty heaps of wood and plaster where sometimes we discovered kittens or snakes, or found ourselves confronted by what we really feared—the ghost of the woman who'd purposefully set her house on fire, a mother-ghost who refused to leave the earth until she was reunited with her three daughters. The girls, trapped inside tubes of smoke, had climbed down the side of the house in their nightgowns. There was no longer a single living member of their family left to describe the tragedy, which had happened long before our arrival. In spite of us never having had anything to do with this story, the village crowned us ghosts anyway. My sister and I were spoken of as spooks, haunted nigger girls who were capable of withstanding flames, smoke, and death. These perceptions allowed the village to see right through us. We could be blamed for anything. We inherited the village's discomfort for the inexplicable. Some of the elders, who despised hearsay and embellishment, said that the girls never actually made it out of the house and had burned to their deaths. Other village rumors insisted that the girls had either fallen from the bluffs into the sea or that, lost and overwhelmed by their mother's madness, they had crawled, afire, across the narrow length of Clove Road where they had then drowned in our pond.

· · ·

THOUGH I RISKED EZRA CHANGING her mind about inviting me to go with her by doing something so babyish, I slid down our bannister to the bottom of the stairs. My sister constantly liked to remind me that when she was my age—thirteen—she hadn't been as immature. Of course, I had to remind her that the only reason I knew how to slide down the bannister the way I did was because she'd taught me. Though I was only thirteen, I was already as tall as her.

Ezra, barefooted and clutching her leather sandals against her chest, stepped lightly down the front staircase, careful to mind the places where the wood would give us away. Our back staircase led directly into the kitchen, so we couldn't take that route.

When Mama introduced us to people, strangers really because we didn't have friends in the village or elsewhere except for the Junkett family, they immediately commented on our height. "Your girls are tall," a person might say, as though they were reading a newspaper aloud and remarking that the day would be mildly sunny with a chance of showers.

My sister and I could never say from whom we had inherited our height. Unlike other people's homes, ours didn't have framed photographs of our relatives on the wall or arranged on the mantel above the fireplace. Instead of family snapshots, my father kept polished stones or bird skulls on his desk for spiritual company. Whenever our grandmother begged Mama to send pictures of us so that she could place them in her family album, Mama declined. While I liked the idea of a grandmother savoring pictures of my sister and me, I understood that her possession of us, even in photographs, was intolerable and painful for my mother to consider.

Ginny, who refused to be addressed as *Mother* or *Grandmother,* still called Mama on the phone, trying to reach her no matter how many times we'd heard Mama's quiet voice telling her to leave us alone. When Mama complained about our wild behavior to Daddy, I sometimes thought it was more about what wasn't right with her and Ginny. In fact, our disobedience had little to do with what was really wrong.

• • •

AS WE CREPT THROUGH OUR living room, we could hear Mama singing beneath a slow ballad that was playing from the radio she kept on the windowsill above the kitchen sink. I paused because I loved Sam Cooke. When he sang "You Send Me" it was like being under a spell. Following my sister's shadow, I thought of Mama in our sunny kitchen, lifting her brown arms, the apron tugging above her waist. She'd have a paring knife or wooden spoon in one hand. In the other hand a drink sweating with ice. Her fingertips would be cold from her glass, where the ice melted into whisky. When Mama was nervous, she liked to have some "medicine," as she called it, and she seemed to get nervous every day. I knew that her feud with our grandmother was some of the reason why she got sad.

Sam Cooke's voice coated our walls with honey. It also helped return Mama to a hidden closet in herself she could never reach unless she got to drinking.

But Mama wouldn't visit that private closet today. Instead, she'd sip her watery drink and switch to lemonade by the time the cooking was completed. She was making the special day-before-the-first-day-of-school dinner she'd prepared for us since we were young girls. It was a tradition that made us feel proud and loved.

This evening we'd have a pot roast with mashed potatoes and wild carrots, all seasoned with the fresh herbs—thyme, rosemary, sage, and lavender—that Mama grew and dried. We'd have her baked, homemade rolls, which were browned on the top but pillowed inside, with butter. To celebrate Daddy's first day of teaching another year, there'd be a lemon cake with lemon frosting.

Ezra twisted around at the front door and scowled. "What I'm thinking is that I better leave your slow behind right here."

I placed my finger over my smiling lips before sticking out my tongue and pushing her a little so that she was out on the porch. The door made a loud sound as I pulled it shut.

We took off running, rushing past the haunted house that did not make us afraid. Recently, Mama had asked us not to do so much racing. *Ladies take their time,* she'd say. Ez and I would look at each other, shrugging. We didn't see any ladies except for Mama and Miss Irene. We couldn't tell our mother that we'd already decided that we would never be ladies. Besides, running pleased us. Approaching the long shadows where the woods led up to the bluffs, we doubled over, laughing. Catching my breath finally, I stood straight and studied the back of the haunted house, which never looked the same because of its perpetual ruin. The ruining was what made us return to it the way we did. The roof had a gaping hole through which an entire tree was growing tall. Like us, the haunted house had a will and way of looking at itself that was unbothered by what anybody else might think.

"Whatever we do on the bluffs today is not something you need to go running around talking about either," Ezra said to me suddenly.

"Who would I tell?"

"You seem just fine when it comes to keeping your own secrets, Cinthy," my sister said. "But when it comes to *my* secrets you seem unable to control yourself."

"Well, this would be *our* secret."

Ez nodded, rolling her eyes. "Last spring, when we got our periods, Ruby and I decided we'd do this thing on the day before school. We're not changing anything now because of you."

"Ruby's coming to school tomorrow?"

"What is that supposed to mean?"

"She got ahold of some soap and water?"

"Cinthy! I wish you wouldn't talk about her like that, treating her like everyone else around here."

Sometimes my sister took on Ruby's problems as though they were her own. I had to remind Ez that the problems white girls have were not the same as the problems she and I knew. That's what Mama and Miss Irene always said.

Ruby, foolishly, believed that it went both ways. Problems, for any of us, belonged to all of us. That sounded fine and could be true, but my sister and I understood that other things were also true.

When somebody treated us like nothing, Ruby walked around dyed in our insult. When she saw us in the village, walking with our heads high the way Mama had taught us, Ruby held her head up like we did, without truly understanding the forces, and there were many, that wanted us headless, lifeless, dreamless.

When Ruby tried to take our side, I couldn't stand her. Ruby Scaggs's life held little rule, and though I thought she was sneaky, there was no real reason for her to be.

"You wearing clean underwear, Cinthy?"

Surprised, I didn't speak as I snatched my gaze away from the haunted house.

"Ez, you know Mama don't like nothing nasty."

"Mama don't like nothing . . . Jesus! I hope you don't hurt yourself thinking too hard about what Mama would do when I already told you this thing is a secret. I keep trying to tell you, Cinthy. The world *is* nasty. Miss Irene says that knowing nastiness, really knowing it, is actually wisdom."

The way Ezra sighed to herself shamed me. There was nothing quite as bad as feeling like I'd disappointed her. Except the thought that my sister might find me boring.

"Ruby is waiting in the woods for me by now," she said.

"Who cares about that white girl? Let her wait there 'til the Judgment Day," I said, putting a hand on my hip like Lindy Junkett, the elder of the Junkett girls. A hand on my hip was the closest thing I had to any authority of my own.

Whenever Mama or Miss Irene was ruffled, she invoked the Judgment Day and then went on about her business. If I'd learned anything, it was that the Judgment Day belonged to Black women who were devoted to calling on it when the present world needled their nerves, dammed their reservoir of tolerance. Our grandmother must've also claimed her rights to the Judgment Day, because I'd often heard my mother's voice lashing out against the receiver of our telephone on this very subject: *Mama you have no right to judge us! You'll never be my judge and you know why.*

Tilting my head, I pulled thick, warm air into my lungs before I spoke again. "Hey turtle-face, hey girl. You feel like racing or what?"

"Yeah," said my sister. Her face broke open like a smiling flower as she took off, calling over her shoulder, "Racing ahead of *you!*"

We scrambled through the woods that edged our property, to an old trail that ran between Ruby's home and ours, then onto another trail scuffed with weeds.

We rushed through the brush until the land opened and we arrived at a clearing where the wind lifted our hair and pinched our eyelids, pulling them into slits against the glaring light. It was half past noon, and the sky blazed everywhere.

Ruby was already waiting for us. Instead of struggling with the wind, she had flung her arms wide, lifted to the raw sun. Her hair was black like her mother's, with the strands cinched into a ponytail that reminded me of a fussy horse. It appeared that Ruby had decided to cut her bangs by herself in preparation for the first day of school. A mistake.

Her parents took little interest in her comings and goings unless they needed her for chores or felt that they should teach her some little lesson that they themselves had failed to understand in their youth. The Scaggs family had a reputation in the village that had been sullied long before the arrival of my family. We'd known Ruby since around the same time we met the Junketts four years ago. Being Ez's baby sister, and wanting all of my big sister's attention, I was offended by Ruby.

In the hot white sun, their silhouettes were almost mirrors. Both Ruby and Ezra had long necks, and the lithe shapes of their bodies were visible beneath the material of their light dresses, which pulled against their bodies in the wind as though they had just emerged from the sea. But where Ruby's ponytail bobbed in place, Ezra's knotty hair flew out from its long, dense braid, and flapped as though it were a reddish coil of snakes that would raise her, bodily, into the flat blue window of sky.

Now Ezra ran forward to meet Ruby. They were laughing for no reason at all. I wanted to keep my distance from both of them until I knew what the game might be.

My shadow moved ahead of me. I stretched my arms like they did, worried that the wind was strong enough to lift me into the air. Dust blew up under my dress, then higher into my face. I tasted my lips; my tongue pushed at the salty grit that coated my gums. Tendrils of my hair pulled free from the plaits on either side of my head. The sun pressed on the middle part of my scalp that halved my head, the dark brown hair thick and oiled carefully by Mama each weekend. But out here the ends of my braids whipped at my ears.

It was all coming loose.

. . .

WE ARE STANDING IN A triangle. Ruby and Ezra face me.

After I watch Ezra remove hers, I hand my underwear to Ruby without looking at her face. Having anyone but Mama touch my panties makes me feel they are touching something they aren't supposed to. I'm both cool and sticky. I shake my hips a little, twisting my body so that the wind can blow against my sides.

Ruby balls our underwear together and shoves the damp lump into the pocket of her dress. She turns her head. Her black bangs look like the visor of a gladiator's helmet knocked askew. Her eyes, deep blue, are darker than the blue sky that somehow feels larger to me now that I've taken off my white cotton underwear.

Ruby sits down on the hot rocks. Ezra sits. I sit.

Ruby stretches her legs into a V, and Ezra does the same, squirming and sliding in the dust until one of her feet touches Ruby's. She jerks her right foot back and forth, irritably, to indicate that I follow.

I push myself back, feeling the skin on my palms scrape against the jagged rock. My legs, too, open into a V. I angle my left foot so that it leans against my sister's. I realize my right foot should lean against Ruby's foot. I don't want to touch Ruby's feet. She isn't even wearing shoes.

I duck my head to look over at Ez, who is staring at me evenly. I can hear Mama's voice cussing in my mind. Her eyes have rolled so far back she can see out the back of her head. *Hyacinth Kindred, what in the Lord's world do you think you're doing? And if you're thinking about what I would say then maybe you already know that you shouldn't be doing it either because where is the good daughter I raised?*

Mama never says anything like that to Ezra, never asks Ez about thinking, because Ez simply does a thing without thinking in the first place.

"Do it already," says Ezra. "It's hot up here."

With force, I shove the sole of my sandal against Ruby's bare foot, hopeful that it will hurt her.

"I'm not touching no white girl."

"Shithead," says Ruby.

"Don't talk to my sister like that," says Ezra quickly.

"She the one messing everything up." Heat pools beneath us. I worry whether ants are capable of crawling between my legs and up inside me. I can picture a thin black trail of them marching diligently between my organs, stomping along the slimy roof of my stomach then through the church of my heart and finally up through the tunnel of my throat right into my brain, which I imagine is inlaid with gems, like a cathedral. How many ants could really fit up there in my head? Then I think about peeing ants into the toilet at home and almost begin laughing.

Ruby's and Ezra's faces have darkened beneath the afternoon sun. They're trying to figure something out for themselves. I don't know what it is except that what we're doing would absolutely mean a punishment if our parents found out. Mama and Daddy don't believe in what Miss Irene calls "switch love." But Ruby's papa, Mr. Scaggs, believes in beatings. He certainly does. He beats Ruby and her mother whenever he thinks they are happy and could live without him.

"Move in a bit," says Ezra, biting her lip.

Ruby grunts, obeys.

I adjust my legs and press forward. My leg grazes Ruby's skin, which is hot. I've never thought about her skin before except to complain about it being white.

I think of Mama, as I often do, and everything she does for us. To keep us safe. In the early evening, before our dinner, Mama will wash our hair and style it for our first day of school tomorrow. Already, I can hear her asking me about the dust, and why is there filth in my scalp, have I lost my mind and been playing in the dirt just to make more work for her. Mama will tug the comb against my roots in frustration. I hold sweat in my hair, especially after I've been playing hard. She says *tangled* instead of *nappy* like I don't know that my hair, especially at the base of my head, is impenetrable when it gets wet. Mama likes our hair to look nice because she knows people, especially white people, are always thinking about our hair. Growing up, Mama had no help with her own hair because she was raised in a convent. Daddy said not to upset Mama by asking her too much about what she was like as a girl. Much of it Mama has buried deep inside herself, and we only glimpse it when she hangs up on our grandmother or goes into the closet of her heart with a glass of whisky and Sam Cooke.

Maybe this is why Ezra and I turn so often to Miss Irene for her wisdom, which she says comes from her mother, her grandmother, and her great-grandmother, who are all still alive. They keep something girlish alive in Miss Irene, while we watch Mama reject our grandmother at each turn. It is hard to not ask our own mother about who she once was, aware that such questions could drive her away from sharing with us what she has made for herself and for us, her daughters.

· · ·

RUBY LEANS BACK LIKE SHE is used to lying down with her legs open and nothing on underneath to protect her. Her legs, which are as tanned as ours, make a shadow. Where her panties would've covered her skin is so pale that it looks as though her privates belong to a different girl, whose skin and manners are fair, more delicate, and prone to bruising easily. I think of how I'm used to seeing Ruby bruised and how it takes time for her wounds to heal because she can't leave her scabs alone.

We copy the way Ruby has rocked herself on her side, roughly gripping the hem of her dress to lift it to her navel.

"Now y'all," she orders us. Her voice goes up like an arrow into the clouds that have gathered and paused to look down on our uncovered bodies.

Our three V's make a strange star.

· · ·

EZRA SAYS THAT SHE'LL LOOK first. Then Ruby. Then me.

The wind has quieted but tingling air still shivers my dress to my navel. I wonder if Ruby and Ezra have closed their eyes like me or whether they are staring up, inseparable from the blue sky that feels as though it is also under our bodies. I can't hear Mama's voice anymore.

. . .

EZRA KICKS ME. THE EDGE of her sandal is hard. It's my turn. Without moving my head, I roll my eyes to the left, where Ezra is spread. Her forearm is draped like a half shield across her eyes. The harsh afternoon bronzes her limp braid a dark red. From the way her calf muscles strain beneath her skin, I can see she's bracing herself against the ground, bracing herself to be seen. I can't remember the last time I've seen my sister naked. Except that what we are doing seems to fall outside the space where someone might point and say *Nasty*, or even *They were naked*. We are the kind of naked that is described in Genesis. The kind of naked that makes God sad.

I shudder, turning to study Ruby, who is using her hand to hide her face while the other hand pulls at forbidden skin below her navel.

Her hand looks like a door of flesh—nicked knuckles, fingernails bitten to pink nail beds, scraped skin. Between the spaces of Ruby's fingers, I can see one of her eyes peering out. Not at me but straight up as though she has been buried under a heap of wreckage.

Ezra and Ruby have both used their fingers to deliberately pull the thin skin apart. Experiment, argument, game, or prayer—I don't know what we're trying to win, what we are pleading for, or what we must prove to ourselves.

I know Ruby and Ezra find shame boring. We have seen it used at school by our teachers. At home, Mama and Daddy use it against Ezra and me even when they don't mean to. While I know our parents are trying to make us into decent women, it feels strange to think they are wrong. But I do. It feels like a secret the way Mama makes something natural seem bad, forbidding me to look at or touch my own privates unless I am holding a bar of soap in the bath.

As I look at Ruby's privates, I feel shame for looking. I feel shame for whatever it was that challenged Ruby and my sister into doing this in the first place. I think again about the shift in their gaits after their first periods last spring. I observed how their eyes sparkled while they complained of aches, cramps, and soreness. While they cupped the place that they called, with absurdly dramatic inflection, the Womb. They shooed me away when I suggested any of the roughhouse games we'd once enjoyed. They claimed that their sudden womanhood allowed them to think more deeply about their future lives, which was why they no longer felt it was natural for me to follow them everywhere. I couldn't know anything about it until I changed too.

I wish Ezra would speak. I need her to confirm that what we are doing is not deserving of punishment but something we are entitled, expected to do. The awareness of our bodies makes me feel like I could cry—the looking has no explanation though I sense it has more meaning than any of us can summon. Our skin near Ruby's skin stirs both fear and irritation in me. I want Ezra to tell me that she feels the same way as me. I want her to say something about our legs being better, stronger, but I know she won't.

She allowed me to join her and Ruby today though I haven't begun to bleed. Maybe that's why I don't know what I'm looking at, why I'm looking, or what is so important about it. If we were all the same color, I wonder whether the whole thing would feel so wrong. But Ezra and I would've never dared Lindy Junkett to play this game.

Then, suddenly, Ruby sits up, digs her hand into her pocket and shoves my crumpled panties at me without warning before she hands Ezra her bright green pair. Ruby is the last to pull her own torn underwear on.

"Boys do worse," she says, staring at me.

2

WE WALKED DOWN FROM THE HIGH BLUFFS, INTO THE WOODS THAT divided our house from the clearing. Ruby and Ezra spoke in low voices while insects hissed. Mama would expect us to be home to have our hair washed and fixed for dinner. I wondered how I could look at her face without her immediately knowing I'd done something so shameful there'd be no way to explain it. Branches poked my feet. In a matter of weeks, gold leaves would scatter through the air, dropping in spirals. That faint scent in the woods would burst open soon, and the odor of warm decay would shift into a fragrance like smoke.

"They really are all the same," said Ruby, as if we'd interrupted her in the middle of a sentence. Her voice was both pleased and annoyed.

"We're late," I said to my sister. I didn't want to hear any more of Ruby's ideas and hoped she would just shut up.

"How can that *be?*" said Ez, as though Ruby had shared the unspoken sentence with her. "It's you and I who got the curse."

"Hers looked cursed too," said Ruby, tossing her head at me. "She ain't even bleeding like us. Not yet. Maybe the bleeding don't matter."

"Matters when it comes to babies," said Ezra. "Matters when we're in the village, and the men who never looked at us before are looking at us."

"Uh huh," said Ruby softly. "Once I get my license as a pilot, I might have me a baby someday too. At least one so I don't have to be some man's slave like Ma says I will. Women in the village say that motherhood makes them free. I don't entirely understand that, but they've been saying it for years. Ma says she's not my slave and makes me do for myself all the time."

"What kind of slave are you talking about, Ruby?" said Ezra, scowling.

"Ma says Papa treats her like a slave," she said. "And he does."

"You wouldn't know what a slave is," I said.

"Shut up, Cinthy," said Ruby. "I ain't saying nothing 'bout coloreds. I was talking about men and women. You're so smart but you know next to nothing most of the time."

"Who is going to let a redneck like you fly a plane?" teased Ezra.

They both spoke as if I weren't there, as if Ruby hadn't just insulted me. Usually, Ezra would give Ruby a warning for talking to me like that, but they were too occupied with what we'd all just done.

Ruby laughed loudly in delight. "I for damn sure won't wait around for somebody like my papa to give me his blessing. Flying's something you take into your own hands."

"Girl, you stuck on a high hook," said Ezra. "They don't let girls fly planes. Be easier for you to have a baby than to get you a pair of wings."

"I aim to fly a plane," said Ruby, stretching her raspy voice until it nearly ripped. I knew they were suddenly close to having one of their frequent disagreements. "If you ain't too pigheaded by the time I get my license, I'll ask you to go up with me first."

"Ha!" said Ezra. "You think they'd let a *Negro* girl get into a plane when they won't even let us sit in the front of the bus?"

"I don't see why not."

"You wouldn't," I said quietly.

"God*damn*," snapped Ruby. "Nobody was talking to you."

My face reddened.

"There must be another reason why adults act the way they do. It can't just all be about this little pee hole," said Ruby thoughtfully.

"Well, what is it?" I said. I didn't intend for them to leave me out of anything ever again after what we'd just done. As far as I was concerned, I'd earned some permanent rights, whether or not I was bleeding yet.

"They don't even know," said Ezra. Her irritation at adults was evident. She sucked her teeth as though her tongue were tart from lemon.

"What if we went around carrying ourselves like boys do all the time?" said Ruby. "Shoot, boys make a game of their things, squirting piss like a fire hose on anything they find! And there's never no trouble, because they're just being boys. What if the truth was that we always have a choice the way boys do?"

"Who wants to be like a boy? They can't *all* do whatever they want the way you say. White boys, sure, but what about colored boys? Daddy says if a Black boy fights it's because he's fighting *not* to be killed for the slightest thing," I said. "Anyway, it's boring to think that all we want is to be allowed to do what boys do."

We were nearly at the path that would lead us to the rear of the haunted house. Relieved, I pictured us saying goodbye to Ruby, crossing Clove Road and walking up the swept, painted steps of our house. I was trying to decide whether I could get away with giving Ruby a good pinch. I knew Mama would be unhappy that we were late. It had to be midafternoon, and it always took more time than she needed to fix our hair and get the table prepared.

"Do you really think we have the same choices as boys?" said Ez, trying to see it from Ruby's eyes.

"Not *yet*," Ruby said. "One day. When we're women."

"Not *ever*," I said. "No one would allow it. Especially our mothers. Especially *your mother*, Ruby."

"Tell your sister not to say nothing about my ma." She spoke to

Ezra, ignoring me. "All I'm saying is I got a right to be free just like a boy. I intend to keep me a freeness, something better than what's been given to the adults. I'd think freedom would be important to y'all too. The way it is to the rest of your people."

When Ruby speaks to us of *our people,* when she proclaims that our people are righteous and mostly good-looking, that our people were queens and kings, supreme athletes and sublime entertainers, the first people who probably walked the earth after the dinosaurs died, we only murmur in response. *Of course,* we have read about slavery and the history of the white man's fear. Who is Ruby to tell us? When she starts her easy talk about the struggle and the Man, when she explains salvation and the uplift of our people to us, we withdraw, fastening our lips together until that kind of talk passes over and Ruby remembers, finally, that she is white.

"What's involved in this freedom you seem to know so much about? Your own papa beats you black-and-blue but you got the nerve to tell my sister and me something about some freedom. Our civil rights are just fine," said Ezra. Without another word, she hurled the splintered branch she'd been carrying at Ruby. It made a whizzing sound before it struck a tree next to Ruby's head, then dropped into a patch of what appeared to be poison ivy.

Ruby made a wounded sound. She lunged at Ezra, grabbing the flesh of my sister's bare arm with her nails. I froze as Ezra easily shook her off. There was a look in her eyes that she'd given other white people, but never Ruby.

"Do you know what would happen to me if I grabbed a white woman the way you just grabbed me?"

"I'm a white girl suddenly? Because of what?"

"You didn't answer me," my sister said. "Because you know what I know. We don't have to live in the middle of nowhere for you to know what I mean."

"I thought you've always told me the truth," said Ruby. Her eyes held tears, as did my sister's. My own eyes burned with how ugly yet inevitable this moment was. Mama, Miss Irene—they'd predicted this for some time.

"Your papa, your ma, my daddy, my mama," said Ezra. "Do you really think they're all wrong?"

"We're different," pleaded Ruby. "We've always said so."

Rubbing her arm where Ruby had left marks, Ezra shook her head bitterly. "We're not."

"But we just *saw*—"

"Ruby, what did you *see*?"

"Ez, *please*."

"We have to go," I said.

Ezra waved her hand at me to hush. But I could sense that what was coming had arrived last spring in Ezra's heart. She'd been carrying it as far as she could, as Mama and Miss Irene had warned her when it came to trusting white girls who would come of age and live inside worlds that were both safe and dangerous when they became women.

"We're not going to grow old together. We *can't*. I know you want to make yourself believe that we're chasing the same freedom, the same life. But we're not," said Ezra carefully. "We're not *sisters*. I have a sister."

Ruby moved as though she would attack Ezra but a force we couldn't see held her back. Maybe it was the sight of me stepping next to Ezra, standing with our shoulders touching, that made Ruby understand, finally.

"I never called you out your name or nothing like that," said Ruby. "I've been protecting you all this time. Even your bigheaded sister. And it's finished because I'm white? This is what you want?"

"Protected me from what? You need protection from your own father, Ruby," said Ezra. "And you know it."

"Papa loves me," said Ruby in a small voice. Her shoulders heaved. I knew she loved Ez, maybe more than she loved her own mama. But Ruby Scaggs had never suffered an insult, even in the name of love. "You say one more word, Ez, and you'll be eating your teeth for supper."

But I knew Ruby would do nothing. Like my sister's, her heart was broken so cleanly they were both breathless.

"Let's *go*," I said to my sister, touching her arm. We were at the edge of the woods in the shadow of the ruined house. "Mama's going to be mad."

3

RUBY WATCHED THE TWO KINDRED GIRLS RUSH AWAY FROM HER VOICE. Their figures turned into smudges as the late afternoon sunlight absorbed their shapes. Turning away from the opening where Ez and Cinthy had left her, she began to pick an unmarked path through the woods that would lead her back to the bluffs.

Ruby resisted the urge to cry. Could she be feeling this way because of what she had seen in her best friend and in herself? It was hard to admit that Ruby had expected there to be a difference between what she had and what the Kindred girls had. The whole world had assured the three of them of that. The inside seemed the same but the outside *was* different. Now that she knew the truth, it felt burdensome to her. Ruby was rarely lonely, though she was often alone. She thought again about crying, but then she pictured her papa, who cried all the time and was the loneliest person Ruby had ever known.

Jonah Reuben Scaggs, after whom Ruby was named, was a man who still possessed the thinness of boys who dove from train bridges to fish when they were hungry and broke. Her father knew how to hold his breath even when he wasn't in the water. For years, Ruby had watched him dive from the bridge of his memory into the wreckage of his past.

His blond hair, nearly white, stood out from his head. His eyes were blue, like a song banging on the door of the blues but somehow his soul couldn't get in to sing it right. These days, her papa's eyes were often closed. She'd come to the crooked porch of their shack and find him preoccupied, busy looking at his past the way a man might pull his finger over an enchanted map that led to buried treasures. Her father scorned the present and the future. It was the past that goaded him to keep living. He was trying to figure out how to name the moment when his life had fallen apart. Ruby had figured out a map of her own so that she couldn't be blindsided by his attacks.

As Ruby came out of the woods and into her family's clearing on the bluffs, she could smell smoke from the meat pit. Her father wasn't home, but he was smoking pork back behind their shack.

Ruby's papa disliked thieves and had no idea that Ruby had become very good at stealing. When she understood that she could die by starvation because she could not rely on her mother or father to provide, she learned how to steal from people in the village. This became another thing for the villagers to gossip about. They spoke of her father's drinking and her mother's dreaming. And now they could mostly say anything about Ruby too, because she wasn't exactly a little child who didn't know better. They didn't think Ruby deserved to be anything more than an unlucky product of the Scaggses' ruinous pride.

Ruby pressed her hands against her waist and thighs, thinking of summer evenings again and the way the last nights of August always felt sad to her because they seemed to know how long, bright days must end.

She wanted endless days of perfect summer blue skies. It was easier for her to dream that way, to picture herself as a pilot inside her own airplane cutting across the sky.

Ruby crossed the hard mud of her yard, cursing at her father's hounds, who raced around her in hunger. It occurred to her that this would be her last year of school. Since last spring, she worried about finding herself stranded in Salt Point, forced to marry one of the six Johns in her class. That was something Ez and Cinthy didn't have to bother with. Ruby had once read a column in one of her mother's beauty magazines about women who complained that, in spite of their desire to find new kinds of love, they'd ended up marrying men like their fathers. When she'd tried to tell Ezra about it, Ez had only frowned and said that her own father was a decent man who had taught her and Cinthy about the stars, human anatomy, Egyptian pyramids, and how to be a good judge of human character.

The only stars Ruby's papa had ever seen were when somebody had gone and knocked him out at the bar. Jonah Reuben Scaggs gave Ruby stars that flushed her skin green and purple. He was not a man who could teach Ruby about what men were made of.

Ruby's mother did nothing but avoid getting knocked out herself. Like her husband, Mrs. Scaggs found her sanctuary in the past. Once crowned a beauty queen at a local county fair, Ruby's mother still walked around Salt Point as though the village were crazy for not seeing her crown.

When Mrs. Scaggs still believed that she was supposed to be a good mother, she'd become severely concerned about Ruby's welfare. It was another way to spite her husband. Too, when villagers had looked at her daughter and said, "That gal should be reading by now," Mrs. Scaggs realized that the blame for Ruby's poor education might be laid at her own feet.

One afternoon, Mrs. Scaggs was in the village with Ruby, buying flowers and making a show of it, when they saw Mr. Hobart. Dressed in a tailored suit, Mr. Hobart had removed his hat and patted Ruby's tousled hair. He asked her age and she'd shyly turned to her mother, who proudly replied, "She's eight or nine." Looking intently at Mrs. Scaggs, he could still see her crown. Or so she hoped. Instead, he only asked her whether Ruby was reading yet, and if Ruby was reading, was she good at it. Batting her eyes as if they were rubbed with pepper, Mrs. Scaggs tried to see whether he might buy little Ruby a bouquet of daisies. His discomfort escaped her attention. Tipping his hat, he wished Ruby and her mother a pleasant afternoon, and added that because he believed that the Scaggs family was a very poor family in need, their daughter could attend his school to improve her future.

That afternoon, Ruby had felt the sting that went through her mother's body.

Ruby remembered how her ma had dragged her away from the village square, taking a rough route back to their shack. The fresh flowers in her mother's old mesh bag were bruised and torn. Ruby couldn't help but notice all of the colorful wildflowers—free—they passed as her mother raged about the man's insult. "He's the poor one, he is. The poorest kind of man possible is one who thinks he's so rich he can pay a woman with petty insults instead of proper compliments."

"Pay for what?" Ruby had asked her mother, who'd replied by slapping her face.

Ruby had sat on the porch, holding her cheek, listening while her mother cried with rage. When Ruby finally went inside, she found her mother eagerly applying Pond's Cold Cream to her face as she spoke about the dangers of tears, how they could ravish a woman's complexion. "At least you'll be in a good school," she kept saying to her daughter while she tried to press those wilted flowers into the pages of a tattered book.

The truth was that Ruby could read. But she'd been put off by the texts available to her. She could find no adventures, ghosts, wars, or fairy tales in her mother's beauty magazines. The only monsters and villains Ruby had ever seen in those pages were menacing heaps of dirty laundry, unhappy husbands, chipped red nail polish, silk stockings with bad runs. Too many damn rules about how to pretend you're something you weren't, like staying in your teens when you were in your fifties. The only things that really unsettled Ruby were illustrations of mothers smiling over blushing babies who seemed safely cared for in a way Ruby knew she had never been.

At age eight or nine, Ruby rebelled against her mother's faith.

She wanted adventures that did not involve feeding men delicious steaks while having to diet. She began to pull away from her mother, whom she loved but who did not see her. While it stung at first, Ruby understood that this was the only way she could have the life she wanted. Whatever it might be. Ruby convinced herself that her parents' neglect had provided her with a special armor. She surrendered what she'd never possessed, and instead found herself enjoying her own company and creating her own adventures.

Ruby had loved the notion of flight long before she, Ezra, and Cinthy saw that annual air show in Briggley. She recalled being mesmerized by seabirds that glided across Salt Point's horizon, and the birds' nests she explored while tramping through the woods; sometimes the sight of a cardinal or blue jay might stop her in the middle of her chores with its color. Ruby knew that flying was *in* her, had been waiting for her to find it and stop feeling afraid that a love like that was possible.

Flying was how Ruby began hearing her own soul.

She told herself that the story of her dream began with the air show in Briggley, a slightly larger town than Salt Point that was just a few miles away. Ezra and Cinthy had joined Ruby, though of course they worried the entire time about what their mother would do if she discovered they'd snuck out. Ruby had laughed and assured them that what they would see was worthy of any punishment.

That day, they'd watched the shadows of planes glide and drop through the blue air like fleets of fish. Like schools of brightly painted sharks, with polished noses and sleek chrome sides. Even the clumsier planes made Ruby tearful with hope. She recalled that this awakening of desire had stirred her the way she'd heard women in the village describe the moment of a first quickening. It sounded both psychic and physical, that awareness of a new presence in a familiar home. And it was *home* that Ruby felt most keenly as she and the Kindred girls stared up into the sky.

At the air show, there were tickets for brief rides on the planes. Ruby had been up in hot air balloons before, when the local carnivals arrived in the old lot at Salt Point. She'd drifted up above the water and looked down at the bluffs. Sometimes she saw the roof of her shack, but none of that felt like home to her. The balloon was too slow. Its operator was bored, uninspired unless he spied a pretty face in his line. No matter how many questions Ruby asked him, she knew he saw her as worthless, even more so than himself.

At the Briggley air show, Ruby had ignored the curious looks directed at her and the two young Negro girls who stayed too close to her. The scornful eyes of men and women had little effect on Ruby. She was too busy looking up.

Though she knew that the Kindred girls had money hidden in their shoes, Ruby elected to steal money from a mother who was busy wiping milk from the face of a wailing child in a powder-blue baby carriage. The Kindred girls weren't surprised at this. Not anymore. Their only fear was that Ruby would be found out and that they would be the ones accused.

When Ruby explained what she planned to do, Ezra called her crazy and smiled. "We're not going with you," said Cinthy. "We're not allowed." Those words were Ezra's sister's constant theme song. They went off to see if they could buy popcorn and candy even though Cinthy began to talk about how expensive dentists would be if their mother discovered they had toothaches, cavities. "We'll sit somewhere where we can watch," Ezra called over her shoulder, grinning. "Just in case the plane goes down instead of up."

Ruby stood in line alone. Her excitement blinded her to the children who were ahead of her, their parents, one or both, tenderly holding small hands.

When she was at the very front of the line, a man who resembled her father looked down at Ruby with bloodshot eyes that were shielded by costume aviator goggles. His round body reminded Ruby of the bocce balls the old men in Salt Point sometimes played with in the village square.

"Got a mother or father?" he said loud enough for everyone to hear that he was doing his job. "If you ain't got one of those, then you ain't going nowhere." He didn't laugh, though it sounded funny to some of the children waiting impatiently behind Ruby.

Scowling, Ruby pushed out her hand with the stolen coins. From what she'd learned from her ma, she figured that he'd take her money and look the other way. But he didn't even look at her. He was standing up, appraising the long line.

"Get lost," he said, and took the money out of Ruby's hands as if it could harm her.

. . .

THOUGH RUBY HAD BEEN DENIED a simple passage to her dream, she did not let that ruin her need to believe that she was capable of flight.

Not long after they saw the air show in Briggley, Ruby stole a magazine out of the school library. Though the older boys usually fought over the magazines with airplanes and cars, this issue had gone untouched. It had a female pilot on its cover.

Harriet Quimby had earned her wings long before Amelia Earhart came into the picture. Whenever Ruby tried to praise Harriet or Amelia, Ezra rushed to remind her about Bessie Coleman, who flew through blue skies too. Ruby was used to Ezra doing this when it came to music or sports, but lately she'd found herself irritated by her friend's need to place a colored woman's name inside a space Ruby felt belonged only to her.

Soon after, their teacher, Miss Burden, mentioned during a history lesson that there were also living women pilots. Their stories wouldn't be found in books, Miss Burden said, but she insisted that her students ought to know that women were also capable of flight. Ruby took it as a sign. It was one of the only times that she was ever grateful for anything she heard in school.

Otherwise, school bewildered Ruby. Even when she gave her teachers the right answers, there still seemed to be something wrong about her.

. . .

ALL OF IT REMINDED RUBY more than she cared to admit about the man at the air show who had taken her money and denied her entry to what she'd wanted most, simply because she was not accompanied by a mother or father. She could not play the game of decency and wondered what that man would've done—pitied her, perhaps—had he looked into her papa's drunken glare.

She was suspicious of the lessons adults gave her, especially men. She found herself being bullied at every turn. Whether it was the man at the air show whose eyes had nearly threatened violence if she considered talking back to him for stealing her money, or whether it was the actual violence her papa gave her in the name of his love for her, Ruby wanted to make new stories where she was a hero. She didn't want to be a princess or a queen or a poor scullery maid transported to a party in a pumpkin. She wanted true stories with pictures that could fill her head. In school, she could not grasp her teacher's rapture for Helen of Troy or women who were punished and wooed by gods disguised as animals. Those things weren't real.

Harriet Quimby was more interesting to Ruby than Miss Burden's silly lessons about mythology. She'd done everything first. First woman who had flown across the English Channel. First woman, on the record, who fell from the sky to her death.

Well, Ruby hadn't focused on the dying part. It was the victory, the woman's triumph, that fit into Ruby's own storytelling. She thought of Harriet Quimby clinging to the sky spinning around her as she was ejected from her seat in her plane, which torpedoed down into a thick grave of mud. Maybe her flying was worth her crashing. Perhaps those women pilots who braced their lives against the sky were less afraid of dying up there than of dying down on the land, inside some awful life they'd never dreamt of but that had found them anyway.

Ruby was thirteen years old when she tore that magazine cover of Harriet Quimby into bitty pieces, then chewed the chalky newsprint, swallowing that woman and her metallic wings. It was the only way to be sure that their lives would remain connected. As she did so, all of her fears flew out of her chest, like thousands of bats from a red cave. Each bite, each swallow, each breath lifted her higher and closer to the sun. One day Ruby Scaggs would have wings of her own.

· · ·

BY EVENING BEFORE THE FIRST day of school, Ruby had finished frying two fresh eggs and cooking the meat her papa had left out in the wood pit behind their shack. She ate very little of it, as he'd complain that she'd taken the best parts for herself, which was slightly untrue. After all, this was often squirrel, possum, duck, raccoon, or venison. What exactly were the best parts? They'd never had the kind of thing Ruby would've preferred, say, a cheeseburger with ketchup and French fries.

Squatting in one of their old zinc tubs, she'd used an old horse brush on her skin and shampooed her hair. Her freckled skin was raw but clean. There was no way for her to repair her bangs but her hair grew out quickly like her ma's; by the holidays nothing of that awful haircut would be left. She'd even allowed herself a finger full of her mother's beloved Pond's Cold Cream. She was becoming a woman and maybe it wouldn't hurt to think of sun damage. Since Ruby began bleeding, she'd told herself that she had to take more care in all things, including her appearance. Being *poor* was of no mind to her because most of the children who attended Hobart were struggling. But to be called *dirty* by her classmates (rarely to her face, of course) meant something different now. Ruby no longer wanted to fight her peers or her teachers if she didn't need to. There were new things for her to consider: flying, a better life. With her belly full and her clothes set out, Ruby couldn't decide whether she was excited or agitated for the first day of school. It was clear to her that her parents had likely forgotten that she would even be attending school the next day. She was relieved to be alone. Ruby would continue to let her papa and ma believe she had no strategy ahead of her that involved leaving them behind.

Ruby was prepared to leave them. It was only Ezra who made her think of recalibrating her plans.

Ruby had watched Ezra and Cinthy walk away from her down the path, and then into their house. A pang had gone through her as she wondered at what it might feel like to have a sister of her own.

At the same time, Ez was as close as, maybe even better than, having a sister. Since the day they'd met at age ten, Ruby was intoxicated. Nobody had ever warned Ruby about the laughter between girls. Ezra Kindred's laughter was like perfume. Ruby had bathed herself in it to the point that she only knew how strong it was when there was distance between them. Ruby liked believing that her own laughter gave Ezra something palpable too. Having her first friend made Ruby feel powerful.

Lately, it felt like work to be near Ez. There was less and less to laugh about. After fighting, Ruby and Ezra didn't forget about the arguments the way they used to. Winning mattered. There were new silences between them. Ruby wondered whether it was because this was their last year of school. Each girl would have to know, *soon*, where and how to be in the world. And the world and its walls seemed to insist that Ruby got to be one thing and Ezra had to be the other. But Ruby refused to believe that this wall couldn't be demolished. After graduation, couldn't they still laugh together?

Ruby breathed deeply, trying not to think about anything except enjoying the sky before the sun sank completely beneath the horizon. Sky gazing gave her peace. She wondered what it would be like to see the setting sun from an airplane. She drifted within herself as the air cooled around her. Images in her head helped her fend off absences in her life.

When the sun was gone, Ruby decided to go down through the woods over to the Kindreds' property on Clove Road. She'd done this each year before the first day of school since she was ten or eleven years old, back when she'd first met Ezra and Cinthy Kindred and realized, in spite of them being Negroes, they lived in a world that was very different from her own.

At her friend's house, Ruby knew that Mrs. Kindred did their ironing, their cleaning, their fussing, and their cooking. Mr. Kindred did the thinking and sometimes, if he remembered, he did the disciplining, except that he didn't really like hollering and giving out punishments the way Ruby's papa enjoyed it.

The Kindreds kept to themselves so much you wouldn't know they existed sometimes. Their religion was privacy. If they were white, Ruby reckoned they'd be exactly the same as her.

The slightest question about their family made the sisters tense, so Ruby learned not to bring up the issue, especially since her own family situation was far from what anyone would call respectable.

Ruby's ma often said that the Kindreds were the most irregular niggers she'd ever seen, except that Ruby knew that her mother hadn't seen too much in her life. Which was why, like other villagers, her ma was slightly fearful of the Kindreds.

Ruby stood up, shivering. She wanted to reach the Kindreds' house before they finished their special supper. She liked to look in at them through the clean picture window of their kitchen. In all these years, they'd never noticed her watching. She wasn't spying, exactly. The hunger was somewhat aimed at Mrs. Kindred's delicious meals but really Ruby knew it was about something else, something she didn't want to explain to anyone, even her best friend. What would Ezra think if she were to know how many years Ruby had found herself picking through the Kindreds' garbage to find her own last-day-of-summer feasts? Ruby made up stories about enchanted spells that would one day be broken to reveal that Ruby was, secretly all the time, the third sister. These tales pleased her and let her believe that while she lived in the wild that surrounded the Kindred home she was, in fact, a daughter who deserved a room and a love of her own in that house. In the past when Mrs. Kindred sometimes set a place at the kitchen table for Ruby to share meals with them, Ruby tried not to let Ezra see how much it meant to her, how she wanted to be seen as part of their family.

Ruby's favorite moment of the night was when Ez and Cinthy and their parents would walk down to that little pond that they fawned over, where they would share stories, wishing on the stars above them. Ezra had spoken of it once and then, feeling embarrassed, had told Ruby it didn't mean anything. But Ruby knew that it meant everything to her best friend. Standing at the edge of the woods now, Ruby observed how the entire family laughed, clasping one another as they looked up, their voices serious in what sounded like prayer.

Ruby had a wish or two of her own the day before her last first day of school. One wish was about flying, really flying, and being brave enough to do whatever was necessary, no matter how frightening, to begin to be who she wanted to be. The second wish, which seemed just as impossible, was that she wouldn't lose Ezra Kindred's love.

4

"YOU LOOK LIKE MY DAUGHTERS AGAIN," SAID MAMA, AS SHE STOOD UP from the chair in our kitchen. She gathered the combs, brush, ribbons, and hair oil, which she kept in an old cookie tin. Her anger at our late return had finally ebbed. For once, I silently thanked that cold glass of brown spirits for making Mama's voice soft. We helped her put everything away, moving quietly as she directed us to set the table for our special meal. She seemed a bit unsteady on her feet but as I passed her, she pulled me to her and pressed a kiss against my fresh braids. I could feel how clean my hair was by the way the air touched my neck and ears, and it was as comforting as Mama's voice.

I still liked ribbon, though Ezra told Mama we were too old for it. Ezra said she wouldn't be caught dead with ribbons in her hair, and it now seemed that she wouldn't want to be seen with me if I wore them, even though I was only thirteen.

"Replace the ribbon with a nice headband," my sister advised.

"Headbands give me headaches, Ez. They poke the skin behind my ears and flip off my head when I do cartwheels," I said.

"You too big to be doing cartwheels. Right, Mama?" said Ezra, narrowing her eyes at me as she used her dish towel to dry the good plates Mama had taken out and rinsed for use at dinner.

"Women all over the world wear scarves and wrap their hair. In some countries, women cover their hair whenever they leave their homes. It's how they were raised. And I bet there are thousands of women all over the world, who are much older than all our ages put together, who use ribbons. You see Irene with her hair wrapped in one of those nice turbans she likes to wear outside. I didn't raise you both to spend so much time thinking about the hair on your head. Your little sister can do whatever she wants," said Mama.

Handing my sister another plate, I giggled and gave Ez my best googly eyes. She was in a bad mood. It was because she knew she shouldn't have said what she had said to Ruby about Ruby and her papa before we parted ways in the woods. Although she and Ruby argued all the time, Ezra could hurt Ruby in a way not even her father was capable of.

Like our entire school, Ezra and I were frightened of Mr. Scaggs.

Over the years, Ruby had shown us many places where he'd bruised her. There were likely other places she hadn't shown us too. I thought about how Ruby would steal whatever she could get away with when no one was looking. She couldn't help herself, even though she knew better. I wondered whether it wasn't something similar about Mr. Scaggs. He couldn't help himself from hurting Ruby even though he had to know better. It frightened me to think that adults could behave that way, even when they knew what was wrong and right.

Without ever offering a full explanation, Mama and Daddy had warned us to never be any place alone where there were white men. Even at Hobart. Should we find ourselves alone with a white man or men, including our teachers, we were to get far away as soon as we could.

. . .

MAMA TOLD EZRA TO HELP her with the starched tablecloth. We laid the table out so finely we could have been seated at a fancy restaurant. Our family behaved like the day before school was as important as, maybe more important than, Christmas.

"Can't we have a picnic by the pond?" asked Ezra. "It'd be easier."

Mama paused, folding her arms across her body. Her yellow dress was spotted with water. She'd removed her cooking apron while shampooing our hair and had forgotten to pull it back on again. Mama had finished with her sadness and returned those feelings that whisky and Sam Cooke gave her to her closet. She'd reemerged as our mother. Though she was not exactly angry, the air in our kitchen was tense. Mama's indignance twitched along her jaw in a code I could recognize from any angle, any distance.

"Seems like you two already had some kind of picnic."

"Mama?"

"Been a long time since I've had to wash so much filth out of your two heads. Where did you go today?" She eyed me, aware that I, unlike my sister, could not lie to her.

"Playing, Mama," said Ezra. She went over to the drawer and began to remove silverware noisily.

"I was calling for you both to help me. Cooking all this food, doing hair right up until the last minute before dinner, cleaning and scrubbing all day yesterday until my back couldn't take any more. You got a nerve to just up and disappear like you think you have a maid in this house. Your daddy and I own *this* house. You don't own a thing, not even the dirt in your head. I want to know where you girls have been and what you've been up to. And I expect an answer that does not insult my intelligence."

Though Mama's words were mostly directed at Ezra because she was older than me and sneaky, I looked down at my clean, bare feet and wished I were outside walking in the wild grass around our pond, which would be cool and damp at this time of day.

When Mama talked this way, it made me sad.

Her voice turned to salt, as though someone else was talking through her mouth. Daddy disliked it too. Sometimes he interrupted her fussing to remind Mama why they'd left Damascus. Daddy said he didn't want to live in a house where his wife threatened to hurt his daughters because it was the only way for her to show us that she cared for us. Mama's whuppings were with words, not belts. What was awful was how tired Mama got after she gave us a good talking-to. Rage made her sick. Neither Mama nor Daddy believed in hitting us. Unlike Ruby or Lindy Junkett, we'd never been slapped across our faces, or had the skin on our arms pinched. We'd never been ordered to go into our yard and pick switches while Mama or Daddy waited for our return. Lindy said that was one of our problems.

"But, Mama, you do know that there's dust *everywhere*," said Ezra. "That's what it is when we have to live in the middle of nowhere."

"Did this dust involve Ruby Scaggs?"

I said nothing, feeling her eyes on me. Mama knew.

"You girls are getting to an age where you need to have nice friends. Friends you can grow up with. Ezra, you're a young woman now. I know you know what I'm talking about. It's time for you to make friendships that can make you stronger, help you get through this world."

"What does that mean?" said Ezra. She stopped shuffling the cutlery. Her fresh plaits slipped forward as she stared at a fixed point past Mama's voice.

"Girls like Lindy Junkett is what I mean. She's reliable. I'm not saying I don't like Ruby. But you're at the age where you and Ruby aren't the same, no matter what you think. I'd prefer you and Cinthy spend more time with Lindy, who is a pretty girl with a good future ahead of her. Nothing distracts that child from improving herself. Irene and Caesar Junkett are going to make sure of it. Keep those babies on the Path."

I sighed quietly so that Mama couldn't hear me. Like most Negro adults, Mama loved the Path. She and Daddy had been talking about the Path as early as I could remember. Sometimes the Path was a mountaintop. Sometimes it was where Moses parted the dark red water so that God's chosen people could get to the Promised Land. The Path was a moral interstate highway for Negroes worldwide. The Path could also become personal, like when Daddy would sigh and say, *I'd watch myself if I were you. Your mother's on the warpath this morning.*

Mama rubbed her palm over the whole shape of her head. Her dark hair, a rich brown that was nearly black, was pulled back into a thick bun at the nape of her neck.

Even when she was scolding, Mama often spoke to us as if we were her friends or her sisters. Truth be told, despite her willingness to give advice to Ezra, Mama didn't really have friends. She'd been an only child, raised by sisters in a convent as an act of local charity after she was abandoned (by Ginny, as she'd learn later in life) in a lonely heap of baby blankets on the steps of a church somewhere in Delaware.

We knew Mama loved us, loved Daddy, but sometimes she went into dark spells. The way she loved Daddy was strong, but there was a haunted house inside Mama whose shadowy intimacy was stronger. Ezra blamed all of it on account of Mama living her girlhood inside a house of God with nobody to talk to but nuns, dust, and Jesus. When these spells struck, we kept quiet, waiting anxiously for our mother to emerge. She was only ever lost for so long. One of the antidotes for Mama was her attention to us and our father. The running of our household held Mama back from the places where living had hurt her. Today her irritation had only grazed us because she was busy and could not lie in bed listening to the radio for hours. Today there was no time for her to pretend she wasn't crying as she washed the dishes. Mama tried not to let us see it, but daughters see such things more clearly than anyone. At least it felt that way to me.

Drying her fingertips on a fresh dish towel, Mama twisted her small diamond wedding ring into place and sighed. "Cinthy, get the candlesticks from the pantry. Make the table pretty."

Smiling, I was relieved that Mama wasn't going to ask us anything else about our whereabouts or what we'd been doing with Ruby, which I still didn't understand. Mama could see that we were safe, clean, and helping her make everything nice for the evening. I hoped that she wouldn't be too tired to walk with us down to the pond, which we'd called the Waterfront since we were very little. We always liked to be near her when she was wishing good things for us on our first day of school. Standing next to Mama, when she was calm, was like standing inside a sunset. Sunset was the only time you could look at the sun without going blind.

The pantry was one of my favorite places in our house. There was a large, crooked window that faced the pond. The other three walls were lined with shelves that were hidden by checkered curtains. We called it the Store. There was a floor lamp in the corner behind the door, which had a white porcelain doorknob that was shiny, the enamel cracked. The ivory walls were yellowy peeling plaster. I could pull a kitchen chair inside and close the door. I'd yank the little chain, turning on the friendly lamp while I read alone or just watched the natural light slide down the curtains until the room darkened. Then I could see all the way out to our pond where stars dropped, like distant silver coins, into the water.

"Girl, are you in there making the candles? What's taking you so long?"

"No, Mama, I'm not making the candles. I was thinking."

"Then bring those candles and their holders out here and place them on the table," she said. "Hell, I'm tired." Her voice slurred. I didn't know if it was from whisky or because she really was more tired than usual. "Maybe we can all walk down to the Waterfront if your father finishes preparing his lessons. It would be a nice thing. I've some wishing of my own I want to see about." She seemed to be herself again, but then she added, "So you aren't going to tell me where you all went this afternoon? What you did?"

We looked away from Mama's sweet voice.

"You really aren't going to tell *me*?"

"There's nothing to tell," Ezra said very softly.

"Here we go," said Mama, shaking her head as if she had predicted this years ago, when she cradled us in her arms. "You're becoming women who have secrets. But I'm not one of your little friends. You can't have secrets from me."

. . .

IT WASN'T A RULE THAT we couldn't speak at the dinner table, but we had to have something interesting to say. Rather, something adults, specifically our father, would deem interesting. We didn't know what interested adults, so we kept quiet and focused on chewing so that we could have our desserts.

We liked when Daddy sat for long periods of time at the table instead of eating quickly and going back to his lessons. We loved the song of his voice, which was gravel and grave. Daddy was a serious man. When he smiled, it often seemed like it took a great deal of effort for him to leave his thoughts and remember where he was and that there was happiness right in front of him.

Our father saved his talking for teaching.

Sometimes when Ezra and I walked through the corridors of Hobart, we'd spot our father striding ahead of us, a weak crown of authority floating above his head, a thick book tucked between his one arm and his long side; we'd barely recognize the loving man he was at home in this man fighting to survive the battlefield of education. Over the years, that distance became something more difficult for my father to switch on and off.

In spite of being bookish, Daddy often spoke about life in terms of cost and price. There were vague things that had, or would, cost him too much. He despised the feeling that his life was for sale. Daddy spoke of the poorhouse as if we could see it from our windows. He mistrusted the world for good reasons.

We'd only been told the sparest details about our great-grandparents, Theodore and Calliope Kindred. Their belief in their right to build a church of their own had made the world nervous. Before my great-grandparents could live long enough to have anything but hope and faith in their hard work, the local white men in Damascus struck a match and sent a flame through our bloodline that Daddy would never admit was still burning in his memory.

He blamed religion for the fires it had set long ago in his childhood. Unlike Mama, our father didn't feel guilty that we didn't attend church every Sunday. Daddy would occasionally drive us to Rising Star, a Black church in Gunn Hill, when he felt we should have God. But it was an unspoken rule that, in our house, religion was not to be used as a means to control our minds or behavior. Our father never ordered us to pray or to repent for our sins.

Instead, we were encouraged to use our intellect to understand why we might say or do a thing. Our father conceded that God was useful, but he was more likely to say, "If we are to analyze the origin of these tears . . ."

In the middle of dinner that night, our father spoke about what he planned on teaching at the outset of our term. My mind drifted towards Miss Burden, who had been my homeroom teacher since I was eleven. I wondered how she was spending her own last night of freedom.

She lived alone in the village, in one of the shabby apartments above a storefront that faced the sea. I don't think Miss Burden was even forty years old, but her face looked as if it had been rubbed with cider vinegar at birth. Her breath made me think that she had slow-kissed whole cloves of garlic with her tongue. On the rare occasions that our teacher smiled, I thought she must be smiling at something that internally amused her, because I don't believe Miss Burden found us, or her life, very funny.

We, as students, were interruptions between the hours when she could be reading. She appeared to me to have a secret life buried in the sleeves of her sober, pea-colored cardigans. There was a degree to which Miss Burden held herself away from us, away from the village.

I was sensitive, and Miss Burden had somehow understood this quality in me. She lent me her own books and created complicated reading lists to match my hunger for stories. Sometimes, if Ezra was at home sick, I was even allowed to sit inside with her during lunch. During those blissful afternoons, Miss Burden and I read silently while enjoying our sandwiches and fruit. Because without Ez's presence, my classmates could be awful, and there would be nothing that Lindy Junkett, or even Ruby, could do to save me from some sort of humiliating prank. Boys pretended not to see me when they threw hard footballs that left marks on my legs. *She was in our way* was the closest thing to an apology Miss Burden could get from them. Inside the classroom, my classmates became artists. I would open my desk or notebook to discover cartoon sketches of myself, my sister, and my father as primates or genitalia. These drawings were only slightly less humiliating than listening to singsong verses about my father's missing arm and African booty scratchers.

As my father went on talking about some of the repairs that Mr. Caesar had had to do over the summer so that Hobart's roof wouldn't collapse, I wondered what kind of summer Miss Burden had enjoyed. There'd been no sighting of her during July and most of August. A few days ago, when Ezra and I had helped our father cover the old textbooks with simple brown paper, flipping through the pages to remove any obscene graffiti, I thought that I'd heard her voice in the hallway, echoing a birdlike greeting to someone in passing. I'd rushed into the hall, unsure as to what I would say, but the hall was empty.

The telephone rang, interrupting my father's dinner monologue.

We'd learned over the years not to stir from our seats to answer it. I watched my father's jaw work in code as his and Mama's eyes met. Our grandmother was trying again, as she always did, to wish us a happy first day of school. Mama usually wouldn't answer this call. She'd try to wait out the noise, her fingers gripping the edge of the tablecloth until her knuckles were visible. Daddy had given up asking Mama to make peace, while our mother insisted that her own peace lived in the fact that she could protect her daughters from the kind of woman Ginny Abbott was. *Nobody protected me,* she said once in a voice so small it kept Ezra and me up after our bedtime for weeks. We'd heard Mama muttering about Ginny being a jail hen, that she wasn't fit to be a grandmother.

Ginny got herself in bad trouble and nobody was surprised. She was a singer, and the devil got into her lungs. Only breath she cared about was her own, from what the old folks said. Soon as she could leave Damascus she abandoned your mama. Didn't look back, didn't even leave her tears for her own child. That's what Daddy told us once, when we asked why we were directed to tell anyone who asked us that we had no living relatives. This was easy, because nobody in Salt Point ever asked us anything about our kinfolks to begin with.

Some years the phone rang only once and that was frightening because it made me think that our grandmother was getting tired of trying to reach Mama, and us.

"She's stopped," said Mama, turning her head to look scornfully at the phone. Then she coughed hard into her napkin. My father offered her his glass of water, which she took gratefully. After she swallowed, her sigh was long.

"Maybe she'd stop if you answered her," said Daddy.

"Don't you start," whispered Mama, wiping her eyes.

"Think of our girls," said Daddy. His voice was patient. He shifted in his chair. Our father was just over six feet tall. He went on speaking. "Think of what you and I never had. They could have their grandmother, Lena. You could have someone to talk to besides Irene."

"Irene's lovely," Mama said, folding her lips into a line before she sat up straight and ordered Ezra to fill our glasses with more lemon water from the pitcher.

"Don't give me a single reason to think of either of you getting into any trouble this autumn," he said to Ezra and me, switching the subject. He took another long gulp of water and cleared his throat. My sister and I received a version of this every term. "We have to begin strong and, well, we have to finish strong. Our pace on the Path is quickening. You're becoming young women. We can't always know when troubles will find us, girls, but if we're on our best guard, playing our best game, then we can't be defeated. We can't be left with our, well, our you-know-what's hanging in the wind. Defeat only happens here," said our father, tapping his forehead, where he'd begun sweating.

Ezra and I were given no special treatment because our father was a teacher at Hobart. As if my sister and I would ever have mattered to any of the other faculty: We were only Negroes. Never mind the fact that when I was younger I'd been skipped ahead two years, and that now Ezra and I always tied for first in our grade.

Ezra, the Junkett children, and myself were the only Black children at Hobart. Our teachers at Hobart rarely called on us unless it was to shame another student, who was always white, into doing better. Miss Burden was the only one who called out our actual names rather than saying, "Yes, you."

"We won't be any trouble," I said, speaking for us both as I stared at the candlelight. Closing my eyes, I imagined the sight of Hobart's golden doors, which glowed like two long commanding tablets of fire.

5

A PAIR OF VILLAGE FISHERMEN DISCOVERED MISS BURDEN, FACEUP, drifting along the shore at low tide in a nightgown that was brand-new. When questioned about this nightgown, the fishermen stated that the price tag was still attached, floating, just a few inches from the dead woman's wrinkled fingertips. The nightgown was spooky, they said, the way it had flowed around the woman, as if she'd already been a ghost for a long time.

Murder was ruled out right away. There were no visible wounds, and Miss Burden had never harmed anyone in the village. She'd had no riches, no enemies, no secret affair. There was no inheritance or benefactor of insurance.

When loneliness was suggested, the men shrugged. They said they couldn't spare a moment to think about our teacher's motives. They were simple men who had spent years in the company of moonlit waves. There were things inside a man's solitude that could kill. They weren't interested in the things inside a woman's solitude. Despair was in their nets now, they complained, because the woman's body had obstructed their usual route, costing them half a day's profits.

There were two deputies in Salt Point. One of them, the chief deputy, was Mr. Hobart's nephew, Charles Hobart. The villagers who'd known him since he was a young man called him Charlie. The other, Deputy Howard Walsh, was known locally as Howie. He was older than Deputy Charlie and had a voice that tilted between warm sarcasm and chilling, precise perspectives about the human condition, like those of a philosopher. His usual jurisdiction was in Gunn Hill, where there were more murders than loneliness. He was in Salt Point to back Deputy Charlie, as he'd always done.

It was the first day of school. Our eyes were fastened on both men, who walked slowly around our classroom in search of clues, armed men turning suddenly on their heels as if a motive might appear at any moment. Sitting at our desks, we wondered silently if, somehow, we had been part of our teacher's woes.

The adults who rushed in and out of our classroom to give statements were irritated and spoke carelessly of Miss Burden, as though each of them had anticipated this day and were annoyed that it hadn't happened sooner. Miss Burden had never made any attempt to ingratiate herself with her colleagues. She hadn't complained about students the way the others did. In fact, she'd held herself at such a distance from the other teachers that they became bitter, and assumed that Miss Burden believed she was better than them. I waited to see whether my own father would come into our classroom to give a statement. But it occurred to me that the last thing Daddy would want to do was insert himself in something as serious as a white woman found dead, floating in the waves with no visible story as to how she'd ended up there. Better for them, as he and Mama always said, to mind their business.

Besides, it was not the first time Salt Point fishermen had fished a woman out of the water. But it was the first time that I'd known anybody that had died.

I met my sister's eyes and saw a strange look in them. I knew she was trying to figure out whether she felt afraid or whether this was yet another instance where she would let the adults sort themselves out without giving up any of her own common sense.

Another teacher of ours, Mrs. Clay, who lived in a dormitory on the school grounds, was being interviewed in the back of the room, near the coat closet, where we couldn't see her face. Her nose trumpeted wetly into her handkerchief. Sometimes she answered Deputy Howie when he barked questions at her. Sometimes she didn't. When neither man was speaking to her, she talked softly to herself, over and over saying, "I didn't know I didn't know I didn't know." It was scary, the way she was going on, even for the boys in our class, who usually mocked her babyish voice and engineered loud bodily noises, aware of her extreme aversion to all scatological matters.

The deputies dismissed Mrs. Clay and began speaking to each other, their voices flicking across the tops of our heads. Our teachers did not bother to suggest to the deputies that they should have some tact in our presence. They knew that Deputy Charlie was the nephew of their employer.

"There must be a letter."

"Wasn't none at her apartment."

"Women leave letters."

"Remember Maria? In '51? She didn't leave so much as a comma."

"Hell, I remember Maria. She walked right into that water in nothing but her nightgown too. Lots of nightgowns at the bottom of that cove."

"I recall Maria being naked."

"Is that right?"

"Maybe. But everyone around here knows it'd be nearly impossible to walk out there like that. Water's too cold. That salt out there is liable to rip the skin from your bones. You'd come back to your senses."

"Well this one was mad enough."

"We can write it up as an accident, long as there ain't nothing she put in writing."

"Not a *parenthesis*. I checked her place. Not much of a life in there."

"What's the lunch special at Linda's today? Cheeseburgers?"

"You never know how people are really living until they die."

"Well, not even then. Especially not then. Hell, they can't tell you. Where was she from? Originally?"

"South of here—Boston, I think, or somewhere near there. There was a birth certificate."

"How'd she get all the way up here? Most women would head south if they could. More husbands south of here, I've heard."

"Didn't seem like she was interested in finding one of those."

"Oh yeah?"

"I think Linda makes spaghetti and meatballs on Mondays. They're decent. My grandmother made the best meatballs. She was Irish. She made Irish meatballs the Italian way."

"What if this one was sleepwalking? Remember that girl Rosa in '55?"

"This one got loneliness all over it. You ever notice that our women never pull this kind of stunt? It's always the ones who come from somewhere else."

"Well hell, you said something there."

Then the deputies remembered us and readjusted their words. "Kids, you just remember that the good guys are here," said Deputy Charlie, fingering the bouquet of dull pencils in a chipped mug on Miss Burden's desk. His voice was thin and bright. "We'll do our job like we always done. We won't let anything bad happen to you." Using the sides of his bare hands, he pushed the sweat from his cheeks back to his ears. The leather of his boots whined as he turned in the spill of red and blue light that poured from our pretty, stained-glass window. The room was once some sort of chapel.

I remembered how Mr. Caesar had spoken of Deputy Charlie's relationship with Mr. Hobart. *Well, his uncle owns his ass* was how Mr. Caesar had described it, which was something our parents told us never to repeat, even if it was true.

Miss Irene called the man a bully. In the presence of his uncle, he used my father's and Mr. Caesar's surnames: Kindred and Junkett. But whenever he greeted Daddy and Mr. Caesar anywhere else,

it was *boy* or worse. Deputy Charlie had made it his business to in-
timidate our family, as well as the Junketts, except that he got little
joy from it when it came to Daddy. It was Mr. Caesar who excited the
deputy. It was Mr. Caesar who was willing to get bruised when the
deputy pulled up outside his house while he and his family sat out in
their yard. It was Mr. Caesar who had no hesitation in warning the
deputy that he, too, was armed.

Ezra, Lindy Junkett, and I stared at the gun nestled in Deputy
Howie's holster. The other children were busy making up stories
of sea monsters that had crawled into Miss Burden's bedroom and
dragged her outside into the water. Or maybe she'd ended up in Salt
Point because she had committed some kind of crime and was actually on the run.

I couldn't take my eyes off the two uniformed men as I imagined Miss Burden being pulled up from the water in a net, like a
mackerel. It could've been an accident, as the officers said. But the
way that they spoke made it clear that they didn't believe it was an
accident at all.

· · ·

THE PRINCIPAL'S VOICE CRACKLED THROUGH our intercom. He was
calling an emergency faculty meeting. Stricken teachers rushed
past us, waving us away with their hands. For once, early dismissal
brought little joy.

Ezra, Ruby, and I stood out in the sunlit circle that curved around
the entrance to the school. Had we made our teacher so miserable
that she'd jumped into the sea? I was sad to imagine Miss Burden
being in pain and having nobody, not even her students, to help her.

Lindy Junkett came over to us, eyeing Ruby. Lindy rarely spoke
to us if Ruby was around. It bothered her that Ezra called Ruby a
friend. Miss Irene had steered her children away from even considering the possibility that some whites could be kind. Lindy said just
enough, without being rude, to let us know that she couldn't let her

guard down, not even for us, in the presence of someone her mother had warned her against trusting. Though Ruby was accustomed to Lindy ignoring her, we all knew that Ruby wanted Lindy to like her and to be friends.

We were often quiet when Lindy spoke. Like the rest of the Junketts, she had a lovely southern drawl that Ez and I enjoyed and envied. She was surrounded by a sweetness that could make God's eyes water. First, she was sensible and pretty. Her fingernails were always buffed to a shine. The palms of her hands were pale and faintly lined. Her large, fringed eyes, dark like Mr. Caesar's, held a light. Lindy's mother, Miss Irene, had taught her to be both plainspoken and mysterious. Indeed, Lindy was her mother's daughter, which meant she had a purpose and understood that. Lindy never quit reminding us that she was a mama's girl. It was the most wonderful thing to her. Next, Lindy had such pride in her daddy, more than any girl I'd ever known, even the girls I read of in books. Never mind if Mr. Junkett cleaned toilets or scraped bubble gum from the undersides of desks and chairs. Her daddy loved her. Lindy reminded us at every moment that she and all of the Junkett family were beautiful and unbothered by anyone else's opinions of who they were supposed to be.

Lindy nodded at us, looking over at Ruby from the side of her eye. "My momma asked me to see whether y'all want to come over to our house on Saturday."

"Let's go find Daddy," I said to my sister. I felt like I was going to get sick on myself. I didn't want Ruby to see that. It was strange of Lindy to be so calm, as if the only thing that mattered was whether our two families were going to get together for barbecue over the weekend. She looked so peaceful standing there in her new starched shirt and skirt. She smoothed back thick plaits that Miss Irene had braided upward into a pineapple at the crown of her head. Miss Burden was *dead*. I knew that Lindy followed her parents' wisdom about leaving white people's business to white people. Still, I would've thought that Lindy would be more moved about our teacher.

Ezra had taken off her new school shoes and socks and was rolling one of her socks into a bright donut. She didn't look at any of us.

"Aren't we going to talk about *this*?" I asked. My eyes tingled. I was crying a little, aware that I risked ridicule from Ruby and possibly my own sister. "I never knew a person we *know* could do such a thing. Not a teacher! Do you think it *is* murder or *what*?"

"Aw, we never knew nothing about that woman," said Ruby. "Ain't no need for you to cry over her, Cinthy, even though we all know you was her favorite."

"Ernest is coming home Friday," Lindy said. "Maybe Friday would be better. He's off from his job for the weekend. Momma is cooking a bunch of food."

"Your brother eats a lot," I said, distracted for a moment. Miss Irene made very good cakes and the thought of a cake was enough for me to quiet.

"Boys eat a lot," said Lindy. Her authority surfaced when she spoke of her brothers, Ernest and Empire. Brothers were something none of us, including Ruby, had. But we wanted them badly.

"Cinthy eats like a hog," said Ruby.

"No, she doesn't," said Ezra quickly and hit Ruby with the rolled-up sock. Then she calmly retrieved the sock and stuffed it into her bag.

"Whatever," said Ruby. "Standing around here is making me hot. Let's go down to the village. It'll be cooler by the water."

"I have to stay here and wait for my father," said Lindy.

"We do too," I said. Bending over, I began untying my new shoes as well.

Ezra rolled her eyes as I stood up with my own folded sock. "No we don't," she said. "Daddy could be in there all day."

"Let's go home and help Mama," I said.

"I'd love to say hello to her," said Lindy.

I nodded, knowing that Mama loved, like the whole wide world did, to see Lindy on the first day of school. Her countenance assured us that she was making our race proud. I noticed that Lindy hadn't taken off her socks. She probably thought it was indecent to show her bare feet in front of a white girl.

In the hard light, Ruby's black bangs cut a blade across her skull. She had pulled her hair into a ponytail and used some ribbon to tie it. I recognized the ribbon because it once belonged to my sister. Ruby slapped a fly away. "We can go see if there are police everywhere."

"I can't believe she did that," said Lindy. "It's a sin."

"Probably the bravest thing she ever done her whole life," said Ruby.

"Why is it a sin?" said Ezra. "She could do whatever she wanted because it was *her* life. She did what she wanted."

"Even *I* know that we're not allowed to do what she did. It's in the Bible," said Ruby, looking at Lindy. "Ez and Cinthy don't know God's rules 'cause their parents don't like God. They're heathens."

"Do you know what the word *heathen* means?" I said to Ruby. My face grew warm. "You better read the dictionary. Because the only heathen around here is *you*."

"That white girl don't know nothing about prayer," said Lindy, moving closer to me to make it clear to Ruby that she hadn't been speaking to her.

"What will we do without a teacher?" Ezra asked. Her eyes were distant in the hazy air.

"We'll just get a new one," said Lindy.

"You don't know people," said Ezra, repeating what Mama said to us at least once a day. "You never know how folks are living."

"Burden knew a lot," said Ruby. "She was a smart woman."

"Smart about what?" said Lindy, frowning.

"Maybe we won't have to read any more books," said Ezra. She sounded hopeful.

"Hell, I'd like to read *Frankenstein*," said Ruby. "I was looking forward to that one."

"You would," Ezra replied. They both laughed.

Their laughter provoked Lindy's exit. Rolling her eyes, she pivoted away from us, calling over her shoulder that we should let her

know whether our family might visit her family on Friday. I wanted
to follow her. It was just as Mama said. Lindy Junkett always walked
in the right direction.

"She wasn't going to go into the village no how," said Ruby.

"Why should she?" I said.

"Because she don't like adventures."

"What are you talking about?"

"She don't go nowhere she isn't supposed to go, always preaching at everybody like she better than us. I can't think of anyone more
boring than Lindy Junkett," said Ruby, speaking slowly to me like I
was a baby. "Cinthy, when you start off on a journey you don't know
what all might happen. That's what's exciting. That's how you get
strong and brave. That's the whole point of not doing what you're
told to do."

"Aren't you sad that she's dead? It's so awful," I said. "We learned
a lot from her. We saw her every day."

"I want to see where she washed up," said Ruby. "C'mon, Ez.
Nobody will miss us."

"See what? There's nothing to see," I said. "She *died*."

But Ruby began walking. Ezra readjusted the strap of her book
bag so that it bounced like a bustle off her butt. Her fingers were
now fretting the braids on her head, unraveling Mama's care. Whatever there was to know in life, their long-legged gait suggested, was
something I should have already known by now.

6

WE TOOK ONE OF THE OLD, ROUGH TRAIL PATHS DOWN TO THE VILLAGE. The angry tangle of branches and roots left our legs itchy and our faces hot. Our uniforms were wet from sweat and the humid sea air. As we came from the trail that placed us on a small street, which led to the main street running along the shore, the glare of the sky met the roar of the water. We walked, half dazed, through watery veils of sunlight that shone above the village square.

We could barely manage to say a handful of words to one another without growing irritable. I spoke the most, as I believed there was still time for me to convince my sister that we had no right to go poking around the details of our teacher's death.

"Who's going to pay attention to you," said Ruby, interrupting me. She lifted her voice to get Ezra's attention. "Let's go to her apartment. It'll be more interesting."

"And nobody would see us," said my sister, nodding.

"Ezra," I said. "That's trespassing."

"Cinthy, you can't trespass when someone's dead," said Ruby. "They don't have no rights or property. You can't get in trouble for that kind of thing."

"Easy for you to say," I said. "You don't understand the kind of attention Ez and I get just for loitering around on the street."

"You think that everyone cares about every single thing you do," said Ruby. "You're giving the world too much of your mind."

"Shut up, Ruby," said Ezra. "The world's got plenty of power."

"To kill us," I said.

"You always jump right to death," Ruby said, shaking her head as she kicked a stone ahead of her, knocking other stones out of her path. "You can't land nowhere in the middle."

"You think we get to live in the middle? Mama says that colored girls barely get to have anything. It's always work. Work to be born at all and work to die."

"What the hell does that even mean, Cinthy?" Ruby sighed. "And Miss Burden didn't live in the middle, did she?"

"These mosquitoes are getting on my nerves," said Ezra, waving her hands around her face in frustration. "I get more than three bites I swear I'm going home."

"There's no point talking about this no more," Ruby said to me. "If you're too chicken to go with us, it shows you don't really care about the woman. You acting like you cared the most about her. If that's true, I don't see why you wouldn't want to find out something more about her life before they toss her in the ground tomorrow."

"That's enough," said Ezra. "Cinthy cares about people. She's just respectful. That's how we've been raised."

"And how have *I* been raised?"

Shrugging, Ezra pushed herself forward, allowing the downward slope of the street to quicken her pace. I could tell she was being careful with Ruby. Maybe she still felt guilty about what she'd said yesterday about Ruby's papa. Ezra had said nothing to me about what we'd done up on the rocks with Ruby either. I kept expecting her to explain it to me, why it had been important for her and Ruby to test each other that way. It was like she was relieved we could focus on our teacher instead of fighting one another. If she had any misgivings about Ruby's suggestion that we check out Miss Burden's apartment, she kept them fastened inside her set jaw. Since we were little girls, I'd seen my sister catapult herself into a kind of stoicism that bordered foolishness. She didn't like to turn back from her decisions.

In the village square, the statue of the Virgin was coated in molten sunlight that made my eyes burn. A strong, salt-swept wind dried the sweat on my face. It was so beautiful, standing there near St. Mary Star of the Sea and letting my eyes glide to where the land fell away into the rolling murmur of thick water. The shadows of gulls traced the ground where we stood. I felt my mind unbuckle itself from its knot. When I looked out at the water anything was possible.

"This is perfect," said Ruby. "It's so hot, everyone's inside. Nobody'll have any energy to give a damn about us. We can just have ourselves a look around and be on our way."

When I realized that Ezra was not going to protest Ruby's easy logic, I said, "I'm only coming along to make sure you don't ruin anything. I don't want my sister getting into trouble on account of you."

"You can't ruin the dead," said Ruby, frowning.

. . .

MISS BURDEN'S DOOR HAD BEEN left standing open. I'd never been in any of the apartments above the storefronts. The room was so plain it was awful. But the view was marvelous. There was a glimpse of a thin ridge of black rock and then green waves, which lapped and surged, lifting rainbow sprays, as water rushed and withdrew, slapping the old pilings.

"You'd think they would've put up a sign to keep people out," said Ezra. "It looks perfectly normal."

"She didn't drown here, dummy," said Ruby, before turning away. But I noticed her tread was light, as though she might snag a trip wire. "Besides, it isn't against the law to take your own life."

"Shut up, Ruby," I said, rolling my eyes because I was both irritated and slightly nauseous. "We don't know what happened."

"Does it matter if we did? Dead is dead."

A watery breeze began to twist the pale, gauzy curtains that framed the windows.

Standing at the window, I looked down at Miss Burden's desk. There was a diary with leather trim and Miss Burden's monogrammed initials. Unsure whether I was tampering with evidence, I opened it anyway. On the inner cover, my teacher had written her name, *Lilac Marie Burden,* and included her birth date with a dash that opened into blank space.

The sea air increased in violence, shoving the sheer panels to the ceiling.

Lilac was a soft name, a word that conjured romance, comfort, and care. I hadn't known that my teacher was also named for a flower. Like Mama, Miss Burden's mother must have cared about her when she was born, cared enough to name her daughter after something natural and distinct. Our teacher had been named for something in the world that had its own perfect smell. Like cinnamon, basil, or oranges, it could not be mistaken for anything but what it was.

"Look at this," said Ezra. She was sitting on the neatly made double bed, holding a picture frame.

"Who is that?" said Ruby, coming out of Miss Burden's bathroom and joining Ezra on the bed.

"What were you doing in there?" I said.

"*Pissing,*" spat Ruby. "That all right with you?"

"Isn't that a curse?" said Ezra. "Peeing in a dead person's bathroom?"

"Oh, Ez, *shut up.*"

"It really could be," said Ezra.

"Then everybody's cursed!"

"Shut up, Ruby. You're a heathen," I said. "Don't tell my sister to shut up when she's trying to help you."

"That her mama?" asked Ruby, ignoring me, as she peered at the photo in Ezra's hands.

"I don't think so," my sister said. "Look how close their faces are. Almost touching."

I came over to offer my opinion. "She's young in this."

"Burden wasn't that old," said Ruby. "About my ma's age, maybe younger than that."

"Miss Burden looks happy here," I said. "I never saw her smile like this at school."

"She's smiling like the woman's her boyfriend."

"Maybe she is," said Ruby.

We were all silent and looked more closely at how the woman's arms were wrapped around our teacher, whose head was thrown back in the middle of a laugh.

"There's a suitcase," said Ezra. She used her foot to tap it, underneath the bed.

I bent down so that I could see it—a sky-blue cardboard suitcase with brass latching. It was plastered with travel stickers. The handle was hard plastic, the color of ivory.

"Let's take it," said Ruby.

"That's stealing," I said.

"From who?"

"It's evidence."

"Of what?"

"It isn't yours, Ruby. It doesn't belong to you."

She sighed, glaring at me. "It don't be*long* to no*body*. You see her family lining up outside the door for her personal effects?"

"You didn't like her," said Ezra.

"She treated me like trash."

"Shut up, Ruby!"

"It's the truth so help me God, Ez, she treated me like the bottom of her foot."

"Will you both be quiet!" I said. "Somebody's on the stairs!"

"Shit!" Ezra said, leaping up to take me by the wrist.

We rushed to the closet together. Three of Miss Burden's dresses hung there on wire hangers. I saw a pair of her shoes. I wanted to cry.

"Shit shit *shit* shit!" said Ruby, hissing, as we heard voices on the other side of the door.

"There's no explaining it," said a woman's voice. "But she paid her rent for this month and next. Paid it on time. She wasn't never late with it."

"You get Judy in here to scrub the place down," replied a man's voice. "Henry says he's willing to paint it for a few dollars. Someone will want it. What, with the view."

"It's a very good view," said the woman.

"Wasn't good enough."

"Charlie said they been trying to find relatives."

"Where was she from? Lila, was it?"

"Yes, Lila," said the woman, sighing. "She never spoke of any people to me. Never had a friend come by and visit. No boyfriend. Nothing indecent about her. That's why I told Charlie she must have done it to herself. Wasn't never no hot flame burning her candles."

"She'll burn in hell just the same."

"Aw, I don't know if she deserves that," said the woman. "Look, here's a pack of cigarettes and a bottle of scotch. So she had some fun."

"Don't look like she got that from around here," said the man, in a thoughtful voice. "That's the expensive stuff. Hell, it shouldn't go to waste. You keep it if you want 'less you're superstitious about that kind of thing. There's a bowl on the floor in the kitchen. Cat lady?"

"Dog, I believe."

"You charge her extra for it?"

"No. It was a stray that took a liking to her."

"Hm."

"It was a quiet dog. I only seen it a couple of times, but she might've had it for a few years."

"I never seen her walking no dog. Reckon I never seen her at all except at St. Mary's sometimes. Seems like if she had religion, she'd have had to know that taking your own life will land you in hell."

"I had an uncle who took his."

"How?"

"Shotgun."

"You get Judy to box all this up. Ain't much."

"Sure," said the woman. "Fred said he'd put an ad in the Saturday paper."

"Howie says they'll have the grave dug by morning."

From the gap under the closet door, we could make out the shapes of their feet as they moved around the apartment. I wanted to get out. I didn't like the hems of Miss Burden's dresses touching my head.

"Leave the windows open so I can air it all out when I get back from my lunch. I'll tell Judy to bring a fan up here while she's getting it ready."

"Sure."

"You see any signs that she did it on purpose? I told Charlie I'd look again."

"Not a single sign in sight. You tell him."

The muscles in my legs and arms were cramped. I hugged my knees tightly against my chest. We couldn't leave the closet yet because there was still a pair of feet walking back and forth on the other side of the door. A woman's dry cough punctuated the slow pace of each step.

My skin absorbed heat from Ezra and Ruby. I thought of Lindy, who never sweated in the heat of the sun. She always kept talc in her purse, just in case. I was sorry I hadn't followed Lindy over to the Junketts', or waited for Daddy's faculty meeting to end, or even walked home alone through the woods to Mama. But because I'd chosen to follow my sister, I was now trapped in the airless closet of our dead teacher, who could not teach anyone anything ever again. I licked the sweat that dripped from the tip of my nose to my lips.

The person who was walking around Miss Burden's apartment opened and closed cabinets loudly. We heard water running in the bathroom and then watched the shadowy steps move across the floor into the kitchen. There was the sound again of water rushing from the tap and down a drain.

The woman, likely the wife of Miss Burden's landlord, didn't make any sound. There was only her presence—a woman silent in her thoughts, unaware that three silly girls were stranded inside a closet. A closet that could, at any moment, be thrown open for her to inspect. For once, Ruby and Ezra did not whisper a single word.

I kept returning to what we'd done yesterday. I saw the ugly star that our three pairs of legs had made together. Perhaps we'd cast some kind of spell on the village by trying to look at one another in a way we weren't supposed to. Maybe it was our fault that Miss Burden had done what she did.

My face burned in the dark. I pressed my heels into the floor-boards of the closet. I could feel my underwear and the skin on my thighs sticking and pulling against the splintered wood. There was a loose nail pushing into my skin. My tailbone was singing. Hiding hurt.

Then a small sound filled the air, growing slightly louder in its volume. The woman on the other side of the door was sobbing. Her cries, thick and guttural, reminded me of a honking goose. Maybe she'd used her hands to cover her face. Had she known Miss Burden personally, or was she simply disturbed by Miss Burden's unsettling story, her incomplete fate?

We heard her cough and sigh. "Enough," she said in a muffled voice, as if she was speaking with her hands covering her mouth. The wooden floor creaked as the thud of her footfalls crossed back towards the front door of the apartment. The sound of her locking up the apartment gave me a chill.

"She's gone," hissed Ruby. "We've got to get the hell out of here!"

Ezra kicked the door open so hard it flew back then slammed shut before creaking open again. I crawled out of the closet on my cramped knees while Ezra cursed. The wind had flattened and the temperature of the room had soared. It was like opening an oven door and being engulfed, immediately, by full heat.

Ruby was already at the foot of Miss Burden's empty bed, strug-gling with the sky-blue suitcase that was lodged underneath it. It was either very heavy or had gotten stuck on the bed frame's broken springs.

Despite her fears of curses, Ezra went into the bathroom. The sound of her piss hitting the toilet was loud.

I had to go too, but I refused to use Miss Burden's toilet. I listened to Ezra soaping and rinsing her hands. She emerged with glittering eyes.

"Look," said Ez, holding out a tube of red lipstick and a pack of Viceroys. The grooved cylinder of lipstick was gold-plated and the brilliant, waxy red had melted at a dull, rounded angle. I'd never seen Miss Burden wear lipstick. I'd never seen her smoke.

"They're just going to throw this stuff away," said Ruby, grinning as she examined the orderly arrangement of lotions and earrings on the mirrored tray of Miss Burden's vanity. Ruby lifted a crystal bottle of perfume and squeezed the small sequined balloon all over her face and neck.

"They should," said Ez.

"I'd like to have her diary," I said, surprised to hear the steadiness of my own voice. I thought of the essays I'd written, and how Miss Burden had taken such care to write out her thoughts and questions to me. I'd saved those papers in a special folder and liked to reread them sometimes, as if my teacher and I were having a conversation that we could never have in the classroom. I couldn't bear to think that she would never write to me ever again. Then I thought of my own diaries at home. They were hidden around my bedroom, so that if anyone tried to find them, they'd have to look hard and lift heavy things. Maybe Miss Burden would approve of me protecting her innermost language from nosy villagers.

"Mosquitoes are going to tear you up," I said, "pouring that stuff all over yourself that way. You smell like a lady."

"She ain't one," said Ez, chuckling. "No matter how much she wants to be."

"Why don't you two get home?" said Ruby, standing up, distracted. "Cinthy, I can put her diary in the suitcase and then I'll bring it over to your place."

"Don't bring that mess to our house," said Ezra. "We'd be in trouble for sure if you turn up with a dead white lady's stuff."

"Nobody even seen this stuff, Ez."

"But we'd be asked about it," I said. "Mama and Daddy would ask about it."

"I bet they would," said Ruby in a dry voice. "But you want that diary, don't you? Think you'll find out what happened? You think she'd leave her little pet a key to her entire life?"

Ruby threw her head back with laughter. I wondered how quickly I could punch her throat. Unlike Ruby, I wasn't a thief. I wanted the diary because it felt like all the adults wanted to throw Miss Burden's life away instead of trying to find out who she was.

"Well, we can always stash everything in that haunted house across the road," said Ruby, talking like she lived with us. As much as she tried, she wasn't our family. She didn't live with us and she certainly didn't live across our road.

"*You* can hide it at *your* place, Ruby," I said. "In that outhouse you call a home. You don't even know what's in that old suitcase."

"I wish your head was in it," said Ruby. "I'd throw your stupid, brainless skull right off the dock out there."

"Shut up," said Ezra, handing the lipstick and pack of cigarettes to Ruby. "We're leaving before somebody else comes. We don't want anything."

"I want the diary," I said.

"Put it in your bag then, dummy," said Ruby. "You sure quick to let me take the blame for damn near everything. You want something, you better speak up."

Shyly, I went to the desk, where I slid the journal inside the opening between my new school notebooks. Taking it felt as if I'd cut a lock of Miss Burden's hair from her head without her permission. The minute I'd fastened my bag and pushed it around my shoulder, a wind swept through the room, scattering envelopes and receipts. It was as though Miss Burden herself had shoved the papers off her desk.

"Cinthy, we're going *right* now," said Ezra.

Following my sister, I glanced back quickly to see that Ruby had

dropped again to the floor next to the bed. Her freckled face puck-
ered beneath the spiky arrows of her bangs. She'd nearly pulled most
of the case out from under the bed now.

The blue box was so brilliant I wondered where Miss Burden had
found such a suitcase. At some point, my homely teacher must have
been a different woman, one who'd once walked into a department
store and pointed at the brazen blue color like she could buy the sea.

7

RELIEVED THAT SHE'D EVADED DEPUTY CHARLIE'S NIGHTLY PATROL OF the square, Ruby slowed as she approached the trail that led to her home up in the bluffs. The man treated her with the same contempt with which he treated her father. In spite of her being a young girl, Deputy Charlie spoke to Ruby as if he expected her to become her father—a sad yet violent drunk. Lately, he'd begun to follow her around the village, "tailing" her. There was no one to protect her from his lewd comments and gestures. No one was looking at her as innocent. Ruby knew that if she tried to defend her reputation, it would be worse for her and for her father and mother. Deputy Charlie reminded her of the man at the air show who had taken her money and dared her with his eyes to fight back. The deputy was like the village men who tried to touch her when she had to fetch her papa from the bar at closing. She feared what Deputy Charlie would do, as he had done her entire life, if he dragged her father to Salt Point's pathetic little prison cell. More than once, the man had threatened to put her there too.

Ruby reached the old route where no one could see her or what she'd carried out of the dead woman's apartment. She threw her weight with every step to keep the suitcase and the sack, filled with whatever else she could grab of Burden's life, from pulling her over. The edge of the suitcase had already cut one of her knees.

She'd stayed behind after Ezra and Cinthy had left, lifting everything she was able—jewelry, a satin robe, two hideous dresses, silver cutlery, a barely touched bottle of Nina Ricci L'Air du Temps that she'd wrapped in the dead woman's clothes, and even a pair of high-heeled sandals. Those had surprised her.

Miss Burden had given Ruby something special even if she hadn't meant to. Sometimes it was after death that somebody could do things for you.

. . .

RUBY WAS PREPARING TO HIDE the sack somewhere in the brush—she'd come back for it later—when a voice called for her.

"Ruby? That you, girl? Ain't you got school in the morning?"

"Papa, is that you?"

"What day is it?"

"Monday, sir," said Ruby. "I've got school every day this week."

"Help me up, girl."

Ruby followed his voice and found her father's shadow under the messy cover of shrubs where he lay prostrated with his arms extended on either side of his limp body. His voice was a strop. He was coiled like a night snake except that she'd never smelled a snake that stank the way her papa did. His drinking spell had worn off him and he was sharp. Ruby didn't dare take off the sack now, even though it was dark. She couldn't see the branches that would snap beneath her burden. It would draw his attention.

As she helped him into a sitting position, Ruby felt the ragged fingernails of his hand against her shoulder. He almost pulled her down on top of him.

"That's it," her father said, using her body to push off and stand on his two legs. "Was you in the village?"

"Yes, sir," said Ruby, hearing the threat of the razor in his question.

"The hell you were," he said. "You just told me you was in school. Which is it?"

"I was in school in the morning but they let us go early."

"Hm," he said. "What's that you carrying?"

"Supplies, for school," she said. "We sure got a lot of work to do to graduate. First day of school used to be a joke, but it ain't no more."

"Your ma at the aunts'?" Her mother's sisters also lived on the Scaggses' property, which was like a disorderly compound.

"Yes, sir," said Ruby. Her muscles felt as though they'd tear from her bones. From the central square of Salt Point, she'd had to take a difficult route, carrying the overloaded sack and suitcase uphill through scraggly brush the entire time it took to get to the bluffs. Ruby hadn't expected to discover her papa there in the raw roots, but somehow he'd seemed, in his stupor, to intuit his daughter's path. She was grateful that her father's hangover had slowed his usual pace. He hadn't noticed the blue suitcase, because of the way she held it on the side of her.

Ruby and her father came through the woods to the clearing where the moon lit their shack; the mismatched shingles gleamed beneath the veil of light draped across their rusting, welded waves. There were no lamps lit inside. When her papa stayed away drinking, and especially when he returned, sour and belligerent, Ruby's ma made no attempt to be his wife. Above their roof, Ruby could see so many stars, cast and scattered like silvery spores across the flat field of night.

Ruby looked at her papa's face as he used his fingers to rake his whitish hair back from his eyes. She could see his mind rattling and knew that all of his thoughts were about his past or how soon he would be able to die. Any minute he'd get to crying about something that had happened to him when he was just a boy.

He fumbled in his pocket until he had a cigarette and lighter in his palm. There was a little bit of blood in the right corner of his lips. His shirt was torn. She'd seen him this way all her life. He was always getting thrown out of the Thirsty Lad, where he drank too much and looked for fights he could not win. She could picture exactly the way Damn Charlie—she'd never call him deputy—would've grabbed her father by the collar, dragging and beating him through the streets for the entire village to see. Damn Charlie behaved as if he and her papa were in a silent movie, their bodies contorted grotesquely in a slapstick routine against the mute set of a maritime stage.

In the dark, she knew they could both feel his rage, his sour mirth. His narrow cheeks puffed once, twice, and then he tossed his head back, squinting up at heaven as though he'd been there before and had found it tiresome. "What's it all for, Ruby? That schooling? I know that son-of-a-bitch Hobart is a worser man than me. He's a crook and his wife's about as brainless as an earthworm's fart. That the kind of woman you intending to be?"

Neither of them spoke for several minutes. Then Ruby understood what he was asking. Her father wanted to know if she was planning to leave him.

"I don't know," Ruby said. At least she was telling him one part of the truth. She knew better than to mention anything about her dreams.

He nodded and seemed fine with that. "You ain't ate up all of that meat, is you? It'll help with my headache."

"No, Papa, there's plenty," she said. Her throat felt thick with the threat of his harm.

Before Ruby went to prepare the meat and fry her papa some eggs, she crept away to hide what she'd taken from her teacher's apartment. Surely, Burden hadn't thought it would end the way it had. Or even worse, what if she had? Imagine a smiling, moon-faced girl looking around inside her life only to realize that all the windows of her dream house had been bricked up before she ever moved in.

· · ·

AFTER HER FATHER FINISHED EATING, Ruby filled the tub she'd used the day before so that he could bathe. She helped him struggle out of his soaked denim while he cursed and threatened to get sick if she couldn't be less stupid. One bare leg trembled in the warm fire-light, the other was still shrouded in dark fabric. It made her think of Mr. Kindred's single arm, and she wondered whether Ezra had ever looked at her father like this, startled by the asymmetry of his flesh. "Get me a towel and wet it so I can wash my chest first," he spat. "Ain't you bathed me enough to know how to do it without making me cuss you," he went on, his voice ringed with tears.

Ruby knew this was the part where her father warmed into hating himself.

As she looked around to see where one of his hounds had dragged the striped towel, she realized that they had been howling out of hunger. They hadn't been fed since yesterday.

"Ruby, get your ass over here," he said. Standing still, bare-chested, he raised his head again and inhaled deeply. "What the fuck is *that*? Ruby?"

"Papa?"

"Where—the—goddamn—have—you—been?"

They were standing in front of the fire pit while the firelight blazed against the metal rim of the tub. Ruby worried it was getting too hot. If her father touched it, his palms would be seared. He would give that pain to her. The hounds picked up the fat of her papa's rage and chewed it until they frothed. Their barking was low-throated, male.

"I'm sorry," she said. "I'll feed them now."

"Girl, I wasn't asking you nothing," he said, "about those fucking dogs. I *asked* where you *been*?" He leaned his face into his daughter's hair. "That perfume? You been with somebody? I can tell. You know I can tell."

Her skin tightened on her bones so hard her breath almost choked her. He'd take her breathlessness for guilt. Ruby didn't answer him. If she stepped back now, she might outrun him before his fingers could find the buckle on his belt.

Ruby could smell herself now too. Sweet Jesus. The roses of her dead teacher's girlish scent had transformed Ruby's body with the allure of gardenia, bergamot, peach, tuberose, orchid, cedar. Blooming jasmine. The stolen perfume draped Ruby's body in a robe of flowers from the crown of her head to her bare feet, which were already roughening from the steep walk home.

"You sure as hell been up to something," he said. "Who is he?"

Ruby shook her head. "Papa, I *swear*."

The wind rushed from her body. Her father's touch turned Ruby into liquid as she fell to the ground. The heavy weight of that sack had left her so tired she couldn't run. Ruby grunted, blowing hair from her face as her father leaned above her. Sighing, he was tearful as he brought his fist through the air into her stomach again and again.

When he finished, he smoothed his hair and lit a cigarette. Since he was a boy his daughter's age, Jonah Reuben Scaggs had smoked Marlboros. Ruby could hear the buckle of his belt as he tried to get his second leg out of his pants. He cursed, struggling with the leather. Then the belt swung in the air.

8

FRIDAY EVENING, EZRA, DADDY, AND I WENT OVER TO THE JUNKETT home to enjoy one of Miss Irene's famous meals. Over the years, we'd all come to hold Miss Irene's meals the way we held the word *Sunday* in our mouths. Sometimes it was a candlelit picnic. Other times it was a bold barbecue, bordering on what could be called heathen. Every time Miss Irene and Mr. Caesar welcomed us to their table it was a good time, and an ordinary thing like our families eating together could feel holy. There were no other tables in Salt Point that welcomed our families to eat with theirs. Miss Irene took these Friday evenings seriously. She mandated joy and stuffed our bodies with spiced meat, fresh greens, cakes made from scratch, and furious dancing.

Between bid whist games and birthday celebrations, there were serious things the adults had to discuss, and we children were often left to ourselves, playing stickball or jumping rope out on the dust road in front of their modest home, which was only a few miles from our own. The feeling of happiness and safety was as palpable as a taste. Being with the Junkett family gave me the same pleasure that school and the sea did. Miss Irene's imagination and love were innate, organic. She gave these things to her children, to us, to herself.

That Friday evening, I felt that she was trying to give us even more than usual.

When we arrived, the Junkett children were already out in the yard, dressed flawlessly in the hand-stitched splendor of their mother's sewing designs. The twins, Rosemary and Empire, wore pale lime-and-pink seersucker outfits. Their skin gleamed with innocence and coconut oil. Lindy was setting out dishes and candles. Her light green sundress featured bold white and gold flowers that reminded me of paintings where young, smiling girls balanced plates of fruits. Ernest was tending to the barbecue. He wore a light blue shirt and a pair of patterned trousers that I was certain Miss Irene had made by hand, as she often did when it came to her family's wardrobe. She disliked buying clothing from department stores. She had an eye for how clothes ought to fit and her selection of colors was unusual; you found your eyes returning over and over to her designs.

As we parked, I noticed Ezra smoothing the skirt of her own dark gold sundress. She pressed her fingers against her braids and applied some gloss to her lips, quickly tapping the balm against her mouth with satisfaction before snapping shut her powder-blue, scalloped compact, a recent birthday gift from Mama. Pleased by what she saw, she tossed it into her small beaded purse, which was a gift from Miss Irene. I wore purple shorts and a white summer blouse that was tied with soft bows at each of my shoulders. My hair was piled into a high, soft bowl. I had enjoyed the drive through the trees to get here. It'd been nice to hold my fingers out against the wind and have the sensation that the wind was holding my hand. My father's profile was so handsome as he'd guided the car down the road. His white shirt and deep green trousers were starched. He'd placed a few wildflowers in the pocket above his heart. He looked like a movie star or a poet. He'd hummed with us as the radio played. I could see that his jaw was unclenching and the muscles around his eyes were less rigid.

Mama had stayed home because she was unwell. All week she'd complained of being tired, though there was nothing specific she could say was giving her pain. *Sometimes women ache,* she had said to me when I'd asked her where the pain was. She had even been tired enough not to touch her whisky. By the end of the week, Daddy had forbidden her to do anything but rest. He told her that we wouldn't stay at the Junketts as long as we usually did, which frustrated Ezra because she'd hoped to listen to some new records with Ernest and Lindy.

Climbing out of the car, I inhaled the scent of Miss Irene's cooking, and the knot that I'd been carrying in the pit of my stomach untwisted.

"Hey, Kindreds," said Mr. Caesar, coming out of the house and down the front steps balancing a tray, which he handed to Ernest with a smile and firm instructions to be careful with Miss Irene's spice-rubbed ribs.

He and my father met in the road, hugging and laughing. Lindy placed the dishes aside, gliding from the yard to us. Her smile glowed as she kissed my father's cheek and hugged us. The twins, sweet as birds, hopped and squeaked towards me, both speaking at once: "Cinthy we're having cake. Momma made us a big, big cake! We can eat our greens first to get them out of the way, okay? Then after we have the other stuff, we'll have cake."

I rubbed Empire's head and pretended to lick sugar from my fingers.

Turning, I saw that Ernest had left his post at the grill to greet my father and Ezra. Even though he was speaking to my father, his eyes were on my sister in her deep gold dress and shining skin. This new way of his, looking intently at her without saying anything, had begun in the spring. We'd all noticed it, though the two of them seemed oblivious or shy or defensive whenever our parents made the slightest joke about young love. Ernest was seventeen and nearly an exact replica of Mr. Caesar, but he had his mother's eyes and curly eyelashes. His voice had changed so much this past year that sometimes, if I wasn't paying attention, I thought it was Mr. Caesar talking. I could see the muscles beneath the light fabric of Ernest's shirt, and the fitted look of his trousers made my face grow slightly warm.

I went into the house, hungry for Miss Irene's voice and her ground-shaking hugs. The walls of the living room were painted in bright blue and yellow. Family photographs smiled out at me in wooden frames that Mr. Caesar had made by hand. There were some of Miss Irene's paintings too: bowls of flowers, seascapes, pencil drawings of each Junkett child as a baby. Family relics from Royal—silver spoons, hand-painted plates, Miss Irene's baby shoes and christening dress—made the living room feel like a cheerful museum of their life. There was even a machete, polished and impressive, which Mr. Caesar said had belonged to his great-grandfather.

In the kitchen, Miss Irene was dancing as she peered into her bubbling pots. That's usually where she could be found, her fingers busy and her mouth even busier with stories from her childhood in Royal. When she was too homesick for such stories, she turned her enthusiasm to the new America she believed was birthing itself against the tiresomeness of white people. Today, without looking up, she cried out a greeting in her melodious voice.

"Miss Irene," I exhaled, almost running into her arms. Her scent was lush and dense, like a paradise from another world. Coconut oil, pepper, mint, lemon, fruit trees, baby powder, sweat. She folded me against her body and swayed before she released me to gaze into my eyes. "How you been, baby girl?"

"It wasn't the first week of school I wanted," I said, knowing that I could say this to her without feeling she would reproach me the way my parents might.

Nodding, she offered me a taste of a new barbecue sauce, which was heavenly. She tossed the spoon into the sink, pointed at a bowl of perfectly shaped lemons, and handed me a pitcher. I knew that whenever I wanted to talk to Miss Irene, I'd be expected to help with the meal in some way. That seemed fair enough.

"I know you must have so many questions," she said, lowering the volume of the radio. "I wish I had answers for you, honey. But nobody does when things like this happen. Strange deaths can overpower life itself, which is even stranger and more important. We can forget how life makes us feel when we hear that someone's death has come too quickly. It feels like a storm that can blow us away, doesn't it? Until the sun appears again and reminds us that it was always there above the thunder and rain. That's how life and death are—they belong to each other even when we think they're at opposite ends of the world. What I want you to do is figure out how to be happy with whatever gifts that woman gave you. When you feel sad about her leaving you, try to remember the things that made you feel like she cared about you."

"There's love you can't even see," said Miss Irene, almost to herself. "You aren't supposed to see it, but you feel it."

Ernest and Ezra came through the back door at that moment, holding huge heaps of greens. They were both smiling above the overflowing tin bowls in their arms. *Greens don't make you smile that way,* I thought.

Ezra greeted Miss Irene with a kiss. It was no secret to any of us that Miss Irene had always held a favorite place for Ezra. Maybe because they both were the eldest sisters in their families. Or because they shared a way of looking at the world, a way where they both refused to give up on themselves and our families. Ernest stood there, handsome and goofy. "Shoo," said Miss Irene, and he backed up awkwardly and fled the kitchen.

Ezra raised the volume of the radio to exactly where Miss Irene had it when I'd come into the kitchen.

"We're going to let some things simmer, girls," said Miss Irene. "And while the funk in my pots gets going, we're going to do something else."

"What?" I asked, twisting a lemon half. I turned around at the sound of Miss Irene's bracelets clicking rapidly. She'd lifted one of her arms in the delicious air and was holding one of Ezra's hands as she twirled her. My sister's smile went through me and I danced over to both of them, shaking my hips and moving my head against the pulse of the music that I couldn't see but felt go through my heart.

. . .

DINNER WITH THE JUNKETT FAMILY helped me feel as though the things that had happened to us during our first week of school were already in the past, and that I had a choice to remember them or let them go.

It had been unlike any week of school that I'd ever had. I was still numb when I thought of all that had happened. I wanted my teacher to be alive. I wanted that pleasant feeling of Miss Burden looking into my eyes when she called on me for the correct answer. I wanted her recognition of my intelligence, our quiet lunches where reading was a feast we both shared. What would I do if my next teacher disliked me, as the rest of our faculty seemed to? I wanted to imagine myself as the kind of girl who could say no when she was asked to do something that felt wrong to her, such as letting a white girl like Ruby Scaggs look inside her private place.

As we prepared to go home to Mama, I saw that Miss Irene had pulled Ezra to the side, away from the long table where we'd feasted. She held Ezra's face between her hands and was speaking to her in a deliberate voice. On a small wooden bench, Rosemary and Empire were entwined, curled into the special, heavenly sleep of twins that seemed as sweet as the homemade chocolate ice cream they'd devoured.

Mr. Caesar opened the gate while Daddy walked beside him. Their baritone voices were warm from the balm of Miss Irene's home cooking. I loved listening to Daddy and Mr. Caesar. It was as if I had two fathers. It made me feel twice as safe and loved. Though my father was more serious and Mr. Caesar more mischievous, I thought that they complemented each other the way brothers do.

With two hands, I balanced a plate heaped with food for Mama.

"We got to watch everything and everybody these days, even our shadows," Mr. Caesar was saying. "That's the way it is. Eisenhower's signed the document. And it is what it is. You read about that yet in the papers? Jim Crow, Jim Cat, Jim Monkey, Jim Mule. White folks don't want to believe that the president's going to make them treat us like anything more than dogs.

"Still, it's a beginning. We getting there. Most of the time, we got it good up here. Imagine if we was at the front of the firing line, preaching that mess about nonviolence while standing up to them pigs in Alabama. I'd probably get myself killed doing something like that. I only learned patience when I realized I had children to raise. God bless this race. Those Negro boys and girls going to be the reason my children will grow up not having to sit at the back of the bus. Drink water from any fountain they want when they thirsty. You know how fucked up you got to be to make a law where somebody can't drink the same *water* you do? 'Cause *you* white and what the hell color is water? Tell me that or don't tell me nothing.

"In my dreams, the white man's always been on notice. Been that way since I was a boy. Too many times I seen a cracker blow a nigger's head off for nothing. Heard about white men going into churches and lighting 'em up just 'cause we don't want to pray like they say they taught us. I was a bitty boy and seen a white man shoot a preacher right in his head 'cause the man forgot to address that devil as *sir*.

"Heron, my man, we got to be ready. The front is going to be everywhere. Already is."

Daddy nodded, speaking quietly, "Lena's been so worried about the girls lately. They're becoming young women. She's worried because there isn't any law here, Caesar. Not really. Or when there is, the law is part of the problem. It feels like the village is seething at the sight of us, from that deputy to the fishermen. All their glaring. Lena and I go back and forth about whether we ought to leave the village once they finish school in the spring."

"That right?" said Mr. Caesar. "Where would y'all go? You'd need a good job where they'd treat you and your family right. Maybe you could find one of them new Negro schools. They got 'em growing all over the country. Colleges and universities that's all about what we need to learn to live for ourselves. That'd be better. Help our people."

"Sure," said my father. I watched the toothpick scaling Daddy's teeth evenly.

"The truth is that we might even send the girls off somewhere. You know, a boarding school or something. We don't want them to stay in the village anymore. Even if our house is paid for. I think I told you one time that I bought it outright. I've never trusted credit, not for a Black man. I certainly don't like the idea of trusting a bank that's miles and miles away from me to keep a roof over our heads. American mortgages are a racket. Lena and I sidestepped that mess and used our savings to get the house. Now we can do what we want. Sell the damn house or burn it to the ground."

I'd never heard my father speak in such a way. I had obviously missed the signs that our lives were spinning away from what I'd thought I understood, which was that we were more or less settled forever in Salt Point.

But the village had apparently sensed our fathers' bitterness because, as Daddy and Mr. Caesar stood on the road, staring at nothing, a single police cruiser pulled into sight.

Deputy Charlie was alone inside the car, and in uniform. Still rolling forward, he leaned over and glared at us through the open passenger window. With one huge hand, the deputy formed an air pistol with his fingers. Grinning, he pressed his thick thumb over and over against an invisible hammer, as though he were shooting at clowns in a carnival game.

"Mother*fucker*," said Mr. Caesar, his voice tucked inside his clenched jaw. We rarely heard Mr. Caesar use bad language, but it sounded right to us in this moment. He raised his voice so that it carried its warning directly to the deputy. "Motherfucking *pig*."

The cruiser stopped.

Helplessly, I turned my head as though this wouldn't be happening if I couldn't see it. Ernest had pulled Lindy against his body to shield her. I dropped Mama's plate of food in the dirt. I was so frightened I could feel wetness leaking out of me. Spots appeared, like red sparks, in front of my eyes. I felt like the deputy's fingers could actually shoot real bullets. None of us spoke until he finally drove away. The tires of the cruiser rolled over the gravel and made a sound like teeth breaking under pressure.

"Jesus *Christ,*" my father said, exhaling. "What the *hell* was he *doing?*"

"Man, he does that shit all the time. We're part of his regular route. Y'all live back off the road, so he ain't bothering with you. Not yet anyway," said Mr. Caesar quietly. "This the first time in a long time he done that mess with my children out here. Next time he point his finger at me I might blow the motherfucker off."

"No next time, Caesar. He can't do this," said Daddy. "He can't terrorize you all. You *live* here. He doesn't have the right."

Mr. Caesar gave a deep belly chuckle.

"Shit, you funny, Heron," he said. "You don't seriously believe these police wouldn't line us up in the square and shoot us all in cold blood? Dump us in the sea with the rest of the Africans. They mad we breathing. All we *doing* is *breathing* and they got their bullets ready at the mark."

"Caesar?"

It was Miss Irene's voice. She'd come outside from the kitchen and now stood in the yard, a new expression on her face I'd never seen. There was a pistol in one hand. With her other, she gripped Ezra's hand. In the dark, their eyes burned identically. I nearly expected Ezra to have a pistol of her own, but she was holding a small leather sachet against her chest that must have been a gift from Miss Irene.

"Ernest, Lindy, take the twins inside right now."

"Yes, Momma."

"I'm sorry, Miss Irene," I said. The words stuck on my tongue like dry bread. "I dropped Mama's food. Broke your good plate. I didn't mean to."

"Cinthy, don't worry about that, baby," said Mr. Caesar, placing his hand on my shoulder. "Irene be over to check on your mama tomorrow. She'll bring something for her then. See if Mama's feeling better." He nodded at my father.

"Ezra, we're going home," said Daddy. He walked out into the road, pausing as he stared in the direction of the cruiser's route.

"He still there?"

"Yes, Caesar, he's gone down just a bit. I can see his taillights."

"Shit," said Mr. Caesar. In four long strides, he crossed the yard and went back into the house. Silently, Miss Irene followed.

Rushing to the table, Ezra and Lindy began stacking plates and glasses. Ernest approached Lindy. He whispered something in her ear before he leaned down and scooped both of the twins easily into his arms. Carefully, he carried them up the stairs into the house.

"Ezra, Cinthy, get your things and get inside the car. Right now."

"Yes, Daddy," I said. It took me a moment to walk around the shattered plate and wasted food, and to climb into the back seat. I tried to distract myself from the wet spot between my legs and was relieved that no one else seemed to have noticed.

Dusk had rolled its gold mouth into night. Ezra hugged Lindy tightly before she walked over to our car. There were lighted candles in mason jars arranged around the yard. The glowing light on the grass, which just moments ago I'd found so romantic, took on a haunted look. Ezra opened the passenger door. "Hey," she said. "Come and sit up in the front with me."

"Okay, Ez." I got out of the back seat so that I could sit next to my sister. The heat from her body surprised me. There was a strong scent from the sachet in Ezra's lap.

"Miss Irene says it's for protection."

"From what?"

Ezra turned her head at my question, but her eyes were shifting back and forth from Daddy to the yard, where Lindy flew around the table cleaning our beautiful meal away. We could see her mouth moving in the flickering candlelight. Lindy was praying.

Then Mr. Caesar came back out. Ernest was right behind him. He said something to Lindy and she went inside. A light from their screened porch came on at the side of the house.

Mr. Caesar and Ernest were alone. They came out to the road, their shirts were darkened with sweat and anger. Ezra's hand hung loosely along the window that was rolled down. Ernest bent down to wish us a good night. He might've thought he was slick, but I saw his hand gently brush my sister's hand.

Against the shriek of frogs and insects, night birds, and the prowl of unseen animals, Mr. Caesar's voice was low and clear. "White men got the right to be fools and presidents," said Mr. Caesar. "But not us. Man, take this piece with you. If that motherfucker pulls you over, Heron, shoot first. I don't plan on burying you no time soon and this world damn sure ain't going to bury me 'til I'm good and ready."

9

SITTING BETWEEN MY FATHER AND MY SISTER, I WAS SAFE, YET THE
blood in my heart was rushing, splashing my bones from the inside.
The scent of magic in Ezra's sachet filled the front of our car as the
night breeze carried other invisible spices. Daddy's hand was tight
on the steering wheel, but his voice was soft. I couldn't see the gun
resting on his lap, but I knew it was there. The incident with the
deputy had shaken something loose in my father. His voice opened
inside our darkened car. The past had been closed away from light
for so long, but now Daddy told us that he wanted us to know about
the church burning in Damascus.

"I hadn't been born," he said.

Like us, he appeared surprised to find his voice filling the car,
pushing the cries of insects to the edges of our listening. "I hadn't
been born when it all happened, but I know it," he said, almost to
himself. "I'm telling you girls so that you can know it. Perhaps it'll
give you the strength it never gave me. I had the audacity to think
that if I made myself forget then it would be erased. But that isn't
how blood lives in us. Your mother and I—we never want you to feel
you're alone. The stories in us speak in you. Maybe you can help me
to not forget how love saved me from my own pain."

"How can we help you, Daddy?" said Ezra. Her voice sounded old, as though she'd lived long ago, before our father's birth. Though we'd never heard the sound of our great-grandparents' voices, it felt that they were inside the hushed space of our car.

"The listening may help," he said. "The remembering too."

The car sailed over pockets of darkness. The shadows of branches flitted dimly against our windshield. The moon splintered light across our arms and faces. I sat forward listening to my father's voice, enchanted like I was whenever he read to me. I thought of all the stories, hundreds, that he'd given me. How he had a way of speaking a story that made it sound as though we were there in that exact moment. My sister held my hand, transmitting to me the steady pulse of her heart inside her body.

Closing my eyes, my father's voice melted into my own voice, the one I heard in my mind that helped me imagine what there was no way for me to have otherwise known. My father's story belonged to me and to my sister. It would be the only way we could remember, in our own blood, what my father had forced himself to forget.

Theodore and Calliope Kindred

IT IS A WARM EVENING IN 1902, AND MY GREAT-GRANDFATHER THEO-
dore Kindred is free.

He walks up a mud path along the Delaware River basin to the
church he is building with his own hands. Next to the church, he
has begun to set the foundation for a school. The education and
preservation of the spirit and the flesh have always been united for
him. My great-grandfather is a young man though he has never seen
his birth certificate and has only used the songs in his heart to trace
the years he has lived in the world. He comes from free men and so
his God has always been free.

The structure, unnamed yet nearly completed, sits on a small
hill in a square that is part of the yellow and olive patchwork of land
he purchased with money he earned and saved from years of labor.
The land is in a place his wife, my great-grandmother Calliope, will
christen Damascus, and is so small that there will never be any official recognition of it.

I see my great-grandfather's reddish eyes praising the earth. My
sister and my father have these earthy eyes. My father, who will not
be born for years, will inherit this need from his grandfather, to own
the land on which he will live. It is why my father bought our prop-

erty in Salt Point outright and rejected the emotional yoke of loans or credit. There is a need for independence that can be traced to the bottom of the Atlantic where our ancestors' voices live in bones that have turned into priceless shells. My father and his father and the fathers whose voices guide them invisibly form a compass in our blood. It will always be important for the Kindred men to have an immediate sense of where they will be buried because they will worship that land more than anything.

Theodore pats his horse, Canaan, as they approach the incomplete church. It has just finished raining, and the great horse's hooves make a sucking sound as each step clops in rich, clotted mud. My great-grandfather worries about places the roof hasn't been properly patched. The sanctuary needs airing before Calliope and her beloved twelve schoolchildren arrive for choir practice and Bible study. My great-grandmother has already poured a foundation of learning into the children she has selected as her first class of students. Their classrooms are the natural world, the kitchen, the garden, and a room in her home whose walls are lined with books and that features an upright piano upon which she has been teaching them how to lift their voices in joy. Though she is not related by blood to any of these children, she has earned their families' trust and love. Their parents have come from everywhere, carrying hope and determination to shape their children's future into a world that is filled with the potentials and challenges of independence. These twelve children have been entrusted to my great-grandmother's care, as the precious seeds of an endangered village might journey secretly across oceans to be sown, watered, and harvested in unknown territories.

Calliope is her full name but to everyone in their new town, christened Damascus, she is ever-always Callie. Mama said that my great-grandparents fell in love when they were five or six years old. They were both raised somewhere in Georgia—Mama wasn't sure of the name and Daddy forgot on purpose. Mama said that when my great-grandfather could barely talk, he said to Callie, "I'm going to marry you." The elders laughed when she replied, in her determined little-girl voice, "Fine!"

So, my great-grandfather is thinking of Callie and his good fortune, and how his life has been filled and bettered by her emphatic *Fine!* while he walks in peace. Soon his wife and the children will fill the sanctuary with their sweet singing. After choir and Bible study, they will all share a cold supper. Under the first evening stars, my great-grandparents will walk the children home, teaching them how to learn a safe path in the dark woods. Then, alone, my great-grandmother will pull her husband's hand to her belly where new stars have joined their dust inside her to make their second child.

The first, a daughter, who will become my grandmother Alma Elizabeth Kindred, is under the tender care of a close neighbor. My great-grandfather is building the school for Alma, working with the vision of his daughter's happiness as his mast. Next, he intends to construct a town library.

Like Alma, Damascus is nearly three years old and growing. My great-grandparents had both tired of searching for home, so with Damascus, they'd tried to create paradise for themselves, somewhere between plantation and Promised Land. Black families arrived in Damascus immediately, willing to invest in a dream that would not kill them, and they were still arriving in 1902. Word-of-mouth whispers told them how to find the backwards river and a small Black encampment that was growing just beside the eastern shores of Maryland, not far from Bucktown. These families were preoccupied with finding ways to live beyond the brutality that had sailed them and their African forebears across the Atlantic.

I see Theodore's hand resting peacefully against the muscular neck of his horse. My great-grandfather was rumored to have been nearly seven feet in height, which was why he needed such an incredible animal.

This evening, Theodore may have relied on the company of his horse and the sight of his well-constructed church for peace of mind.

As his acreage increased, he had gained unwanted attention from a group of whites that had initially laughed, waving their hands dismissively when they laid eyes on the small, underdeveloped Black settlement. When those men returned to survey what they hadn't anticipated surviving, much less thriving, they began an incessant campaign of sabotage. Disbelief and derision were quickly replaced with rage as these Christian men asserted their divine rights and economic supremacy.

Theodore had seen this awful art of rage his entire life. Every colored man in America had received, against his will and his soul, this piss-poor education. Recently, he'd discovered Callie crying over her ravaged flower beds and trampled vegetable gardens. No animal but a white man had the teeth, the hunger, to pull up her roots and seeds so viciously.

Another evening, husband and wife had stood inside the door of their house, staring at the faceless, darkly hooded men who lurked, armed, in their yard. A flickering huddle of muffled voices vowed to threaten my great-grandparents with rope, bullets, flame, or worse. Reviewing his mental index of white terror, my great-grandfather was aware that, at some point, their cowardly talk would turn to action.

Those that gathered under my great-grandfather's faith embraced the god who lived in the daily dignity of their own faces. Many of them had forgotten what that pride looked like until they stood in the Kindreds' half-hewn sanctuary. Their recognition of that pride now meant that none of them was willing to turn back from what they were building in Damascus.

Still, tonight, he wonders whether he should have allowed Callie and the children to walk alone in the afterlight of the storm. But white folks did their worshiping on Sunday just like everybody else, said Callie. Hopefully, they would also be at rest.

Alma had been fussy when he'd kissed and nuzzled her satiny forehead before handing her over to Mrs. Whitaker, whose cooing made his daughter's face brighten into a full, dimpled smile.

Alone, he and Canaan had walked along the backwards river before cutting into the woods, towards the hills where the sight of the simple church always filled his heart with joy. It was nearly time to make a naming decision, and Theodore trusted Callie to choose well. He had ebullient visions of bringing up both of their children in this new church, in their new town, named by their mother.

After Calliope Kindred's death, the townspeople will find a slip of paper in my great-grandmother's journal expressing her wish that the church be named Hinder Me Not.

. . .

AS HE TIES HIS HORSE, Theodore hears Callie and the children approaching.

He calls to his wife, then walks around to the front of the church to greet her while the children stream inside to dry off from the sudden rain.

Callie's hair is braided into a soft bowl on her head. She wears a green shawl around her slender shoulders. The black eyes that look out from her oval, freckled face are intelligent, sensuous, and warm.

Theodore presses her wrist against his lips. Their four hands rest on her high, round belly. She asks him about Alma, and he tells her that their baby daughter is fine. Mrs. Whitaker will be waiting for them to pick up the child on their way home. When he turns my great-grandmother's face up to kiss her, he can see Callie at every age they have ever shared a kiss. One of his sharpest, first memories was trying to kiss her and getting punched squarely in his nose before she kissed him back.

On this evening in 1902, Theodore can feel the full, wet artlessness of Callie's lips in their youth; he remembers the taste of buttercream frosting left on her lips from the shared slice of cake on their wedding night—a night in spring when magnolia petals blew through the windows of the hotel he'd saved his paychecks to take her to, onto the white, cool sheets where they'd first made love. He remembers, too, the salt on her lips from her labor, which lasted sixteen hours; she kissed him when she finally held their daughter, Alma, in her aching arms. He can recall the full and easy kiss he gave her when she agreed that it made perfect sense for them to build a town from scratch, a town where they could grow old together in freedom.

More than the building rising in front of them, Calliope is his church.

He listens to her beloved schoolchildren giggling as they watch him and Callie. He smiles back, waving at twelve shy faces. He says he will light the lamps to keep the mosquitoes from tasting their sweet blood. "Better mosquitoes than the devil," he adds while Callie pokes his rib at the place where his heart has burned for her his entire life.

. . .

FROM THE SOUND, THEODORE KNOWS Canaan has suddenly turned two-legged, rearing and dropping down, printing the earth with a warning. The stamping is percussive, fearful, so much so that he can hear his great horse above the upright piano where Callie is playing sideways because of her swollen belly.

My great-grandfather marks his place in his Bible. His eyes meet my great-grandmother's knitted frown. Getting up, he tells the children, who have stopped, wide-eyed, in the middle of their prayer song, to keep going with the music.

Alone, he goes down the rough, unpainted steps at the entrance of what will later be christened Hinder Me Not. Rounding the muddy corner, he walks quickly along the side of the church. A wild animal must have provoked his horse. He regrets that he doesn't have his rifle to fire a warning shot because he doesn't like to have his gun near Callie and the children for no reason.

My great-grandfather has not seen the man who is standing in the shadow. The butt of the man's gun against his neck sends him to the ground. A wheel of red stars burns his eyes as he is yanked, with some effort, to his long feet.

"Git up, Preacher Man," says the voice, which belongs to another man who jabs his own gun into my great-grandfather's side. Theodore shuffles forward. Tears form in his eyes when he hears Canaan snorting and whinnying in distress. "Had yourself a choice, didn't you?" the voice is saying near the temple of his head. "Ain't no choice now after all those warnings we gave you. Bet you wished you'd listened to us the first time, you hardheaded preaching son of a bitch."

Theodore wonders how many of them are standing in the shadows. Sweat pours into his eyes. "Go on then," says my great-grandfather, smelling kerosene. "Burn me up. Hang me. Shoot me. Eat my balls if that's what you're planning. But please, spare them. They're innocent."

From the shadows he can see men flinging the kerosene over his dear friend. Theodore's voice goes hoarse from shouting at them to let the animal live: "Take him alive, won't you? Worth more to you alive, even if you sold him right off. Go 'head and let 'im live! He ain't done you a harm. Let 'im live and he'll be worth more than this! Jesus, let 'im live, let 'im be!"

"Bring him over here, boys," the voice says. "I'm going to make him eat his goddamn horse."

When he hears the match, my great-grandfather does not bow his head but looks directly into the broken, bleeding eyes of his friend to ask forgiveness.

The great horse shrieks, leaping like a man, as the fire rides his back. Soft ears flatten against his skull. Heat engulfs the animal from nostril to belly, until, in defeat, Canaan kneels, dropping in a single bow onto his side. Dark flames work over the marvelous body. Theodore sees their friendship collapse in the dying creature's eyes.

When Theodore turns in horror away from Canaan's scorched body, he spots Callie's face in the window. He mouths the word *run* but one of the men is watching.

"Kindling," he says, laughing.

. . .

THEY DRAG THEODORE MOST OF the way back to the church. It takes four or five of them to get him through the entrance because of his resistance. When they have shoved him inside, they laugh and bar the door from the outside.

Callie, pressing her palms against her belly, sinks to her knees and calls her schoolchildren to her, gathering them into the center of the sanctuary.

Theodore begins smashing the windows opposite from the men. He can push the children out, one or two at a time, so that they can run and hide in the woods. "Don't come back for us," he tells them as they cry.

He is reaching to shatter one of the windows with a blunt broomstick when a bullet tears through the crown of his head.

Then, torches begin to whizz through the broken windows. Landing in green and red rage, the flares instantly begin to chew the church apart.

Weeping, my great-grandmother crawls away from the children and struggles to pull her husband's body back towards their circle. The sleeves of her dress rip at the shoulders. She has never carried the full weight of Theodore. Callie closes her eyes and pulls him with all her strength. His broken skull leaves a slicked comet of blood. Some of the bigger boys, crying and coughing, get up and help her to move him while the beams of the ceiling whine in agony.

She coughs, feeling the baby kicking frantically inside her. Callie spreads herself on the floor next to her husband. In the glass gaze of his dead eyes she can see the furnace of their dreams and faith. Callie kisses him intensely, as she has always kissed him, tasting again the beautiful years they shared. Then her fingers close his silent eyes.

· · ·

BETWEEN HER DEATH AND CROSSING, Callie recalls her own mother and father kneeling in southern cane fields deep in Georgia. She remembers how a white man once dragged her mother away from their table at suppertime, and how her father was forced to let his woman go.

Callie can see her mother now, walking out of the dark moonlight to beckon her daughter. Her eyes are red as rubies. She holds something like a basket in her hand.

It is her master's head.

The fire climbs Callie's hair. It licks her ears, parting her skin from her skull like the crimson sea a prophet once parted to free his enslaved people. Later, those fugitives would become tribes. The hands of twelve children fasten to Callie's sides. The burning hands of twelve children become millions.

Then she thinks of one child: her daughter, Alma.

My great-grandmother's last breath is her daughter's name.

The entire roof of Hinder Me Not collapses. The innocent night, revealed. Callie breathes a single word until it sings its memory back to her—Alma?

Alma!

Alma?

Alma! Alma!

Al—

Like a scream, she crosses with one word to the underworld.

· · ·

CARRYING TWELVE BURNED CHILDREN IN her arms, my great-grandmother Callie meets her husband, Theodore, at the river of eternity.

He explains to her where they are and what they must do, as he always has. "We must cross now, honey," he says. "The children are too young. They don't have as much time to cross as we do before they are lost."

"*Alma?*" says Callie. She is still refusing to die even though her soul is with Theodore and the schoolchildren.

"There's no time left to say goodbye," my great-grandfather says, unable to let himself think about their other child, their unborn child, who is unable to cross, lost in the cinders of darker earth.

My great-grandparents are at the mouth of a roaring river. Theodore sits on the saddle of his beloved horse, Canaan, whose sockets are blinking green fire. My great-grandfather takes the children into his arms, places others across his broad shoulders. Some of them are too small to cross over. They, too, are lost. He must help the rest, so that ancestors can hold them, breathe their short songs into starry symphonies.

Before stepping into the river, Theodore and Callie turn, looking over their shoulders to see their old world, and nestled within it, a small raw speck named Damascus, where they meant to make their own freedom.

10

IT WAS SATURDAY MORNING, AND THERE WERE ONLY A HANDFUL OF people besides Ruby on the local bus. The sunlight pressed against her face, and she closed her eyes, savoring the shadows that dotted across the inner red glow of her eyelids. She wasn't sleepy, anything but. She clutched the small bundle wrapped in a canvas bag on her lap. Her skin was scrubbed clean, and she'd washed her hair, though that didn't matter because no one could see it. Ruby had pushed it up inside the sweat-stained mesh cap that her ma used to make her own black hair lie flat, before she tugged on the bouncy, blond wig that Ruby called the Bombshell. *I'd give Jayne Mansfield a run for her money,* Ruby's mother always said. She'd bought it after she and Ruby had gone to the Gunn Hill Cinema to see *The Girl Can't Help It.*

Ruby's scalp itched, but she was afraid to scratch her head the way she wanted to, worried that her fingernails might disturb her ma's well-preserved coiffure. She'd seen her mother rub her face against the hair as if she were rubbing her face against a kitten.

Ruby thought about the money she hoped she'd get from selling a few of her teacher's belongings in Briggley. There were a few pairs of earrings and necklaces that appeared to be valuable. There was an

old watch, perhaps given to Miss Burden by her father or a male relative. There was a checkbook too, but Ruby knew there would be no
safe way, not yet, to explore what might happen if she wrote herself a
check. She'd need to learn how to write a check, to begin with. And
maybe the bank already knew that Miss Burden had died. Trying
her luck with the woman's valuables made more sense. Nobody in
Briggley would have a clue about how Ruby had gotten her hands on
these things, and more important, nobody at a pawnshop would care.

If Ruby had money, she could begin saving for pilot school. But
there would be things she'd need before that—better clothes, three
hot meals a day, a room in a boardinghouse where she'd be viewed as
a decent, hardworking young woman. She shook away a memory of
herself lying exposed on the rocks.

As the scenery blurred outside the window, Ruby's mind loosened into vivid daydreams. She tried to imagine climbing onto the
bus and looking down the aisle at a young, plain-faced blond girl
staring dreamily out of the window. The girl's dress was old but clean.
Because she was sitting with her arms pressed tensely against her
sides, the holes beneath her armpits were concealed. Her tousled
curls looked as if she'd just lifted her cheek from a pillow (not a wig
box). She wanted anyone who looked at her to think she was a star in
a love story. She was in pursuit of the possibility that her love interest might love her back. The place where the hair was matted and
darker at her nape could not be detected from the way she held her
head high above her bladelike shoulders. Her sense of determination
was palpable, heady as the pungent scent of marigolds. There was
something lovely and awful about her.

Ruby stood, blinking and shaky, when she realized the bus had
pulled into Briggley's depot, which was already crammed with loud
mothers and their hollering children. Ruby remembered that on Saturdays, most normal families went to the market, or had picnics with
their relatives, or enjoyed double feature matinees together.

As she descended from the bus, she liked how women smiled
at her. It was like she was Cinderella, but instead of wearing en-

chanted glass slippers she had stolen her mother's magic wig. And why couldn't she be both princess and pilot?

. . .

SHE SAT ALONE IN A red plastic booth at the Cedar Street Diner. The sunshine poured through the large square window. No amount of wiping could make the table look new. Dulled tin cutlery gleamed on a thin napkin. Waitresses in daffodil-colored uniforms danced between the kitchen and dining room, as the frequent chime of a bell sounded and a greasy, bored male voice called out orders.

"Honey? Aren't you pretty as a doll! Your parents joining you?"

"They're shopping," Ruby said quickly. "But they gave me money to have some lunch."

The waitress nodded, smiling. A rumpled notepad was wedged in her palm. Without a beat, she set a sticky menu in front of Ruby, winking as she spun away. "My advice to you is a milkshake, honey. We got the best malteds. Ask anyone."

Ruby looked at the menu, but her mind was on the woman's compliment. She *did* look like a doll, didn't she? With her ma's hair and the new dress she'd bought next door in a small boutique that reminded her of a dollhouse? Everything had worked as smoothly as she had hoped. The man at Second Chance Pawns had carefully appraised the earrings, bracelets, and necklaces Ruby had offered him. The only thing that wasn't costume was a delicate sapphire ring that she'd been tempted to keep for herself because the man at the store said it matched her eyes. Instead, she'd walked away with seventy-five dollars. A fortune.

When she'd turned the corner at Cedar Street, thinking about her rumbling stomach, she'd been startled by her yellow-headed reflection in a storefront window that displayed rich, jewel-colored dresses and tweed suits for ladies. Ruby had serious-lady money tucked in the waistband of her underwear. If she could wear a wig that drew smiles, what would a decent dress do? A nice dress needed new shoes, a new hair ribbon, perhaps a scarf with a lovely print. The dress might match her eyes, which she'd always secretly felt were her best feature. *This ain't you,* a voice in her head growled. *Don't fool yourself, Ruby. Not a bit of this lady stuff got a thing to do with you.* Another voice countered: *Well, what if it does now? I can't get nowhere in life without looking like I got a good life.*

"Won't you come in, dear," a woman's voice had floated towards her. Ruby took her eyes away from the wonder of her reflection and found herself greeted by a slender, auburn-haired woman who wore a brighter-than-money green summer dress. The elegant, thin gold belt that cinched the woman's middle-aged waist sent a spiral of envy through Ruby as the woman extended her bare, freckled arm and her pink manicured nails to take Ruby's hand in hers.

"I'll help you, dear," she said, as Ruby sighed softly, stepping into the embrace of air-conditioning and rose-scented sachets. But it was the way she'd been called *dear* that made her feel as if she were soaring towards the sky, the feeling of warmth and hope in a single, polite breath. *I'm dear,* she'd thought. *I'm dear enough to be seen as such.*

Now Ruby removed her hand from the shopping bag that sat closest to the window so that she could use her finger to mark the menu's prices. This was a special day. She didn't have all the words to explain why. Rather than wait to see some signs that her life was changing, she had provided those signs for herself.

She wanted the milkshake, oh yes. But there was a decision to be made between a cheeseburger and French fries or a grilled cheese with sliced tomato and a pickle. Would the waitress think she was greedy if she had a milkshake *and* a bottle of Coca-Cola? Ruby tapped the menu with her fingers. Already, she'd spent more in that ladies' clothing store than she'd intended.

"I'll have a cheeseburger, French fries, a strawberry milkshake, and a bottle of Coca-Cola," she said to the waitress, enjoying how rapidly the woman wrote up her order.

"Where you going to put all that?" the woman said, grinning before she vanished.

Smiling, Ruby leaned her elbows on the table so that she could cup her cheek with her hand, which was soft from the rose lotion the saleswoman had encouraged her to rub into her sunburned skin. *Dear, dear, dear.* She'd given her a sample, which Ruby had taken, but she thought of how her papa had responded when he'd gotten a whiff of her teacher's perfume. He'd accused her of wearing it for a boy, and there'd been nothing she could say to convince him that she was innocent of any flirtations. Her papa had threatened to walk her to and from school from now on so that she wouldn't be able to sneak off to see this boy, whoever he was. Ruby blinked away her memories, recalling how she'd prevented that nice saleswoman from assisting her in the fitting room. The sight of her bruises would have ruined everything.

Instead of her papa, Ruby imagined what it would've been like to sit in a booth like this with Ezra. Two girls, well-dressed, playing at being young women, excited for their futures. Ruby closed her eyes for a few moments and lost herself in their laughter. They would play the jukebox and share a slice of cherry pie just so they could linger at their very own table, making up stories about whoever walked in. They used to make up stories about villagers in Salt Point but Ezra had complained about doing so when Ruby insisted it was just for fun. Ezra had grown tired of pretending what life was like for white people. The stories pushed Ezra somewhere that Ruby didn't have to go because she looked like the people whose blank faces were like open pages for her own moods. It was strange now for Ruby to make up stories about her own life, her own reality, whatever that was, without the presence of her friend.

Ruby opened her eyes and noticed that a man at the counter was watching her. She drew her elbows off the table and turned her head sharply from his direction. When she was certain he'd swiveled back to his plate, she tilted her head for a look. Even from the back, she could tell that he was young, probably not a teenager but not nearly her papa's age either. He was wearing a leather bomber jacket despite the heat. His dirty-blond hair looked windswept. Lowering her eyes, she saw that he was wearing clean denim pants and work boots.

The waitress set down Ruby's order, wishing her and her appetite a good time. Before turning away, she flicked a thin slip of paper beneath the saltshaker and told Ruby she could pay the bill at the counter register. "Leave the cash tip on the table, honey."

Nodding, Ruby took her napkin and spread it over her lap. *Honey, dear, honey, dear.* Suddenly, she worried about her dress and the grease—the fries, the burger. Even the bun was slippery. And the ketchup—she couldn't skip the divine ketchup. Arranging herself, Ruby leaned forward, so that she could have a sip of her strawberry milkshake. "Jesus in Heaven," she whispered, as the cold sugar went immediately to her head. The whole meal was going to be better than religion.

As Ruby was finishing the last of her French fries, she took the bus schedule out of her old bag. The saleswoman had begged Ruby to buy a new purse and had even offered to make an arrangement for Ruby to purchase it with credit. She'd almost said yes, bewitched by the idea of carrying something like that around with her that everybody could see. *A proper handbag tells the world everything and nothing,* the woman had explained when Ruby asked whether having a proper purse made thieves think about trying to rob women.

The man who'd been studying her earlier turned his head slightly to smile at her as he crossed to the register. The full sight of his face was a vision. Ruby's face grew warm. She put her French fry down as if she'd been ordered to freeze. Snatching her napkin from her lap, she tried to wipe away the grease smeared on her lips and chin.

The man laughed at something the waitress said as she gave him his change. He was taller than Ruby had thought. The air moved away from him, leaving the sensation that there was nothing cooler. He handed the waitress what seemed to be a stack of brochures.

After he said goodbye to his friends at the counter, he grinned at her again. Ruby pushed her food scraps away, wishing she'd had grilled cheese. She felt like burping.

As he passed the edge of her table, he slowed and looked down at her.

"I'm Cullen," he said. "You local?"

Ruby managed a weak shrug as she cleared her throat. "Maybe."

"You don't know where you're from, Sunshine?" he said, laughing. "That's new."

She stared up at his sparkling green eyes. His shirt was open at the neck and she saw that he was wearing a gold chain with a little hot air balloon charm that battled a pale tuft of hair along his collarbone. She was nervous that he'd seen her slip the bottle of ketchup and the glass cylinder of sugar, with its curved silver top, into her bag. He bent down closer to her, so that his breath licked the side of her face. "We got a new thing going in town if you'd like to read about it. You look like the kind of girl who isn't afraid of heights."

Ruby nodded as he slid a brochure down next to her sweating bottle of soda. She could barely believe it when she saw a colored illustration of a plane bridging the horizon and the sea. She knew this was a sign. It had to be; and it didn't matter that she hadn't given it to herself. *Sunshine, honey, dear.* Lifting her chin proudly, Ruby laid her rough, rose-scented hand on top of the paper.

"You know where the airfield is, don't you?" Cullen asked.

She nodded, keeping her hand on the brochure, fearful that he might snatch it away.

"Walton's got a sale on ketchup *and* sugar," he whispered in her ear before she could ask him how much it might cost to take a ride in one of the planes at the airfield. "You can get some mustard too, and some better manners, for next to nothing."

. . .

AFTER THE BUS UNLOADED PASSENGERS at Gunn Hill, Ruby found herself nearly alone again. In the very back row, she'd bent herself in half, pulling off the Bombshell. She stuffed it deep into one of her shopping bags, worried now about where she could hide her purchases from her parents. The brochure from the Briggley airfield was folded around the damp bills of cash that she had rearranged inside her bra. She was nervous about the dress too. There was nowhere for her coins, and nothing for her to change into, as she'd allowed the saleswoman to stick her lovely, manicured fingers through the armpits of her dress and *tsk tsk* at the broken zipper that revealed some of Ruby's back. *There isn't enough here for rags,* the woman had said, carrying the dress away to the back of the store. Ruby hadn't been thinking then, too transfixed by the new Ruby that gazed back at her in the trio of full-length mirrors that made her blond image recede into infinity.

Now she ran her fingers through her sweaty hair; droplets rained down from her hairline. The wig was soaked and had a bad smell, but she couldn't fix that. Her face grew hot again as she thought of Cullen and how he'd complimented and insulted her at once, as if he knew exactly who she was. *Sunshine,* he'd called her. It was an odd feeling, to want to see him again. It was more than just the idea that he might fly planes. He'd made her feel seen. She couldn't tell whether that was good or bad or something else. Ruby thought of Ezra's eyes and how she and her friend could read each other's thoughts. They'd always seen each other clearly. Without those words *bad* or *good*— they'd spent their times together close to the bone, raw and natural as the wind that blew against their skin. She wondered what Ezra would say if Ruby could describe all of the ways she felt about herself. It would be like breezing into the Kindreds' house and calling out for her sister to share a secret. It wouldn't be about eating from their garbage. Instead, she'd have something to say that would make Ezra proud. She missed their laughter. And she wanted to show off her new dress.

She'd walk up through the woods over to Clove Road. The anger she had been feeling about Ezra's comment about her papa had finally worn away. Maybe Ezra would apologize to her, allow Ruby to accept the apology, and then they could go on as before. They should've spoken about what it had meant for each of them to see the other naked *that* way, which was not how they'd ever been before, when they'd seen each other as naked girls. Maybe Ezra needed to talk about it or had feelings that she needed Ruby to understand. Ruby only wanted to hug her, tell her that she was beginning to have a different life, as they'd always imagined.

Still, Ruby wasn't sure that Ezra would have approved of the Bombshell approach, or the pawnshop.

She just had to trust that Ezra would see that Ruby was trying to improve herself, to get the help that Ezra and her sister already had because their parents cared about them in a way neither of Ruby's parents ever had. Maybe they could spend the day together, and she could be the new Ruby without leaving the old Ruby behind.

. . .

WHEN RUBY EMERGED FROM THE woods opposite Clove Road, she was surprised to see that the wide front door of the Kindreds' house, which was usually open with the screen unlocked, was pulled shut. At least the windows had been left open, so that the pretty, hand-stitched curtains puffed in and out in the slow wind. Even with all of those windows open, Ruby knew that there were never flies in the Kindred house.

On the porch, Mrs. Kindred swayed in a wooden rocking chair. Miss Irene was seated in the other. The two of them moved like blurred colors inside a painting. Their voices carried in the lazing, gold air.

"She can't come out," said Miss Irene before Ruby or Mrs. Kindred could say a word. Miss Irene held a pistol in one of her hands. She hadn't bothered to stand and say anything friendly. Ruby was reminded of the women down in the village who carried guns around while they did errands. But Miss Irene, as Ezra had often said to Ruby, was a different kind of woman. What had happened since Ezra and Cinthy left her alone at Miss Burden's place? Tension drenched Ruby's face with more sweat, which she resented because the cosmetics that the saleswoman had applied to her face were surely ruined.

Politely, Ruby walked to the bottom of the steps, half smiling up at Mrs. Kindred, whose face was partially hidden in the shade of the oak. Ruby spied two rose-painted glass plates on a low table between the women. Lord, she could smell the cornbread. Mrs. Kindred watched her closely before speaking.

"How is your mother, Ruby?"

"I guess she's fine."

"And where is your father?" asked Miss Irene. As usual, her voice was hostile for no reason Ruby could tell. And she rolled her eyes the exact way her daughter Lindy did whenever Ruby tried to say anything at all. She wondered if Miss Irene was the one to blame for the small but noticeable shifts she'd been noticing recently in Ezra's attitude towards their friendship. In many things, the woman's wisdom had overtaken Ezra's opinions until sometimes it seemed like Ezra had no thinking of her own. *Don't be alone with white men. Don't trust white women, especially when they say they mean to help you. The only thing you can trust is God and a gun. If you keep your mouth open too long, flies will lay maggots on your tongue. Always pray in the evening that you'll be lucky to pray in the morning.* And then all the things the woman had crowded into Ezra's head about ancestors when the Kindreds didn't seem like folks who gave themselves over to hauntings.

Ruby had only ever seen Miss Irene's hair plaited, but now it was loose and formed a puffy crown around her head that coiled to her breasts. Sunlight picked up the hair oil Miss Irene used, so that the nest sparkled.

Ruby shrugged in response to Miss Irene's question. "I believe he's still sleeping, ma'am. Reckon he's got himself a righteous hangover today."

"This child is running all over the village," said Miss Irene to Mrs. Kindred. "She go missing, the first place the police going to be is over at our place, threatening to shoot *my* babies, or right here threatening to kill yours. Right up and down this dead-end road looking for this girl. Let one of my babies go a-missing and the world, that devil-of-a-deputy, would be just fine with the dead-end part."

"Damn Charlie won't do no running," Ruby said. "Not after me anyway."

"This *girl* is part of our trouble," snapped Miss Irene. "Don't need but one eye to see it."

Her words were outright mean, but Ruby didn't say another word as her eyes filled with tears. Her day had been nearly perfect until she returned to Salt Point and realized she was still old Ruby. She'd come to Clove Road in need of friendship only to find herself insulted. Anyway, Ruby knew all about the trouble because Ezra had shown her Negro newspapers. They'd listened to Mrs. Kindred's radio in the kitchen. When her papa wasn't around, Ruby listened to the national news for hours, out on the edge of her porch with her eyes closed, trying to imagine Black people in Alabama being hunted and hosed down because they demanded equality. Her mind conjured growling canines ripping freedom songs from the throats of Negroes who refused silence. She knew her imagination was useless because what had just happened in Little Rock, Arkansas, was real.

Ruby had seen firsthand how Negroes were treated in Gunn Hill, especially in Sweet Bay, a rough Negro section of Gunn Hill that respectable coloreds looked down upon. Those Black folks had funerals almost every weekend of the year. When they got tired and fought back there'd be two or three funerals on Sunday at the same time. Funerals all month long, with whole families singing while carrying shovels, flowers, and shotguns.

Ruby could still recall the moment, two years ago, that Ezra showed her a picture in a magazine of how Mississippi sent that Till boy back to his mama in Chicago. So Ruby knew what Mrs. Kindred and Miss Irene saw from their porch: They saw Carolyn Bryant, crying crocodile tears down in Money, Mississippi. They saw the whistling shadows of tree branches. Sweet Jesus. It made Ruby angry that they wouldn't ever give her a chance. It made her angry that she understood why they couldn't.

"Can I come back later this evening, ma'am?" said Ruby. "To talk to her?"

"Ruby, I don't think so," Mrs. Kindred said finally, covering her mouth and coughing. Her hair was pulled back hard against her head. The skin under her eyes was dark, pressing discolored flowers above her high cheekbones. Even though it was warm, she pulled her shawl tightly across her shoulders. Mrs. Kindred didn't look good at all. Maybe that's why Miss Irene was being so dicty. Mrs. Kindred looked like a ghost.

Ruby wondered why Ez hadn't told her that her mama was sick. She knew Negroes could be fearful of doctors out here in the country, but there was a hospital for coloreds in Gunn Hill. Mrs. Kindred looked like she needed to see somebody about that cough.

"Ma'am, I didn't know you was ailing," Ruby said. "I wouldn't have troubled y'all."

Shaking her head, Miss Irene rolled her eyes again.

"She's just a girl," said Mrs. Kindred in a soft voice. "Poor girl." Shakily, Mrs. Kindred came down the steps of the porch. Her face was the beautiful, poised face Ezra's would grow into one day, and in it, Ruby saw the truth: Ruby Scaggs and Ezra Kindred would not grow old together, as best friends, because Ezra's mama, and Ruby's mama, and everybody's mama, weren't going to allow it.

Mrs. Kindred's kindness was clear to Ruby. It was also insulting. The old Ruby and the new Ruby bristled together. She disliked being pitied by anybody, especially someone who, in the village's opinion, was as bad off as Ruby was, if not worse. Why had they made her *beg* to see her only friend? Why hadn't these Negroes even offered her a glass of water when she'd visited their home? Miss Irene wasn't the only one who could say something that wasn't nice.

"Ma said can't nobody in the world be poorer than niggers," replied Ruby, wiping her lips before she spat on the steps, barely missing Mrs. Kindred's tired feet.

II

OUR SUNDAY MORNING HAD BEEN QUIET UNTIL MISS IRENE PHONED, insisting that we attend services with her and the Junketts that morning. Daddy had sighed at Mama's suggestion of prayer while he instructed us to finish with our breakfast and change into our church dresses.

We only went to New Hope of Rising Star, a Black church in Gunn Hill, when Daddy and Mama were sure that the Junkett family would be attending services. Heavily lotioned and tight-lipped in our starched dresses, my sister and I observed the Junketts' parish as it hollered and shuddered in joy.

Invariably, Mr. Caesar would get himself worked up so fervently he would leap into the aisle, hopping in measured rhythms like he was whipping an invisible jump rope over his head and under his feet. Miss Irene could be counted on to hurl her snowy handkerchief into the air over and over, with the understanding that Lindy or Empire or little Rosemary would crawl around on the floor, without getting dirty, and pick it out of the fleet of other ladies' handkerchiefs that sailed through the air like the wings of doves.

The Rising Star pastor had explosive ways of speaking and dancing at offering times. Once, he'd thrown two whole checkbooks that personally belonged to him into a basket as an example of what he owed Jesus. Daddy complained about the pastor's antics, but Mama teased Daddy, saying he was bothered because our household only had a single checkbook and it belonged to *her* most of the time.

We especially enjoyed the ending of the Rising Star services, when the entire small building vibrated from a symphony of heels beating against the ground, joining the choir in a rapturous scream, accompanied by the trilling of gold tambourines. The church could barely hold a hundred people but there were always people outside hollering *Amen* and *JeezUs* through open windows, which were not stained glass. Through it all, our family remained glued to our seats, but there was nowhere else in our lives that Ezra and I could see Black people worship.

After the service, our family clung to the Junketts while every-one, smiling and sweating, shuffled into the little hallway that led to a reception hall where we didn't bother trying to claim any of the re-served metal folding chairs, given we weren't regular parishioners. Instead, we allowed ourselves to be greeted by the sweet voices of the Rising Star lady ushers who were assigned to distribute paper cups of coffee and cookies that tasted like they had been baked back when Jesus, bless Him, might have appreciated the miracle of a baked good.

It was so nice to be called *little sister* and to hear our father and mother addressed as *brother, sister*. We were complimented, then promptly ignored as the congregation, who really knew one another's business, began to gossip and complain about white people, their day jobs, their night shifts, and a complicated assortment of petty injuries to their youth, including bunions, corns, hammertoes, pulled nerves, last nerves, and loose teeth. When the Junketts dissolved into their perfumed and powdered flock, we'd lose our nerve, slip out, and drive, in silent relief, back to Salt Point.

It'd been some time since it had happened, but if Mama was feel-ing particularly buoyed from the service, she might actually phone our grandmother and talk for a few minutes, before she remembered that she couldn't forgive her mother's abandonment of her.

Daddy said little or nothing about the pastor's sermons, or how sometimes Mr. Junkett tugged on Daddy's good shirt, trying to pull our father up on his feet so that he, too, could dance his way back to the Promised Land.

. . .

WHILE THE RADIO PLAYED AT low volume, Ezra and I dried the Sunday evening dinner dishes. The back door of our kitchen was open so that we could smell the changing air.

At dinner we'd all noticed Mama's fatigue. In the middle of talking, she'd leaned her cheek against the back of her hand and closed her eyes instead of inspecting our plates to be sure we weren't wasting any food. After our simple meal, we didn't linger at the table. Mama had asked Daddy to help her to bed immediately. Perhaps the service at Rising Star had tired her.

"Or she's pregnant," said Ezra. Even though I hadn't said anything aloud, she knew we were both thinking about Mama.

"How could she be?"

"Cinthy, she *could* be. She's *young*."

"Oh," I said, trying to imagine Mama cradling a child that would be my sister or brother. I sighed. It was too hard for me to picture.

"Miss Irene once said that she was exhausted all the time when she was expecting the twins. She was carrying *two* babies, so that makes sense. But I think women can get really tired from carrying one baby too."

"Oh," I said, aware that anything I knew was less than my sister. In fact, whatever I knew about babies and how they were made had come from Ezra.

Ezra kissed her teeth with her tongue. "Could you *imagine* having a little brother?"

I stuck my dishcloth inside a glass and twisted it around to dry away the moisture. "A brother would be all right," I said. "I don't know if we need another girl."

Ezra chuckled. "What's wrong with you?" she said. "You can't ever have too many sisters."

Laughing with her, I wiped my eyes. Ezra sang to the radio, while I listened to her voice mingling with the sound of insects, twinkling cymbals, and tender strings. Then we were both quiet for some time while we concentrated on cleaning the kitchen the way Mama would. If Mama came downstairs in the middle of the night for a glass of water or whisky, we didn't want her seeing that her kitchen wasn't clean enough, then trying to do it herself.

I was coming out of the pantry, holding my dishcloth, when I saw Ruby's face behind the screen.

"Hey, y'all. Hey, Ez, it's me."

Ezra shot me a glance. I didn't move to unlock the screen door.

"What's wrong with y'all!"

Ezra and I exchanged looks. My sister leaned across the sink filled with sudsy water to lower the volume of the radio. The wild sounds of nightfall suddenly grew loud, threatening to invade our house. We went close enough to the door so that Ruby could not mistake what we had to say.

"Mama said you're no longer welcome here."

"What you mean, Ez?"

"*We* have to explain it?" I said, locating my tongue so that I could speak. "To *you*?"

"What y'all offended about now?" Ruby asked, sighing. "You talking about that mess with your mama yesterday? I was just feeling mean. Wasn't personal. Ain't like y'all ain't been called niggers before. It must've been my nerves jump roping from this heat. That's all it was."

"If you don't think calling my mama and Miss Irene out of their names isn't personal, I don't know what to say except that you can't be my friend," said Ezra. Her eyes were slits and her voice was icy. "Not now or ever again. You think I'd be all right with you calling *me* that word? How would you feel if I walked up to that toilet you live in and spat on it? How quickly would your mother or father punish *me*?"

"Gosh," said Ruby. "I didn't mean nothing by it, but that Miss Irene don't care for me. She always lets me know it too. I never done nothing to that woman."

Shaking my head, I sighed. Ezra held up her hand and gave me a look.

"What you *said* to them . . ." said Ezra. "And you don't spit at somebody's mother, I don't care *what* color she is. I wish I'd seen you doing what you did. You're lucky we didn't jump you as soon as you walked up to our door and beat you blue and black."

"Y'all picking on me like you and Cinthy never say nasty things about my ma. You think you can do that 'cause she's *white*?"

Ruby tried the door as if she was going to open it and come into our house.

"We're not messing with you anymore," I said.

"I said I was *sorry*," Ruby said slowly with clenched teeth.

"Mama was trying to be nice," I said. "You lucky Miss Irene didn't just *shoot* you."

"Cinthy, don't say another word," said Ezra.

I worried that Daddy would come down and see Ruby's face and hands pressed against the screen. We weren't supposed to put too much weight on the mesh because it was delicate. Replacing screens was expensive. If Ruby ripped the screen we'd get into trouble. If Mama or Daddy saw Ruby on our property, I knew we'd be punished on general principle. Mama hadn't told Daddy exactly what had happened with Ruby, but Miss Irene had stayed at our house for another hour. Her warpath wasn't like Mama's. Miss Irene's warpath was a galactic battlefield. We'd had to listen to her voice raising itself into full nuclear alert until we thought the glass of lemonade in her hand would shatter. At some point, Mama had gently taken the pistol from her, worried about how she was waving it around. Miss Irene was still upset from the night before, when the deputy had cruised past the Junketts' home, threatening us with his ghost trigger. Apparently, he'd returned, much later, driving back and forth up the road past their house all night long. None of them had slept. *We can't even have a Friday night anymore,* Miss Irene kept repeating while she'd paced across our porch. *The devil not going to have my babies scared. Evil don't have nothing else to do. I ain't scared of evil. Do you hear me?*

And we heard it. All Saturday afternoon until Mr. Junkett drove over to pick up Miss Irene and take her home to her children, who missed her.

Ezra walked silently to the door, standing just inches away from the screen that separated her from Ruby. She shut the door. Then locked it. Her hands were shaking as she pulled Mama's eyelet curtains over the small square window. When Ez turned to face me, the tears in her eyes did not fall. "Can you finish this, Cinthy," she said, sounding weary like Mama.

I nodded, looking over at the pans. I didn't like washing pans, but I'd be sure I did a good job tonight. Without saying anything else, Ezra went up the back stairwell with a gait that made her seem older than our parents. There was an unseen weight that bowed my sister's shoulders the way chronic aching can make old people walk like they're about to fall over. I felt like I was falling too.

As I stood alone in our kitchen, the sensuous music playing from Mama's radio made me shiver. There was nothing lovely left in the air. I turned the radio off. Silence crashed over me while I listened to droplets of water leaking from the faucet and the chirping second hand on our plastic wall clock that always made me think of crickets. Blinking, I put down my cloth and went to the front door, which I unlocked before scanning the tall grass to see if Ruby was still on our property.

When I sensed that Ruby had taken off, I went outdoors, creeping through the underbrush that surrounded the haunted house. Leaves and insects slapped my face as I came out at the back of it. There was a little moonlight to see by, but I didn't need it. Ruby, in her disorder, was predictable enough. So I knew exactly where she'd hidden Miss Burden's suitcase.

In a few minutes, I'd wrestled it out of a gouged hole in the wall where Ez and I once hid our toys. I was convinced by the events of the past week that the luggage was bad luck, an evil omen. Mama sick and tired. The deputy's harassment. Ruby's cruelty, which I could see hurt my sister so deeply. I thought of the three daughters of the burned house, whose bodies had never been found, and how the village believed that we were haunted. Perhaps Miss Burden could not rest until what was stolen from her was returned. I wanted a return to our quiet days that felt safe and endless. Maybe, somehow, if I destroyed the suitcase, things could go on as they had before. I held the case against my pulsing chest for a moment before I turned, sprinting up the scraggly slope in the dark to the road.

It took less than five minutes for me to reach our pond, where I walked quickly to the edge of the little wooden dock; it trembled and creaked beneath my tread, but the water took the suitcase without protest.

12

A NEW TEACHER TOOK OVER MISS BURDEN'S FORMER APARTMENT BY the sea. Apparently, the hiring interview was brief. When Daddy came home and told Mama about Miss Dinah Alley, Mama rolled her eyes so hard it looked like it might hurt her.

But nobody had asked us about our opinion of Miss Alley, pronounced *ally*, whose name alone was the perfect, ripe fruit that should've given the boys in our class permission to taunt her with pranks, but none of that would ever happen because most of our class, if not the entire school, had fallen in love with her.

Not me though. Sitting at my desk in the classroom later that week, I realized Hobart was no longer my haven. Maybe it had never been. I was often lost in my thoughts, oblivious to Ezra poking and pinching me to snap out of it. Unlike with Miss Burden, who I'd wanted to believe had glimpsed something special in me because I loved reading and writing, I now found myself, along with Lindy and my sister, tossed to the anonymous ranks of "Negro girls." Every day, we were overlooked by our teacher, and picked on by our peers. Unlike Miss Burden, our new teacher did not stop my classmates from making monkey noises whenever I got up from the desk to sharpen my pencil. When boys flicked wet spitballs that landed in my hair, it could take an entire period for me to realize my hair was filled with them while the girls with sleek, pert ponytails laughed with tears in their eyes. Our teacher frowned whenever she had to pronounce any of our names. Sometimes I think she was doing it on purpose though. Hyacinth is as easy to pronounce as Rose or Lily—the names of white girls who sat behind me in the second row because they could barely pass their exams.

Throwing Miss Burden's suitcase into the pond had done nothing to return our world to its former order—the arrival of our new teacher made that clear.

Whenever Miss Alley called my name, I didn't know whether she would ask me a question or simply order me to cease to exist. My shame was a parquet floor, a polished grid where my new teacher danced and spun, her patent leather heels sliding across my confidence until I felt dull.

. . .

OUR CLASSROOM SMELLED LIKE SWEAT, socks, and sunlight. With windows and a corroded fan circulating rusty air, we bowed our heads over our notebooks, holding the arrows of our sharp yellow pencils, as Miss Alley gave dictation.

From the corner of my eye, I watched her sip her coffee cautiously. Her shiny, red mouth met the rim of her ceramic mug and then, without any semblance of an accident, she released it from her hand. Her face furrowed mysteriously as the liquid splashed to the floor.

It was now Miss Alley's second week of work, and she had increasingly been breaking cups, hiding chalk, and complaining of mice and black mold in the corners of our classroom. These minor repairs were part of Mr. Caesar's many responsibilities. He didn't have a staff. Sometimes Ernest or some Negro boys from Gunn Hill would come up to the school to help him with painting or more complicated jobs. But mostly, Mr. Caesar handled everything himself.

I always liked when Mr. Caesar came into our room. Tall in his crisp uniform, he would wink or nod at Ezra, Lindy, and me when he finished his task, right before whirling himself and his bucket or tools away. His arrivals and departures left the air around me charged, like I had just been witness to a real-life superhero, a strong man whom others were incapable of recognizing for who he really was. Until now, I hadn't given his frequent appearances in our classroom much thought.

But this was Miss Alley's sixth, seventh, or twelfth cup that had crashed to the floor. What did she want from Mr. Caesar? He couldn't laugh or complain outright about Miss Alley. He couldn't cuss her. He couldn't have Miss Irene showing up without her earrings, the cuffs of her housedress rolled back like armor, and her cowrie shells jostling and gleaming in preparation for war.

When Mr. Caesar arrived this time, his face was a mask. He looked like drawings of pharaohs in a history book Daddy had once shown me in his study. Mr. Caesar only nodded tensely when Miss Alley offered her usual script, blaming her clumsiness in a dripping, Shirley Temple–like voice, while pointing to the floor where a steaming puddle reached its burning, black fingers across the floor that had been mopped how many times already that week. The wasted coffee made a dark animal shape.

Ezra, Lindy, and I exchanged looks. This was the first time he had ever not looked or smiled at us. Black specks climbed up the edges of my vision.

There was a slight smile on Ruby's mouth, as if she was uncertain what to do with her face, whether she should be entertained or enraged. It occurred to me, looking over at Ruby in her clean new dress and hair ribbon, that she looked like the rest of those ordinary white girls and less like Ruby Scaggs, the girl who'd assured us she would be the pilot of her own freedom one day.

"Nerves, I guess," Miss Alley was saying.

Mr. Caesar moved the mop in rapid jerks across the hardwood boards as if she weren't speaking at all.

"You the only boy they got up here to take care of this whole big school?"

"I—"

She smiled up at him encouragingly.

"I sure am," he said, visibly frowning.

"You look very capable," she said.

Mr. Caesar didn't reply.

My sister, God help her, decided to answer for Mr. Caesar. With her hands on her hips and eyes like glinting arrowheads, Ezra resembled Miss Irene more than Mama.

"If *you* were more *capable,* you wouldn't have made the mess you've been making for him for the hundredth *time*."

Disbelief sizzled like an egg, cracked, on the pale skillet of Miss Alley's face. Lindy covered her face, and I didn't know whether she was cackling from nerves or from crying. My own face reflected the knowledge that Ezra would probably get the first beating of her life. My sister had gone too far. In spite of my pride for her I closed my eyes in vertigo.

"Ezra," said Mr. Caesar. He tried to put his hand out gently to gesture at her to sit.

"Don't you *touch* me!" shrieked Miss Alley. She surprised us with this tactic, directing her fury at Mr. Caesar rather than Ezra. She bounced on her heels, shrieking. "You *tried* to *touch* me! You've been trying *all* week!"

Lindy and I were activated at the same time. Ezra couldn't get into the ring, because she already had something coming to her, and we knew it would be bad. So we jumped up, throwing our high voices into a single screeching fist.

"Nasty! He *didn't*! Don't nobody want to touch you!"

"He *didn't*! He *didn't* touch her!"

Our teacher rushed to the intercom panel. Frantically, she pressed all of the buttons that connected our classroom to other rooms, including the main office.

"Excuse me," said Mr. Caesar, speaking calmly. "Ma'am, I was trying to settle the girls. There's no problem here. The mess is all cleaned up, see?" Mr. Caesar whipped the bucket around quickly and gray, sudsy water sloshed out. I could see where sweat stains had erupted down the back of his uniform and beneath his armpits.

"Daddy!" said Lindy, pushing her chair away so she could reach his side.

He turned sharply. "Stay there, baby girl," he said. "Sit down, Lindy. Learn these books, these lessons. That's what I need you to do."

A male voice whined from the speaker. Mr. Caesar rolled his bucket and mop expertly out of the room before our teacher could order him to stay.

"Good afternoon, Miss Alley, do you need some assistance with your class?"

She pressed the button, resuming the false, cloying sweetness of her strawberry voice. "Everything is just fine in here, thank you, Mr. Mitchell," she said, fixing her eyes on the floor where Mr. Caesar had scrubbed away the black animal shape before it left any stain.

. . .

IT WAS CLEAR: MISS ALLEY was a bully. Ez and I had decided not to tell our father when these moments happened to us. By now, there were too many.

At recess, Ezra, Lindy, and I stood apart, saying little, while we watched other children kicking rubber balls across the gravel circle.

"She *really* getting on my nerves today," said Lindy finally. "That woman is *this* close to me breaking my foot off in her ass! Cinthy smarter than her! Cinthy could teach the whole lesson by *herself* if she wanted, and we *know* it. I *hate* bullies! Miss Alley ain't shit. Shame on her." Lindy's voice was flat. Even with the dusty wind her clothes were immaculate. Dust could not touch her.

"Ever since she *got* here," said Ez.

My eyes burned as I recalled how Miss Alley snapped at me earlier for no reason at all. I could hear my name—*Hyacinth*—in her mouth and how she made it sound like spit-up.

"White folks picked her," said Ez.

"Mm-hm."

"But picking on *my* sister?" said Ezra. "Oh no, she's not going to do that."

"No," said Lindy. "She can't do that. She's not even a *real* teacher."

"No, she isn't. Sweet Jesus. Did you see her doing the numbers?"

Lindy giggled at Ezra. "My father said she's a niece, or whatever, a distant relative of Mrs. Hobart. That's how she got the job."

"Well, that explains it," said my sister. "Miss Irene would knock her head off and use it for kickball."

We were quiet again, comforted by this image.

Recess would end soon. Not that it bothered me especially. Years ago, our parents had given us rules about recess: Recess was for white people. During that period, Ezra and I were to read or wash the chalkboards for our teachers. It's not like we had friends to play with anyways, especially now that we weren't talking to Ruby. All these years at Hobart, we'd never been invited to any of our classmates' homes or birthday parties in the village. Our parents had never permitted us to have such parties either, because it would've meant inviting our classmates into our home. We didn't want to go into white peoples' homes because it would be neither safe nor fun. We didn't want white people coming into our house and treating it like their own.

We stared at our classmates, whom we didn't want to play with and who didn't want to play with us. Then Ruby appeared from green bushes that edged the gravel lot where we stood. As she approached, I sucked in my breath and folded my arms when I realized that she intended to speak to *me*. I had no control over what Miss Alley might do to me, but I surely had some control over Ruby Scaggs.

"I know you got it," she said, not bothering with any greeting for Ez or Lindy.

"Not anymore."

"What'd you do with it, Cinthy?"

"First of all," I said, "it wasn't *yours*."

"Shit, you don't got a say about what belongs to me," said Ruby.

"Get lost, why don't you," Ezra said, tossing away the stick she'd been fooling with.

"I can't get myself prepared for pilot school if I don't have my money. I put some in that suitcase, which I'm sure you would've found when you took it from me. I need my money."

I could hear my blood ticking as I stared at her. "Is that my problem?"

Lindy let out a *hoot-hoot* laugh. "Girl, *please*! Y'all, did she really say *my money*? Ain't nobody in this whole wide world would *ever* put the word *money* near the word *Scaggs* with a straight face and that's the truth. Honey child, I hope somebody takes *all* of that money. Standing here talking crazy like we all don't know how you be stealing. You too *stupid* to have somebody's money."

Ruby pushed Lindy. Or tried to.

"Girl, please," said Lindy. "Push me again and see what I do."

"You got 'til the end of the day to give me my stuff back."

"Or *what*?" said Lindy, laughing in Ruby's face.

My sister spoke in a low hiss. "Cinthy didn't *take* anything that belonged to *you* in the first place."

"What do you really know about it?" said Ruby to Ezra. She wiped angry tears from the corners of her eyes. I noticed that there was a bright ribbon, not ours, in her hair. She was wearing a gold necklace with a little hot air balloon charm that glowed against her skin and a funny-looking gold belt cinched around her waist that reminded me of something somebody's grandmother would wear. It didn't suit her. "What I know is you're a *coward*, Ezra Kindred. You was never worth being my best friend. You got to listen to who your mama say you can be friends with like you can't think for yourself. No matter what you believe, I ain't your enemy. I ain't never caused you no harm!"

There was a whistle, signaling the end of recess, and then the bell at the entrance to the school rang three times.

"Ruby, you have no idea what harm is," I said.

"Come near my sister," said Ez, "and you'll be coming the closest you ever been in your life to your last breath."

I thought about going to the nurse to see if I could leave school early. I was dizzy and my stomach was queasy. I'd tell Mama what I'd done with Miss Burden's suitcase. I'd tell her how Ez and me had shown our privates to Ruby. Because maybe that was the reason Miss Burden had died and why the deputy thought he could drive by the Junketts' home and pretend to shoot at all of us for no reason. I'd tell Mama everything. Mama would find a way where I could just be Cinthy instead of growing into a womanhood that felt so strange, bewildering, and certainly didn't suit me.

13

AS RUBY'S CLASSMATES STAMPEDED OUT OF THE CLASSROOM AT THE end of the day, Miss Alley asked her to stay. "A word with you," she said. Ruby was surprised but nodded, aware that Ezra and Lindy were watching with their dark eyes narrowed to slits. Cinthy had gone home early for some reason, probably to mess with Miss Burden's suitcase again.

The classroom blazed with end-of-day sunlight. Ruby could detect the very faint fuzz of downy hair on Miss Alley's face. Thin, fine hairs had slipped past her foundation of chalky pressed powder. Her old teacher, her dead teacher, had never seemed willing to get this close to her.

"Ruby Scaggs," said Miss Alley, her voice soft and mysterious as she strolled around the edge of her desk. Her blond hair bounced against her shoulders, reminding Ruby of her ma's Bombshell wig, which had never regained its shape and luster after Ruby borrowed it. Miss Alley wasn't a natural blonde either.

"I see you're wearing a rather nice dress and ribbon today. Did your mother get that pattern from a magazine?"

"Ma don't give me nothing," said Ruby. "And I don't trust nothing in them prissy papers she always reading night and day. They're worse than candy rotting my teeth."

Miss Alley threw her head back, laughing pleasantly. "Why, Ruby, I believe you're smarter than all of us!"

Ruby liked this attention. It was new—her teacher telling her *she* was smart. *Sunshine, honey, dear.* She'd never had another woman, not even Ezra, tell her she was special.

"I can tell you everything you need to do to have everything you've ever wanted. It's not as hard as it sounds, dear," Miss Alley said, looking around the classroom as though they were on the top of one of those great skyscrapers in New York.

"What do you really want, Ruby? May I ask?"

"Ma'am?" It was hard for Ruby to hear her own voice when Miss Alley's filled her head with height.

"What do you want from your life?" she said.

I want the feeling flying gives me when I think of it, Ruby almost said. She wanted to tell Miss Alley the truth. But she didn't know how to trust anyone but Ezra Kindred, who could no longer be trusted.

"You're very special, Ruby," her teacher said when Ruby didn't answer. "But you must apply yourself in school from this moment on. First—your attendance. It's not too late for you to graduate in the spring with enough education to get your life going the way it should. I used to be like you, but I *applied* myself. I'd be happy to come to your home to speak with your parents about your potential." When she'd said *home,* a ripple of ice-splitting dread went through Ruby.

"Oh, that won't be necessary," Ruby said quickly. "My folks live deep in the bluffs. It's rough ground up there. If you don't know your way, you could step on a snake or find yourself cornered by a pack of wolves. Maybe I could visit you in the village."

"Well, dear, I'm counting on that," Miss Alley said. "Still, I'd need your parents' permission first, for some of my ideas. I wouldn't want them to think I was trying to influence you in any way that defied their own plans."

Ruby pressed her hands over her mouth so that she didn't laugh in Miss Alley's face. To her teacher, it probably looked as if Ruby were going to cry.

"Behind these rough ways you pretend to have, I know there is a sensible young woman who wants something better than the hand she's holding. Leave it up to me, Ruby."

Ruby's face grew hot as she pressed her fingers against Cullen's golden hot air balloon charm. He once asked her to truly consider the potential she had to improve herself. He'd told her that he believed in her because she was unlike any girl he'd ever kissed. Ruby thought of her freedom, pleased that she'd finally beaten Ezra at something, or at least that was how it was all feeling to her.

"Why would you want to help me?"

Miss Alley nodded, as if she'd anticipated Ruby's question. "Besides my aunt, I don't have anyone in my life. No husband, no daughter, no sister, no cousins. I arrived here and I guess I found myself taken by your guts. I'd want to have a daughter just like you, or a younger sister I could dote on, an angel I could protect."

Ruby smiled without thinking. The woman made her tingle the same way Cullen had when he kissed her that very first time. Everywhere Ruby looked suggested a kind of dizzying romance where people wanted her, saw that she could be something else.

"There it is!" her teacher cried. "A one-hundred-watt smile from Ruby Scaggs! That wasn't so hard, was it?"

Striding quickly to her desk to open the creaking drawer where she kept her purse, Miss Alley spoke to Ruby in a friendly voice, as though they'd known each other since they were girls. "I'll walk you outside, dear."

Ruby stared at the corner of her teacher's wallet, which she could see peeking from her purse. She thought of all those spilled coffees. The woman was careless, an easy mark. Grinning, Ruby allowed Miss Alley to take her arm, hooking it with hers.

"Off we go," her teacher said brightly.

· · ·

OUTSIDE, RUBY'S FATHER WAS STANDING alone in the schoolyard. He squinted nervously when he saw a pretty, well-dressed girl who resembled his daughter floating down the steps next to her teacher. He'd arrived at Hobart hoping to catch his daughter sneaking off to some pock-faced lover. She'd been more absent than usual, and Mr. Scaggs had no intention of letting his daughter think she was free to do whatever she wanted with whomever she wanted.

Because there was no one else in sight that could've been Ruby's father, Miss Alley waved at the tall yet hunched figure. Calling out to him, she paused when she noticed Ruby had pulled back, shrinking into herself.

The sky suddenly split into a war of light. Half of the horizon threatened downpour while the other half sparkled, ignoring the rapid pace at which the darkening clouds moved, like horses prancing towards the center of a gray battlefield.

Rooted there on the steps of the school, Ruby took in her father's appearance, worried that his usual lack of care for his clothing and hygiene would make Miss Alley reconsider the alliance she'd offered. But to her surprise, Ruby's father wore a simple blue button-up shirt with no stains or holes in it and his good pair of gray pants. His whitish-blond hair fell neatly around his face. He'd shaved. Ruby didn't know what to think. Was her papa putting on the face of a loving father so he wouldn't be judged by her teachers? Or was he preparing to threaten harm to the imaginary beau he believed Ruby was secretly seeing? When Miss Alley presented her hand to him, Ruby's papa shook it kindly. Except for not having a proper hat, he looked like a simple man on the rather handsome side.

Miss Alley introduced herself, easing all of them into shallow chatter. Smiling and amiable, she spoke of Ruby's good behavior, exaggerating little things Ruby had said or done so that it made her sound like a leader, like she was at the top of her class. She likened

Ruby to a member of her family. "She's like the daughter I've never had," her teacher said. "She's such a star pupil!" The image of a marvelous girl none of them had ever seen appeared right in front of Ruby's eyes. *Sunshine, honey, dear.*

"Ruby got a mother," her father said. "She ain't never said she needed no sister or brother neither. I don't know what kind of yarn she's spinning now but she ain't a orphan. Just to be clear—Ruby can get lost in that backwards head of hers so I'm here to steer her straight," her father said. "Even decent young girls can find themselves in the hands of devils quicker than the wings of angels. I was a young man once. I figure if some bastard is going to try and get something from Ruby she should only be giving to her husband, they'll have to think about me first."

"Well, I certainly understand that," said Miss Alley in an encouraging voice as she shifted her body to face Mr. Scaggs. "I wouldn't dream of letting a nice girl like Ruby walk around alone, what with the way that colored boy showed himself off to me. Those nigger girls are even worse."

"That right?" said Mr. Scaggs, running his hand through his hair. He went to the left pocket of his trousers and took out a cigarette. Then he offered Miss Alley one. Turning to look at the windows of Hobart over her shoulder, Miss Alley ducked her head shyly before she accepted it. Understanding her caution, Mr. Scaggs pointed to a far corner of the impressive lawn. The three of them walked a bit away from the entrance of the school. Ruby watched her papa offer her teacher the light of his match before he flicked his wrist to light his own cigarette.

"You mean a boy like Ruby's age?" he asked.

Miss Alley shook her head at him. "The cleaning nigger."

"Oh," said Mr. Scaggs. Ruby could tell he was listening carefully.

"Today, he almost attacked me," said Miss Alley. "I spilled a cup of coffee, so I had to call for him on the intercom. I could've cleaned it up myself, the way he took his time coming." She lowered her voice. "I was raised to appreciate the basic, human rights of Negroes, of *all* peoples, but I was truly shocked at how he was staring at me. The outright contempt. No decent man has ever looked at me the way he did. I might as well have been naked." Miss Alley had no idea that she was touching one of Mr. Scaggs's deepest nerves speaking about Mr. Caesar that way. Ruby didn't dare risk correcting her.

"Hm," said Mr. Scaggs, pushing his hair out of his face. He'd lifted his eyes to take in the branches of the trees above them. Neither of them behaved as if Ruby was there. "He's a cocky son of a bitch," said her father. "That wife of his walks around here like the queen of the jungle."

"I suppose she'd have to be a savage too," said Miss Alley, "to let a brute like that love her."

Soft autumnal air surged around their thoughts. They were both quiet as they smoked.

"What do you all do around here when you have a nigger who's out of line?" Miss Alley continued. "He has to know his place, otherwise all of them think they've got the run of things. Surely you take action?"

"We don't *do* nothing," Ruby said, blurting the words out before she'd fully thought them through.

"Ruby, just shut up," said her father. "You're in a hell of a lot of trouble. I didn't catch you today but I'm going to. You and whoever this boy is—I'll catch you right on your back. You can be damned sure of it."

Miss Alley turned to take Ruby in before she looked back through her lashes at Mr. Scaggs. "Is Ruby trouble?"

"Not more than any of you women are," Papa said without a note of humor.

Miss Alley coughed. "Those colored girls in the classroom are downright *brazen*," she said as though she hadn't heard his remark. "Had I known niggers could sit next to girls like Ruby in the same classroom and be treated as if they were capable of learning what Ruby is learning, I'd have applied for a position elsewhere."

"What is Ruby learning exactly?"

What Ruby now knew was that Miss Alley was a liar. She was trying to decide whether she minded. In her head, Ruby heard again how sweetly Miss Alley had spoken to her in the classroom. She imagined the two of them being close like sisters, or good friends. She tried to think of the kind of life she could live with a mother like Miss Alley. Ruby didn't want to give that dream up just yet.

Then the sky broke through her thoughts.

Warm water fell hard through the branches above, welting their faces and arms. Miss Alley shrieked and laughed while Mr. Scaggs smiled in spite of himself.

"It's a good soaking, ain't it," said Mr. Scaggs, looking at Miss Alley's mouth as he flicked his cigarette away. Her lips were candied with rainy light and tinkling laughter. Ruby's eyes drifted again to the chunky purse pressed between the side of Miss Alley's body and her bare arm.

"Oh!" said Miss Alley, as she tucked her purse high under her armpit. "God has broken *loose*!"

Miss Alley's powder and foundation had rinsed away. Her blond hair deepened to a dark white helmet. Ruby could see the color and fabric of her teacher's bra through her blouse. It was red like her mouth.

"I've got to walk down to the village in this rain because I missed the bus," Miss Alley said. "I admit I don't feel safe walking alone."

"We'll walk you if you want us to. You shouldn't be afraid," said her father, using his hands to slick his hair behind his ears.

Whichever way Miss Alley turned her head sent a jeweled spray of water. A woman in a downpour was always marvelous. Even if she wasn't too pretty.

Miss Alley took Mr. Scaggs's arm, and Ruby crossed to her other side. Miss Alley removed her purse so that she was closer to Ruby's father, then handed it to Ruby to hold, without thinking twice. Ruby felt the modest weight of it in her hands and it reminded her of Miss Burden's suitcase, which had only been slightly heavier. Almost tenderly, Ruby thought of her dead teacher's gifts as she tried to calculate how much cash might be in this woman's wallet. The way that her teacher had made her papa look at her lips had sent a twinge through her and she remembered how Cullen had teased her when he first laid eyes on her. When she saw him now, which was infrequently, she worried how to cast a spell the way Miss Alley did, so effortlessly it felt natural to anyone who looked at her once. She could make people into mirrors. She had the face of a woman who came from millionaires. *Dear, dear, dear.*

Indeed, Ruby realized that Miss Alley could teach her a few things.

Jonah Reuben Scaggs III

ALL HER LIFE, RUBY HAD EAVESDROPPED ON HER FATHER'S NIGHT-mares, listening to the fragments of his life that he screamed out just before dawn lifted him out of his terror. In trying to understand her father, Ruby had to use her imagination, placing seams and zippers where the stitching had been ripped out. Ruby tried to put together what had happened to her father because she loved him. But love was not a story that had ever provided Jonah Reuben Scaggs with any happiness.

Jonah was just thirteen years old when his father drowned in a boating accident, lost to the waves that battered Salt Point's streaked banks. Less than a month after the drowning of his father, his mother threw herself from the bluffs into the sea. Her grief had infuriated the villagers, who blamed her desperation and unnecessary display of passion on whatever made her skin that deep olive complexion. They'd refused to retrieve what was left of her and claimed that the wind had carried her away, down a cliff into the sea to her husband, for a reason they had no intention of disturbing.

Young Jonah was a half-empty child, easily filled by whatever power poured itself into his immature shape. Gruff men, friends of his grandfather, whom he was named for, called him *boy* and pressed the tips of their callused fingers into his shoulders. One day, with these adults, he'd stood on a green square in an ordinary rural town far south from Salt Point watching a Black man's body burn, and learned what kind of man he was expected to be.

As they insisted that Jonah Reuben Scaggs III would have a good life—*their life*—the boy realized that the last thing he wanted was to be a man at all.

He'd never forget how his grandfather's friends, *brothers* they called themselves, savored aloud their memories of killing, one murder reawakening memories of the past.

Remember Willie, that son of a bitch whose neck wouldn't break until the third time? Oh yeah, who could forget that stuttering son of a bitch! Heh, he cried and called for his momma, that one. Balls as wide as my palms, that one. Remember Esau? Paul brought his wife and children over for ice cream. That sure was fun, wasn't it? Old times, you know? The good times, as our daddies used to say. And the good ain't all the way disappeared, I guarantee you. I guarantee you.

Jonah observed those Christian men whistling merrily as they spoke about their livestock, their crops, God, broken truck engines, bitter wives and better-than-nothing mistresses, and what was in the papers—war, war, war—while one or two would go over to the pyre, eyes glittering, and unbutton his pants to piss on what had, too, once been a man. Then, chuckling with pleasure, they turned their talk to going to find barbecue they could actually eat, maybe over at Regina's. She was a Texas nigger who made the best barbecue for miles and miles around. Before they wandered off in search of crisp pork belly, biscuits with gravy, and smoked ribs, they patted Jonah's head and mentioned something to his grandfather about poker and whores later.

Turning away from the smoldering corpse, Ruby's great-grandfather asked whether Jonah would like some ice cream. Jonah made himself smile and say that he reckoned ice cream would be fine thank you, sir. *That's my boy, that's my boy. You'll be a good man too, coming from the stock you do.*

At the glass counter, eyes smarting, Jonah was handed a strawberry-and-vanilla scepter. He didn't turn it down, though Jonah wondered what might happen if he found the strength to smack the confection away. But his discomfort dissolved on his tongue as he lapped the sweet, cold scoops. He tried to convince himself, nearly succeeding, that none of what was happening across the street had anything to do with him. As with Negroes, Jonah reasoned that there were different complexions where his own white skin and stock were involved. He wasn't the same color as those men and their bonfires.

He observed his grandfather scribbling on the back of something that looked like a postcard. When the old man lifted his head, grinning, Jonah could see his grandfather's skull beneath a grid of veins that crisscrossed his polished, speckled skin like a brown and pink galaxy. His fine hat rested next to a rack of postcards: crudely reproduced photographs of rope, neck, torso, hips, groin gouged out, slack feet hovering inches above the ground. Long dark toes curled like petals of flowers.

Jonah kept licking at the cone he held in his hand. He was numb as he watched his grandfather push the card over to him. He shifted the cone to his left hand, so that he could use his right to sign his name next to his grandfather's grand, looping signature. The postcard would be mailed back to Salt Point, where Jonah's grandmother would place the keepsake alongside many others in a secret album at the back of a long drawer.

As the cashier began to fill the air with local gossip, his grandfather flicked his hand, indicating that Jonah should finish the ice cream on the sidewalk.

Jonah stood outside in a little alley where he could turn his back on the square. When that didn't feel like enough, he squeezed his eyes shut too, focusing on the softening strawberry ice cream. When Jonah finally opened his eyes, it was because his tongue had reached the firm rim, where the pretzel part of the cone became a slimy wall of crude, uneven ridges. Pleased, he tilted the cone to his teeth. This was Jonah's favorite part, the private chewing apart of what was left. So it shocked him to find himself being watched.

The black eyes of a girl held his stare from the entrance of the alley.

She'd been to church. The hem of her white dress grazed the depthless black skin of her calves. On her feet were white patent leather shoes with modest heels. Long limbed, she was taller than he was. Her fingertips were shielded from his gaze by wrist-length white gloves. Jonah longed to see her fingernails, whether they were delicate or broken. It would tell him what kind of work she did. A white satin sash, stitched in lavender thread with a single word, *Lily*, clung to her small waist.

Was she waiting for him to let her pass down the alley? Wasn't she supposed to defer to his path? Jonah didn't know the rules, not yet. He looked at the rainbows inside oil-slicked shapes along the curb and thought about her good shoes, but he didn't move.

She tilted her head, neither irritated nor docile. Jonah watched the girl—Lily must be her name—reach her hand into the pocket of her silent, white dress to remove a blue handkerchief. She pressed its brightness, like sky, over her nose and her mouth, which were pearled with sweat. Eyes trained on him, she held the cloth over her nose and mouth. Then she passed.

Lily had walked through him as though he were a bad smell. What was he, if even a nigger girl could walk imperiously past him?

With a rage that he could make no sense of, Jonah shoved the girl and her silence into the street. She stumbled but did not reveal any shock or surprise. She jerked back towards him, as though she would strike him in return, but she didn't, and maybe that was the thing that would hurt him for the rest of his life. They didn't have the right to hurt the same. Or so he would believe.

He'd never considered that perhaps Lily had covered her face against the depraved scent of burning flesh. Perhaps the odor of his birthright was too sickening for her to inhale.

But Jonah Reuben Scaggs III would never recover enough from that day to stay a boy or become a man. It was not the dead that had made the infinite shame rise in him but the living eyes that did not water in pain or fear when he'd pushed her body into the street with all of his strength. Jonah could still feel his grandfather's fingertips pressing their poisonous warmth into the blades of his adolescent shoulders. Had Jonah said the first thing he thought when looking at her, that she was the most beautiful girl he'd ever seen, it would've earned him his grandfather's eternal loathing.

One afternoon years later, in late autumn, Ruby's father spied a striking brunette at a local county fair, a beauty queen crowned in a sty while country people gulped caramel apples, drank rye, praised the fine snouts of their livestock, and admired the innocence of their children.

He married Ruby's mother then waited for the hour—days, weeks, then years—when she might say she loved him, might reveal her inner life. But his wife had been taught not to trust men who asked for such confessions. Inside the voluptuous, velvety body Jonah had vowed to cherish until his death or hers was a spoiled, indulged, and manipulative child.

Of course, Jonah was no better. He couldn't bring himself to be a husband since he was still bewildered by being a man. Inside his adult body was a boy who stood licking an ice-cream cone while he stared at the mute shadow of a dark girl on a sidewalk.

Out of all the kinds of men Ruby's father could be, he chose the sad, raging drunk. Jonah learned to bellow, to weep, to stagger, to cuss, and to crash.

He emerged from his fog long enough to hold a baby on each of his hardened palms, his whisky breath baptizing a pair of twins—a daughter and a son. The son was stillborn, a curdled blue dream, whose body reminded Jonah of a cerulean cloth a girl named Lily once held over her face. Even as he'd wept, Jonah was relieved that he had no "stock" to share with his silent son.

Ruby's father and mother chose the sea for burial, dropping the lifeless bundle into the water. Turning their oars back towards shore, they remained both married and entirely separated. Jonah blamed the death of his son on his father and his grandfather. He thought of his father's drowning and how selfish his own mother had been to follow her husband into crashing waves with no thought of Jonah's future. They were all at fault. He also blamed it on the dark gaze of a nigger who'd walked through him. Jonah believed she'd cursed him with impotence. That was why the little boy had died before Jonah could show him a different life.

Those eyes had shut him completely out of her existence—and his own. The way she'd covered her face—that gesture had assured Jonah that he'd had no right to look at her. Not then, not ever. Still he couldn't let go. Over the years Jonah saw her black eyes in his mind wherever he went. A wordless haunting. Sometimes he felt her eyelashes against his cheek, wet with tears from silent, mocking laughter. Or he dreamt that the tips of her lashes were red with his blood. Other times the eyes were dry, hard, and unforgiving as a jury. But he was most bothered when her eyes were closed, as though she was uninterested in looking at him at all.

Jonah loathed his need for the memory, which had, after so many years, turned into something that was entirely about his failure to embrace the empire he was told belonged to him. He could not keep steady jobs and the men around him refused to extend to him their complaints about manhood. In their presence, he could not whine about mortgages, too many mouths to feed, the stockpile of resentments between himself and his wife, or his lost youth. His lust was thin-blooded and he was always broke, which made it impossible to keep a woman privately, for pleasure, as his grandfather had done. He could not get loans and bobbed, like a busted barrel, in a pool of debt. His days were shallow crypts—fatherhood soured in his mouth when he realized that it was expensive, more than he could have ever afforded, at least for a daughter.

When the old man died, Ruby's father had rejected his grandfather's will and everything that the will contained—its confirmation that its living benefactor, Jonah Reuben Scaggs, was a white man, deserving of all the amenities and articles that would rightfully indicate to which people and which race he belonged. At the funeral, his relatives had watched in rage as his grandfather's lawyer handed him a thick envelope with his name typed there in block lettering. He'd held the paper in front of his eyes, ripping it apart with his fingers. The will fluttered across the exposed dirt, the petals of his grandfather's last wishes carried away silently.

Refusing to take any part of the future his grandfather may have intended for him, Ruby's father lived between his cowardice and his courage. It made him contradictory. His life leaked away, siphoned each season by turns of his pleasure and repulsion.

So it was a shock when Ruby's father told his daughter he would kindly accept Miss Alley's invitation, on behalf of the Scaggs family, to spend their winter holidays at the Hobarts' home, just beyond Salt Point, in Amity.

14

"POTATOES DESERVE TO BE PEELED WITH AS MUCH CARE AS A PEACH," said Miss Irene, speaking aloud as she turned down the flame beneath a pot on her stove. She had asked Daddy to bring Ezra and me over to her house so that she could "share some words" with us. This invitation was as serious as if she'd threatened to find a switch long enough to whip both of our behinds at once.

Daddy told us he'd return for us in about an hour. Walking into the Junketts' kitchen, I was surprised at the quiet. The bedroom doors were firmly shut, and there was no laughter from the twins or teasing from Ernest, who was sitting in a corner of the living room holding a Bible and studying it so hard I knew there could be no way he'd be doing anything but eavesdropping and praying for us, especially Ezra, who was in the most trouble after the incident with Miss Alley.

I looked around for a bowl of potatoes that I expected Miss Irene wanted peeled but couldn't see anything.

"Sit down, young ladies," said Miss Irene. She waved at Lindy, who was surely terrified to be invited to sit down in her own kitchen. "I'm not going to talk *at* you at all if that's what you're hoping. I'll let white folks do that. Because that isn't *my* work, you understand?

I'd rather place my voice, my hopes for you *in* you because when I look at you three girls all I'm hoping right now is that you grow some sense, and quickly, between your two ears, before I knock you each into the middle of the next week."

"*She's* the one who was trying to make Mr. Caesar clean up after her, working him like she *owned* him," said Ezra.

"Girl, if I asked you to speak in my house you'd be speaking," said Miss Irene. "Were you asked to *speak*? In this *house*?"

Ezra shook her head, and I knew she wanted to cry because *I* wanted to cry. Lindy was already crying.

"My work is to *love* you," said Miss Irene. "You can't make that hard for me, but you can make it hard on yourselves if you don't re- alize how ready this world is to tear you up and use your bones for bonfires. See, I can understand how you felt it was your job to defend my husband from your silly little teacher, but Caesar's a grown man. Three Black girls against one raggedy white woman is just about the sorriest thing I've ever heard of, but let me tell you that it ain't noth- ing new.

"Now, Irene Junkett don't give up on nothing she put her love on, you understand? And Lena Kindred didn't bring her daughters this far to lose them at the hands of some white-woman mess that don't make no kind of sense. When you're up in that school, *close your mouths* and *keep your eyes open*. You don't *live* up in that school. That school was never about *loving* you, never mind *liking* you. Stay on the Path. 'Cause it ain't nearly as well traveled as we'd like to be- lieve. Keep it dignified, ladies. Keep it funky. This world will press every dream out of you before you can spell the names we've given you. A beautiful poet spoke of something someone once told her. She shared these words: 'What they call you is one thing. What you answer to is something else.' Y'all better get busy with your own call- ing or you'll end up looking for your name in somebody else's mouth."

"I'm so sorry," whispered Ezra. Her hands covered her face.

Miss Irene went to her, pulling her hands away so we could see her tears. "Don't cover up your face for us, for *anybody*. Just remember who loves your face. Your lives are my favorite stories. Can you remember that the next time y'all want to act like you're grown? 'Cause ain't none of you nearly grown enough to mess with a woman like that. Too many of our women gone so that you all could live the next chapter. That's not a debt or guilt I'm talking about when I say that. It's love."

We embraced Miss Irene. Beneath her flowing tunic, I could feel her shaking. It made me sad that she'd been this worked up about our behavior. I was worried about Ezra, who was having a harder and harder time letting things go. Ezra's temper lacked any kind of moderation, unless she thought we could be hurt as a consequence. Even then, I realized my sister couldn't always help herself.

Miss Irene asked us to set the table with her special wooden dishes and spoons. She'd made a healing stew, she said, filled with nutrients to replenish and restore our self-esteem. I'd been so afraid of what Miss Irene was going to say to us, I hadn't noticed the rich scent of the stock simmering on the stove.

"This has potatoes and peaches in it," she said.

Having no idea, really, what she was talking about, we only nodded, and went around the table quickly arranging bowls and spoons and cups before our father would arrive to take us home.

. . .

MY FATHER WAS RUNNING LATE. Ezra and Ernest were seated in the screened porch on the side of the house. Miss Irene had the door open so that she could see and hear everything. As I helped rinse and dry the smooth wooden bowls, I snuck glances, just in case he tried to ask my sister to do something dumb like marry him or be his girlfriend. I was certain my parents wouldn't have allowed Ezra to do so at the age of fifteen, even if he was respectable and very handsome. The evening wind carried Ernest's words into his mother's kitchen where they blew like fine grains of sweet rice.

"Can I give you a song? I didn't write it."

"Oh, *please*," my sister said before her voice turned shy in a way I'd never heard before. "What do you mean?"

"Nah, nah, I been thinking about it for some time now," he said. "I want to give you a real song, the kind of music that doesn't end."

"People don't just go on singing and singing," said Ezra teasingly. "I didn't take you for the kind of brother who believes in magic. Plus, who wants to listen to the same song forever and ever. Boy, please. Sounds corny to me."

"First of all, I'm a man," he said. "Well, a *young* man."

"Says your mama!"

"That's right," he said, chuckling. "Says my momma. But she knows my heart." There was too much quiet, so I went to the edge of the door. "I want you to know my heart too, Ezra. If and when you want."

I thought of vomiting but realized that I'd be throwing up Miss Irene's rice and stew and fresh-baked bread, which had all been delicious.

"Tell me what our song would be," she said to him.

I positioned myself at an angle from which I could leap onto the porch, just in case Ernest could move faster than Miss Irene. I saw him press something into Ezra's hand. Then he touched her hair, smoothing it back, as she lifted her cupped hand to her ear. Her eyes were closed as if she'd tasted something sweeter than cane sugar.

"It doesn't end wherever you take it," he said, his voice going out to the edge of a whisper. "It's the only thing that's smaller than my heart but way bigger. I thought that was cool, and yeah, it's probably a bit corny. I'm hoping you won't mind 'cause I spent the entire summer looking for the right one to give to you. None of them are alike."

When she opened her hand, I could see the most perfect seashell resting there.

. . .

IT WAS THE FIRST DAY of Ezra's suspension, which would last for two weeks. I woke up thinking of this and could not believe it again. The board had brought their gavel down against my fifteen-year-old sister and her "questioning" of Miss Alley's treatment of Mr. Caesar. After her suspension, they would then vote to decide whether she could finish out the year. If they forbade her return it was likely we could not graduate together as we'd always imagined. Sensing my anxiety, Ezra surprised me by coming into my bed and gently plaiting my hair for school. The smell of the hair oil on her fingers was so nice. I sighed in pleasure as she used the edge of the comb to slightly scratch my scalp. "You're the smartest girl in the entire class," said Ezra, as if we'd been in the middle of discussing that very subject. "That's why that witch is on you all the time. Remember that."

Chewing my lip, I finally spoke. "It won't be the same. Nothing is any fun without you."

She laughed. "Cinthy, you know what? Mama is going to have me up in this house washing walls with so much bleach you'll smell it all the way up there. One day, you're going to have to know how to learn and to do without me. I might not always be around to tell you to trust yourself. You've got to love your own feelings, defend them at all costs. Can you remember that when someone hurts you?"

"I'll try," I said, smiling so that my tears wouldn't fall. Ezra could always keep her tears in a deeper place, far down where they couldn't betray her.

"All this time ahead of me with Mama bossing me around, I'll be more than ready to be back in that funky old classroom," said Ezra, grinning.

I smiled before growing quiet again. I had to ask Ezra what had been on my mind. "Mama's sick, isn't she?"

"She'll be better. Don't worry, okay? Once we know what's wrong with her we can help her heal." Ezra's eyes darkened but she blinked away her feelings before they trickled down her cheeks.

"Daddy says we'll have to take her over to that Negro doctor in

Gunn Hill," I said. "I heard Miss Irene and Daddy talking. Nobody here would care about Mama living or dying."

"Don't say that," said Ezra. Her voice was sharp. "Mama's full of living. She just needs a rest. Miss Irene says Negro women ought to take rests whenever they can since they're always working. Miss Irene says when a Negro woman is smiling she is still working. I think that's true. Miss Irene ought to know."

"Mama isn't the same as Miss Irene, no matter what you want to believe."

"I know how strong Mama is because I know how strong I am," she said. Her eyes left my face as she withdrew into her own thoughts. "I know how strong I am and what my work is. I'm going to protect us no matter what it takes," said Ezra. "We have to be brave. Look at everything that's happening right now in this country, okay? It's on the radio, in the newspaper, every day. Mama and Daddy might be too tired to pay Mississippi any mind, but I'm not."

"Oh," I said. Then I remembered how Ezra had begun to listen to Martin Luther King, Jr.'s speeches on the radio at our house and over at the Junketts'. Two years ago, while the sight of planes whizzing above us at the air show had inspired Ruby's passion, my sister was riveted by bus boycotts in Montgomery. But I'd only been eleven then and couldn't understand how deeply it had consumed her. And Ezra rarely mentioned anything about it in front of my parents. I think she knew it made them nervous to think that she might leave Maine and head south to prove her devotion to our race.

"Hey," she said to me, "go downstairs and get us some of those biscuits I smell. I hope I'm allowed to have biscuits even if I'm supposed to be in trouble. And when you walk into that fake school, let them know what your work is."

"Okay," I said, unsure as to what my work was at all, except to obey my parents because I was only thirteen years old.

"Mind-whupping outlasts an ass-whupping any day of the week. A mind-whupping doesn't stop hurting. That's what Miss Irene once told me."

"Hm," I said. Standing at my desk, I slid my books into my satchel. "Is that what I think it is?"

Ezra pointed to Miss Burden's diary on my desk.

"Remember? I took it from—"

"Let me take care of it," said Ezra, pushing her voice over mine. I wished she hadn't seen it, but a part of me was relieved. I didn't want to think about Miss Burden anymore. I didn't say it but Ezra could see that I was thinking of us—her, Ruby, and me—with our backs flat on those rocks. I'd done it because I'd wanted my sister to think I was fearless, the way she was. It hadn't ever been about Ruby for me, though I realized now that whatever had happened that afternoon had changed the two of them. My sister had changed, which meant I was changed too.

"Let all of that go," said Ezra, reading the shadow in my face. "Ruby comes near you, I'll take care of her. Focus your *soul*, Cinthy. Everything we do is right, do you understand? Miss Irene says that our ancestors have already paid for our passage. We're not enslaved. We're not suspended. We are not stupid or wrong. Miss Alley is the slave, as is Ruby, as is her papa and her ma, and this whole damn village." Ez touched my shoulder with her hand. "Come back and tell me what you've learned so I don't fall behind. Get the stupid homework for me."

"We are already ahead," I said.

"That's right," said my sister, smiling as she guided me out of the bedroom. "See? You already know the most important thing."

I nodded but I didn't know what that meant for me. The entire school looked at us—Ezra, Daddy, and myself—as if we were finally starting to become the niggers they'd always believed we were. I could see the triumph in the eyes of my teachers and classmates.

Yesterday evening, when our father had answered the phone, I'd first thought it was our grandmother calling to bother Mama. Daddy was being excruciatingly polite to whoever was on the other end of the line, like he always was to Ginny. But our father's face had darkened when he returned to his chair and his eyes met Mama's puzzled glance over their cups of coffee. We hadn't had time to have our dessert with the Junkett family, so we'd brought huge slices of Miss Irene's red velvet cake home with us.

"Ezra's suspension may directly affect her chances of graduating with honors," Daddy announced. "At this time, she will not be permitted to enter the property of the school for any reason. Should she consider any form of trespassing, she faces the possibility of expulsion and arrest."

What surprised me was that Daddy didn't ask Ez what had happened. He didn't ask me either. Except for Mama's involuntary coughing, the silence at our table was like fine, wet gauze stuffed into my mouth.

Bewildered, I watched Ezra set her fork and knife down calmly beside her plate. She wiped her mouth with her napkin before excusing herself to her room.

"She didn't do anything," I said to Mama and Daddy, wondering why I hadn't been suspended. Or Lindy. If our principal had called Mr. Caesar and Miss Irene about a punishment for Lindy, I didn't know about it. We'd both raised our voices to our teacher too. Then I recalled how Miss Alley enjoyed humiliating me, while Ezra just seemed to fluster her. Any action taken against Lindy Junkett would involve a confrontation with Miss Irene. But Daddy wouldn't argue. It upset me to think that our father wouldn't fight for Ezra, that his inaction implied that he felt Ezra deserved suspension.

"She didn't *do* anything," I repeated.

"Hush, Cinthy," said Mama, leaving her untouched slice of cake as she rose from the table. "It doesn't matter."

. . .

SITTING ALONE IN THE CAR with Daddy on the way to school, my disappointment in him expanded in my stomach like yeast. I picked at the warm biscuit wrapped in a cloth on my lap and studied my father's profile as he constantly checked the rearview mirror. The only thing trailing us was a tail of cloudy gravel. He wasn't a good driver like Mama. It was too easy for him to wander off in his mind where his thoughts drifted like the ancient boats tethered down at the village pier. This morning his mind was anywhere else but at the wheel. My father pushed his wing-tipped shoe against the accelerator. He was driving too fast.

"Slow down," I said to him. "I need you to talk to me. I don't understand anything, okay?"

He cleared his throat and I leaned towards him, expecting him to say something.

"Daddy?"

"I'm driving, honey," he said, swallowing with effort. His voice was thick with what I sensed was both anger and resignation.

"Why didn't you ask *us* what happened at school yesterday? Don't you want to know our side of the story?"

I turned my body a little so that I could see more of him.

"This job is the only job I'll ever have where I can afford for us to live the life your Mama and I wanted for this family."

"But couldn't you at least try to speak to someone at the school about what really happened? Couldn't you ask Mr. Caesar? He was right there. Lindy was there. I was there. We all saw it."

My father used his flat palm to swivel the steering wheel, pulling the car over to park on the shoulder of the road. He didn't cut the engine, but he placed his foot on the brake before facing me. His starched white shirt and skinny black tie gleamed.

"I'm sorry that your sister forgot her place and earned herself a suspension. That's all there is to it. I'm pretty sure I know she spoke out for the right reason, and I'm completely aware that Miss Alley is a dangerous, foolish, unqualified woman. These things are the facts," Daddy said. "But my god, Ezra's old enough—and you are too—to understand the notion of action and consequence in this world. So if you're asking me about logic, then that is the logic. If you're asking how I feel, well that's another thing. I'm disappointed in your sister, sure. I'm also frustrated because I'm not, and will never be, in a position to overrule the people who pay my wages without risking an even greater punishment than your sister is experiencing. I suffer indignities I intend never to pass down to you or your sister—or your mother, for that matter. In case you haven't noticed, there aren't any favors in this world for a Negro man. I can't count on anybody to speak or act on my behalf. I can't count on anybody to feed my wife and my children or keep the lights on in my house. There are other jobs elsewhere, but at what cost?"

"Daddy, Miss Alley *lied*," I said, in spite of his words. Tears smarted in my eyes. "She *picks* on me." I sobbed. "She's not—not a teacher."

"Of course she isn't!"

I drew back sharply.

"Your sister knew *exactly* what was coming to her. Mr. Caesar knew too, which is why, should that woman decide to break every glass, cup, and plate in that goddamn school, it would *still* be his job to clean up the shards with a goddamn smile on his face. Do you understand? Mr. Caesar knows what his job is, so *he does it*.

"Now, maybe that's my fault for having such high ambitions for my daughters but I'm telling you this, and Jesus Christ we're going to be late now, but I hope *you'll* have the sense to keep your head down and not have this godforsaken woman get you suspended too!"

I said nothing.

"Cinthy, there will be no suspension for me should I challenge Miss Alley on your behalf or your sister's. Instead, there will be Mr. Hobart pointing his lousy finger at the door. He'll be smiling while he does it. Sweetheart, that man will go home, have a drink, and put his feet up." The sigh that came whistling through my father's lips was so bitter. "It'd be just another day of him being a white man."

Pressing more tears from my eyes, I was so confused. A day of being a white man was nothing I could picture. Except that all my life I'd been told that a white man's day was worth more than mine and my father's.

"Baby girl, the reality is that they don't want us here. Never have.

They don't want us here, but they don't have a real reason to make us leave. Not yet. The last thing I need is for you or your sister to give these people any reason to run us out of Hobart, out of Salt Point, before you both get the chance to graduate. Then all of these sacrifices we've made will have been in vain. There's not enough time for us to start all over somewhere else. Not right now, not with the way your mother—"

The biscuit had turned into crumbs because I'd been clenching it so hard. Daddy stroked my cheek. "Please don't cry, honey," he said. "Help me by behaving like the young lady I've raised you to be. Keep your head down, will you? I'm sorry to speak harshly to you but you must know better. Can you know better for me?"

"What about Mama?"

His face crumpled as he snatched his glasses off to press his fingers against his eyes.

"Daddy, what's wrong with Mama?"

"Honey, I don't know."

My father's truthfulness was so awful that I had to open the door quickly so that I didn't vomit down the front of my clothes. The wind picked up the savory, greasy crumbs from my lap and blew them away while I heaved acid from my stomach into the dust. My emptied belly hungered for the feeling of safety that my mama and daddy had once built for us, the taste of which I'd known my entire life.

Whatever had blown into our village from the sea at the end of summer seemed intent on swallowing everything we once believed had made us who we were.

Daddy had made me understand his powerlessness by three simple words: *I don't know.* Maybe he really couldn't protect us from the world.

• • •

AT SCHOOL, I SAT AT my desk, aware that the only friends I had were the lined notebook spread flat against the abused wooden desktop and a sharpened pencil I clung to as though it were the oar I'd need to row myself away from this place I no longer trusted.

Lindy was absent. Perhaps Miss Irene had simply decided not to allow Lindy to be further subjected to Miss Alley's lessons.

So I was alone.

My classmates' light eyes flickered brightly over me, as if they were relieved that there was only one of us left. Everything in the room felt flipped. For example, Ruby sat in the front row instead of the back. Her dress was clean, and her skin was scrubbed. She chewed on her pencil instead of her fingernails. She even put her hand up in the air when Miss Alley asked a question.

The next time she turned to stare at me, I rolled my eyes so hard she whipped herself around and didn't move her head to look at me again.

I pictured Ezra scrubbing our walls at home and wincing while she helped Mama chop onions. The kitchen radio would be vibrating with opinions about what was happening elsewhere in America—nine Black students had walked through a mob of whites to the entrance of a school in Little Rock. I imagined my sister pausing to listen to the list of their names—Ernest, Elizabeth, Jefferson, Terrence, Carlotta, Minnijean, Gloria, Thelma, and Melba. Maybe when she got tired of thinking about the world beyond our village, Ezra let herself daydream about Ernest Junkett's shy smile while she hummed "The Very Thought of You" or "You Go to My Head." Closing my eyes, I saw Ezra leaning inside our door, waving to me as I came up Clove Road with our homework. Just then, I forgot how awful school was because, in the eyes of my sister, I was seen and loved. *My sister will be waiting for me* became the seven words I'd repeat to myself the rest of the day. Each repetition was armor, salve. At recess, I sat alone, enjoying a beautiful apple Mama had given me for lunch, and I felt more like myself.

The bell signaling the end of recess rang too soon. Miss Alley stood at the entrance of the classroom while we presented our faces and hands to her for inspection. Some boys wandered away before even reaching our teacher. But when I got to the front of the line, Miss Alley's eyes swept carefully over my outstretched palms.

"Hyacinth, please wash your hands."

Blinking, I looked at my palms. Where was the dirt? I had been very careful eating the apple so that my fingers weren't sticky with juice.

"Excuse me, Miss Alley," I said. "I wasn't even playing. I didn't touch anything."

"You are filthy," she said wearily, folding her arms across her chest. We both knew she meant something else when she said *filthy*. "Any further disobedience from you will result in a suspension as well."

Ruby sailed past me, slowing down at the last minute so that she could enjoy my shame. She offered her hands to our teacher for approval.

"Thank you, Ruby," said Miss Alley with such care they almost seemed related to each other.

. . .

MISS ALLEY GAVE ME NO more of her attention that afternoon. She dictated an easy vocabulary test to us, and at my wooden desk, my mind drifted, a crowing loneliness flapping in my head.

One of the boys broke through the classroom's stale silence.

He leapt to stand on the seat of his chair before scrambling to the ledge of our sunny windows. Shouting, he waved his balled fists. "They arresting that coon! They got 'im now!" His words soared and an army of boys tugged their bodies up to kneel beside him on the wide wooden sills.

I stood and walked to the window. When I came closer, the others shifted away, shoving me forward so that I was pressed against the glass. I noticed neither Ruby nor Miss Alley had moved.

It was hard to see clearly from the second floor, but I was fairly sure I was looking at the top of Deputy Charlie's head. Roughly, he pushed Mr. Caesar ahead of him, forcing him to shuffle in a straight line. He kicked Mr. Caesar with each step, knocking and sliding his black baton across Mr. Caesar's back. I couldn't understand how Mr. Caesar didn't fall to his knees at such force.

"Oh my God," I said, turning around. "He'll *kill* him."

There was Ruby sitting carefully in her seat, staring at Miss Alley as if she and that woman could speak to each other wordlessly, the way I could with Ezra. I realized they were likely responsible for whatever was happening to Mr. Caesar. Ruby's back was unusually straight against the hard chair; she looked smug and vulgar. An air of purpose wavered around her. In the set of Ruby's jaw, I knew that Ruby had finally understood what her white skin was capable of.

Then I imagined my sister standing in our kitchen with squared shoulders, a warrior holding a dripping rag in her hand. Her chest lifted and fell in a steady rhythm, her hairline edged with sweat and defiance. Ezra had spoken the truth when Miss Alley had lied about our Mr. Caesar. In doing so, she had accepted the consequence.

Thinking of my sister's bravery, I flew from the room, running as fast as I could. I skidded around those sharp corners, shoving away teachers who tried to grab me, pushing my entire body from Hobart's tall entry doors. Surging forward, I leapt from the top of the steps, clearing them in an instant.

I saw Mr. Caesar's face through the window of the police cruiser. His handcuffed palms were pressed and spread against the glass. His eyes widened when he saw me coming. I didn't know how I'd free him, reach him, but I would. *I had to reach him.* Mr. Caesar moved his head violently. His mouth was moving but I couldn't hear his voice.

Crying, I banged my fist against the glass, feeling it rattle. He'd placed his fingers on the glass but our fingers couldn't touch. Blood streamed from Mr. Caesar's nose and the side of his head.

The deputy was already in the driver's seat of the cruiser. He swiveled clumsily to look at me. His thick head shook in warning and something like boredom seeped from his glittering eyes.

He brought his baton back in one firm move and smashed it into

Mr. Caesar's face, knocking him out. His deep brown hands went silent against the window. Screaming, without thought, I reached down to snatch a stone sitting in the gravel. I tried to shatter the entire window with the stone that was now in my hand. If I could only crack it. Again, I struck the window and the force of the stone in my hand made the glass give way. There was sparkling glass everywhere. Small pebbles of glass hit my face as I tried to reach through to touch Mr. Caesar's bloodied hands, which were studded, like my own, with glass. Pain winged through my fingertips, my knuckles, the bones in my hands. His fingers slipped in our blood. I couldn't let him go.

"What the *hell*?" the deputy said, twisting himself to get out of the car. He was breathing hard as he rushed around the side of the cruiser. "What the hell you think you doing? You one of them Kindred niggers, ain't you?"

By the time Daddy appeared, the deputy had drawn his gun and had it aimed at me. My father jerked me back, roping his single arm around me. This was no longer a ghostly gesture, a miming of violence: The deputy held his pistol close to my father's face. I could feel Daddy tense his entire body; he was ready to shield me, to push me out of the way. I could feel his arm tightening as hard as he could, as if he could stop the bullet from going through us both.

I stared up at the deputy's face from my father's arms.

"You've no right to arrest that man or to point a loaded gun at my daughter." His voice was harder than I'd ever heard it in my life. With his firm grip Daddy pulled me behind his body as he backed away, one step then the next. "We'll surround that bullshit jail of yours until you have evidence—and I am certain that you do not—that Caesar Junkett is a criminal."

Deputy Charlie peeked over his own shoulder to glance at the pulp of Mr. Caesar's unconscious face. After a moment, he returned his pistol to its leather holster. Then, almost casually, he got back into the car and turned on the engine.

My knees gave and I sank to the ground, where rocks teethed my knees. Somewhere above me was my father's voice. *Cinthy, you could've been killed! Killed! What did you think you could do? Jesus, you could've been killed. Both of you! Oh, your sweet hands. Baby girl, are you here? Stay with me, honey. Can you hear my voice? Cinthy, stay with me. It's Daddy, honey, I love you.*

I felt my father's arm gather me up. Lifted with such power and gentleness, my body went limp.

As a young girl, I'd frequently had a dream in which a tall, red-eyed man gave me his word that he'd carry me on his horse across a strange river one day, when I was ready. I hadn't had this dream in so long, but it filled me.

For the first time, I realized that the man was my great-grandfather, Theodore Kindred, and that his love carried my father and me, had always carried us, so that we did not burn alone inside the fires of this world.

TWO

15

DEPUTY CHARLIE DEMANDED THAT MY FATHER PAY FOR THE COST OF replacing the glass of the police cruiser. Daddy agreed that Mr. Hobart could dock his pay until a new window was installed. At home, my father didn't complain about any of it, but we all could see his worry. If he protested in any respect, he was certain that Mr. Hobart would fire him. It was winter and the holidays were ahead of us; my father was not the kind of man who trusted that things would work themselves out or that God would provide if he were to quit outright, which was what I'm sure a part of him wanted to do.

Despite his efforts at appeasement, there had been a shift in the environment. The faculty had tacitly agreed that I should not roam around the school. My presence was dangerous because I could now be cited as having issues with rage and adult authorities; I was still permitted to attend my classes, but no longer could I linger anywhere on the campus of the school without supervision.

It was worse for my father. He was asked to take his lunch in his own classroom rather than sitting alone, as he usually did, in the faculty's shabby dining lounge. Sometimes Mr. Caesar invited Daddy to join him out in his woodshed, which he'd made cozy with a small woodstove, a couch and chairs, a table set; there was a large adjoining room filled with tools, kerosene lamps, turpentine canisters and paint, ammonia and innumerous supplies, which Mr. Caesar kept in immaculate order. Most days, the Junkett children, Ezra, and I also took our lunch there. The entire school had seemed to sigh in relief that we had finally begun to know our place.

What disturbed me most was that life continued.

It made me question whether the whole thing that happened between Mr. Caesar, Daddy, myself, and the deputy was a real event. It took me some time to figure out that Mr. Caesar had been arrested after being accused of stealing Miss Alley's purse, which was never found. It was rarely mentioned when our families visited. Like the adults, I tried to go on as best I could and be grateful that nobody had been killed. Mr. Caesar had had three of his ribs broken and there was a gash from the impact of the deputy's baton that fractured his skull. He'd come close to losing four of the fingers on his right hand. Daddy and Mama discouraged me whenever I asked why wasn't there a way to challenge what that deputy had done to Mr. Caesar; I couldn't let it go.

Mr. Hobart had forced his niece to drop the charge of theft against Mr. Caesar, who, to my surprise, was not fired. There was no follow-up investigation of any kind. In fact, the day after the incident, Mr. Hobart had phoned Mr. Caesar to ask if and when he'd be returning to the school to handle an infestation of mice in the dining hall. Rumors claimed that Mr. Hobart had expressed his personal displeasure over his nephew's behavior, threatening to use his own gun if Deputy Charlie couldn't handle his duties in a more civilized way. We didn't know if this was true, but the deputy no longer regularly drove past the Junkett home.

When my father suggested to Mr. Caesar that he find new employment over in Gunn Hill, Mr. Caesar declined. He didn't want to work in a factory and have a white manager breathing down his neck all day and night. *Won't be the last time a coward like that tries to bash my head in,* Mr. Caesar said one day. *I got children to raise. I got God and Irene to love*. He folded the entire matter up carefully inside him, like a man folding a rare two-dollar bill inside a wallet.

It seemed naïve of my parents to believe that, if we only minded our business, we could escape the deputy's menace, but our time in Salt Point went on: indistinguishable days lifting and bowing against cool air. Winter seeped away our hours of light. I rarely thought of Miss Burden anymore. The "game" we'd played on the rocks seemed like the kind of thing children could do with one another without realizing what harm could come of it, even if it was years away. The harm between Ezra and Ruby had come much sooner. I couldn't stop thinking of it as the moment I'd lost something of my own innocence that was unrelated to having my period.

Each evening our yellowing lampshades stenciled tallowy circles of light on thick oval rugs where Ezra and I sat quietly, as crisp air pressed against the panes of our home. Nat King Cole's voice filled our hearts, and Mama's favorite Sam Cooke records were played frequently to cheer her spirits. From our perch, we also listened to the radio and tried to prophesize where our nation was headed. Eisenhower continued his recovery from a mild stroke, while the Cold War picked up heat. Huddled together, my sister and I tried to imagine how machines from earth could be launched into space. One day, the radio advised us, humanity would reach the moon. Stranded on earth, Ezra and I searched to find news programs that featured the voices of Negro preachers and activists like Medgar Evers who, above a backdrop of shouting and applause, insisted that Negroes were human beings. Because there were so few Negroes far up in Maine where we lived, there was little attention given to the ways we too were being menaced by the police in Salt Point, in Gunn Hill, and even in Briggley. Still, the radio connected our family to a call to arms. We wondered how the spirited actions of the NAACP would ever reach us.

Out there in a nation we couldn't fully comprehend, Black swarms marched unafraid. They sang of freedom, lifted their sweet bodies into dark picket lines, danced between fatal crossfires, and did not waste their breath on white grace. Who was our grace for, if not ourselves and those who sang before us?

Ezra and I listened to freedom stories, and when our parents drove over fifty miles away from our village to Piney Hollow, for Mama to see a specialist, we stole our father's newspapers before he could burn them. He was fearful that someone in the village would suspect the truth, which was that my father and Mr. Caesar were much more educated about their civil rights than what was assumed. Eisenhower had signed the Civil Rights Act of 1957 in September. The aftermath of the law had set the nation on the brink.

When we all gathered together for meals, my parents and Mr. Caesar pored over issues of *The Crisis* while Miss Irene shared pamphlets that were given to her in Gunn Hill. These very talks were happening around the tables of Black families everywhere. If we dared to interrupt the adults about a glass of water, or something else to eat, the slight, hard glance of irritation we received was more devastating than anything a belt or hairbrush might do. But while the rise of the movement spurred Mr. Caesar and Miss Irene into action and purpose, my father still mostly worried that he could lose his job. Mama, who grew more and more tired after these strong-voiced dinner discussions, withdrew from them early for the sake of her health.

In our bedroom, after these high-tempered suppers, I listened to Ezra read aloud from the notebook where she'd transcribed many of the Junketts' political tirades. It made me nervous to listen to Ezra reciting Miss Irene's ideas in her own voice. But beyond Salt Point, there was a world that required our courage and a resolve to change; and we were trying by ourselves to learn the things that would arm us appropriately.

The first problem, then, was that Ezra and I couldn't go anywhere.

We walked with our chins lifted to the edge of Clove Road then turned around and walked right back to our porch. We pretended to hold hand-lettered signs in our arms, above our heads. Across our barren winter fields, we mapped a grid of the Capitol in Washington. We conjured sidewalks, parades, and main streets where we stomped and sang and scrambled into huddles with other Black people when the gas was thrown, the dogs unleashed.

In the cold, my sister and I marched double time until we could do it without panting. It was a game, we told ourselves. Ezra showed me some of the self-defense tactics Ernest had shown her. *But they aren't nonviolent. You'll get yourself killed like that,* I reminded her. My sister's face went distant as she shrugged away my words.

Using her pretty voice, Ezra might sing a spiritual to distract me: "Wade in the Water," "Lay Down Body," "Amazing Grace."

I could never remember the words, so I couldn't harmonize. But when I heard them, flames grew inside me, a lick of smoke on my lips.

At home, I was too focused on Mama's health to spend any extra time wondering how a person like my old teacher could decide to die. I was more concerned about my father and how he'd nearly sacrificed himself to save me. When I went to sit quietly in his study while he corrected papers and listened to some of his blues records, he didn't shoo me away or say that the blues was only for grown folks. I'd never heard him play such music before and I felt that I was learning something of my father's troubles.

. . .

THAT WINTER, EZRA WAS QUIETER than usual; I couldn't tell whether it was the cold or the strangeness of accepting that she was a young woman that made her mute. She spoke up when she needed to, but otherwise appeared to be saving her energy and strength for something ahead. I missed her.

After putting away the dinner dishes one December evening, I stood alone in the hallway's stillness. Ezra had shut the door of her

room, which was a sign that I wasn't to pester her. There was a loneliness in me that I couldn't describe, except to say that it felt like the
entire house was also lonely.

My parents, who usually closed their bedroom door when they
went up to their room for the night, didn't seem to realize that it was
cracked open. Quietly, I went as close as I could to it so that I could
listen to their conversation. I was tired of how quickly they would
stop talking whenever Ezra or I came into a room.

"To this day she refuses to apologize," I heard my mother say.

"We don't get to pick our mothers," replied Daddy, mildly. His
voice was both sorrowful and good-humored. I could picture him
in his white T-shirt and slacks. He would be sitting in the wingback
armchair that once held a bright rose pattern in the fabric.

"At least your mother didn't abandon you," said Mama.

"She abandoned me in other ways."

"Who could *do* such a thing—leave a newborn baby on the
steps of a church," said Mama as if my father hadn't spoken at all.
"I could've died, and it wouldn't have meant much to Ginny, long as
she kept her dance card filled. Trifling. All I've seen my entire life is
a proud woman who chose herself over everything, even her daughter. I'd never do that to Cinthy or Ezra. Or you. Because I know how
to love. My mama doesn't know a thing about it." My mother's fit
of coughing silenced whatever my father was about to say. I heard
Mama moan the word *water*. I pictured my father, moving from his
chair to their bed, and holding Mama against his chest with his arm
until the spell passed.

"Baby, you're getting yourself worked up, which is about the
worst thing you could do," said Daddy. "You're not well enough for
that rage. It'll make the symptoms worse. We've got to get you strong
enough to take the surgery. If Ginny's offering to help, we may need
to accept it. Until you're better."

"Until what?" asked Mama bitterly. "I will make peace with my
God while I make my last arrangements."

"Don't talk like that," he said.

"I can't help it. I didn't expect my life to—"

"Your life is *here*."

"Heron," Mama said. Her voice was clear. "I'm not sure I'm willing to let my mother have the chance to hurt me ever again. Even if I do need her."

"Call your mother, forgive her, put up with her, and let her love you finally," said my father. His voice was muffled. Maybe he'd pressed his mouth against Mama's cheek the way he often did. When he cleared his throat, it sounded like he was sitting up. "Maybe she's ready to explain."

"Did your mother ever?"

"Ever what?"

"Explain," said Mama.

"She couldn't," he said. "I killed her star."

"God took him," said Mama. "You were just a boy."

"I was at the wheel," my father said.

Alma Elizabeth Kindred

ALMA ELIZABETH KINDRED, MY PATERNAL GRANDMOTHER, WAS ALWAYS only called Comfort. When a child receives a nickname too soon it can be ruinous. My grandmother, even as a baby, was destined for contrariness. Before she could even make tears of her own, the people of Damascus placed the tears they wept for her murdered parents and their lost children inside her. Anointed with their legacy, she was a walking death, a breathing ghost. Whoever she might have become on her own was lost.

Inwardly, Comfort sighed when the people of Damascus dangled heaven, hell, and paradise in front of her. Salvation and sin, Satan and saints, bored her. Too intense, solipsistic and childish, she thought. The dusty pendulum of punishment, sacrifice, and reward made her sneeze. Maybe she was allergic to the air in the Promised Land.

Sometimes my grandmother stood in the sanctuary of Hinder Me Not, staring at the framed photograph of her young parents, trying to make her eyes water, but she had no imagination to reenact their death.

Comfort's strangeness, so unlike the temperament of her gracious mother, Callie, unsettled the women of Damascus. She was

a force they could not define. But in spite of the shallow conceal-
ment of their dislike of her, they were loyal to her strangeness. Words
like *hussy, heifer,* and *tackhead* were swallowed, because their aging
ears could still recall the light green laughter of Calliope Kindred. At
times, they caught themselves wondering if Alma "Comfort" Kindred
enjoyed their unease just a little bit.

Comfort grew. Lovely, separate. She was raised by these wom-
en's hands, until one day, when the Hinder Me Not ushers gave my
grandmother a metal ring, shining with a pair of keys to her parents'
home, which had been kept locked, cleaned, and revered. *You grown
and got to make a way,* she was told.

Instead of continuing to preserve the house as a sort of museum,
Comfort threw open the windows to let out the old-timey smell of
mothballs, old marigolds, and mute bleach.

First things first, she needed to breathe. Then she wanted to
fuck. How could she do either with a crucifix on damn near every
wall, including three in the biggest bedroom? Could she ever be delicate enough with her mother's china set to drink whisky over the
morning newspapers like she wanted? Where would her own clothing fit, tight and bright, mostly shades of red and gold, if she didn't
remove her mother's faded calico and muslin dresses from the carved
mirror wardrobe?

The sweat and submission of fucking (the submission not and
never hers) made each breath she took her ecstasy. After sex, she
soaped her body and sighed with relief that she'd given nothing up,
given nothing away. Men could find softness only in her skin. Nothing else in her would yield.

When two different men each gave Comfort a son, her eyes flickered outward briefly, then returned to the island of her inner self,
where her thoughts ripened like untouched fruit, falling alone inside
silent groves. Sometimes she caught herself looking down at the two
beings she had made, terrified. She couldn't bear to tell them the
truth, which was that she had next to no interest when it came to
their fates.

No wonder, then, that my teenaged father and his baby brother took off, stealing one of her old boyfriends' cars, which had lain deserted and opulent next to the butterfly bush.

They didn't get very far.

The crash was written up in all the local columns. The name of the younger boy who died never appeared in print, because it was such a beautiful name it made Black people weep. Even white people stopped talking while they were reading the tragic story.

The eldest boy, my father, was hurled halfway through the window, so hard his arms were torn into tentacles of muscle, his bones broken and splintered under the enameled steering wheel. The baby boy, who was Comfort's favorite because he was similar to her in his aloof temperament, was discovered in the branches of a tree beyond the wreckage, headless. His arms were opened like the wooden wings of a cross. The head had rolled some distance, and it would take time for it to be found.

The elders of Damascus wept and shook their heads. Heron Kindred had mangled his and their legacy. Killed his brother. Behind my daddy's back they called him Cain. And the townspeople who worshiped the ashes of Theodore and Calliope Kindred couldn't bring themselves to hint that maybe some of the new tragedy was Comfort's fault. That those young lions had been in need of attention.

From that day forth, my father, Heron Theodore Kindred, had to do the living of both sons.

My father's car accident took place the summer before his senior year. As Daddy recovered—he ended up convalescing for much of the school year—he completed his assignments alone at home. Once or twice a week a fellow student, or one of the Hinder Me Not ushers, would come by and pick up his work to take it to his teacher. When girls came by, he could see the word *freak* squatting on their tongues. With adults, he could almost taste the word *murderer* in their spit.

His mother, Comfort, fed him. She taught him how to bathe, dress, and heal himself by staying reserved and untouchable by the old folks who said he ought to spend each day of his life in hell. These lessons were offered swiftly before Comfort returned to the remote archipelago of her own mind. Daddy tried not to be a nuisance or needy, until he realized that his mother's emptiness actually prevented him from irritating her.

They never mentioned his younger brother, each aware of what could happen if they did. My father hoped that if he mentioned that name, perhaps forgiveness could follow. But my grandmother's silence told him there was no real reconciliation on offer. Uselessly, he tried to push her, tried another angle, but eventually they both recognized the futility of it.

So he crawled into books.

My father lifted his lanky, tender body into sentences, stories, dictionaries, almanacs, astronomy, and bizarre anatomies of endangered creatures. In his mind, my father visited indigenous villages and the horizons of other continents. The more miles he trekked across paper—histories of world wars, incomprehensible genocides, inscrutable pages of lost languages—the more he mistrusted the whole God situation, which seemed to ask humans to forget and forgive too much.

This felt especially true once a year, when the entire congregation gathered in a little patch of earth behind the new Hinder Me Not to pray over the spot where the old church had been. They screamed the names of the children that Calliope Kindred held in her burning arms. They pressed their fingers down into the earth and said they could feel the bones of God poking out.

While they never required my grandmother or my father to speak, it was essential that the last living Kindreds be present to witness the stations of their devotion. They spoke of Theodore Kindred, a great man struck down too soon by white folks. They wiped tears from their faces with the sides of their hands and said how much Callie Kindred, a fine woman in all respects, gave of herself to her husband and his vision for Damascus. The whole thing never lasted more than a few minutes, this shuddering and wailing, before shortbread cookies and lemonade appeared.

A year had passed and my father was a high school graduate, crippled in body and spirit, as he attempted to appraise his future. The summer had revived the young things that teemed in his body against his will.

He did not have the easy, lusty glow of other boys his age. At school, he never threw his arm lazily along the delicate, angora-soft shoulders of a sweetheart. He was never found slouched inside an arrogant posse of boys who chuckled about what they'd done or seen. He was never invited into the boys' washroom, where they studied their long young dicks. He was not invited to tread the coarse yet silken vocabulary of getting some. When he heard the easy wonder of the word *pussy,* he turned away in shame.

After the accident, if he opened his eyes for too long, Daddy would glimpse what those good-looking girls of Damascus saw when they bothered to look at him at all—an aloof, one-armed freak who'd killed his own brother and whose family was cursed so bad the parents of these girls kept saying, behind closed doors of course, it would've been better for the whole family to have been burned alive in the church.

One day, early in summer, after the annual memorial to his grandparents, my father spied a tall, intense-looking beauty at the edge of the church lawn. Her arms were folded across her chest as she studied the church. Their eyes caught, then hooked together in a conspiratorial gaze.

When the young woman at the edge of the church lawn shifted her arms to reveal a book pressed against her breasts, he was breathless. My father then observed a striking woman approach the girl and begin talking to her. Together, they turned and vanished onto a path that led to the farthest parking lot.

Daddy knew the woman. She was Virginia Abbott, often simply called Ginny in town. Ginny Abbott was known for her exquisite pie making. Still, he wondered where she'd hidden such a beautiful daughter. How hadn't he paid attention before?

That afternoon, hope flashed its wings through his melancholy.

Standing in the cemetery of his grandparents' vision, my father felt that maybe there was something to prayer after all if he could only see that lovely girl again.

Alma Elizabeth "Comfort" Kindred would be dead from a heart attack not long after my parents ran away to Salt Point, as soon as they could after Ezra's birth. My father had worried that the flame of the past threatened their new happiness, still burning brightly enough yet, to make good on its old curse.

16

ONE TUESDAY EVENING, JUST OVER A WEEK BEFORE CHRISTMAS, THE Junketts came over to our home for dinner.

Sam Cooke's "You Send Me" played from the radio, and when it was over, Ezra and Lindy ran into the living room and put on the record. I spun and twirled the twins, each one claiming a hand, while Ernest dipped my sister. She had a new laugh I'd never heard before and I only heard it whenever Ernest was whispering into her ear. For Mr. Caesar, we played Eartha Kitt next. Mr. Caesar took Mama carefully into his arms and said things that made her laugh, while Miss Irene and Daddy sailed around the room so elegantly they looked as if they were floating. The smell of rich food, butter, and sugar filled the kitchen. Our troubles felt distant. There were candles burning, and by the end of the week our front window would be filled with the flickering silhouette of our holiday tree.

When the Junketts finally left, Daddy suggested that we gather in the living room. This evening, he told us, was the last day that *The Nat King Cole Show* would air. He'd read about it in the papers and, though we had no television, we had plenty of Cole's records. We could celebrate the man anyway, our father said.

Mama sat at the piano as I placed the needle to the vinyl, careful not to scratch it. "Forgive My Heart" filled our living room with Cole's voice. She played along softly, pressing the keys with her long fingers.

Daddy invited Ezra to dance. Giggling, she took his hand and began to do a sweet two-step before she turned and gestured that I take her other hand so that we could both dance with our father.

He mouthed the words. His white shirt and black tie glowed in the low light of our living room. Barefoot we traced a path around our father. With closed eyes, he turned slowly in place, smiling. Ezra slipped away so that she could sit at the piano and keep playing in Mama's place.

Mama stood, trembling, and I pressed her hand to Daddy's. Without opening his eyes, he kissed Mama's hand, holding it against his lips.

After checking that the fire was strong, I went to my low stool near the window to watch my parents. The way they danced like they would never let go of each other thrilled me. How could they look so strong and fragile at once? My father's head was almost bent entirely against the top of Mama's hair, which Ezra and I had helped her curl. Her navy dress was nearly black, and her long legs slid like liquid beneath the silk of it.

Ezra left the piano and crossed to the window, sitting on the floor so that she could lean against me. Nodding to the music's gentle rhythms, I tried to imagine Nat King Cole wearing one of his beautiful smiles as he waved farewell to his unseen audiences, gathered in their living rooms across America. I hoped they were dancing to Cole's shining voice.

"There's school tomorrow," said my father, opening his eyes.

"What a beautiful evening," said Mama, still standing inside my father's arm.

Without complaining, Ezra and I got up.

"Wait," said my father. His voice sounded slightly broken. He lifted his arm and we went to him and Mama. His arm was long enough to encircle us. We swayed together, embracing as one. I held on to my father's shoulder and to my mother's waist. I could smell Mama's hair oil and perfume. We were all warm and soft. I forgot about the last weeks, months. They didn't matter. We were sheltered in our joy.

"I love my girls," my father said to us. He was crying a little.

. . .

EZRA ALLOWED ME TO SLEEP in the twin bed in her room. Down the hall we could hear our parents' voices murmuring behind the walls of their bedroom.

"They're really in love," said Ezra, yawning.

"Yes," I said.

"Maybe everything will be all right."

"What do you mean?"

"Things have been hard, or haven't you noticed? How are your hands?"

She climbed out of her bed and came over to me. Her voice was suddenly close to my face. "Let me see." She turned on the lamp on the nightstand between our beds.

"I'm fine."

"Stop," she said, shoving her hands beneath the quilt to pull mine into view. "That was brave what you did. Does it still hurt?"

"Sometimes," I said, not looking at her face. "I don't think about it."

"Of course you think about it."

"Not tonight," I said, feeling a flash of pain in one of my hands. "I didn't think about it at all tonight."

"Good," she said. "I've been thinking about it every day. Even tonight. Remember when Daddy was a boy? His arm went through glass and he lost it."

"Well, here are my hands," I said. "I didn't lose them."

"But you could have."

"But I didn't."

"I hope you don't ever do something that stupid again," my sister said. Pulling my hands to her face, she rubbed her cheek against the scars. "You scared us all, Cinthy. We could've lost you."

"But Mr. Caesar—"

"Is a grown man," she answered.

"Yes," I said.

"I'm not afraid of many things," said Ezra, "but I was afraid when I saw all the blood. *Your* blood. I was frightened. I thought when they took you to the hospital—"

"It hurt," I said quietly.

"I know," she said.

With care, she placed my hands down on the quilt and pulled it up to my shoulders. Then, instead of returning to her own bed, Ezra stayed. Snapping off the lamp, she curled in bed next to me. The weight of her arm on the cover made me sigh as though I'd been holding my breath for weeks. Down the hall our parents were laughing, and I smiled in the dark. Mama was strong enough to laugh, so maybe Ezra was right. Maybe things would be fine. Besides, I'd heard Ezra's admiration and respect for me in her voice. That was enough for me to face anything. There was a trace of music again from the radio Mama kept by her bedside. Closing my eyes, I listened to Ezra's breathing and imagined my parents slow dancing in their bedroom.

"I would do anything for you," my sister said, her voice surfacing as though she were speaking to somebody in a dream.

• • •

SCHOOL CLOSED FOR THE CHRISTMAS holiday on Monday of the next week, December 23. My father would drive Ezra and me home and then go back to Hobart, to pack up some books and other materials he wanted at home. Mr. Caesar and the Junkett children would still be there, as Mr. Caesar intended to get ahead on cleaning so that he didn't have to think about the school, about white people, over the holidays. As my sister and I waved from the car, Mr. Caesar had laughed his full laugh and spoke of Miss Irene's lucky pot of black-eyed peas. "Y'all always invited when it comes to good luck," he'd said. My father hadn't wanted us to stay at the school with him because he knew that Mama would be trying to clean and cook by herself. "Help your mama with things," he'd said. "You know she thinks she can do it all when it comes to Christmas."

"We'll help Mama," said Ezra. "Don't worry, Daddy."

Our father's handsome face was streaked from the yellow lights that shone from our first-floor windows. I saw his smile even in the dark. A beautiful feeling went through me. I realized I was safe, even if my mother and father couldn't always keep the world from going after us. It was love that made me feel this way. A love the world couldn't take from me or from our family.

"Give your mother a kiss from me," he said, laughing a little. "And make sure the fire's hot when I get home."

. . .

THE DECEMBER WIND WAS RAW and could drain the heat from a man's skin in minutes. My father guided our car into one of the parking spaces between the main building of the school and Mr. Caesar's woodshed so that Mr. Caesar would see that he was there working too. As he climbed out of the car, pulling the collar of his deep navy wool coat around his neck, my father was greeted by sweet shouts from the woodshed. Turning his head, he could see the silhouettes of three Junkett children against the light of the janitorial shack: Lindy, Rosemary, and Empire. Ernest was back at the house, having been given his holiday from a Black carpenter with whom he apprenticed in Gunn Hill. Miss Irene was in Gunn Hill for Rising Star's evening service followed by choir practice and a women's dinner to discuss more details for the church's annual New Year's Eve prayer gathering.

Calling out to the children, Daddy warned them to stay inside.

"Keep the door locked," he said suddenly. Mr. Hobart often had his nephew patrol the grounds.

He went through the side entrance of the school. Pausing, he looked down the darkened halls, nervous that someone might suddenly call out to tell him he no longer belonged in this place. That he'd never belonged.

Since the "theft" of Miss Alley's purse, Mr. Caesar and my father were no longer given free rein when it came to staying alone at the school. Mr. Hobart had encouraged some of the teachers who resided in the women's dormitories to "keep an eye" on the men's comings and goings. He'd even made Mr. Caesar return some of the tools that he'd been allowed to take home and make use of elsewhere, when he picked up odd jobs in nearby towns.

Listening for Mr. Caesar's whistling or radio now, my father walked swiftly to his own classroom. The lights were already on and the floor had been recently mopped with the lemon mixture that made the room smell like sunshine. My father was grateful, again, for Mr. Caesar's friendship. My father had drawn a division between him being a man of books and Mr. Caesar being a man of brooms. But the tension of the village had made each man equal to the other and, in the eyes of the white people, equally inferior. They'd become closer since the deputy's wrongful arrest of Mr. Caesar. The faculty's implicit barring of my father from nearly all communal spaces opened my father's eyes to the reality of our future in Salt Point. For many evenings now, he'd listened to Mr. Caesar and Miss Irene go back and forth about heading south. They spoke of Royal, where they were from, and tried to get my father to speak of Damascus. He'd skirted them, but now my father was seriously considering an idea they'd suggested about all of us going south as one family, and finding a town that was big enough, Black enough, and safe for all of the children. My father didn't think such a place existed. Not in America. Perhaps not anywhere. Miss Irene's immediate word was *Africa,* but my father couldn't bear to think of the strain of such a move, not with his wife being so ill.

Sighing, my father pressed his gloved fingertips against his right temple. He'd have a headache if he didn't focus on what he needed to do: tidy up his classroom, organize his books, wrap hidden Christmas presents for his family, and help Mr. Caesar with whatever cleaning was left so that they could all leave as soon as possible.

Just then, a large mouse crossed the dry floorboards of my father's classroom. Cursing aloud, my father thought of how meticulous Mr. Caesar was about rodents in his school. But this was no longer *their* school. It was delusional to believe anything else.

Sharp wind from the bluffs rattled the windows, and my father shivered. Mr. Caesar had probably turned the heat down to save money. He thought of the Junkett children out in the woodshed, where it'd be warmer.

Daddy hung his coat in the small cloak area on its familiar peg. He allowed himself to anticipate what 1958 might contain for himself and his family. Daddy sensed that there were changes coming and that they would require him to be careful in a way that excluded his usual reticence. For a moment, he stared at the empty desks that faced him. The absent jury of young white children left him a brief, haunted feeling he'd never had before. Shaking away the sense that he was being watched, Daddy chided himself and reached for the worn case that held his beloved fountain pen. He would take some time to read, to fill a notebook with questions and declarations. Gathering the familiar, frayed comfort of logic around his thoughts, he invited reason and fact to guide him, as they always had.

. . .

THE EDGE OF THE WIND carried the acrid scent of smoke, which made my father rush abruptly out of the chamber of his mind. He could make out a huge halo of orange light beyond the warped, antique glass of the classroom windows. Leaping to his feet, he dashed out into the hall. He lifted his voice and called out, hoping his voice would find his friend. "Caesar! Caesar! Caesar!"

My father heard nothing. He raced down the eerily lit hallways, his feet pounding like hooves on the uneven, polished wooden floors. Arriving, panting, at the side entrance, he found that the door had already been locked with a key. This was unusual, as Mr. Caesar would've seen my father's car and known that he was still inside the building.

Daddy wasn't panicking yet. He didn't know what exactly he'd seen from the window. But what else could that glow be? Out by the woodshed. The woodshed.

Pivoting around unlit corners, Daddy ran down a long, black corridor that led him to the front entrance of the school. He could see that the tall doors were shut but he knew Mr. Caesar usually locked them last.

My father pushed one of the doors open using his shoulder. The blistering wind from the bluffs nearly knocked him down like a scream.

He stumbled towards the lot where he'd parked the car and where he'd seen the bright yellow light near the woodshed. My father couldn't explain why this felt so familiar, like a dream, as if he'd lived through this race before and had always woken up before knowing whether he'd won or lost.

As he rounded a bend of low, pruned brushes, he stopped abruptly. Underneath the black shape of a tree, he could just barely make out the shadow of man atop a huge horse with flaming green eyes and a burning tail. The man's face, my father marveled, was nearly identical to his own but younger. The sadness in the man's shoulders, which were crowned with strange, writhing shapes like hundreds of wings or hands, brought sudden tears to my father's eyes. Because he knew this man. When my father blinked away his tears, there was no figure. He shook his head and ran directly towards the radiant light.

It was an inferno. The woodshed was afire. My father could hear the screams of the Junkett children, who were still inside. He recalled that in the winter Mr. Caesar kept the windows of the woodshed locked, to prevent any mischief or theft of tools. He thought of the neatly arranged canisters of gasoline, kerosene, turpentine, and propane that his friend kept labeled. The stacks of matches, wrapped in small towers of cardboard. The entire thing was a tinderbox.

My father could see the thin, black shadows of three children dancing through the windows. One part of the roof was entirely engulfed and sparks, grotesquely festive, sprayed high into the dry, freezing air.

He called out again for Mr. Caesar, aware that the man could be in an entirely different wing of the building.

My father ran to the shed, which reminded him of a church he'd never seen.

The roar of the fire reminded him of the sea down below the bluffs. He used all his strength to push open the door he'd instructed the children to lock. Inside, he felt the Junkett children clinging to him and stopped thinking of anything but how to save them. The air was thick with dense chemical smoke.

Looking back over his shoulder, my father saw that he wouldn't be able to get the three children out by going out the front door he'd come in through. He'd need to get them out through the glass. Covering his face, he used his elbow to bang at the hot panes. The locks were already melting. Two of the windows were impossible to reach. The children shrieked, and he saw the fire reflecting his fate in the shine of their eyes.

My father lifted Rosemary to his right shoulder and Empire to his left. Raising his voice, he ordered Lindy to hold on to him no matter what.

When he stood at the last window, my father used his foot to kick out the glass. He pushed Empire out into the icy embrace of air. Then Rosemary. He lifted Lindy's semiconscious body, whispering soothing words to her while she moaned. She'd lost consciousness yet had still managed to hold on to him. As he passed his arm, holding the girl, through the glass, he was surprised to feel strong, firm hands gripping his own, pulling Lindy through to the other side.

My father smiled as he heard somebody shouting his name. It

was the fire, or his friend Caesar, or the smoke in his blood from years ago that had never been put out. The wind breathed a surging gale of scorching heat, and he clearly heard a woman's voice burying him inside her name. *Alma,* the voice said over and over, until it was sure he was listening, remembering. A vision of a woman whose name had also been Comfort, but who never was, flared in his racing heart. He was close to melting. The fire danced across his sweating back and along the white sleeves of his good shirt. *Alma, Alma,* he called back to her with hope. His mother and hers and hers would save him.

As my father reached out, his fingers nearly touching what he assumed were God's own, a blazing wooden beam crashed down onto him, crushing my father's mind.

17

ON THE MONDAY BEFORE CHRISTMAS, RUBY AND HER PARENTS HUD-
dled in a limousine that would take them to Amity. Ruby's papa had
agreed to a holiday dinner with Miss Alley and the Hobarts. Her father said that it was "big" of him to have accepted the invitation; he
said he couldn't argue with the fact that it was kind of the Hobarts to
want to help Ruby improve herself. He'd seemed lighter in his moods
since he'd told Ruby that he'd decided to accept Miss Alley's good
intentions for Ruby's future. Ruby's papa no longer accused her of
having illicit affairs with village boys but Ruby was terrified that the
affair, so brief, she'd actually had with Cullen had changed her life
in the exact way her father had threatened.

Her ma, being told about the special dinner in Ruby's honor,
pouted for some weeks and could focus only on her own "debut."
Her eyes smarted when she thought of how Miss Alley's uncle had
treated her and Ruby so many years ago. But she wouldn't stop thinking that Mr. Hobart needed to "pay" for the compliments he'd never
delivered to her in her prime. Ruby's mother was not distracted from
her scheming, giving little attention to her husband's whereabouts,
even when her own sisters suggested that Ruby's father had been
seen down near the lighthouse with a woman far above the kind of

lusty village woman who would do him a favor. Each of the Scaggses had lived in the uneasy whispers of rumor and innuendo so whatever might be said, about *any* of them, had likely already been something ugly that pleased the villagers' scornful lies.

But Ruby had also wondered whether her father's wicked thoughts about Miss Alley had a lot to do with this generosity. She didn't want to think that her teacher was using her or her father. But she found herself thinking it over often—whether the woman really wanted to "adopt" Ruby as a daughter, a sister. What if this was just some sort of besotted charity ruse? In the pages of her mother's magazines, she'd read about the kind of women who were so rich they could afford to buy poor people, treat them like prizes, and then abandon them. More than anything, Ruby feared abandonment now.

She was too worried about her future to find out whether Miss Alley was spending more time with her papa on her behalf. In the limousine, Ruby noted that her father had managed, without her knowledge, to see a barber.

"This all is for you," he said. "Whenever you doubt me, I want you to remember that I'm trying to help you." His hair, his voice, his temperament, were abnormally even. "So you can have a chance."

"She's had chances," said Ruby's mother in a petulant voice. Pulling a nearly bald fur around her body, she rocked her thighs into a solid throne so that she was sitting up very straight. "We all have."

"Ruby's different than us," her father said, producing a pained smile.

"I reckon I need every chance I can get," Ruby said. It was awkward to hear her papa speak of her as being different from her ma and himself but maybe he was beginning to think it was true. Her eyes settled on her mother's ill-fitting wool dress. Ruby had tried to excuse Ma's presence at the dinner, but Miss Alley had insisted that both her parents accompany her to the Hobarts' home, because she had an announcement to make.

"*I* had a chance once," said Ma. "*I* could've been somewhere else, being someone else. God knows I'd be *with* somebody else too. Somebody deserving. But here I am."

"Shut up," said her father, "and think about something more than yourself."

"At least I *do* think."

"Says who? Don't start with your lousy lost beauty queen routine. Don't you fucking start."

Ruby's mother shifted, turning her head to the window again. She'd fluffed her thin hair into an awful bouffant. Ruby could see her fine cheekbones beneath the dimpled jowls that no cold cream could hide. Still, in profile, it was clear that Ma had been a beauty.

"I can't see what these people want with Ruby. They got to want something. And whatever they want they probably want it for free. I just don't understand—why Ruby?"

"You wouldn't," her father said.

"I'm as good as anybody," Ruby said. "Ain't nobody better than me. Ain't nobody worse than me."

"You can't expect nobody to tell you you're good or not," said her father tersely.

"I can depend on myself, Papa."

He slapped Ruby hard across her face. Staring down at his hand as if it were an unrecognizable face, his eyes were sad. Then her father took the edge of his hand across her face twice more. "You gone depend on whatever I say you gone depend on."

As the limousine ascended into the soft hills of Amity, the rough land of Salt Point shifted into a groomed landscape of seasonal shrubbery, formal hedges, and gilded lanterns that were already lit. A thin red belt of sunlight banded dusk. As if on cue, a shiny powder of snowflakes twirled down inside the twilight. It was unbelievable that the two places were barely twenty miles apart.

Amity looked like a movie set except that it was real. Ruby had never seen anything like this except in the double features she and her ma used to go to. Ruby had hated these excursions because she and her mother often fought—Ruby asked too many questions, often during the movie, or begged for popcorn, candy, and other sorts of sweetness her mother couldn't afford. The fights destroyed the dreamy feeling of movies for her. And when she said she didn't want to go to the cinema anymore, her mother accused Ruby of having no capacity for dreams.

Ruby resisted pressing her face against the glass window of the limousine. She had eyes of her own and told herself to give this new world a good hard look. The sight of curtains in lamplit windows made her eyes sting. She disliked the rich longing that swelled inside her throat.

Moving into the farthest corner of her seat, Ruby could feel the leather under the crinkly layer of crinoline beneath her dress, which Miss Alley said was a dress she herself could no longer wear because of her age. It was the best secondhand dress Ruby was ever given. There was a scorched smell in the air from the curling iron Miss Alley had used to curl her hair into ringlets. Ruby remembered how delicious, and a little scary, it was to have her hair curled. The sweetness with which Miss Alley blew on every curl and how Ruby had looked into Miss Alley's vanity mirror and seen her teacher's smile reflected back to her. Despite the mood of intimacy, she'd kept quiet about Cullen while Miss Alley giggled about men. She spoke pointedly about Mr. Hobart, her aunt's husband. Ruby couldn't tell whether Miss Alley fancied a rich, distracted man like him for herself, or whether she craved a devastating heartbreaker, the kind of no-good heartthrob that made her ma swoon at the movies.

During an earlier visit to Miss Alley's apartment, the woman had conspiratorially asked her about her period. Ruby had lied, figuring it wasn't the kind of thing a teacher was supposed to ask, which meant Ruby wasn't obligated to tell the truth. But the truth was that Ruby hadn't bled since September.

By now, Ruby knew that Cullen was a lying sweet talker. He hadn't taught her to fly. He hadn't taught her a thing except how to open her legs. His touch was forceful, strong, breathtaking, and, Ruby admitted to herself, so brief she was perplexed as to why adults made such a fuss over something that took less time than brushing her teeth. Being called *Sunshine* was all right, but Ruby really wanted to know about getting a pilot's license. She'd pestered him about whether a girl like her had a chance to soar like Harriet Quimby and Amelia Earhart. How long would it take?

When Cullen began to talk about taking good care of her, Ruby only half listened. The last time she returned to the small, dilapidated hangar where she'd been meeting him, she asked if he'd at least take her for a short ride in one of the planes he owned. Then she discovered that he didn't really own a single one of those planes. She saw a maintenance report in the hangar office where he'd signed his name in crude letters beneath one of his employer's evaluations of his skills and performance as an employee. Cullen only washed and repaired the planes. Like cars. He was more or less a handyman of the sky. Still, she begged him to get her up there in the clouds on the sly. It was probably safer than driving off in a car that didn't belong to you, she had said, not realizing she'd insulted him and that there was something unbecoming in her to ask him to risk his job for her single wish. She'd tried not to feel embarrassed when he made up some excuse about the weather changing. When she attempted to ask him when might be a better time, his voice went cool and his eyes were green with farewell. There was no more Sunshine. Cullen shrugged just before he said, "Never."

This exhumed uneasy feelings from that spring when, like Cullen, Ezra had turned away from her when the trees were clad in white flowers and the air carried what Ruby had mistaken for hope. Ruby and Ezra had compared when they'd started their periods, each within days of the other. And there was the last grief, when they'd looked between the spaces of their bodies only to discover that they were, and were not, essentially the same. The grief was that each girl could ignore neither her own body nor how her body was valued. Because they could never share the same values. It'd be impossible for them to think of each other as sisters.

This, the missing of Ezra, was what remained of the innocent part of Ruby, the young self who'd once held newspaper clippings of female pilots, arms akimbo, standing boldly in front of airplanes. Who'd chewed their pictures with her teeth so that she could ingest their freedom.

. . .

IN THE BLADE OF HER knife and the stem of her fork, Ruby admired the reflection of the chandelier shining above the long table where servants set monogrammed plates on the tablecloth so deftly they did not make a sound.

In spite of Ruby having attended his school for most of her life, Mr. Hobart's eyes flickered absently over her and her parents as he sipped his cocktail. The remaining black blades of his hair had been combed across his skull, pasted down with slimy pomade. He was wearing a tuxedo. They were inside, with fireplaces burning on either side of the room, but Mrs. Hobart would not remove her fur.

The grand dining room, with its velvet wallpaper and domed glass ceiling, floated around Ruby as she tried not to gulp the champagne in its stenciled flute. When offered whisky, Ruby's papa nodded too eagerly. Ruby tried to catch Miss Alley's eyes to warn her about her father and his drinking, but she couldn't. For the first time she sensed that her teacher was deliberately *not* looking at her. Miss Alley, who had declared herself to be as close as a sister to Ruby, now held her face back in what reminded Ruby of a mask. Painted with heavy cosmetics, Miss Alley's face was unfamiliar. She wore rose chiffon that looked like it belonged in a Hollywood nightclub.

Ruby's mother couldn't look at anything else but that outfit. When she'd finally pulled her bulging eyes away from Miss Alley's powdered face, sparkling jewelry, and satiny, peekaboo kitten heels, Ruby saw her mother's sadness full-on, in a way she never had before. It turned her stomach inside out. She remembered all those years ago how her face had stung after her ma slapped her, before spending the rest of the day in tears while she rubbed her face with cold cream. Ruby now recalled it was Mr. Hobart who had sent her ma into a fit of rage and desperation. Shame and a small flicker of anger flared through Ruby. Would the millionaire remember that day, or were Ruby and her ma so insignificant that he'd forgotten that unpleasant scene right away? In her mind her papa's judgment of Mr. Hobart—as a crook—blared between her ears. What had changed her papa's mind?

When a pair of groomed caramel spaniels trotted imperiously into the high-ceilinged room, Ruby's ma flopped down to adore them, shrieking with affected delight. Everyone could see the gaping hole in her mother's stockings and that she wasn't wearing any drawers. The champagne was sour in Ruby's mouth, but she couldn't spit it out.

They sat down to dinner quickly. Ruby sensed that the Hobarts seemed eager to get through the evening as quickly as possible. It felt like everyone, including her, was holding their breath. She kept finding herself looking to Miss Alley to tell her what to do, which fork to pick up, which water glass was hers—they each had four glasses before them, so she kept swallowing champagne because it was flute-shaped, easily distinct from the rest.

Ruby watched how the Hobarts chewed, how her parents smacked their lips, how daintily Miss Alley pushed the fatty goose around on her plate. Her eyes darted at the grandfather clock near one of the fireplaces. The Hobarts made Ruby look at Miss Alley in a way that pulled away some of her teacher's veneer. Miss Alley kept exchanging looks with Mr. Hobart. Ruby was startled when she looked down to see what the pressure was on her thigh, near her knee, and realized it was her papa's hand. He thought Ruby was Miss Dinah Alley. She pushed his hand off, assuring herself that this was an accident, but she realized that her papa was drunk and likely thought it was her teacher's legs that he was stroking.

Nobody was speaking but the sound of the cutlery echoed, deafening, in the long hall. Any attempt on Miss Alley's part to bring up Ruby's future was greeted with a rapid string of farts or curses from Papa. Her ma then took every opportunity she could to point out his failures as a man, as a father. She couldn't help but repeat her own past, being crowned for her beauty and how her husband had always been drawn to good-looking women.

Later in the meal, when a Negro woman came out through swinging doors, Ruby understood that her father was very drunk. In a moody silence, he only stared at the Negro woman, whom Mrs. Hobart addressed as Marvella, and who had the darkest skin Ruby had ever seen. The closer Marvella stood to the stiff white table-cloth, the blacker her skin became. In the firelight, the woman's oval face reminded Ruby of photographs of African bush women Ezra had once shown her in Mr. Kindred's study. As the woman moved to hand Ruby's father a spoon, he gripped her hard by her wrist, pushing her hand back sharply to the tureen she carefully balanced in her other hand.

Marvella stared directly at him, moving her eyes between his hand on her wrist and his face. The woman looked insulted, bored, and entirely aware that it would be Papa who would lower his eyes first. Marvella had the bearing of a woman who'd never lowered her eyes except to sleep.

"You ain't serving me."

Miss Alley smiled nervously. Then she began to speak a bit more loudly in a voice that seemed to plead with her aunt and uncle to ignore Ruby's father, who was obviously, as she'd already mentioned to them privately, a local savage, unaccustomed to fine dining.

"Marvella, please bring Ruby another glass of champagne," said Mrs. Hobart. She pressed at her frizzy hairline as if she only had so much tolerance, so much charity, left in her life to give away. When Mrs. Hobart smiled at her, Ruby winced. Maybe Miss Alley was just like her aunt and Ruby was, in fact, a vanity project—a living charity.

"My niece has been singing your praises," she said. "Which has brought us all to this evening. I'm so pleased to hear you and your poor family have agreed to think about your future. Not all families are as sensible when asked to consider an offer as generous as ours for their daughter's future."

"We weren't asked nothing," said Ruby's father, whose eyes were fastened to the swinging doors. Like one of his hounds, he'd trained his attention on the back-and-forth appearance of Marvella, who had decided to ignore him as she served. She'd set a dish down near his plate so that he could help himself. Ruby could see the fisted muscles in her face. "We can't agree to nothing without being asked properly. We want to do best by our Ruby, within reason."

The dew of champagne she had no business drinking settled in Ruby's stomach. She was filled to her gut with gas. The seams of her dress stretched. Ruby lowered her head to study her small pink belly poking out from the rose sash that cinched her waist too tightly. It was the same shade as Miss Alley's outfit. Ruby realized that she'd been dressed to match Miss Alley. Like Ruby belonged to her teacher and not her own parents.

Then Mr. Hobart asked, in a slurred voice, to whom should he write his check, and Ruby's mother immediately spelled out her full name for him. Shrugging, Mr. Hobart inquired as to why the man of the household shouldn't be the one to have the money deposited into his account.

"He's never had any account," Ruby's mother said. "He don't trouble himself in that respect. Ain't got the head for a piggy bank. Wouldn't you agree, Ruby?"

Her face flushed as she shrugged helplessly, staring at her mother. What was happening? No one had asked her anything about her future.

"Papa?" Her voice quavered, her eyes were tear-filled as she turned her head in fear to him. "Papa, *please,* what's happening?"

"I've got a pig for a wife," Mr. Scaggs said without missing a beat. "The kind of queen who'd sell her own daughter, *our only daughter,* and think I'd swallow it without a fight." Pausing, he pointed his finger at Ruby. "You set me up, didn't you? You, your ma, and that slut over there who can barely spell her own name. Now, I ain't saying I'm the best father but I know I ain't never been a crook. Devil's got plenty lines in his book for the lot of you. *Ruby, this is a crime.* It's called kidnapping."

All Ruby could feel were gold bubbles popping and hissing in her head. Panicking, she thought of a baby that could be growing somewhere under her skin, inside her blood. Could mothers become pilots? She'd only let Cullen touch her twice, yet maybe that was all it took? He'd never even asked what her name was, calling her Sunshine, and putting his lips over her mouth whenever she said something that wasn't, Ruby sensed, in his own script.

But Ruby couldn't let herself fully feel that shame, because she was even more horrified at what was unfolding at the table in front of her. Her parents, it seemed—her mother really—had settled on a price, a finite value, for their only living child.

Ruby's ma gestured at Marvella for water. The flick of her hand sent her wineglasses crashing in a row. Hiccupping, she took a sip of water and licked her lips before stating what she thought was a fair number.

Ruby stared at her ma's face, swollen from years of failure and frustration. The figure was about payback; Mr. Benedict Hobart owed her something she had never had before—respect. The price of Ruby's esteem suffered, as she tried to guess her worth. None of them had told her. Ruby felt as though she were staggering under the weight of trying to carry her mother, and her father, up a vertical incline. They seemed fine with this, as if, as their daughter, she had always owed them something. She thought of how that man had looked through her that day at the air show, taking the money she'd stolen, stealing it from her as if she could harm herself by dreaming of flying.

Ruby's ma, Miss Alley, Mr. and Mrs. Hobart, were all talking, their voices stiff with the unpleasant iciness of negotiating Ruby's potential, as though she were human cargo. They were using the word *investment*. Nobody was smiling.

The anger that bubbled inside Ruby also confused her. Miss Alley had just bought Ruby out of her own life.

When Mr. Hobart rang a little bell, Marvella returned to the table with a sheaf of legal papers and a new checkbook, and Ruby's mother elbowed her husband. Not because he was objecting to the low sum of money they'd accepted for Miss Alley's adoption of their daughter, but to keep her husband from falling drunkenly, face-first, into the main course of their first and last formal holiday dinner as a family.

. . .

THE NEXT MORNING, RUBY'S UNHAPPY head rested on a silk pillowcase. She'd had the worst sleep of her life. Her dreams disliked the delicacy and fuss of silk. Her stomach twisted with cramps from the rich food and champagne she'd consumed. She thought she was going to vomit as a spell of vertigo went over her body. Pushing herself up against the elaborate brass headboard, Ruby pressed her back flat against it.

"Good morning, Ruby," Miss Alley said, entering the guest room. She pulled the heavy powder-blue velvet drapes back so that she was standing in a cloud of chalky light.

Marvella was right behind her, carefully carrying a pressed navy dress with an ivory collar, ivory cuffs, and ivory lace hem. The getup matched Miss Alley's dress, which was navy silk.

Looking Ruby over, Miss Alley gave Marvella directions as if Ruby weren't there. Her teacher began with her hair, chastising Ruby for sleeping on her beautiful curls. Why hadn't Ruby asked Marvella to wrap her head properly so that she'd keep those nice ringlets? Ruby tried to explain that her hair was thin and that curls were hard to keep with hair like hers, but Miss Alley interrupted to tell Marvella to pull Ruby's hair up on the top of her head. Ruby hated buns, but when she protested, her teacher only threw her head back and laughed. She wanted Ruby taken to a salon in Boston where a lady she knew would bob it. She ordered Marvella to make the appointment as soon as possible. A bob would be easier and more suitable for the girl she imagined Ruby would be. The next thing Ruby needed, Miss Alley said, was a morning bath.

"I don't want to bathe in front of nobody," Ruby mumbled. "'Specially not her."

Miss Alley turned from the window to focus her full attention on Ruby. Her feet were hidden in white calfskin boots with brass heels that reminded Ruby of a photograph of her hero, Harriet Quimby. "I'll be the judge of that," her teacher said. "The more you fight the harder it'll all be for you."

"All of what?"

"You'll see," she said, deploying a cold smile. Nodding at Marvella, she departed from the room.

"Miss Marvella, I ain't taking no bath," Ruby said, pulling the coverlet back in one motion.

"Do as you please, Miss Ruby. You go right 'head."

"Good."

"But you going to get in that tub right now," said Marvella. "You don't pay *my* bills. Miss Dinah and her folks do. Since you don't pay nobody's bills and don't know nothing about who you got yourself mixed up with, you better think about who you can trust to help you."

"What's your full name, anyway?"

From her height, the woman looked down at Ruby. "Marvella. Period. That's my name. I ain't your employee. I got no interest in your feelings neither, and I sure ain't your friend."

"Where'd you get a name like that?"

Marvella tilted her face, frowning. She saw that Ruby wasn't going to let it be. "I ain't been called my name since my mama died," she said with a softer tone in her voice. "I don't want nobody in this house calling me by my name, especially not some poor trash like you."

"What I done to you?"

"And don't you never call me *Miss* Marvella again," she said sharply. "What's the matter with you? Trying to rile up the whole house with that mess. Don't think about me. Don't feel nothing for me. Nothing at all. You may be thinking you mean good by showing me some respect or whatever you think respect is, but I respect myself just fine."

Ruby's eyes watered as though she could smell the thing that made the woman's face pucker so sourly. "If I'm poor trash, then what are you?"

"I'm myself, Miss Ruby," Marvella said, sighing and rolling her eyes. "And that's a whole helluva lot more than you or any one of these fools is worth."

18

MR. CAESAR AND SOME MEN FROM RISING STAR SMOKED ON OUR PORCH.
The cold didn't distract them from passing a flask. Across our road,
the Junkett twins shrieked, flinging snow above their heads. The
haunted house was crusted with snow. It was Christmas Eve.

I was sitting in my bedroom on my seat by the window in a
nightgown, though Mama and Ez had each warned me separately
that the next time one of them came upstairs I'd better be dressed.
I'd barely slept. I was in a living nightmare. My mind flashed with
pictures from the night before. I couldn't stop hearing my mother's
scream just before she collapsed. Mr. Caesar had driven our car
home. Across the back seat, wrapped in tarp, was my father's body.
An electrical fire due to faulty circuiting that Mr. Caesar hadn't had a
chance to repair. My father had saved Lindy, Rosemary, and Empire.
He saved my children, Mr. Caesar kept saying. His entire body was
covered in filth, smoke, sweat. Dousing himself in water, Mr. Caesar
had climbed through a window and pulled my father's body out of
the burning building. When he opened the back door of our car the
odor of burned flesh made me so sick I'd almost fainted. *I need you
girls to go inside,* he'd said gently.

Then Miss Irene had pulled up just behind her husband, and the three Junkett children, still in their soot-black clothes, had run to embrace us, to take care of us. *He saved our children, our lives,* Mr. Caesar kept saying to himself.

Feeling ill again, I wiped my eyes on the hem of my nightgown, tapping my toes together inside a pair of wool socks I'd taken out of my father's shoes, which I'd found arranged neatly on the floor near his closet. I thought of his words to me just before he'd driven away, about keeping the fire hot. We'd been at home helping Mama with the holiday preparations, as he'd asked us.

I suddenly saw Ezra and Ernest standing in the middle of my bedroom. I hadn't heard them come in. I was having trouble hearing words or voices unless they were very close to me.

"Cinthy, *please,*" said Ezra. "We need you downstairs."

"Where is he?"

She knew that I meant Daddy.

"Miss Irene said that Mr. Caesar and the men from the church are going to take Daddy over to Gunn Hill to have him dressed."

"Dressed for *what?*"

"Momma says that the Negro undertaker in Gunn Hill works three hundred and sixty-five days a year," said Ernest. "Christmas Eve is no exception."

"Can I go with them?" I said.

"He's in God's hands," said Ernest. His voice broke on the word *hands.* In that breaking, I could hear a glimmer of the boyhood he'd abandoned for this grassy, mannish baritone. He was holding my sister's hand.

"Mama needs help," Ezra said. "Miss Irene and Mr. Caesar say they've had to bury family all their lives. They say it hurts too bad to do it alone and they'd be happy to help."

The word *happy* sounded odd to me. I was shaking again.

Ernest came to the window where I'd curled into a ball. His maleness, dense and distinct as the smell of cinnamon, made me cry harder. I wanted my daddy. I wanted to hear his voice. Instead, it was Ernest who was speaking gently to me. Even though I was long-legged and way too big to be held, Ernest easily lifted me, wrapping his arms around me. "C'mon, be strong, baby girl. I know you're hurting real bad."

Through the uncombed cloud of my hair, I saw Ezra wiping her red eyes. Seeing her tears made something happen in me. In a quiet voice, I thanked Ernest, pushing my body away so that I could stand on my own.

"Ez, can you help me?"

"Always," she said, managing to smile. Her arms hung at her sides but her eyes were bright inside raw lids.

"My favorite sweater is in the closet."

"We'll be downstairs in a moment," she said to Ernest.

"Sure," he said. He brushed his fingertips against my sister's hair as he passed us. He turned and I could see Mr. Caesar's eyes, almost identical, in his son's face. "I'm sure sorry about your daddy. He was real smart. And a good man. My daddy say that's a rare combination. Little sister, we all family here. We was always family. Try to remember that."

· · ·

OUR HOUSE WAS FILLED WITH voices we knew and trusted. But it was hard to trust the world, which had taken one of the most important things from me with no warning. Weeping, I listened to the soothing voices of men outside. It was bitterly cold yet their voices rose in hot harmony. They sang the old words, songs that had raised them their entire lives—"Roll, Jordan, Roll." Their faith wafted through the bald boughs of the oak outside my window. I wondered what kinds of songs had raised my father in Damascus, where he was born. I remembered that just before he died my father had turned to the blues.

When Mr. Caesar and the men stopped singing, Ezra came and stood behind me. Delicately, her fingers gripped a comb to pull my hair back from my face. The touch of her hand on my neck was so soft I wanted to cry again. Instead, I pushed those tears down where they spilled into other parts of me. Turning my head carefully, I could see my father's profile in the mirror fastened to my closet door. In the mirror, I watched the lips speak with a woman's voice.

"What will happen to us now?"

19

THE SIGHT OF OUR ARTIFICIAL PINE TREE WAS GROTESQUE ON CHRIST-
mas morning. It was burdened by joyous ornaments, tinsel, garlands
of stale popcorn, the chunky bulbs blinking colors from ramrod
limbs. As I stared past it, I could see Daddy stretching his arm up to
the tree's tip, balancing a crude, three-sided cardboard star dipped in
gold glitter that I'd made years ago, our cherished crown. Because of
his height, Daddy always crowned the tree, making sure to tease me
about my refusal to make a newer, shapelier star.

There was Daddy's armchair with the high, scooped, oily dent
where his head had rested for naps. There was our shiny black piano,
a lovely baby grand, which Mama played less and less as we'd grown.
Sixteen years ago, my parents had purchased the piano together as a
wedding present. Shock overpowered me. Our family had only deco-
rated this tree last week. Daddy had been laughing. When the tree
was finished, Ezra made up a pan of hot chocolate. We'd listened to
Nat King Cole albums while nestling before the fire. The new, blinking joy that came with the end of another year and the birth of the
Son of God always made us look around our living room as though it
had become something else.

It was Christmas morning, but I'd never hear my father say another word.

The fire had gone down again, leaving a chill that was not yet unpleasant. Sitting quietly on the couch between my sister and my mother, who were both crying through closed eyes, I forced myself not to think about Daddy, whose body was wrapped in a cloth, like a mummy, in his study.

In a few moments, Mr. Caesar and Miss Irene would arrive from the early Christmas service at Rising Star. Usually, they spent their entire Christmas Day in Gunn Hill. This year, the Junketts would spend their holiday with us. They would bring their feast and their singing. Miss Irene said we'd need to have food near us to keep our strength, even if we looked at it and felt ill. There'd be a moment, she assured us, when a plate of home-cooked food would be exactly what we wanted, would be the thing to unloose the places where tears pooled inside us. Miss Irene said that she would keep coffee brewing, have tea ready. She said she and Mr. Caesar would help Mama with what everyone kept calling "the arrangements."

Mama was too catatonic to protest, and Ezra accepted their kindness because of her dogged devotion to Miss Irene. I'm certain Ernest being so sweet on her was part of it too. Serious and shy, he followed her with his eyes less discreetly when he understood that she'd welcomed his smiles and the light, respectful touch of his hands. For my part, I knew it would've made everyone unhappy if I'd said that we needed time to ourselves. But I had feelings that I couldn't speak of—my father had died because he'd saved the Junkett children. I didn't want a *hero;* I wanted my *daddy.*

Mr. Hobart had fired Mr. Caesar, citing his carelessness and the destruction of school property. I'd overheard Mr. Caesar, Miss Irene, and my mother talk in low voices. *We'd better get gone before they set us on fire next,* Mr. Caesar said. *I couldn't work at that no-good school anyways, not if they paid me a million dollars.*

I let my eyes drift across the living room.

Our wallpaper was Atlantic blue with ivory flowers twisting and

unfurling from green-and-gold-leafed vines woven across the silhouetted bodies of well-bred horses, goats, foxes, birds, and pale stags
pasted in a harmonious zoo. Mama had once seen similar wallpaper at an estate auction in Amity. She'd searched and discovered a
cheaper imitation of it in a catalog. Because of the cost she'd only
been able to paper half the living room, which always made it feel
unfinished. Mama said that in Damascus almost every home had a
blue ceiling or blue wall somewhere inside, because the blue would
repel ghosts. It was also why, Mama added, in Damascus most of the
headstones in the small cemetery were painted in shades of blue.

I told myself that Daddy was still in the house with us, his soul
surrounded by the books he'd studied and loved. I pictured his silent
head, wrapped in a thick veil on the pallet Mr. Caesar and Miss
Irene had made for him. They'd used clean strips of cloth to bind
his body tightly. Beneath those cloths was some sort of herbal poul-
tice that had a strong smell of lavender and something similar to incense that I couldn't identify. But it didn't make the scent of burning
go away.

· · ·

"THEY'RE HERE," SAID EZRA, OPENING her eyes. The way the watery
light glowed against our windows meant it must've been just after
twelve o'clock.

Instead of the usual hollering, the Junkett family entered our
house speaking in hushed voices. Lindy and the little ones carried
paper sacks of food past our living room straight to the kitchen, as
though Miss Irene had already given them their orders. In gold-and-
ivory matching outfits, the twins were dressed like angels. Lindy was
wearing lipstick that made her lips look stained. Instead of greeting
us, she was silent. Miss Irene said that Lindy blamed herself for our
father's death. She hadn't been able to help him get the twins out of
the window because she'd passed out from fear and smoke inhala-
tion. Mama roused herself to insist that Lindy wasn't to blame her-

self for what had happened. I didn't know what to say to Lindy but I didn't want her to feel bad that she had survived.

Outside, Mr. Caesar and another man were in the process of reversing a vehicle that resembled a delivery van. They angled it along the side of our house near the glass doors of Daddy's study.

I didn't need to guess what the van meant but the sight of it made me dizzy, as if I were riding in a car with no steering wheel, no brakes, no windshield.

·   ·   ·

AROUND THREE O'CLOCK, MISS IRENE laid out the food in the kitchen with Lindy's help. Her dress flowed as she darted around with a gold silk flower pinned behind one of her ears. Loudly, she called for everyone to gather together.

I opened the pantry door where I'd been sitting. I was stiff from slouching for so long against the back of the hard chair. My head ached, but I tried to smile as the children bounced up and down at the sight of the shining haloes of pineapples that blessed a cherry ham. Their eyes lifted in adoration at the marvelous vision of browned, whipped marshmallow peaks that crowned creamy sweet potatoes in a glass dish.

"All mercy is God's mercy," said Miss Irene, closing her eyes. "May our beloved Brother Kindred feast at the Lord's great and everlasting table in his new peace. May we never forget our brother's bravery and the kindness he gave us. May we remember him, as a new angel, to keep our passage safe in a world that has forgotten God's love. Forever and forever, may we remember that love is God and may we always give God to each other, as God has given us this food today. Amen."

"Amen," said Mama, before everyone else.

"They'll eat it all if you don't get a plate, Cinthy," said Lindy gently.

Miss Irene held her hand out to me. The brass and wooden bangles on her arms knocked together musically. "Try those sweet potatoes, won't you—they're irresistible. Your daddy never said no when I made them for him," she said. Before I could say anything, she was making my plate.

"Sit where y'all can sit," she said, and everybody scattered.

I'd never been allowed to sit with food anywhere but at our kitchen table, but now I went to the steps of our back staircase, balancing my plate on my knees. In the evenings, I liked the stairwell because of its mysterious purplish and olive shadows. When morning arrived, the plaster made a blinding tunnel of light. I sat, unable to deny how perfect Miss Irene's sweet potatoes were, so quietly that the adults didn't notice me when Mama and Mr. Caesar finally returned, joining Miss Irene in the kitchen.

"Caesar, Irene, thank you so much for everything you're both doing," said Mama. "I thought that it'd be me laid out before him. We'd planned to go ahead with my surgery after New Year's. There's a hospital down in Boston. We wanted to tell the girls once the cancer is treated. Now, I know you think I shouldn't delay it, but I'm going to wait. If there are any complications, I'd be forced to stay in Boston for God knows how long. The girls need me."

"I don't know if you should play with time that way," said Mr. Caesar. "Cancer can move like the flames that have taken our brother Heron away."

Miss Irene nodded and spoke hesitantly. "Can this cancer be treated? These doctors so quick to take the knife to us before there's any time to think about all the options. Seen it happen in my own family. I don't want to see you suffer."

"*Suffer?*" Mama's voice broke in astonishment as she breathed out the word.

"Have you decided?" asked Miss Irene, switching the topic. "About Heron?"

Mama's voice faltered. "I know you all mean well but we, he—wasn't religious like you and Caesar. Can't we bury him here on our property? Then he'd always be close to us. We *own* this land."

"Ground's frozen," said Mr. Caesar. "And these parts ain't good for burying bones. Not ours, anyway. White folks vandalizing us everywhere and death ain't no exception. Bones need to be safe. Need company. Should you and the girls move back south, for whatever reason, you'd be asking me to dig him up. I don't dig up no bones once they down six feet."

"I see," said Mama. She'd been saying *I see* all day, but I knew that was an empty phrase. It was a person saying *I'm fine* while they stand next to the place where a fire has burned everything they own and care about to the ground. "Well, what other options do we have?"

"Cremation?"

"Oh, no, I couldn't do that."

"Look here," said Mr. Caesar, as he accepted a plate from Miss Irene and maneuvered so that he could place it on the counter. "Let me take him south to Delaware. You can trust me to take him home to your people."

"Put him back," said Mama in a strange, absent voice I'd never heard before. "In Damascus, they'll put him back. That's what they call it instead of burial. They think death is as familiar a place as life. So when a soul is 'put back' it's like they've been returned to something they already know. The folks who raised us say it's got to be by noon the day after the death, but we're already too late."

Miss Irene glanced at Mr. Caesar.

"Warren is outside in the van. You give him a little something for his time, he can help Caesar with the arrangements," she said. "Give us some good shoes, and we'll have him prepared. You got a map to your people's place? 'Cause these men won't know the way. I'm thinking that if Damascus is a place like Royal, where Caesar and I grew up, then it's not on any map."

"That's true, Irene. You won't find it on any map, that's for sure. I'll call Mama."

"*Wait*," said Miss Irene. "You mean to tell me your mama's *living*? Lord have mercy, girl, you've never said anything to me all these years about your mother!"

"Yes, she's living, I suppose," Mama said. "She'd probably have a different word for it." She went to the stove and poured herself some coffee. "My mother never wanted a daughter, so I've never pretended to be one."

"Coffee's cold, honey," said Miss Irene. "Let me warm it up for you."

"Irene, I can't really taste anything anymore. It's fine."

"The girls doing all right?"

"They're good girls."

"Sure, I already know that," said Miss Irene. "I'm asking about how they're *doing*."

"They're shocked, just like I am."

"We are *so* sorry," Mr. Caesar said. "What he did for us—Heron couldn't have known when he ran into that fire he'd be giving up his life for my children. Only God could've known."

"Maybe that's right," said Mama. "Guess I'm grateful I'll never have God's kind of knowing. It'd make living impossible."

"Don't speak that way, Lena," Miss Irene said. "Don't let grief boil your tongue."

"I'll call Mama. Maybe she could get here by tomorrow morning, depending on the storm. Then she can ride back with Caesar to show them the way to Damascus. I don't know if I know it well enough anymore to give clear directions."

"Sure, she can ride back with us if that's easier," said Mr. Caesar. "'Less you think it'd be good for her to stay on for a bit with you and your girls."

Mama gave a dry laugh, shaking her head at the last part of Mr. Caesar's suggestion.

"You want some more sweet potatoes, honey?" said Miss Irene, noticing me at last. "Plenty macaroni and cheese over in the oven. Cornbread."

I shook my head and heard myself speak up. "That's not Daddy's home. He always called this—*us*—his home."

"Hyacinth Kindred, this conversation is for adults," Mama said. "You aren't grown. I'm the mother. You're the child. Am I making myself clear?"

"I'm sorry."

Miss Irene gently took the plate from my hands and ran her fingers across the crown of my head.

I wanted to say that adult clarity was meaningless, useless. Not even the air that went in and out of us lasted long enough to be clear.

. . .

INSTEAD OF JOINING EZRA, ERNEST, and Lindy upstairs, or curling up alone on the couch, I slipped out the front door. Mr. Warren's shadowed, sleeping head tilted against the window of the van. Rushing down the steps, my arms wrapped around me, I went around the side of our house and entered Daddy's study through the unlocked glass doors. Walking to the side of the table where my father's body lay, I kissed his veiled head. "I miss you already," I whispered.

The sight of my father's death comes into full view.

His body is enclosed in his finest suit, his neck collared in a starched shirt. His head is shrouded in a veil of black velvet. Daddy's single hand, encased in a white glove, folds against his chest. Beneath the cologne, there is his dying, burned odor that makes me wrinkle my nose. Though his body is horizontal, all I can think of is my father's height. When I was a small girl, the skyscraper of his body shadowed the earth. I hear his tread again, how his footsteps parted high grass. I hear again how he hummed pleasantly under his breath while the sun lapped at our skin when we sat together, peeling oranges and sharing stories, in the small, sturdy boat we floated, year after year, in our pond. I thought of the wishes he'd made for my sister and me over so many years and, while I couldn't remember any of the words exactly, I still held the cadence of his faith and voice in my guts. My father encouraged me to climb tall trees, to trust old boughs. He kissed my scratches and tickled the bottoms of my feet.

He called me his star and his favorite story. How marvelous it had been to live in the company of a person who knew what a story was and what it was supposed to heal. He often said we were his delivered miracles.

I see his quiet, inspired hand racing across blackboards, gripping a wand of chalk. My father devoted himself to an institution that deserved neither his mind nor his laughter, which gave my heart ease in a dialect I will never find in any corner of the world.

In the hushed room where my father dreamt and read and shared his ideas with me, I stared at the intimate museum of stones, feathers, bones, dried wings and flowers, cracked kaleidoscopes, broken compasses, and a telescope, wondrous relics of his body and its imagination.

I kissed his silent, gloved hand with a daughter's love. It was his gentle hand that allowed me to know what any daughter could know of her father's heart.

Then I sat down on one of my father's faded love seats. The pressure of the springs beneath the cushion comforted me as I rested my head against my arm. The black shape of my father's head blurred in front of my eyes as I sank into a dream that made me feel orphaned because I knew I wouldn't wake up and share it with my father the way I once did with my dreams.

I wished I'd told him more of my good dreams and was grateful he'd encouraged me to look up the visions I had in his dream books. *You may very well have a gift for them,* he'd once told me, as we looked up the appearance of a color or animal or number that I carried from my dream into my morning thoughts. When I asked him about his own dreams, my father only cleared his throat and cited his lack of memory, his need to empty his mind before he laid his head on his pillow. *When your mama kisses me good night, I always feel like I'm dreaming,* he'd said once to my sister and me. Then he'd kissed us and said we were the best dreams a man like him could have.

· · ·

THE SIGHT OF DADDY'S BODY bewildered me when I lifted my head from my arms, where I'd fallen asleep. I thought he was shouting inside that black material wrapped around his head, but it was another man's voice. Mr. Caesar's. There was noise in our house, approaching my father and me. The sound of rapid stomping. Ducking my head, afraid because I couldn't move my father, I rushed to the far corner of the room just before the door of Daddy's study flew open so hard the knob stuck in the plaster of the wall.

Miss Irene and Mama tumbled together into the room, then scrambled to get back on their feet. The candles sputtered in their holders. Miss Irene had arranged them and bowls of herbs and incense all around the room. The calming smell made the air feel charged, clean, yet my chest tightened as though the room had been flooded with smoke. Flattening myself against the far wall, my body became so shallow it was easy for me to leave it, to scurry away like a spider in the empire of its web.

The deputy stood in my father's study above his body.

"Please," said Mama. "Please leave my home at once."

"Shut up."

"Get your cracker ass out of here before I *make* you get out," hissed Miss Irene.

Deputy Charlie stared, confused, at my father's body. "We were told he'd been burned alive in the fire. There were no remains. Whose body is this? Who told you that you could remove this body from my uncle's property?"

Nobody answered him. In a slow circle he turned to stare at us, his eyes shiny with the understanding that he couldn't control us. By the time he completed his second rotation, his eyes were set in cruelty. His sight shackled to the contempt that edged his mean lips.

The deputy glanced at the orderly shelves of Daddy's study. His face twisted into a smirk as he tapped a white envelope against the side of my father's shrouded head. Later, I'd learn that the sealed envelope conveyed the official termination of my father's employment, which was to be delivered, by hand, to my mother. Mr. Hobart had been worried about Mama bringing a lawsuit against him or, worse, trying to squeeze the school for some sort of death settlement. Earlier, I'd heard Mama discussing Daddy's life insurance policies with Miss Irene and Mr. Caesar. I wondered if the arrival of this white man was about taking that from us too. But it was the sight of the church van from Rising Star that roused the deputy's curiosity. He'd known that our household had never leaned into the arms of any religion.

"There's some rules about this," he was saying.

"Do you mean the law?" said Mr. Caesar. "We haven't broken the law."

"That's for me to say."

"Say what you have to say and leave us alone," said Mama. Her eyes were scalding. "Let me bury my husband in peace."

The deputy shrugged. "Folks been tired with the bunch of you for some time. They might feel they have a say."

"Is that all?" said Mr. Caesar.

"No," he said. "That isn't all." Without any warning, he snatched the veil from my father's face and spat on him. Wiping his mouth, he staggered back from the table, his hands shielding his eyes. "Sweet Jesus." When the deputy moved his hands away, the barrel of Miss Irene's gun was at his temple.

Quickly, Mr. Caesar dragged her back, his arm around her waist, whispering urgently into her ear. Ernest, Lindy, and the twins were at the door now. They stared with me at the black, charred hole of my father's face.

"You know killing a white man 'round here will get you lit up like a Christmas tree." The deputy raised his eyes first to the children and then to Ernest, who'd stepped closer, holding his fists at his sides. The deputy readjusted his holster and rushed out of the room. We could hear him gagging as he slammed our front door.

"Have mercy," said Miss Irene, crying. She rushed to my father and tried to cover what it was too late for us to have not seen. Mama slid down the wall she'd been using to hold herself upright.

"Coward," said Mr. Caesar. "No respect for our dead."

Lindy led the twins from the room as Ernest embraced Ezra, his arms tightening against her rigid body. From my angle, I could see her eyes; the rage there was as inscrutable as the fire that had taken away my father's face. We held each other's gaze, my fire meeting hers until I found myself blinking, aware that I was closer to being a full woman than I'd ever thought. When Ezra finally closed her eyes, the tears spilled down her cheeks. Above the candlelight and pungent scent of incense, Miss Irene's voice filled the room with her praying.

I went to Mama, kneeling so that I could help her stand again.

20

AFTER THE DEPUTY'S VISIT, MR. CAESAR INSISTED ON ALL OF US SPEND-
ing the night together. He and Miss Irene drove to their house, returning with pajamas for the twins and Lindy, as well as two shotguns
that he held as he stomped up our steps, the snow shaking from the
tips of his work boots. Inside, Mr. Caesar's and Ernest's footsteps
formed a percussive rhythm for what felt like hours as they walked
a path downstairs between the back door and the front door. "He'll
come back and when he does, it'll be me he tries to kill. That man
want me laid out next to our Brother Kindred," said Mr. Caesar. "But
he ain't going to stop us from what's God's will. I have to take our
brother south so he can rest with his people. I'm not going to fail
this man. He saved my children, saved our lives. Son, show me again
how to load that thirty-eight like your life depends on it. You'll need
to help your momma 'til I can get back."

In spite of it being well after midnight, Miss Irene had brewed
more coffee. The scent of coffee was odd so late at night. Its strong
odor went through our house like a call to arms. I knew it was supposed to make us feel safe. When I went down to get a cup, Miss
Irene's hand held one of the machetes that usually hung on the wall
in their parlor.

She set it aside to embrace me. "Come up and help me with your mama," she said. It must have been close to two or three o'clock in the morning. I followed her upstairs, watching how carefully she pulled the covers around Mama's sleeping, tearstained face. Then she guided me and the children who were still awake into our beds, praying over us before she placed herself, like a soldier on night duty, in the study with our father's body.

. . .

IN THE BLUE MORNING AIR, I woke to hear the tread of tires clenching the muted snow. Pulling a pair of jeans up beneath my nightgown, I heaved an old sweater over my head and tugged it down to meet the waistband of my jeans. Scooping a pair of yellow rubber boots into my arms, I stepped over Empire, who was snoring lightly beneath a quilt. Rushing into the hall, I shimmied a foot into each boot as quietly as I could. I decided to use the back staircase, which was close to Mama's bedroom, so I wouldn't wake everyone up. But in the kitchen, there was already coffee brewing, and gusts of wind from an opened door told me that I wasn't the only one who was early to rise.

I found Mr. Caesar and Miss Irene standing, coatless, on the porch. They were staring at a sleek car coming up the road.

The car stopped in front of our house. When its passenger door opened, brass music could be heard pouring from the radio.

A woman, wrapped in scarves, stepped out. The driver, a well-dressed man, got out too, cursing the snow. He stumbled to the trunk before the woman had to say a word. She was tall, bottle-shaped. Without bothering to close the passenger door, she waved hello with the red sleeve of her jacket before she slowly said three words: *How y'all doing*. Her lips were painted holiday red. As she approached us, she began unpeeling herself from her travel garb. Gloves first, then two scarves while she noisily climbed our steps.

Miss Irene greeted her in a friendly tone, but this woman only nodded in reply, smiling approvingly at Miss Irene's sweet voice. Unable to pin down the drawling notes in her speech, I waited for her to speak to me too.

Wrestling a suitcase, the man came to the foot of our steps. Placing it down on a mound of snow, he swiveled around with his arms stuck straight out so that he wouldn't lose his balance. The feather in his fine red hat trembled at a jaunty angle in the growing light.

"Thank you, Jeremiah," she called out.

Bewitched by her voice, I stopped shivering.

"Good morning and God bless. Are you Lena's mother?" Miss Irene said politely. "You must be—folks seldom get themselves lost on this old dead-end road. Lena and the girls will be so glad to see you."

"Lena *who*? I got a baby named Jolene."

The last words could've been the blues, the birdsong of a blackbird who feels pity for the fates of the mockingbird, the rooster, and the parrot.

"I got a baby named Jolene," she said again, raising her eyebrow. "Hm, when that baby called me, I thought I ought to get here soon as I could. In Damascus, you don't never share no bad news on the phone if you can help it. Don't ask me why. But soon as we hung up I knew this was something heavy. Called Jeremiah and packed a bag. In Damascus, what you don't say can be heard just as clear as what you do. It is what it is," she stated, sailing past Mr. Caesar and Miss Irene into the house. Her voice drew itself through the air like a sunbeam. "All I know is that she can't be dead 'cause she called me late yesterday, but I can certainly see with my own eyes that this house got some death in it."

I thought the woman hadn't seen me but as she came farther into the house, her face wrinkled. She took a deep breath, exhaling as though she'd been running a long distance.

"Lord, Lord, *Lord*." She turned around in a circle, then stopped, fixing her eyes on me. I couldn't tell if she was frowning or smiling. She had lipstick on her teeth.

"Daddy died in a fire," I said. "The day before Christmas Eve."

She nodded, loosening more of the cloth that was bundled around her body. *This woman is my grandmother?*

"Shit, he lasted longer than I thought," she said to herself, tossing her coat into the living room, where it landed on a chair as if she'd already memorized where everything was arranged. The way she spoke of Daddy made my stomach clench with ice. She and her opinions could turn around and walk out the way they'd come.

"I go by Ginny," she said. "Government say Virginia, but I keep the government out of my business just as much as I can." She looked over at me, kissing her teeth. "Shit, what happened to you?" Without any patience or interest in what I might say—but what could I say to such a question?—Ginny walked straight ahead, into our kitchen.

In a loud voice, she inquired about coffee, toast. Without being asked, she started talking, drawing Miss Irene, Mr. Caesar, and me into her firm opinions over her loose teeth, black ice on the turnpike, how white people drove versus how Jeremiah could drive, how wonderfully Jeremiah could handle speed, how he was so good he knew how to slow down when he ought to when he was driving. Especially in places like her bed.

She said something to Mr. Caesar that made him laugh easily. She kept on talking as though she'd visited us frequently. She said our house reminded her of the homes of white folks who kept the temperature low on purpose when they could afford to have heat. This house was too cold for her 'thritis, and sometimes if she found herself in a house as cold as ours, it affected her bowel movements and could leave her constipated. In fact, our house was constipation itself, she said, opening Mama's drawers and peering at our polished cutlery. Kneeling, she opened a cabinet to inspect Mama's pots and pans. She pressed her finger against Mama's cast-iron skillet to examine the slight proof of oil. Using that same fingertip, she reached for the knob on Mama's radio, adjusting the volume so that a low torrent of strange, formal voices spilled into the room. There was news about Elvis Presley receiving his draft notice and more details about a murderer named the Butcher of Plainfield, who'd killed and decapitated a woman.

As she stared out of the high kitchen window above the sink, I felt like I was looking at a more mature version of Mama. "Girl, can you take a hint? Get in the living room and light that fire before the blood in my veins turns to ice," she said when she saw me studying her. "This hussy got the whole nerve to stand here looking at me in *my* face like she been grown long as I been grown in the world. Hm, she ain't grown. Hey, go on, girl, and get that fire going in here before I lose a tooth. Two witches' tits couldn't light a cigarette between them with the draft. I can look at you and know that you the one 'posed to keep this house warm, aren't you? Way I came up, long before your daddy was a little boy, I was told you Kindreds got a thing for fires."

"Would you like to see Brother Kindred?" said Miss Irene. "Before your daughter comes down?"

Ginny washed her hands in steaming water at the tap. When she turned to speak over her shoulder, there were tears in her eyes. She and Mama cried the same way. She spoke the way Mama did too, now using a wearier, intimate tone. "Lord, honey, I don't never look at death first thing in the morning if I can help it," said the woman who was supposed to be my grandmother. "You look at death in the morning you can't be surprised when that nigger show up talking about sharing your pillow. Much as I like myself some regular male company, I don't never encourage no niggers to share my pillow. You hear me? Hell, I ain't about to share *my* pillow with nobody's death no time soon."

21

GINNY SPENT MOST OF THE MORNING IN MAMA'S BEDROOM.

I crept to the door and pressed my ear against it. I wanted to be in the room with Mama, nestled beside her in Daddy's space.

Downstairs in the kitchen, Ez, Lindy, and Miss Irene busied themselves with warming up plates for the children and preparing food for Mr. Caesar and Mr. Warren to take along with them for the hours-long drive south to Damascus.

Miss Irene lifted her eyes, smiling at me in welcome as I wandered in half-interested in the delicious scents that came from the stove. She was wearing a lilac sweater and a pair of striped men's trousers that were a deep burnt orange. Miss Irene often looked like a painter or someone who lived in a city like Harlem, where clothes were worn for the sake of beauty, daring, and not necessarily for utility. When she laughed her wonderful laugh, it quieted the voice in me that was uneasy with that woman upstairs, who'd given birth to Mama.

Miss Irene spoke to us about her birthplace—Royal—and described how Ginny would've fit right in with the Royal women. That's why Miss Irene and Mr. Caesar knew how to laugh when my grandmother said something prickly.

"Slice a bit more from that bread, Ezra. Lindy, did you wash that potato? *You did?* Well, wash it again and if it can't get no cleaner than that put it over by the bread. That poor potato looking too tired to go in my potato salad. Where are those twins?"

"Across the road," I said.

Miss Irene nodded. "They might as well play. We haven't had a single moment to give them their new toys yet."

"We could take them back to your house so they can have their gifts," said my sister, pushing her hair away from her face as she concentrated on making identical, thick slices from the fresh loaf.

"Where is Ernest?" said Lindy.

Miss Irene cut her eyes at Ezra, whose face had immediately flushed at the boy's name. "He and your father are sitting with Brother Kindred. Mr. Warren's on his way over from the church."

"They're taking Daddy *tonight?*" I said in a voice that was too high to sound normal.

"Taking him *home,* baby. Putting him to rest with your people. Best you think of it that way," said Miss Irene. "You see this storm is getting worse and worse. Too bad your granny is going to have to turn right back around and get on the road. You've barely had a cup of tea together."

"He isn't going to Rising Star?" said Ezra, closing the pantry door.

Miss Irene shook her head. "This storm's made up its mind. There's no time. We've got to hurry. Caesar and Mr. Warren will only have so long down there before they'll be stranded."

Then Mama and Ginny came into the kitchen.

Right away, I noticed Ginny's eyes were red. Her tight dyed curls drooped along her hairline. Her scant edges struggled to stay flat. The red paint on her mouth had also faded, settling into the chapped skin of her lips. Lines of smeared kohl rimmed her top and lower lids along her true lashes. The artificial ones my grandmother had been wearing when she arrived, which reminded me of tarantulas, were nowhere to be seen.

"Could you please pour your grandmother a glass of water?"

"I'll do it, Mama," said Ezra, smiling shyly at Ginny.

"Lord, girl, if this ain't your child," she said, her eyes fastened on Ezra. This was our grandmother's first time seeing my sister. "Jolene, I hope you won't take it no kind of way, but I really don't know which one of these girls of yours is stranger."

"Oh, Mama, *please*."

"Please what? And didn't I tell you about calling me Mama in front of people? These my grandbabies, right? Well, they haven't hugged me or said a kind word yet. I ain't too old to hear a kindness." She pouted, looking over at me. She rolled her eyes. "That one over there is about as kind as a stroke."

"There's nothing wrong with my daughters," said Mama. "First of all, they don't *know* you. They're shy girls, very smart and very loving."

My heart calmed for only a moment before my grandmother picked at me again.

"Hyacinth, are you a good girl?"

"Yes," I said, hoping she would believe me.

Frowning, Ez handed Ginny the water and looked over at Miss Irene for guidance. Unlike Miss Irene and Mama, we hadn't been raised in places like Royal or Damascus. We weren't used to the forceful voices of women like my grandmother, whose moods could swing from sugar to acid in seconds. These women, adorned in a finery invisible to everyone but themselves, seemed to carry themselves around with an air of impenetrable strength even as they complained about nobody else being competent to hold the world together the way they always had. It wasn't something to be taught. But there was also a sense that these older Black women had been hurt, sometimes fatally, at the hands of the world, even the hands they'd nurtured with love and loyalty. How could they be so loyal, so *sure* of their sovereignty, their grace? What harms had grazed their dreams when they were my age?

We'd been raised in Salt Point, never finding ourselves in the company of such women except for when we handed out holiday meals in Sweet Bay or attended one of Rising Star's lovely church dinners.

"Auntie, I have a plate here for you," said Miss Irene. "I know it's dust compared to what you're used to, but my husband and our friend Mr. Warren from the church will be back any moment. I don't want you leaving here hungry after you've come all this way. Probably won't get home until the middle of the night or early tomorrow morning, depending on the roads."

"Is Mr. Warren single?"

"A widower, I believe," said Miss Irene, winking at us as Ginny settled herself at the kitchen table.

"I'd appreciate a cup of tea with some lemon if y'all got some," she said through a mouthful of food. With uncloaked horror, I looked into her gnashing mouth longer than I was supposed to. My grandmother extended her tongue, studded with chewed wet crumbs, at me before she twisted around, calling for Mama, who had slipped away.

"She's going to sit with Heron," said Miss Irene quietly. "Got to get moving. Blizzard's full of spit, for sure. We could be shut in for a few days without electricity. Every year there are outages, but Lena and the girls are alone now."

"Hm, we don't have storms like this in Damascus. We don't have nothing nearly as mean, at least in terms of weather," said Ginny, swallowing her food. Her face opened into one of the most radiant smiles I'd ever seen. She licked her lips, squealing in delight. "*Oooh, girl*—you sure winning with this goddamn cornbread! Ezra baby, wrap the rest of that up for me. Yes, *all* of it. This lovely woman has won me over and that's not easy. Why, this cornbread alone could make me come north, and I've always said there was nothing above Baltimore that was worth my time."

Laughing, Miss Irene pointed to the boiled eggs that she wanted Ezra and Lindy to peel.

"He was a good-looking boy," said Ginny in a soft voice, pressing her napkin against her suddenly wet eyes. "Glad Alma crossed before this day come. Lord, Lord, *Lord*, putting your own baby back before your time is un*bear*able. Nobody can help you understand it."

"Amen," said Miss Irene.

"Jolene got her ways, but she was always good about love," said Ginny. "I hadn't laid eyes on him for so long, for so long. Now I never will. He took after his grandfather, Theodore Kindred. Now *that* man was mighty easy on the eyes."

"I'll help Mama," I said.

"No," said Miss Irene and Ginny at the same time.

"You go work on that raggedy fireplace before we all end up like stiffs in the church van they done drove over here to take your daddy home," said Ginny, sitting back in our kitchen chair. She pointed at me with a manicured finger. "The minute I came down those steps my teeth started hurting something bad. Shouldn't be feeling like the outdoors indoors, you hear me? My 'thritis already gone give me high hell riding in a van for that long. Lord have mercy. Put my scarves and coat on the radiator to warm. Last thing I need from this mess is the 'neumonia."

Miss Irene nodded at me.

As I excused myself, I could hear Ginny's brassy voice curl into a tigerlike purr as she began to speak to Ezra and to Lindy about their Futures.

"The single threat to you having what you want in life is having the idea that you know anything at all. The greatest danger in this life is yourself believing you don't deserve to want yourself. But you have to want yourself, above all else, and that's a hard knowing no matter how you think you're living. Peel them eggs without breaking them up, Ezra, hear me? Have mercy, where did my daughter find a name like *Ezra* and think it was a good idea for a girl? Keep your eyes on those eggs before I knock them out of your head for rolling them at me. I got hindsight, foresight, and insight. I don't miss nothing, you understand?"

Virginia "Ginny" Abbott

MY MATERNAL GRANDMOTHER, VIRGINIA ABBOTT, WAS SIXTEEN WITH A good voice when she gave birth to her only child. Her description of my mother's birth made the entire story sound like a love song or the blues, especially the part where my grandmother abandoned her newborn baby to run off after a dream that suggested her four-octave voice would place her on every stage and nightclub between Paris and Tangier.

But before that happened, Ginny told anybody who would listen about how her daughter's birth had ripped her open so she could smell herself. She spoke of the nether scar her stitches gave her. She recalled how streams of shit streaked her landlord's sheets. Between clenched teeth my grandmother had panted and pushed. *Imagine giving birth, making a life, and you don't even own the sheets you sleep on,* she'd said in wonder. My grandmother said that the midwives, who were both interlocutors and divining rods, smiled at Mama's first shriek and surrounded her bed: "Praise God, sister. Praise God for the life you have and the life you have created. It is God who gives."

Laughing, tears spindling her tongue and spilling from her eyes, Ginny had pressed her face against her new daughter's cries. Lifting her head, my grandmother's body stinging in its miracle, she said,

"Shit! Praise *who*? Shit, praise *me*. Praise me. My whole goddamn self!"

During the first weeks of Mama's life, my grandmother sang to my infant mother constantly, her eyes fastened on the empty road outside the window of the boardinghouse where she was waiting for a sign. While my grandmother waited, she took the time to name my mother Jolene Abbott. The baby absorbed her attention until her stitches healed.

Back then, the downtown area in Damascus was a small grid, with only one or two paved roads. The main road was paved up to Fourth Street, where it became gravel and dust before leading to a rocky path, which thinned into a tunnel of trees that stopped at the lip of the backwards river. On this side of the river, there was Booby's, a joint where Ginny had been singing since she was thirteen. The Pearsons, who owned the bar, also owned the building where they rented my grandmother a room that she shared with another girl, Ernestine. By the time the Pearsons took the rent out of my grandmother's wages and deducted all of the little extra things they could think of, they more or less owned her.

Once my grandmother had Jolene, though, the church got involved.

The men and women of Damascus had a word they thought of whenever they saw my grandmother. Sometimes they said it to her face but mostly they traded it with one another: *That Fast-Ass girl. Fast. Baby-already-out-her-ass. That's how Fast. Well then, when they born like that what you going to do? What can you do? She was always Fast. Whose child is she anyway? Child of God, sure I'll give you that, but the Fast part? Who gave it to her and why we got to live with it? Surprised she ain't gone yet, Fast as she been all this time. Remember when she was young and used to rub on herself in the pew? Talking 'bout how good God felt? Her mama was an angel but the wings this child got need glue.*

Now there was a baby, whose innocence could not be tossed to the easy, gold-capped teeth of hip-grinding heathens. Hinder Me

Not passed their brass plate around and got some money together. Times were tight in Damascus, as they'd been since their original church had burned down in '02. Still, they collected enough money to place the baby safely elsewhere.

Then a tour of musicians arrived and ruined everything.

In the evenings, Ginny dropped Mama into Ernestine's arms and didn't return to their room until the morning. Hair slicked with moonlight's lust, her skin sweating whisky or worse, Ginny's voice grew hoarse with dreams of Harlem, Chicago, Detroit, St. Louis. Every city on this side of the Atlantic, and Rome and Cairo, consumed her. Champagne-laden dreams filled my grandmother's head, washing away the duty of the cord that once tethered her to my mother's navel. My grandmother went on and on about them to Ernestine while her friend laid Ginny's hair into meticulous finger waves. As she tugged her girdle up her hips, my grandmother shrugged away the cries of her child in the cradle. Plugging her baby's mouth with a bottle while she poured herself a stiff drink from the bottle of moonshine she hid in her closet, my grandmother couldn't stop describing the music that would raise her voice into the spangled life she had always dreamt of—a life that excluded motherhood. Meanwhile the women of the church accused Ginny Abbott of being fast, simple, and only capable of nursing one person in the world, which was herself.

Ginny craved sequins, sex, and slow songs that let her show all of her teeth when she smiled. Her voice, her legs, her high, perfect ass attached to indefatigable thighs. My grandmother was a prize! That's what Jimmy, Johnny, Eddie, maybe Freddy, kept saying. She'd begun a habit of taking a different man to bed each night and rolled her eyes when the women of Hinder Me Not reminded her of her stitches, her duties. Ginny despised homespun lullabies about stealing away to Jesus. She told Ernestine that the old folks used Jesus against her like they used the heels of their Sunday shoes to crush roaches.

To claim herself was the sweetest and most dangerous theft. To snatch her sovereignty back from the Almighty and those pinched mouths who clung to and worshiped their own suffering and sins every Sunday was far less offensive to the Savior than the oppressive catechisms that were intended to protect and save her. Sometimes Ginny felt like the pastor was no different from the police. My grandmother's defiance was nearly criminal in the sanctuary of the very parish that held the lives of its congregants in its living air.

One Thursday afternoon, Ginny cradled her daughter in her arms. The sight of her baby's two front teeth startled her as if a clock had chimed. As she stared into the creamy miniature of her own face, admiring the round, darling eyes and wet lips, Ginny knew that as soon as something shiny danced down the empty road wearing alligator shoes, she would chase it.

Aware of how exactly the church would raise her daughter, the young girl only shrugged and wished the baby girl luck.

Ginny thought of Ernestine, of asking her to "hold" her baby for a year or two, but doubted the church would deem Ernestine a proper guardian.

Ernestine was a known adulterer. Ginny knew that Ernestine had kissed too many women's husbands, had worn fire-red dresses at Hinder Me Not's non-holiday services, and was not to be trusted if someone was foolish enough to leave their purse or wallet visible in her presence. Ernestine wouldn't lie about who she was. If asked to return something she'd stolen, she'd look at you, hurt and wide-eyed, and then she'd give it back to you—if she still had it to begin with. She also cried when she saw field mice smashed by tires in the paved section of the street, and wept loudly when birds flew into the glass windows of a storefront, dying instantly and vividly on the sidewalk alone. In the small square, Ernestine fed pigeons, and that pissed everybody off because it was something white folks did. Who had bread and crackers to waste on birds that ended up shitting all over everything nice that people tried to keep clean? Who had the time to grieve the senselessness of death? When a blackbird flew into a storefront window, instead of being useful and picking the thing up with a shovel or broom, Ernestine would fold it into her hands while the women and men, who worked night shifts and day shifts and cut hair on the side in their kitchens, watched her and itched to slap her face.

Ernestine was just like those birds. All of her life, she'd crashed into mirrors when she thought the path was clear. Sometimes it wasn't her fault but after a while there was something to be said about a girl who couldn't see her own reflection, even in the presence of light.

My grandmother looked at the half-lidded doll in her arms. Maybe she'd come back when it made sense. But Jimmy-Johnny-Eddie-Freddy said she'd forget this swamp. Except when she was singing. Then Ginny could bring the memory of Damascus to the surface of her music like a vein. Otherwise, it was best for my grandmother to learn new music, new melodies that would set her free.

It was time for my grandmother to get hers—salvation, ecstasy, and a sleek shiny car filled with good-looking colored boys, who reminded her of Easters and Juneteenths, singing and whistling in their marvelous bodies. She welcomed their easy laughter and the hardness buried in their laps. Humming and sighing each day, Ginny stared through the windshield of her future, listening for the cue to her solo.

During the Thursday evening service at Hinder Me Not, Ginny bounced her daughter on her lap and sang *Jesus, oh Jesus.* She wiped her tears against her baby's skull. As she left the church, she reapplied her red lipstick, which was now smeared like a fateful mark on my mother's brow. Ginny felt like howling, she was so alive. The baby on her arm was heavy as an old woman's pocketbook. Ginny wanted to put her down and go and sing. Humming, she nodded at the parishioners who looked at her funny as she whispered, perhaps too loudly and impulsively, to the sleeping baby in her arms. "Jesus, don't let nothing bad happen to what I made. 'Cuz I love what I have made."

When Ernestine woke up on Friday morning, Ginny was gone.

. . .

ERNESTINE TOLD MIRIAM PEARSON THAT she was taking Ginny's baby to the doctor and needed to borrow her car. The woman had eyed her without looking at Jolene, and tipped her head to say *go on*. Ernestine placed Jolene inside Miriam's car. The baby rode shotgun. Because those Black folks were occupied with working, minding their business, soaking beans in a pot for Sunday luncheon, and preparing for the sky to fall, they did not notice Ernestine at the wheel.

Rolling along the turnpike, Ernestine spoke the names printed on signs aloud to the swaddled baby sleeping on the seat next to her. Perhaps Ernestine thought that my mama would retain them, would remember the sound of Ernestine's loving voice replacing my grandmother's careless crooning.

Ernestine kept the engine running in the alley where she pulled in next to a church with a stained-glass rose window. The town had a biblical name she'd forget immediately—Calvary, Hagar, Bethlehem, or New Christ.

The doors of the church were open, which assured Ernestine that this was the right god, the right entrance for an orphaned child. After writing *Jolene* on a slip of an envelope, she signed her name and then Ginny's. They were her mothers. Pinning their three names deep inside a generic white baby blanket, she gathered the bundle into her arms, rocking her in apology. Then she settled my infant mother inside the front doors of Sacred Heart Roman Catholic Church. Ernestine hoped she'd be forgiven for leaving Jolene in God's hands. In a moment of guilt, she took a pencil out of her purse and scribbled the word Damascus and a postal code under the baby's name.

As she hurried away from the tiny cries of a daughter who was not hers, Ernestine prayed no one would see her. Her heart spun, sick with possibilities, accusations. Damn Ginny for placing her and the baby in this predicament to begin with. There'd been no note from that girl, no plea for Ernestine to have patience. And there'd been no money either.

Ernestine thought again about the baby, a sweet new life that couldn't survive without the care and love of another human being.

There was a full tank of gas in the car. Ernestine reasoned that Miriam wouldn't mind losing what she could replace. The Pearsons bought themselves new cars every two years. Ernestine pressed the gas pedal hard. As she sped off, she spoke the names of towns aloud bemusedly to herself, with the windows rolled down and the radio hollering.

. . .

AT AGE FOURTEEN, WHEN MAMA began to bleed, the Daughters of Divine Charity, who had raised her, hinted that it was time for her to return to her own people. The only blood that they could honor was the white blood of Jesus, the Son of God. Their own periods were distant in memory, as most of the women of this sect were well over sixty years old, and the Daughters of Divine Charity found themselves in private agreement: A colored girl's blood was nothing but trouble. Once the bleeding began, they whispered, a Negro girl was liable to steal, fornicate, dance, and preen, to lie to their faces.

The very first time her period happened, Mama had been able to launder her own sheets, unnoticed. But the next month Sister Loretta discovered her in the washroom. It was the second time Mama had wakened, before dawn, and sensed the wetness leaking from her. In the dark, her fingertips sticky, she knew that she was no longer a child.

Sisters Loretta and Prudence also noticed that Jolene's presence began to arouse the attention of those who came to worship. They noted the watery eyes of priests and monsignors. Deacons lingered as Jolene retreated from the sanctuary. The sisters watched Mama. They worried that they had no words for the things inside them that made them afraid of her dark skin, even as they claimed that she, too, was a daughter of God. This tension could not be prayed away, so they secretly blamed all of their fears on the ripe smell of her blood.

Given the good education Jolene Abbott had received in their midst, and her skills at scrubbing, praying, and playing the organ, they thought it'd be good for her to marry, attaching herself to a pastor and his parish. My mother spoke French and could read some German. She'd set tables for bishops and cardinals, whose heavy jeweled rings shone against the ornate knives they used to slice fine cuts of meat, even as God's daughters sipped weak broth and chewed dry toast in the kitchen.

The Daughters of Divine Charity had treated Mama as a pet, training her against her own mind, her feelings, and her body. They plied her into kneeling positions whenever they could, threatened by her rapidly increasing height. When she grew as tall as she did, they found other ways to make my mother small. There was a quiet satisfaction in the burns on her hands and arms from cooking and baking in their sunny industrial-sized kitchen. Mute, useful, and gentle, Jolene Abbott, the Daughters decided, would be an ambassador for her race.

· · ·

ONE DAY, WHILE DUSTING MOTHER Superior's private office in the library, my mother found herself opening a metal cabinet that had always been forbidden to her. Mother Superior, who'd recently begun to be absentminded, had left the key in the lock instead of keeping it on the chain that she wore at her waist, which clanked with shining keys. In the cabinet there was an olive folder with a typed label: *Jolene X.* The file was as thin as a fingernail. The first sheet of paper was the official intake that contained information that the nuns had never concealed from her. In feminine handwriting, the words *Jolene, Negro, Abandoned* were written in large letters. But on the second sheet of paper was a postal code with the word *Damascus* printed inside parentheses. No number given. There were two names written in pencil: *Ernestine* and *Ginny*.

Mama's eyes blurred upon the word *Damascus*. Why had the Daughters of Divine Charity kept this location from her for fourteen years? Quietly, she went back to work. Later, though, she'd look up

the town and how to get there. When she was forced to kneel and
to give confession each morning, my mother fought against the fits
of rage that danced like holy tongues above her head. These wom-
en's veils of order, of purpose, of sanctity, had concealed the world
from her. Like medical tape, it'd been ripped away from her skin so
quickly she was breathless.

As the sisters were trained to detect moral turbulence, they
sensed my mother's self-knowledge. They were irritated by the fury
she could barely suppress. Because of their sincere affection for
Mama, some of the younger sisters actually grieved what they knew
would come next.

One evening during dinner, Sister Loretta inquired indirectly
about Mama's temperament, alluding to the weather of her heart.

"You had an address for me," said Mama, without any pretense.
She was finished with their vague dialogues concerning weather re-
ports and the will of God. "I came from a *real* place."

Their thin lips squeezed together to suck up the steaming soup
without checking first to see if it would scald them. "We believed this
would be a better home, dear."

"Cooking and cleaning day and night for you?"

"Not us, dear," said Sister Anne. "This is the Lord's work that we
do. We take our vows in the name of our Father."

"But I'm not like you," Mama said.

"Well, you were always colored. We'd always thought as much
in terms of your future," said Sister Maria, setting her spoon down
with a frown. "We might as well be clear about it. You've received the
kind of education and upbringing your people would've never been
able to give you. When you were sent to us—abandoned by your own
mother—we saw another vision, another way to continue our mis-
sion as servants of the Lord. We've given you what we could, given
the vows we've taken. We gave you the life God could've given you
had you been born differently. Had you been born with the choices
we have."

Mama heard what was not said but suggested. If she'd been born white rather than colored they could've offered her another life, perhaps a family who would've wanted her for their own. But being Negro meant nobody, including God, wanted her. The sisters had viewed themselves as her last resort.

"Jolene, you have a choice to make right now," said Sister Loretta. Her usual melodious voice flattened. "You can choose to stay with us, share this sacred roof of simple living, and continue to work together, with us, to serve God. Or should you prefer to return to your own race, we'll write letters on your behalf. We'll help with your enrollment in a fine Negro women's college somewhere in the south. We've sent girls like you to Tuskegee, Atlanta, Mississippi. It's likely you'd qualify for a scholarship, dear."

"Oh, a scholarship," said another of the older sisters. "A scholarship is always nice."

Sister Loretta cleared her throat. "The third choice is for us to take you back to the poor dust where you came from. Should that be your wish we won't be able to help you anymore."

"You'll punish me for wanting to know who I am?"

"God is our home," said Sister Loretta. "God's will is how we live, where we live, and for His will we live. We do not live for the fruits of this world. We know there is another."

"Damascus," said Mama, her mouth filling with blood, as she tasted the word and its memory, "is only twenty miles away."

"Heaven is much closer," said another sister. They began smiling and nodding. "Heaven is much, much closer."

. . .

THE DAUGHTERS OF DIVINE CHARITY dropped Mama off at the post office.

Mr. Davis, who was sitting on a bench, raised his eyes from his newspaper to watch my mother, striking and long-legged, climb out of a modest station wagon filled with four white women. They drove off the moment the girl got her suitcase out of the trunk, as though they expected at any moment to be held at gunpoint or worse.

Amused, the old man slapped his knees with the paper and used his tongue to move the toothpick, which had been resting between the gap of his teeth since sunup, to the gummy corner of his mouth. He'd observed that one of the religious women buried her crumpled face in a white handkerchief as the young girl turned to wave farewell.

Mr. Davis said hello to Mama.

The only men who'd spoken to Mama for the last fourteen years of her life wore collars around their throats and spoke to her in voices coated in phlegm. Sure, sometimes a man spoke briefly to her at church, or some of the delivery boys asked her questions about repairs and groceries, but she'd never been alone in a man's presence, much less a Negro man's company.

"Good afternoon, how you doing, sister? You visiting people here?"

Mama nodded, wiping her face with her hand.

"You got a tongue in there? Ain't no mind readers 'round here."

"Sisters say that this is my home," said Mama. "I was born here in Damascus, sir. I'm fourteen. I think I'm fourteen."

"You tall for fourteen," he said, smiling. "That's good, that's good. Tall woman is a strong woman."

She found herself smiling as she gripped the handle of her valise.

"What they call you, gal?"

"Jolene, sir," she said. "I'm Jolene Abbott, I think. Tried to look up my mother's name in the phone directory before they brought me back. Her name is Ernestine or Ginny."

He sat back, rearranging the aged jelly of his thighs, shaking his head. "Hm, well, it's one Abbott here. She run off long ago then come back. Virginia. And if you call her that she'll cuss you out. Goes by Ginny. Heard she did some time in Alabama before she called herself coming home. Live far out off Owl Mill. Been there a long time. Didn't never hear nothing 'bout her having no chirren though."

"Well, maybe I'm wrong about that woman," she said, flushing at the thought that her mother was a criminal, or had been. "So my mother must be Ernestine, sir," she said. "Ernestine Abbott."

She took in how his face darkened.

"Can't be," he said. "You too pretty."

"The sisters said that there were two names given—Ginny and Ernestine. I saw the paper myself. The sisters said one of them must be my mother."

"What's what they say got to do with it? They don't care nothing 'bout you, quick as they drove off like that. Didn't stop to see whether you had something to eat or a place to lay your head come sundown. Them nuns there going to tell you anything but the truth. But me? Shit, I already know what that is."

"I have to find my mama."

"I already know who that is too."

"She's alive?"

"You're the baby that went missing when Ernestine stole Booby Pearson's car. Nobody was looking for you, assumed that girl threw you in the river and kept on going to Chicago or wherever. But you wasn't hers. You belong to Ginny Abbott. All I got to do is look at you to know."

Mama stared down at the ground.

"Ginny a different woman since she came back," he said. "More smoke than spark now, but she's an original through and through."

"Original what?"

"She'll tell you," said the man. Chuckling, he stood up and shook out a ring of keys from his pocket. Patting his belly, which dropped over the band of his crusty denim pants, he smiled again at her. "You had anything to eat, gal? Your height is fine but your width ain't near where it ought to be. We going to get you a proper appetite."

"I want to go home," my mother said. "I've been gone fourteen years, sir. My mama's missed me. I hope she's missed me."

"Well," he said, "you ask her about that too. Everybody 'round here know that Ginny Abbott is a generous woman. Sings like an angel. Most of 'em that take off always come back just 'fore they 'bout to die. Surprised she came back sooner than that.

"Got herself a job over at the factory. Got herself some boyfriends, so I've been told. Got a side business—baking pies and selling 'em. Them pies of Ginny's will cure just about anything that ails you—only woman 'round here who can really cook a meal the way we used to eat coming up. People stingy now when it comes to using real butter and will salt every goddamn thing 'til a tomato will taste like a steak and a plate of spaghetti might as well be a chocolate cake. These women too tired to think about they kitchens the way they used to. Hell, I don't blame 'em a bit.

"She come back after prison and who knows where. If Ginny Abbott *is* your mama, you lucky. She'll get all that nun mess up out of you. Ginny Abbott is a delicious woman and won't nobody say I'm lying.

"Women like that got to protect who they is."

22

MR. CAESAR, MR. WARREN, AND MY GRANDMOTHER HAD DRIVEN OFF IN that ugly van, taking Daddy away from us. It was like cutting off all the electricity in our house and asking us to figure out how to live by firelight.

As I'd watched my grandmother fussing while she bundled herself against the weather and the journey, I wondered if I'd ever see her again. Watching the way she'd treated Mama with such tenderness had moved me, and it was hard to think of her as an enemy. There was no doubt that my mother and grandmother needed each other. When she whispered to Mama, "I'll be seeing you, baby," I was reminded of the sad ballad on a Billie Holiday record Mama played all the time when I was a child. As Ginny said the words, Mama nodded her head before she threw her arms savagely around her mother's body, squeezing her eyes shut, her lips parting as she mouthed, *I love you, Mama*.

After she made my mother eat something, Miss Irene mopped and wiped Daddy's study, removing the candles and evidence of her incense and dried flowers. Checking our refrigerator again to be sure we had plenty of food should our appetites want it, she told Mama she had to take her children home. The little ones needed baths

and their own beds. Miss Irene worried about Lindy, who continued to believe she was responsible for Daddy's death and the loss of
Mr. Caesar's job. Her children would all have nightmares about the
fire for a long time. And she wanted to be sure her own house was
stocked against the menacing approach of the storm. She offered to
have Ernest stay with us, but Mama smiled gratefully and waved the
invitation away. "You'll need Ernest with you and the kids, Irene," she
said. "Don't worry. That deputy won't be thinking about us. It'd be
too much of a risk. Even for him."

Nodding, Miss Irene hollered for the twins and Lindy to get into
the car and handed the car keys to Ernest, who hugged each of us
before he went outside to warm the engine. I pretended that I didn't
see him linger, whispering to my sister. I liked how he made her
smile.

"He's driving?"

"That boy's seventeen," said Miss Irene. "Seventeen going on sev-
enty. I guess I shouldn't complain. He's hardworking. Always been
like that. He's got patience I don't have, that's for sure. Even when
he was a baby, like he was waiting for me to figure out how to be a
momma. Rarely cried or gave me extra work to do."

Ezra nestled against Mama's birdlike shoulder. Her eyes were
swollen, her mouth raw. The way they'd driven Daddy away had
taken all words from her.

"This is the last thing," said Miss Irene in a low voice. She took
out a small, gleaming pistol and set it down on the unsteady table
where our father once piled his books and papers.

"Irene," said Mama softly, their eyes meeting. "Oh, Irene, I—"

"Ezra knows how to shoot because I taught her."

"Shoot what?" I said, feeling nervous.

"Long ago, my mama—Ginny—taught me too. It was one of the
things I was happy to immediately forget when we left," said Mama.
"Used to be a lot of shooting back in Damascus. Probably still is.
Mostly it was white folks shooting. But colored men shot for food,
for defense of their property. When they had no choice and it was a

matter of white folks going after their wives and children, they used their weapons for other reasons."

"Well, my sister, let's hope there won't be no reasons tonight." Miss Irene kissed Mama's cheek and the tops of our heads. Her eyes swept over our scrubbed walls, which were traced by the light of flames. Then she and the Junkett children went off. The gnawing tires of their car made loud mashing noises as the wheels rolled across dense planes of snow.

· · ·

THE EVENING FIRE BURNED HOARSELY in our living room, which was very hot. I thought of our grandmother's loose teeth and allowed myself a small grin. She wouldn't have been able to complain about it being too cold, though it was clear that she was equipped to complain about just near anything.

Seated in my father's frayed armchair, I attempted to fit the back of my aching head inside the shadowy shape of his skull, the proof that he was still with us. Yawning, Ezra was trying to stay awake. Exhausted, Mama's body folded inside a light sleep at the other end of the shabby couch.

The quiet, save for the sputtering of our fireplace, gave me an uncomfortable feeling, as if I'd eaten too much food. Instead of letting myself drift in the warmth with my sister and mother, my thoughts sharpened as I tried to imagine how we could ever bear such evenings with no father. Questions exploded in my head, sparking from one to the next. When would Mama have surgery for her cancer? How much time did we have before she'd need to go to that hospital in Boston? Maybe Ez and I would stay with the Junkett family. Except that Mr. Caesar's termination from Hobart meant it was likely that the Junkett family would move on, perhaps returning to Royal, which would please Miss Irene. I tried to imagine finishing my school year in a place like that. Daddy wanted my sister and me to go to college, but there'd be no way we could ever leave Mama alone, especially not here in Salt Point.

The sound of another pair of tires approaching pulled me out of my worry. Immediately, my eyes went to the pistol. It was as shiny and black as the enamel of Mama's piano. Ezra was already standing with her head tilted in the direction of the car. Her body was tense. Placing her fingers over her lips to indicate that we shouldn't disturb Mama, she lifted the pistol and pushed it deep inside her dress. We squeezed ourselves in the space next to the holiday tree so that we could see out to the far end of our road.

"Is that a *hearse*?"

"Hush! Don't wake Mama," said Ez, pulling me out of the living room. Opening the front door, we stood side by side in its frame.

"It looks like a hearse but it isn't," I said, squinting through veils of snow that twisted like sequined sheets around the porch. Our visibility was limited. "Is it Deputy Charlie?"

I thought of the gun buried inside my sister's dress. Ezra's jaw was clenched like Daddy's. Around her eyes were fireworks of fragile muscles twitching and vibrating. Each nerve signaled alarm, a frantic transmission on a switchboard somewhere deep inside my sister's furious head. "It's a limousine," Ezra finally said.

We hadn't heard her, but the heat of Mama's body blazed behind us. As I turned my head, our eyes met. In the dark, clean air I saw that Mama, Ezra, and I all shared the same steely fire in our eyes. She nodded as if to remind me to remember this.

Then she placed her hand on my shoulder as the three of us tried to make out the visitor approaching our house.

Miss Alley.

The woman, for some reason, had risked driving in a blizzard all the way from Amity to Salt Point. There was something like joy in the way she'd stepped out of the luxury car, its doors opened by a white-gloved colored man.

"Evening, Miss Dinah, I wonder what could be so important as to bring you out here in such dangerous weather. Won't you come in?" Mama's voice was clear, the nerves in her body alloying into a metallic tone that told us not to insert ourselves into what she would say. Our mother could be shattered by our father's death, but she wouldn't tolerate Miss Alley's foolishness in her own living room.

Ezra and I remained outside on the porch; with our mismatched clothes, we probably looked like vagrants. Standing near the car were two Negroes, a man in a chauffeur's uniform and a woman whose dark eyes took in our shivering. She scanned our half-lit house before nodding a gentle greeting.

Ezra tried to peer through our front window, but the ugly, glowing tree obscured any view of what was happening between Miss Alley and Mama.

"Can she expel us?"

"Cinthy," sighed my sister. "Her aunt and uncle own Hobart, which means she practically owns it too."

"But how is that fair? We shouldn't be suspended from school because of what's happened to Daddy. He *died*."

Ezra shook her head. "That's the *reason*, dummy. They don't have to do a damn thing for us anymore. We've lost any leverage Daddy might've had and he didn't have much to begin with. If Hobart wasn't such a crook, Daddy wouldn't have had this job for as long as he did. It's rare to see a school with a Negro man teaching white children. Miss Irene once said that our situation was always compromising. Well, she was right."

Daddy's voice filled my ears. Education had meant everything to him. He always said that it had saved his life and that knowledge was the only thing that could save us. Being expelled from Hobart would threaten what Daddy wanted us to have, what he'd worked to give us. So it wasn't fine by me, but I said nothing.

The back door of the limousine opened again. I feared that it would be Mr. and Mrs. Hobart, or worse, Deputy Charlie himself.

Instead, a girl wrapped in a long coat with fur trim peeked out of the car. The Negro driver nearly slipped and fell in his hurry to hold the door ajar for her.

The girl couldn't have managed the door herself, because her hands were hidden inside a fur muff. Dark ringlets blew around her

face cinematically, the staged way we'd only seen in movies. She was
wearing polished leather boots that barely left a trace of her prints
on the ground. As she waited for us to recognize her, she raised her
head, taking a few more steps. I thought that perhaps this was one
of the haunted daughters who'd never been discovered at the bottom
of our pond.

For several moments, we all listened to the wind.

I watched the breath that streamed from the colored woman's
nostrils. She had to be freezing. I wondered what her life was like
and why it was her job to stand there like a soldier guarding this
spoiled girl.

Ruby came up as if she owned our steps, owned us. She sat right
down on the edge of one of the chairs where Mr. Caesar and the
Rising Star men had been sitting, singing to Jesus on Christmas Eve.
The voice that came out of her mouth struggled with the freezing air.

"I thought I'd come and pay my respects to your family when
I heard about you losing your daddy," she said. "I'm sure sorry he's
dead. Died like a hero, saving them children the way he did."

Ezra was shaking her head. "How dare you."

"Keep our father's name out of your mouth," I said, wondering
whether my spit would freeze before it landed on her.

"Be careful," said Ruby, rising from the rocking chair. "It's far too
cold out here for me to be insulted this evening. Marvella, would
you mind joining us? Given my condition, I can't have these niggers
threatening my nerves."

"What is it, Miss Ruby?"

The woman came up the steps, clearly irritated at being ordered
to do so, and stood on the opposite side of the porch, away from
the three of us. The idea that Ruby could command a grown Black
woman to do what *she* wanted her to do made me grow hot inside
with rage and shame despite the blustery air.

"*Miss Ruby?*" I said in a mocking voice.

"You'd know my life has changed if we was—well, if we *were* still
friends."

"What's changed?" said Ezra. "Filth is filth."

Ruby blinked away her disbelief. "I come to see about *you*! Guess I was feeling sorry for Mr. Kindred. Without him working at the school, I don't know how you all are going to afford to stay on in the village. I suppose your mama might get a job—finally—but that depends on her health, doesn't it?"

"There's nothing poorer in this world than you," I said.

She nodded at me, smiling. "Ez knows how to survive, like I do, but *your* little world has been destroyed. You're the one who needed school more than all of us; you don't even know who you are unless there's some kind of book telling you you're alive."

"You've been getting good lessons from that white woman," said Ezra. "If you want to talk about somebody needing something, let's talk about that. You had to have a white woman show you how to be white, is that it? 'Cause your ma's white wasn't working out? Or maybe you really knew what you were all along and Miss Alley told you it was okay to admit it. Looks like you need her to tell you who *you* are more than anybody, especially if you believe that she's going to care about you once she has what she wants—whatever that is."

Instead of Ruby replying to anything my sister had said, she went on in a voice that we'd often heard adults use. It was the tone of a person who is only ever interested in the business of her own voice. I heard my father's voice in my head, talking to us about compassion. I pictured Ruby's shattered eyes the day we'd left the air show. She'd always been hungry for something she hadn't been able to share with us, even as we shared so much, prowling through Salt Point's wilderness together. But perhaps Ruby had finally understood that we could not share our blackness with her. We could not offer what was between our legs or the love behind our eyes that made us love each other's faces. We could not give Ruby the blood from our ancestors' throats and songs. Ruby had to sing alone and that was a sad, sorry thing. But we owed her, and ourselves, no apology.

Ruby lived in a new wilderness now and I tried to have some sympathy, some hope that she'd be able to get out of it alive. But her refusal to leave us alone made it hard for me to see her as anything but pitiful. I hadn't been raised to turn the other cheek.

"The charity show is over," said Ruby. "Mr. Hobart will be in some important negotiations right after New Year's about selling the whole school off and heading west. It'll hurt the village, but they'll get over it. He's been bleeding money trying to keep that school in the black. He says that California is the place for him to be. One day I'll go there too. Maybe I'll be in the movies."

"You want to talk about charity? We've just put the trash out in case you're hungry," said Ezra. "You didn't think I knew about that, did you? How it made me feel so bad because I had to pretend I didn't know you were hungry?

"And here you are now. You got a nerve, a real white nerve. Speaking of luck, where is your papa and why is he letting you be Miss Alley's lapdog?"

"Miss Alley's taken a special interest in me," said Ruby. Her trembling chin jutted out in the amber light that spilled from the fireplace through our front window. The comment about our garbage had left a hairline crack along Ruby's new face. She shifted a bit so that we could see her. "She gave Ma and Papa some money to invest in my future. There's talk of adoption. Miss Alley's always wanted a daughter like me."

"So they *sold* you," said Ezra. "Go on, tell us more lies. Wouldn't be the first time you lied to yourself."

"My future is worth any investment! I'm going to travel to Europe with Miss Alley. We're going to a fancy ball in New York and from there we'll set sail for our new adventures. I'm going to have all the things I've ever wanted, and I won't ever come back here unless I want to."

"What about being a pilot?" I said. "I thought that's all you wanted. Being free?"

"I've already got my freedom," said Ruby. Bowing her head, she pressed the muff against the felt belt tied around her waist. "And more." The wind picked up again as though Ruby had choreographed the elements of her disclosure. Her face shone with hope as she enunciated two clear words above the hissing cold.

"I'm expecting."

"Expecting what?" I said.

She didn't answer but fixed her eyes on Ezra, as if she still held on to the possibility that they could love each other.

"I'm going to be a mother, and there's going to be something sweet in the world that will be depending on me not to fall. Miss Alley had a private doctor visit me in Amity earlier today. I never been to the doctor before. You should've seen Miss Alley's face! They kept asking me, but I know it doesn't matter *who* the father is. The more I've thought about this baby, the higher I feel myself lifting. I can be free by loving my baby. It's the simplest thing. I don't know why I never thought that way before.

"Listen, I can help you all. I know what hard times is like and trust me when I tell you that you all are facing them. We can go to your pond and wish together. Just like sisters! Things might get worse before the sun appears again," Ruby said. "Damn Charlie's talking about the village running you and those Junketts right on out of here by New Year's. After Miss Alley spoke with her uncle, he thought it was best, as they're worried that Mr. Caesar could be the father of my child."

Ezra shoved Ruby. "That's a goddamn lie!"

Instead of scrambling to her feet the way she once did, Ruby took her time getting up. The Negro woman Ruby had called Marvella spoke with a sharp voice that snaked across our porch. "Girl, don't you lay a hand on Miss Ruby again. You don't strike nothing that's carrying life in it." It was Marvella's voice and her protection of Ruby that made us wonder whether Ruby wasn't a liar, not about the baby at least.

"Did *he* do it to you?" said Ezra, folding her arms across her chest. "Lindy used to tell me how your ma left you and your papa alone all the time. Maybe she couldn't compete with you for your papa's love."

"Ma didn't *abandon* me!"

Ez stared at Ruby's belly as though she could see through the fashionable cashmere coat, through Ruby's pale skin, to where a tiny clot of life was contracting, breathing and exhaling in its own jelly. "Where is your father, Ruby? Where could he be that would be better than saving you from what you're doing to yourself?"

"Passed out by the woodstove like every Christmas," said Ruby. "Oh, Papa's gone mad since I won't come back to him. Why would I go back to *him*? I'd rather live in Amity. It's like being in a movie. Poor Papa. Damn Charlie's had to lock him up almost every day for intoxication. He's saying Ma tricked him into giving me up. Says I been kidnapped. Says he got rights."

"Are you really going to have a baby?"

Ruby took in my tone and lifted her chin. "Maybe. Well, yes. I—I don't bleed no more."

"I thought you loved your papa," said Ezra. "He'll end up in prison, a real penitentiary, if you don't help him."

"He'll end up dead if I'm lucky," Ruby said in Miss Alley's voice.

"We'd give anything to have our daddy with us," I said. "And you can fix your face to wish something as terrible as that on your papa."

"Marvella, help me back inside the car," said Ruby, closing a shutter over the dark blue window of her eyes. "This air ain't—*isn't*— good for me."

"Yeah," said Ezra, her eyes narrowing. "Get your ass in that car and don't ever drive down this road again."

"Miss Dinah coming," said Marvella.

"Can't you wish me well," said Ruby, face quivering. "Be happy for me? I'm not sure when I'll be back here after we take the steamer to Europe. Miss Alley says we'll celebrate New Year's at sea. I may never come back. Nobody's given me a reason to. I was just thinking—"

"Be happy for you?" I said.

"You grow up or you give up," she said, leaning on Marvella's arm.

"Did you give up on your father?" said Ezra. "Or did you give up on yourself first?"

"If you don't get your tail in this car . . ." said Marvella, pulling Ruby. "I ain't about to lose my good job on account of you."

"We didn't see it the same way, did we, Ez?"

"What are you talking about?"

"That day when we looked," she said. "We could've never."

It was that wildness in my sister that had attracted Ruby—that unsettling and unpredictable loyalty. The coolness. Between Ruby and Ezra, an unfamiliar womanhood sprouted, arriving amid late spring and the end of summer. Beneath that rough sunlight, their girlhood lay blanched on the rocks. There was barely enough time for my sister and Ruby to wish their girlhoods farewell. A new language sprung like a barbed fence through which they stared at each other in faint recognition. Ruby's period had signaled her availability to be married and to have a family. Though she was poor she'd still been rich because of her skin.

For my sister, the maturity of her body meant something dangerous to everyone around us. It had worried our parents that Ezra was suddenly in the line of sight, of fire, of ugly histories. For my sister, there was no guarantee that she would ever be granted the kind of dignity or respect that indicated she could be safe anywhere, even in her own home.

I remembered Ruby's spiteful scorn against the world as she snatched our damp panties into her hands that day, taking this most intimate article from each of us. None of us had known that when we pulled that thin garment back over what we had been warned to see as a weapon, it would already be too late to forget what we had seen.

Ruby let herself go limp under Marvella's fussing. Just before she ducked into the limousine, she raised her head to speak. Her hands, in their black muff, looked as if she were imprisoned in a straitjacket.

"He couldn't never be the father he told me I needed. So sad and wild and mean. But sometimes wild things leave you or you let them go," she said. "Even if they're part of you."

23

THE NEXT MORNING, IN OUR PARENTS' BED, THE SCENT OF MY FATHER was an unseen caul wrapped around us. I'd fallen asleep on Daddy's side with my back facing outward. Mama's chest rose and fell gently. Breathing slowly in her sleep, her body turned inward, fetal. It was comforting for me to rest inside the memory of my father's weight. I'd been born in their big goose-feather bed. When we were small girls, Mama had often pulled us against her in this very bed until Daddy finally insisted that we had to sleep by ourselves.

Now Ezra was tucked between Mama and me. The night before, while we tumbled into sleep, Mama sang to us as if we'd each been placed at her nipple again. "Goodnight, Irene" became a mourning lullaby. The blue plea of a woman's name ebbed and hushed us into the oceanic rocking of waves. Mama hummed *I'll see you in my dreams, I'll see you in my dreams,* until we melted together into a liquid reverie, protected from what threatened us beyond the walls of Mama's grieving voice.

As I blinked against the morning's silence, I heard Ruby's warning in my head again, like an icy drip of water against the warm folds of my thoughts. *The village running you and those Junketts right on out of here by New Year's.*

By the time Ezra's eyes flickered open, I was in a terrified trance. Though I hadn't seen her crying, Ezra's slightly swollen eyelids gave the proof of her own grief, which she tried not to let me see. So close to her face, I was startled how her eyes, identical to Daddy's, took me in, as she tapped her finger against my mouth. She cupped my face, letting the heat of her palm flow into my head. Her finger traced my nose and eyes, then the entire shape of my face before she pressed her finger back to her mouth and smiled with her eyes. When I was young, my sister did this with me all the time. I swear I could remember being in my cradle and looking up into her large brown eyes as her fingertips glided lovingly across my face.

Throwing my legs over the edge of the mattress, I was revived. Ez scooted to my side of the bed and stood up too, stretching her long arms. Together, we pulled the quilts over Mama, who moaned in her sleep and rubbed her cheek back and forth against the pillow, which perhaps, in her dream, was my father's breathing, unbroken chest.

· · ·

EZRA BREWED COFFEE WHILE I checked on the sunny squares of cornbread I'd placed on a cookie sheet in the oven. Setting fresh butter on the table, I was grateful to feel Miss Irene's presence. The food she'd made for us was almost like her voice filling our kitchen. The radio played at a low volume. We strained to listen to the urgent male voice repeating the forecast: impending blizzard with expected loss of electricity along the coast.

"The fire is good," said my sister.

"Plenty of food," I said. "I have flashlights by the front door."

"If the pipes freeze, we can bring in some of the snow and boil it."

"I've got matches right there," I said, pointing over at the rectangular box with its coarse strip pasted along the edge.

"We'll be fine until Mr. Caesar returns," said Ezra. "There are extra batteries in the drawer, so we'll have the radio for company. We have what we need. Later, we'll go out and shovel, as much as we can. We can salt the front steps and the path. We can salt the back steps too, if they freeze. . . ."

Her words trailed off. We were both thinking of Daddy. Instead of giving up, we were trying to do what Daddy would've wanted us to. I remembered hearing other people speak of the dead this way, as if the dead still had a say, as if the voices of the dead could be heard and heeded from the darkness.

"She'll probably sleep through the worst of it," Ezra said. "Maybe we should give her hot milk instead of tea. That might be better with the cornbread so that she's not wide awake."

"All right," I agreed, kneeling at the cabinet next to the stove to find the beloved, dented pot we used to warm milk or soup. I measured out a little more than a cup so that I could have some of the milk too.

"But what if we have to leave?"

"Leave what?" Ez said, focusing on the coffee.

"Salt Point," I said. "What if the deputy tries to run us out of our home?"

"This is a little old trifling place," my sister said. "They can't run us anywhere unless we let them. Colored folks are standing up all over this nation. Did you forget that? Protesting, putting their lives on the line for the right not to be run off from what we built with our sweat and blood. We're running *into* power not *away* from it. Black people can't wait another minute for white folks to arm us with a freedom they've never wanted us to have. And you know what? Miss Irene says they don't even *have* freedom, not *real* freedom without us. We have the will. We are the deed. White people have debts to pay, not us. So what if we can't graduate from that silly school. We're old enough to teach ourselves. Don't forget that we're sitting on the best library for miles and miles. Daddy made it for us. His books are right here. We can be our own teachers. We can see our lives for ourselves. They don't want us to be the heroes in their stories? We have our own land here. Our own story. Might be better this way."

She was so sure of our fate, but I felt ill. Briefly, I thought again of how Miss Burden had drowned and how the world—or fate—had burned my father alive. The people in my life who had seemed to be the smartest were dead. I didn't want to be my own teacher. I worried that this meant that I wasn't as strong as my sister, and that if she got herself free, she might leave me behind.

"Might be better this way," said Ez again, touching my hand that held the spoon.

The milk would burn if I didn't keep stirring it. I nodded at her words, wondering how I'd ever be able to hold my father's books in my hands without falling apart, let alone learn from them.

. . .

INSIDE DADDY'S STUDY, BRUSHED LIGHT marbled his silent books. The hands on my father's clock struck noon. Mama said that the dead of Damascus are always put back at twelve. I tried to imagine Daddy's grave being filled in a tiny town I've never seen. The people in Damascus would etch his full name into blue stone, where it would live with his bones amongst the graves of his ancestors, and mine.

. . .

IN THE LIVING ROOM, MY sister's piano playing went silent. She was no longer distracting herself with complicated chords. She was screaming.

I rushed to the front of our house, where the front door was open. Cold air shoved me back as I went towards a figure silhouetted against daylight. For a moment, I thought it was our father. But then Mama was rushing down the stairs past me, and she and Ezra were pulling the shadow inside our house because they recognized that it was Ernest Junkett who was standing in the center of our living room, unable to open his left eye or his lips. I could smell his terror beneath the scent of snow.

"What's happened," Mama said.

"Momma," he said finally.

"Irene?" said Mama.

"Jesus," he said. "Momma."

"Where are the children?"

Sobbing, Ernest shook his head and pressed the bottoms of his palms against his mouth. My mother wrapped her arms around him as best she could so that he wouldn't fall. Her voice was clear, her own pain escorted away, out of her eyes and mouth. "Ernest. Where? Are? The? Children?"

"Deputy pull up talking 'bout Ruby's daddy saying she'd been kidnapped. Had Ruby's daddy in the truck too."

"Wasn't it the police car?"

"No, ma'am," Ernest said. "They was in a truck. The one from school my daddy use for his work errands and such. Came into the house talking about Daddy taking Ruby. When we said Daddy wasn't with us, they said it was because he'd taken that girl somewhere and done God knows what." He paused for a moment, shaking, as though he didn't want to say it in front of us. "I tried to tell them that Daddy left out yesterday with Mr. Kindred to bury him proper, but they say they had the right version of the story," he said bitterly. "It don't make sense 'cause the deputy ought to know that his uncle's got Ruby. It's like that don't even matter 'cause the man kept saying he was going to help get her back. And Ruby's daddy ain't right at all. Eyes was all messed up drunk and crazy. Deputy talking about we didn't have the right to leave the village with Mr. Kindred's body. Talking about paperwork and outstanding fines and the death certificate not being signed. Momma told him they didn't own Mr. Kindred's dead body. Said something about us not being slaves to pigs. When she said that, deputy hit Momma hard."

"No," said Ezra.

He gulped more air. "Momma got up like she been hit worse in her life. Said we didn't know nothing about Ruby's whereabouts.

Then Mr. Scaggs started ranting something awful. Calling us niggers, saying he was going to kill all of us, that killing all of us wouldn't come close to what Ruby was worth."

Mama sat down quickly in Daddy's armchair.

"Momma took out her machete and I had Daddy's gun—but I ain't never really shot no gun before and—"

Ezra buried her face in his sleeve. I could feel myself floating away, rising up to the ceiling.

"They grabbed Lindy. Deputy put his pistol to her head. Said that if Momma didn't go with them, he'd blow my sister's head off right there in front of us." Ernest's voice was almost a whisper. "So Momma put the machete on the table. I put the gun down. Soon as I done that, Deputy snatched it away, talking about it was going to be real good evidence if Ruby don't show up safe. Took my daddy's gun and beat me in my face hard as he could 'til Momma began screaming that she'd go with them if they'd just leave us alone. They went off then, dragging Momma. Put her in they truck."

"Where were they going?"

Ernest's face shone with new tears. He shrugged like a little boy. It was hard to look at his face without thinking of what the deputy had done to us when he'd stormed into our house, ripping away the shroud from my father's face.

Ezra lifted her head. "She keeps a gun in her pocket. They don't know that."

"Yeah," said Ernest. "But it's two of them. She by herself."

"She's a good shot," said Ezra.

"I left my brother and sisters in the house."

"You drove here like that?"

"Yes, ma'am."

"I don't want you driving anywhere else. Your eye looks bad, honey. I don't want you to lose it. Let me stitch it up with some thread. Cinthy, bring my bag with the peroxide. Soon as the storm's calm, we'll get you over to Gunn Hill General. I was expecting Caesar to return by nightfall, but this weather could change everything."

"What about Miss Irene?" said Ezra. "What about her, Mama? What will they—"

"Oh, Ezra, we can't—we can't go after her. Irene's on her own," said Mama. "God isn't going to drop her down. Irene will prevail. It isn't her time.

"All I can do is what she'd want me to do, which is take care of her babies. We can't do more than that right now."

"That isn't enough," said Ezra, folding her arms against her chest. Mama took Ernest by the arm.

"Cinthy, you're going to have to drive Ernest back into the village. Right now, I don't trust your sister to obey me."

"*Drive?*"

"You can do it," Ezra said before I could say another word. "Get them back here before the snow gets worse."

"It *is* worse."

"I'll tell you what to do," said Ernest. His voice was both desperate and determined. "Because if I have to crawl back to town by myself, I will. Empire and Rosemary can't walk far in this cold. Lindy, I don't know. They was crying bad, didn't even want me to leave in the first place. But I told them to hide in our house and wait for me. I didn't know if that deputy would trap me somehow if he saw me on the road. Thought it'd be better if I was alone. I said I'd come back for them. By the time those men come back, I'm going to be there. My daddy told me what to do."

"Lord have mercy, I need to make some calls," said Mama. "The pastor at Rising Star. Ernest, do you have his number?"

Ezra's teeth fastened against her tongue in a loud kiss. "*Calls, Mama? That's it?*"

"Girl, you better use your common sense talking to me in that tone."

The skin on Mama's face stretched into a mask. "Irene's going to make it. We have to be ready for whatever she needs, what these children need. Do you understand me, Ezra? Don't let your mind go off into the wild. We need you here.

"Soon as I get this boy fixed up," continued Mama, whipping her body around so that she was staring into my eyes, "you need to be ready to go. Steady yourself, Cinthy. You girls get outside. Salt the road. Dig out the car. Snow's still light so it won't take you long. We have to use our wits. No telling what we'll have to do by the time it gets dark."

"We'll be sitting ducks by dark," said Ezra.

"Enough!" Mama's voice was a hiss as she guided Ernest into the kitchen.

Ezra gazed at me, concentrating as she stared at my face. Each of her eyes was a hive. "In the Bible there are hunters," my sister said, the bees beneath her eyelids breaking free.

· · ·

I COULD SMELL MY FATHER in the wool of his sweater, which I wore beneath a large fisherman's coat that had also belonged to him. I felt Daddy wrapped around my body, his scent my talisman. Most of my hair was shoved inside one of Mama's knitted wool caps, but beads of snow mixed with sweat pearled my hairline, my edges, and the nape of my neck where the cap kept lifting.

Against frigid gusts, I stabbed the blank snow with the rusted bow of our shovel. Panting, I circled and circled the car, attacking the grainy, pristine dunes. Wearing gloves prevented me from gripping the handle properly so I pulled them off. My palms were quickly raw, blistered. The knees of my jeans were wet and cold. Water had seeped into my yellow rubber boots. The loss of sensation in my feet forced me to walk on what felt like two frozen stumps. Fear kept my stomach and bladder in a tight ball. I tried to keep my head up, resisting panic. *Do as Mama told me to do. Shovel the car out of the snow. Drive the car. Do as Mama told me. Shovel the car out of the snow. Drive the car.*

With watering eyes, I kept the shovel moving. The wind caught my memories of my father's voice, lifted the elegy of his breath into strands of lonesome clouds. *Keep going, Cinthy-girl. Keep going on.* When I finally dropped the shovel, I gazed at the land which had dissolved into a battlefield of banked white hills. Across from our home, stunning in its destruction, was the haunted house, squat and black even through the snow, with Ezra walking out of it towards me.

I hadn't seen her leave the house and wondered how she could've had any time to go poking around across the road when Mama had given us her orders.

"Get in the car," she said to me.

"What?"

But she'd already gone around to the passenger side without replying to my question. My fingers were numb as I fumbled with the chrome handle. When I finally managed to get it open and sink myself into the driver's seat, I couldn't help but think of Daddy again. Outside the car, the wind howled while inside the quiet was odd. Our breathing made little clouds that dissolved quickly. Ezra offered me the key. Dull and familiar, it sat on her palm and was warm to my touch.

"Get some heat going in here already," she said, rearranging herself so that there was some space between us.

We were silent as the car sputtered to life. I couldn't bear to look at the back seat and remember how Mr. Caesar had arrived at our house with Daddy's burned body wrapped in tarp.

"Don't think about that," ordered my sister. "I need to talk to you, but I have to make sure you're listening. At any given moment of your life, I've watched you walk around with a hundred miles of thinking going on in that head of yours, but right now I need you to be here with me. Can you do that, Cinthy?"

Nodding, I blew my breath on my fingers. My face was hot. I didn't want her to be angry with me, but she was right. It was hard for me to focus, partly because of the cold, but mostly because of the blizzard of memories that seemed intent on blowing me away.

"I'm going to find Miss Irene," said my sister. Then she removed the gun Miss Irene had given our mother from her coat. She held it with her fingers firmly against her lap. I began to shake, feeling that Ezra's new womanhood had taken her, and us, hostage.

"Mama said—"

"I don't give a good goddamn *what* she said," said Ezra. "I asked you to *listen* and right away you want to talk about what Mama said. Can't I trust you?"

"Yes," I said immediately, though my eyes were on the gun. Like my father's death, its awful silence filled the car.

"You know I love you more than anything, don't you?"

"What?"

"Love, Cinthy," she said. "I need to know you know me."

"I *think* I know you."

"So you know I'm not going to just sit up here in front of the fireplace while those white devils do whatever they're going to do to Miss Irene," said Ezra, returning the gun to her pocket. "I'm going out there, and I'm going to get her back. I need your help."

"How can I help you?" I asked fearfully. "How can I help you when you know what could happen?"

"I don't care what happens to me," she said. "If I have to lie, I'll lie. If I have to kill, I'll kill. If I freeze, I'll freeze. But I'm going to bring Miss Irene home. She's our mother too."

"You'd kill?"

"And quick."

"You know Miss Irene is grown like Mama said," I told her. "You could *die*. She can take care of herself, Ez. She's not going to let them win."

"Winning has nothing to do with this," said Ezra. "This is about *living*, not dying. All this talking we do, all this learning we say will help. All this mess about defending and protecting ideas that we can't even see because we can barely see each other without being afraid and mad most of the time. Miss Irene has survived a lot and I'm not about to let that cop or Ruby's father take Miss Irene from us. I just can't sit here and cry and pray. I'm not saying my way of being is better but it's the best thing for me because I chose it, for *me*. I'm about *doing*. Because that's living to me."

"Oh," I said, nodding my head as if I knew exactly what she meant. "Do you think Miss Irene would want you to do that? She's always telling us to hold our souls up in the light. What will happen to yours?"

"I don't want to say much more," said Ezra. "The less I tell you the better." Then she took my hand and pressed it against her face before she guided it to the wheel, squeezing my fingers into position so that I was gripping it.

"You can do this," she said. "Daddy will show you how."

24

MAMA AND ERNEST REARRANGED DADDY'S STUDY BECAUSE IT WAS THE only room in our home that would allow the Junkett children to sleep together. Ernest devoted himself to Mama, striding back and forth, insisting that he do the lifting of Daddy's furniture by himself. Earlier, it was his adrenaline that had guided me at the wheel to the outskirts of our village, using rough back roads to reach the Junketts' house. Ernest and Lindy had carried Empire and Rosemary out into the cold, placing them in the back seat of our car while I shivered behind the wheel keeping watch. Should any car approach the house, Ernest had ordered me to immediately drive away.

Now, up and down the back staircase, Ezra carried quilts, sheets, and extra pillows to Daddy's study. Her face was a stony mask. Whenever I tried to say anything to her, she only looked at my own face as though she was intent on memorizing it. As nervous as I felt, we both knew I wouldn't say anything to Mama. What could I say really; Mama was using all of her strength to take care of the small children who seemed nearly oblivious to the dangers rising around us.

In the kitchen, Lindy and I poured hot chocolate into the children's mugs, careful to fill the cups only halfway. They brought their sweet faces towards the steam, listening intently to the music they'd been allowed to choose on the radio. In the low light of our kitchen, I could see both of their parents in their faces. It made my eyes ache.

"Lindy," I called out softly.

She raised herself out of her thoughts to take me in, eyed the plate of cornbread in my hand, which was extended to her, and shook her head.

"I won't eat nothing 'til Momma's here," she said. "Nothing."

I understood that her refusal to eat something she really loved was part of her private sacrifice, her prayer to have her mother returned safely. If God would only deliver her mother, she would allow herself comfort.

"Once they've got it set up, we can spread out the quilts. Get the room warm," she said automatically. "Momma will be coming back from the cold. It was cold when they took her."

I couldn't, and did not want to, picture Ernest's description of how Miss Irene had stumbled through the front door of her own house, dragged by her hair through the snow, before being flung into a truck by those white men. But looking at Lindy's face, I could see that she was replaying it over and over.

When I came into my father's study with the last of the pillows, I pressed my hand hard against my stomach. I hadn't prepared myself for Daddy's room to be deconstructed yet.

Quilts had been piled, to insulate the room from the drafty doors. Daddy's worktable was placed like a barricade against one set of glass doors. His desk was pushed far into a corner. On the floor, there was the rectangular outline, like a door or grave traced on the ground, where his desk had sunk into the floorboards after being unmoved for years.

"Nothing's been thrown out," said Mama, looking over at me. She was panting lightly as she swept and tidied. "It's just been moved around. Please don't look that way, Cinthy."

I nodded, backing away.

"Tell Ezra we need those quilts. Get the ones from my bed too. I'll sleep on the twin in her room. Ernest and I can drag the big mattress down once I get up this dust. Mr. Caesar should arrive before midnight. He'll be tired, hungry."

"Yes, Mama."

"Have Lindy put a plate together and leave it covered on the stove. Then help your sister. Those quilts are heavy. Don't have them dragging on the floor either."

"Yes, Mama."

She bent down again to roll up one of Daddy's thin rugs into a tube. When she stood up, her words were bright and hot from the firelight, and she put her hand on her hip. "Girl, if you don't go get those quilts like I told you!"

I spun away, dashing through the kitchen and up the back staircase. In the little stairwell, I stopped so that I could push the tears away with the sides of my hands. But there was nothing I could do to keep the vomit down, so I ran, holding its sour taste against my teeth until I got to the bathroom, where I dropped to my knees at the basin of the toilet I shared with Ezra.

Chunks of cornbread and clots of butter caught in my throat. I wrapped my arms around my knees, folding myself into a ball.

Mama was wrong and right.

Everything I once knew had been thrown away, had been moved from its usual place. Everything was heavy, yes. Being smart could kill you, could drown you, could get you burned alive for no discernible reason. Some kinds of intelligence could make you sick with cancer from the inside. The world could make you believe that it knew who you were before you did. The flames of death could make you a hero. Loving yourself could mean a white man, in the name of the law, might drag you out of your own house in the view of your own family. Nothing and nobody could save you.

After rinsing my mouth and face, I went into my own room only to find myself greeted by a flat, freezing palm of icy air. My bedroom window was open. It could've only been unlocked by someone inside our house.

Dark spots appeared at the corners of my vision. My heart

climbed the slimy well of my body. Breathing deeply, I looked around
my room before walking into our hallway where I flicked on the electric overhead light.

I tried to mouth her name, a single word. The shock rose through
me like water in a sinking ship.

It would only be a matter of time before Mama would call for
Ezra and expect her to appear. I didn't want to think of what would
happen in that instance, whether I'd be silent about what I knew or
pretend to be as surprised as Mama would be when she realized that
Ezra had snuck away. Even if Mama interrogated me, there was no
way I'd tell her the entire truth, which was that Ezra was ready to
kill a white man if it meant Miss Irene's safety. Terror filled me as I
tried not to think of what was also possible, which was that my sister
could be killed by one of these men. Gathering the quilts as carefully
as Mama had instructed, barely able to see over the lumpy heap, I
stepped numbly down the back staircase into our kitchen.

Lindy was seated at the table with Empire and Rosemary. She
looked at me strangely as I rushed by her, afraid that she might ask
me about Ezra's whereabouts.

I took another breath before my body pushed me to the entrance
of Daddy's study. In the doorway, I was silent as I watched Ernest
lean over my mother, pressing some sort of compress across her
brow. When she saw me watching, Mama pulled her handkerchief
away from her mouth. Her lips and teeth were stained with blood.

"Didn't I tell you and your sister—"

"I'm going to go back and get the rest right now," I said. "This was
all I could carry by myself."

Mama coughed again, her body shaking. She closed her eyes as
her breath racked her body. Slowly, she wiped her mouth again with
the cloth. Her eyes were still closed. "Why isn't Ezra helping you?"

Ernest stared at me. Had I said the truth aloud? No, no, I spoke
as calmly as I could, making my voice mimic the way I'd heard adults
sound when they had very bad news that they weren't prepared to share
with their children. "We have a system," I said. "It's easier this way."

I waited for Mama to reply, which she did after some time. Instead of looking at me, Mama stared at the red mouth of the stove and then lowered her eyes to the cloth crumpled between her clenched fingers. Her gaze studied the scarlet language blooming and drying in stains on her handkerchief.

"You know I know when you lie to me."

I decided I'd risk whatever voice I had left to protect Ezra. But the lie broke my heart.

"Mama, I wouldn't do that to you."

. . .

ERNEST APPEARED IN THE DOORWAY of my sister's bedroom while I was sitting on one of her twin beds and staring at the floor. Mama was down in the kitchen. I could smell food cooking. The radio was turned to a news program and for the first time in a very long time I knew that Mama wouldn't run off inside her heart with Sam Cooke and her whisky. She wasn't furious with me because she didn't yet know what I knew—Ezra, her elder daughter, was out, and armed, in a thick storm of ice and vengeance. Downstairs, I could barely lift a glass or plate without shaking, so I was hiding out up here.

The small lamp on Ezra's nightstand gave off its girlish, coral-colored light. I hadn't turned it off because I worried that if Mama came upstairs, it would've been strange to walk past the dark bedroom. Mama probably thought my sister was sulking over what we hadn't done to help Miss Irene. She didn't have strength to deal with Ezra.

"Where is she?"

I shrugged at his voice, wrapping my arms around my torso so that he wouldn't see me shaking, but the thing about Ernest was that he had two sisters of his own. Pulling the door nearly closed, he came into the room and sat down on the bed next to me.

"You knew she'd run off to help Momma, didn't you?" He stood and walked to Ezra's closet, which I'd left open while I was gathering the quilts for the study. Wiping away anxious tears, I watched him fingering the fabrics of my sister's dresses, sweaters. He peered at the mirrored tray on Ezra's vanity. After a moment, he lifted the seashell he'd given her. He didn't seem as goofy to me as he had before. His tenderness made my face flush. He loved her.

"We was going to rescue Momma together when y'all went to bed. Guess she went on without me."

"I'm not telling you anything."

The hurt on his face made me feel sorry for him. I knew that Ezra cared deeply about Ernest. He was part of Miss Irene, and Ezra loved Miss Irene. Whether she might love him the way Daddy and Mama loved each other was another thing. Still, if Ernest knew what I knew, perhaps he could help Ezra and Miss Irene return to us, safe.

He repeated himself. "She went on without me when she told me we'd go together. She didn't wait."

"You know she couldn't tell you what she was going to really do," I said.

"What you mean?"

"Ezra knows all the secrets in this place. Well, enough of them," I said, trying to soften my voice. "You'd be in more danger than she would. Ez knows that. You're a Black man. The deputy would've aimed at you first."

"At least she wouldn't be out there by herself. Anything could get her."

"Yes," I said. "But Ezra isn't alone. She's like your mother that way. Miss Irene said she's surrounded by her ancestors and a fatal amount of common sense. Miss Irene has faith that's natural. Can't be taught. Remember what my mama said about Miss Irene? God's not going to drop her down. Well, maybe Ez learned that from her. Don't worry about my sister."

"What we could do is get in the car and go looking."

"It's dark," I said. "With this weather, we'd sail right off a cliff."

"We need light," he said, almost to himself.

"You know as well as I do if Deputy Charlie were to catch us alone out on these roads . . ." I paused. "Well, us sailing off a cliff into the sea would be better."

"She's already dead," he said, "if she's gone after that cop."

"It wasn't him she had in mind," I said.

"What the hell are you talking about?" Sighing when he realized I wasn't going to say anything else, Ernest closed the door of Ezra's closet, then walked over to her desk. Lifting a framed photograph, he brought it close to his face as though my sister might tell him what to do next.

It was a snapshot of our family. Daddy clasped me on his lap while Ez leaned against Mama's arms, my sister's mouth spread in a laugh. It'd been taken so long ago that Mama said I wasn't walking yet. Daddy had carried me everywhere. A dreamy flare of sunlight blotted out any background of where we were, and Mama said she couldn't remember where it was taken. Daddy said it didn't matter, that all that mattered was that we were clearly happy.

"Man, y'all was beautiful," Ernest said.

"From a long time ago," I said.

. . .

WITH MY POKER, I BANKED the fire, tossing corkscrews of newspaper into the pit. I realized that I was burning the last newspapers my father had ever read. The papers had always been so meaningful to him and now he would not ever need their news. Then I pressed the edge of the quilt around the curve of Mama's chin—she'd fallen asleep on our living room couch—and sat in Ezra's usual spot next to her.

Ernest sat in Daddy's armchair with his arms folded across his chest. Even though his eyes were closed I knew he was awake and listening.

In this late hour, long and empty as an outstretched palm, we waited for the return of our families. We listened to the stinginess of time passing in that unforgiving darkness.

I tried to inhabit my sister's perspective but found myself shut out by her innate privacy. Though I knew Ezra loved me, I recalled how lonely I could sometimes feel even as I walked next to her.

In my mind, I conjured the village under veils of snow. She could be anywhere—the lighthouse, the school, the woods, or out on the bluffs. I wouldn't have been surprised if I walked across our road and discovered her, squatting and armed, in the frozen air of the ruined house.

It was that wildness in my sister that had convinced her she could rescue Miss Irene from white authority. Guided for so many years by Miss Irene's own radical beliefs, Ezra wouldn't take the manners, fantasies, or systems of white people into any serious account. Especially when Negro women were involved. Miss Irene belonged to us, and always would be ours, as much as we belonged to ourselves.

· · ·

WHEN I NEXT OPENED MY eyes, Mama was walking into the living room. Placing a finger on her lips, she pointed to Ernest, who was snoring. I got up and followed my mother into the kitchen. She'd put on a pot of coffee and a kettle for tea.

"That was Mr. Caesar on the phone," she said, pushing her hair out of her face. Her eyes focused on the kettle as though it could do more than boil water. "The storm's delayed his return."

"Did you tell him about Miss Irene?"

"I didn't need to tell him," said Mama. "He could hear it in my voice. He's going to get some of the men together from Gunn Hill. They'll find her. Some of them are on their way here. They have a sort of secret society of men at Rising Star that handle these kinds of matters. They take justice into their own hands."

"What about the police in Gunn Hill, Mama? They can't all be like Deputy Charlie."

"They're worse," said my mother. "Everyone in the county knows their kind of justice. Do you understand me?"

"Yes, Mama."

"Your daddy and I wanted to keep all of that away from you and your sister," she said, pouring steaming water into my cup over one of her homemade tea bags. "Yet here we are."

· · ·

MAMA WAS ON HER SECOND cup of coffee when the doorbell rang. Her eyes lifted quickly without focus as if she'd been shaken suddenly from a deep sleep. I gripped my hands around my lukewarm mug of tea. *We can't take any more,* I thought, wondering who it could be at the door. We practically lived at the end of the world. I got up and followed after Mama, remembering that part of my responsibility was to take care of her.

· · ·

THE COLD CAME IN AGAIN like a landlord, its icy fingers open against my face as I pushed the door shut against the wind. Locking the door, I tried to breathe deeply. My heart was like a metal box in my chest.

In the living room, Mama and Miss Irene held each other. The kind of cold that came off of Miss Irene's body made me wonder if she was actually a ghost. But when she let go of Mama and pulled me against her, I felt her warm tears and the heart in her chest.

Mama ordered me upstairs to get fresh clothes and towels. "Don't wake up the children," she said to me in a shallow breath. But it was too late.

The twins rushed into the room, with Lindy and Ernest behind them. Lindy's body shook as she, Ernest, and the twins sank to the floor around their mother, covering her in the blaze of their love. Inside the quilts, Miss Irene whispered their names while they wept. Her face was scratched and cut, from what looked like branches; and the exposure to the elements had battered her.

"What happened, Irene?"

"They tried to scare me," she said to Mama. "They couldn't."

"Do you need a doctor? Caesar's got some men from the church who say they'll try to get here as soon as they can. Storm's picked up now."

"I'm all right," said Miss Irene. "They took me for a drive. Down to the lighthouse. The cowards threw me out on the side of the road."

"You could've died," said Lindy, crying hard.

"But I didn't," said Miss Irene, kissing her. "When I got to our house and found it empty, I knew where you were. I had to get here to you all. And I did. Ancestors carried me."

"Oh, Irene," Mama said, covering her mouth. She was pale.

"I got to get this chill out of me."

Lindy leapt up, pulling me with her. "C'mon, girl! Help me get the towels, the clothes. We need hot water."

"I'll get the ointment too. Bandages," I said. "I can warm the soup."

"*Cinthy!*"

Miss Irene's voice was low but like a steady arrow. The twins were in her arms. Their eyes were sleepy. I was glad that maybe they'd grow up with none of these memories. Dropping my hand, Lindy stopped a few steps ahead of me.

"*Cinthy*," Miss Irene repeated, pushing herself up, "where is your sister?" Her unblinking eyes flashed at me from their dark lids. "*Where is Ezra?*"

Her voice cracked in fury as she spoke Ezra's name. The light from the flames dancing on the wall grew as if under her command.

"She wanted to save you," I whispered. "She said that she could."

25

EZRA RACED THROUGH THE BARE TREES TO THE BLUFFS. THE BLOOD IN her veins shoved the cold winds from her skin. Her mind was a fist. She wouldn't let herself think of her father, who wouldn't have understood what she was going to do. He was a gentle man, averse to retribution, repulsed by rage. She'd often wondered whether she'd been born into the wrong family. This wasn't a questioning of her love for her parents and her sister, but an inner recognition of who she really was. Ezra would never be the kind of woman who turned the other cheek or agreed to suffer the world's dismissal of her existence. She *existed,* needing no affirmation from her teachers, the villagers, or even her family. Ezra knew it was strange, but it was a truth that she was prepared to defend with all her strength, with her very life. Perhaps this was the thing that had bound her to Ruby Scaggs and was, also, the very thing that had made her pull violently away from Ruby when she slowly realized that the paths of their lives were barely parallel, and certainly not identical. She had seen it herself the day she, Cinthy, and Ruby sat up, blinking in the light, staring at one another in silence. Ezra had tried to ignore the contradictory things between herself and Ruby—it was Ruby who was poor, who ate from Ezra's family's garbage, whose parents treated her with something that was worse than negligence or abandonment. Ruby sometimes said there was a mix-up—*she* was the one who should've had Ezra's life, which was closer to the life young white girls were expected to receive: nurturing, attention, and protection. Ruby's general opinions about freedom, Negroes, and friendship were more ignorant and dangerous than Ezra had realized, until they began to bleed like women.

Ezra resented her parents' insistence on keeping silence at the center of their home, acknowledging that their lives were peripheral in relationship to the village. They didn't want to attract notice from the village, yet Ezra wondered how they could've ever thought that they had power in maintaining their invisibility. She resented the need in their house for an education that Ezra felt had enslaved her dear father. She'd detested those dusty books, aware that their authors were white people who assumed Negroes were mostly illiterate.

Ezra stood in the clearing, trying to make out Ruby's shack through the thick veil of snow blowing wildly all around her. The dark reddish hair on her head was plastered to her skull. Her heavy coat was soaked, nearly pulling her to the ground. Her freezing fingers touched her pocket. She thought of Miss Irene, who'd always seemed to be her soul mother. Miss Irene had taught her how to love herself, to defend what she loved, and to go towards good and evil with a warrior's courage.

There was evil in front of her now. She couldn't stop thinking of Ernest's description of the deputy knocking Miss Irene to the ground and dragging her out of her own house. Had he or Mr. Scaggs killed her? This possibility was as unbearable to Ezra as the death of her father. Ezra needed to feel that she had the power to change what her father or mother would have quietly accepted as fate. Ezra was prepared to shoot Fate between its blue eyes.

She would demand that Ruby's father tell her where Miss Irene was and what they'd done to her. Stumbling forward through drifts of snow, Ezra pictured her father's shrouded head and the smell of Miss Irene's Egyptian hair oil when she'd hugged Ezra, reminding her that God would keep them safe. Ezra would take God into her own hands.

She saw low candlelight through one of the windows. Trembling, she remembered all those days she and Ruby had spent playing in this mud-packed yard. Ruby intended to float away on a large boat to a new life without looking back. She could become anyone, maybe even herself. Ezra knew Ruby would never return to Salt Point. And neither would she, not with what Ezra was prepared to do if Ruby's father said the wrong thing. She thought of the man, with his sad eyes, and how Ruby spoke of loving him in spite of what he was.

Miss Irene had helped Ezra understand that there would always be differences between Ezra and Ruby. Sitting in Miss Irene's kitchen, hearing stories of how she was raised in Royal, how the liberation of Black people could only be achieved by Black people and green money, and how Ruby would change, whether she wanted to or not, Ezra was filled with feelings she knew she couldn't share with anyone, not even Cinthy. Her sister was too sensitive, too young in spite of her old eyes, too concerned with a kind of obedience that Ezra had never understood.

She heard the distant whine of hounds somewhere behind the shack. Her blood pounded in her ears as she went up the snow-covered steps.

He was there. Staggering back and forth across the filthy floor. A film of snow blew through one of the open windows. There was an overturned trunk near the little woodstove whose intense heat surprised Ezra. She'd anticipated coming into this place and finding Miss Irene tied up or worse. Instead, it was Mr. Scaggs alone. When he turned to Ezra, she saw that half his face was opened to the bone. One whole hand was stained red. Ezra could smell the sharp scent of liquor as she looked at him tottering in pain. Her anger rose in her throat. Miss Irene must have wounded him, but had he wounded her too? Ezra gripped her pocket. There were bees in her ears, smoke in her mouth.

"*Lily?* Is that you come to see me again?"

"Where is she? What did you do to her?"

"Can't remember," he said. His mouth gurgled with blood. "I think Charlie threw her into the sea."

Ezra pulled Miss Irene's pistol out of her pocket. Her hand was steady in spite of the tremors that ran through her body.

His metal eyes flashed as he laughed at her.

"You finally going to kill me? Shit, you did that long ago."

"Who is Lily?"

Ruby's father spat blood on the floor. "You know damn well who you are. You know what I am, because you gave me this pain."

"You don't know anything about pain," said Ezra.

"Ruby put you up to this? She ain't never coming back. I seen her eyes."

"I'm not Ruby. I'm not Lily. I'm Ezra Kindred."

"Ain't you her friend? Is that who you are, come to put me in my grave?"

"I'm here about Miss Irene."

"Did you help them kidnap her? It's a crime what you done. I told that rich son-of-a-bitch I'd work to earn Ruby back. I'd be his slave. But it's too late."

"I'm not here about you or Ruby. I'm here for Miss Irene."

"That bitch tried to cut my face off," he said, dropping his hand from the deep slash along the side of his jaw. Blood dripped from his fingertips to the floor. He spoke softly. "Shoot me in my heart, Lily, so I won't see the truth no more.

"I always thought I'd die by my daughter's hand. I was just fine with that. I put my hands on Ruby's dreams, put my fists through her, and Christ if she didn't keep telling me she still loved me, until she didn't. Ain't that something? See, I wasn't like my daddy or my grand-daddy. All my life I been punished for not following in their fucking footsteps. Didn't want granddaddy's evil to pay for my life. Tried my best to take myself out of the family's fate, but everything I tried to earn on my own fell apart. It's easy for a man to become nothing, easier than people think. Everything I told myself I was going to be melted in my mouth before I could taste it. Couldn't never be my own man 'cause everywhere I gone and everything I tried to do—it was all the same."

"You watched him throw her into the *sea*," said Ezra, taking a step closer. "You did nothing. Because you are nothing. Do you know what you deserve?"

"Lily, do you remember that Sunday? On the sidewalk? Sweet Jesus, that silence of yours and how you knew it would insult me. I could've killed you and we both knew it. They'd have thrown you atop the ashes of that other nigger, but I kept our secret. I couldn't ever confess how much I needed you. Why did you make me remember what I was?"

Suddenly, he whipped his body around like a belt. Mr. Scaggs held a gun of his own. His other hand was a red, dripping fist.

Ezra drew back, screaming. As she covered her face, she saw that instead of firing at her, Ruby's father had pulled the trigger of his gun inside his own mouth.

The room filled with silver dust, the odor of blood, the stink of gunpowder.

In terror, Ezra folded to the ground, shaking. She'd walked alone through this blizzard, convinced she had the power to end a white man's life. But she hadn't. He'd taken that power for himself. Dropping Miss Irene's pistol to the floor, she looked down at her hands as if she'd held them above a hot flame too long. She thought of how sheltered the life she and her sister lived had been. She was fifteen. Her parents had built a home, a dream in a world that was entirely flammable. Miss Irene was likely dead, her Daddy too, and Ezra feared her Mama wouldn't last until spring. Anger flushed her soaked clothes. Each of them had shown her so much, yet Ezra felt it was inadequate. Life wasn't a pile of lessons folded into the heart. She felt her own spinning inside her chest. The last part of her girlhood left her, as a sweet, milky breath. She wondered if that was her soul.

Ezra crawled across the room to Ruby's father. His mouth was a spattered hole. As she leaned over his body, she saw Ruby's eyes, their blond lashes tipped in blood. His darkened gaze stared silently at something above her head, as if he'd finally witnessed something fair, a fate that belonged only to him. He'd done a thing by himself. Jonah Reuben Scaggs III could turn away from his past having brought himself to justice. Haunted by his life, he could go elsewhere, into his future perhaps. His dead eyes brightened with the thought of a long journey.

THREE

———

26

IT WAS SUMMER AGAIN—JULY.

Despite living with Ginny for the past six months, Mama and I weren't used to her ways. Damascus bewildered us in the rare moments it was able to puncture our long hours of despair. Most of the time, I thought of Ezra's new life, which was far from us in Royal with the Junkett family.

After Mr. Scaggs's suicide, Mr. Caesar, Miss Irene, and Mama decided we could no longer fool ourselves into believing that Salt Point meant us no harm. They'd worried that Miss Irene's pistol would be discovered by the deputy whenever they found Ruby's father.

But by then, we would all be long gone. Mr. Caesar convinced Mama that we should split up, to keep Ezra safe. She'd go to Royal with their family, while Mama and I traveled to Damascus to stay with Ginny.

Every two weeks since January, Mr. Caesar had phoned my grandmother's house to speak with Mama. He called her from different towns, just to be safe. He'd discouraged us from writing letters or leaving any possible trail for the authorities to trace. He told us that Ezra missed us, that she was growing rapidly in height and consciousness, and that she rarely complained of anything. Ernest had decided to apply for college and Miss Irene was making quilts and could barely keep up with the amount of orders she received. She was teaching Ezra how to use her own hands, to keep herself busy with thread and needle, with kneading bread and washing greens.

I couldn't forget that evening when Ezra returned to us, assuming that Miss Irene had been killed. When she came in, shivering, she was shocked by the sight of Miss Irene standing to open her arms. Ezra ran, weeping, to the woman, nearly knocking her over as they embraced. We all wept then, as Ezra described how she'd barely been able to make it home in the storm. Then we wept harder when Ezra told us how Ruby's father had swallowed the mercy of his own gun. Though I said nothing to anyone, I wondered if there was any meaning to the fact that we'd lost our daddy and Ruby had lost hers too.

· · ·

MY BIRTHDAY, WHICH WAS IN May, meant that I was now fourteen years old, the same age Mama was when the Daughters dropped her back in Damascus. I tried to imagine Mama as a young girl, walking around this place. Already, I'd spent many afternoons along the backwards river, and had watched its thaw in spring.

One sunlit day, when the ground was sweet-tempered again, Ginny drove Mama and me to Hinder Me Not so that we could place flowers on Daddy's grave, a deep blue headstone that held his full name—*Heron Theodore Kindred*—as Mama had wanted. The first time I saw his name on that rock was bludgeoning.

Something in my spirit fell with a thud and wouldn't get up. After that, I began to do most of my talking inside my head. There was no one else listening to me anyway.

By the beginning of June, Ginny ordered me to stop walking over to Hinder Me Not and sitting in the graveyard like I wasn't flesh and blood. "You ain't nowhere near your six-feet, little sister," she'd said. "Don't let me hear somebody else say they seen you over in that cemetery neither. Remember, your daddy's bones might be there but his soul ain't. His soul is in you and in your mama upstairs, fighting for her life. His soul is in your sister too, wherever she is."

In spite of the warming weather that usually made me happy, my heart grieved. I couldn't stand the sunlight for too long without feeling sick inside. The edges of my immediate memories of Salt Point had begun to curl like the family photographs I'd ripped out of our albums when Mama had ordered me to pack as many of our things as we could fit in the car.

Though it had been months since we fled Salt Point, I still had a tendency to take on the traits of a fugitive. I was fearful of speaking too much in front of anyone. I had terror-drenched nightmares of Deputy Charlie or other white men finding Ezra in Royal and harming her and the Junkett family. But to our knowledge, the authorities weren't searching for us.

We'll go back when it's safe, Mama said often when we first arrived.

But that was a lie.

I'd known it even as I filled suitcases with our belongings.

My days in Damascus were occupied with unanswerable questions and memories while Mama faded upstairs in a room, her head barely leaving its dent on the pillows. Mama was sometimes so still in her bed that Ginny kept a small mirror on the nightstand to check my mother's breathing.

So I spent as much time as I could on the porch.

When July came, the heat made the air in Damascus waver as though it were combustible. The flies dove at my face, and I flicked mosquitoes away until I was too hot to be bothered if they covered my arms and legs with bites. Around my grandmother's porch katydids and crickets filled the air with chirping. Butterflies circled large vases of wildflowers on my grandmother's porch. When a dragonfly hovered, I'd look up from my stupor and marvel at it, remembering how my father loved to watch them. There was a collection of assorted bottles, all blue, because Ginny liked what the bottles did in rainstorms, or when a simple breeze fluted its breath over those glass rims. These ordinary objects became an orchestra of sublime instruments that brought colors alive in my head. Inside my grandmother's house there was no room that did not have a wall or ceiling painted some shade of blue.

Months ago, at the beginning of the new year, when I'd asked Mama why we had to go to Damascus, she spoke of her need to be put back. She couldn't ignore the voice that called her home anymore, and she'd waited too long to have the surgery the doctor had claimed might give her more time.

I too had long given up insisting things could be done to save her life.

· · ·

TODAY WAS A BAKING DAY. Ginny had pie orders to fill. Inside the house, dishes clanged and clattered in her kitchen. When I offered to help, as I had done for months now, she always rolled her eyes or said *hell no* without looking up to see the hurt on my face. Unwelcome in my grandmother's kitchen, I staked out my usual territory on the porch swing.

Rays of sunlight drew sweat along the edges of my hairline as I stretched my legs, pushing the swing back and forth. I focused on calculating how far I could go without banging the swing against the side rails, which would bring my grandmother outside, her cheeks flecked with flour, to complain and cuss. That distracted me from thinking about all the things we'd had to leave behind.

I couldn't let myself remember Ezra's last words to me before she'd climbed into the overloaded car with the Junkett family, clutching a brown hard-shelled suitcase. She was wearing Mama's green felt coat with its velvet lining. The material no longer swallowed her inside its shape. She was exactly Mama's size. It was too much. I could still feel her fingers cupping my face, my tears.

"If I don't get to you before Mama should—"

"Please stay," I cried, shaking. "Please."

"I'm always with you."

"Love you, sister," I said, feeling her warm breath on my cheek.

"Don't love your pain," said Ezra, gripping my fingers before she pulled me into her arms. She blinked away tears and smiled like summer. "This world promises us harm, and there's nothing you can do about it, except to have the nerve to love your life."

· · ·

DAMASCUS WAS VAIN. THE ENTIRE valley surrounding Ginny's house bragged of its beauty. The flowers did not tremble but beckoned the air to flush the wind with the sweetness. The green leaves on the trees gave delicious shade between hard patches of sunlight. In the mornings, before it grew too hot, the peonies were so lusty they made something tingle inside me when I inhaled them. I knew that I was close to my own time, when I would be changed from youth to young woman. I was following my sister and wished I could hear her voice. She appeared in the murmuring rustle of swaying branches. Seeds danced and seethed in the air. The land rolled its lush girth along the horizon at dawn. Beauty dried her mouth on everything it tasted.

But I craved Salt Point: that smell of the sea rubbing the rough air, and the way summer light swelled, leaving whorls of golden light inside long days. I thought of my father and my sister until my throat ached, my broken heart spinning like the chimes that tinkled from their hooks on Ginny's porch.

Over the past months, Mama's helplessness allowed me to disappear, lost in plain sight. I found myself steeping in resentment at the way so many adults seemed to tolerate pain, however high, until it became ordinary, just another clause in their acknowledgment of a world beyond one's control. My mother's eyes had the look of someone who was waiting for something final to happen to her.

27

GINNY LIVED SO FAR OUT FROM THE DOWNTOWN DISTRICT, IT WAS A long walk just to go on a simple errand. For Mama's sake, I tried to figure out how I could belong in Damascus. Back in February, Ginny had gone over to the school and told the principal I wouldn't be attending school again until next fall. In the meantime, I was to spend some part of each day reading, which was fine by me. When I tried to thank her, my grandmother only waved me away. "Abbotts don't do all that thankfulness shit. We prefer common sense. Anybody with sense can see you ain't in no shape to be sitting in nobody's classroom. You got too much grief. Only Abbotts left now is me and Jolene. Poor thing. She didn't harm nobody. Lived sweet as she could, her and your daddy, loving each other."

Ginny lifted her eyes up to the ceiling. "You best spend all the time you can with her. Don't sit up there crying and carrying on in her face. Don't make her feel your troubles if you can help it. Bring her your brightest smile if you can, little sister. Tell her what's going on out here in the world. Jolene's casting the net of her next life, but she's holding back. She's holding on for you and your sister. Tell her about the sun shining, the birds a-singing, all the blue you seen in a single hour. Tell her about the orchards and the river. Tell her about the fresh air and most of all, tell your mama you love her and that you always will. Tell her she can go on. Sing her away. Tell her it's safe to leave you."

. . .

I BEGAN TO SPEND MORE and more hours exploring the land that edged the backwards river. Most afternoons, the river was gold with whitish-green caps. The water helped send a cool breeze for a few miles. I had been warned not to swim in it because I didn't understand its moody currents. But when I dipped my fingers into the river for the first time, a sensation went through me. The river recognized me and greeted me with easy warmth.

Mama told me that she and Daddy shared their first kiss in the currents of the backwards river. They met after dark because Daddy had been shy, and a little vain, about his missing arm back then. In the night, they'd waded, naked, into the river beneath a metallic moon. The shadows of their bodies were silver, liquid shapes on the nearly still surface of the water. Mama said that when they'd kissed, they drew some of the moonlight into themselves, swallowing its taste. When I went alone to the river, I liked to think about Mama and Daddy alive in love. Mama hadn't told me about the naked part, but when I stood at the river, the water told me.

There were only birds, insects, and shadows to survey me. When I pressed myself flat against the wet stones, the earth came up through the river and the rocks and went into me. Gold foam frothed across my bare feet and ankles. Clouds passed over my closed eyelids as I settled myself against this new world, relieved for once, to accept its older wisdom. *Come back,* the water seemed to say whenever I left.

As I walked from the river back to my grandmother's house, I thought about the last time I'd secretly visited Hinder Me Not. I'd seen a shovel leaning against my father's indigo headstone. I couldn't forget the rusted shovel, left casually by one of the maintenance men near a rectangular patch of land that had been roped off next to

Daddy's plot. Hinder Me Not was prepared to bury Mama. I knew I couldn't beg heaven to turn Mama away. She was close at the gate. The evidence of this silenced me for days.

. . .

ONE JULY EVENING MAMA AND I sat together in Ginny's good parlor. Often, it was Mama who now leaned against me, because it was too much for me to put my weight against her. It was strange, thinking that my body was the heavier one and could make her tired. We held hands. Since leaving Salt Point, there were many things I wanted to ask my mother, but I'd learned patience. My mother's helplessness flickered in the veins beneath her hands, so I pretended to be brave and believed, as my grandmother advised, that one day I would claim my strength. Bravery insists on repetition. It meant that I had to be vulnerable every day without letting anyone see. Rubbing Mama's hands with oil, I tried to distract myself from her suffering by being useful.

That evening she whispered for me to sing to her.

"But I'm not Ezra," I said, staring at the hand-painted blue flowers on Ginny's blue walls. "I can't sing, Mama. I was never good at singing."

"You could try anyway," my mother said, sighing. "It makes you feel good even when you're blue. That's what really makes singing good. It's not about whether your voice is better than somebody else's."

"How long can the blue protect us, Mama? Are there other ways for ghosts to get inside this house?"

Mama pushed herself up with care. "Your grandmother was afraid the nuns would come back and take me away. Or the foster care people. She was also afraid of her old ways. She was afraid her old self would come back and rob her of her new, chosen life.

"We've made our peace about all of that, so it does no good for me to pass our injuries on to you. My mother has worked all her life to keep from going back to prison. Maybe one day she'll tell you about it." She made herself say the last part softly, "When I'm not here."

I couldn't speak for a moment, and when I did speak again, I couldn't say anything about Mama's death, so I changed the subject.

"Sometimes when I go outside, I keep seeing blue when things aren't blue. It takes time for me to see what things really look like. I have to blink and squint until the blue goes away. It's like looking at neon signs. I almost feel sick. Maybe it's too much."

"Is it too much? I like that Ginny's beliefs acknowledge the things we can't always see. Especially things like evil. It's lovely, the way old folks can be, that my mother believes she can distract or ward evil off as if it's real. But look at what my body's doing to me."

"Mama, I know."

"The only thing I can do with all of this blue is enjoy it. Because this blue is about our belief in goodness. Maybe you should try to enjoy it too. You know that this will be your home, don't you?"

"I don't *know* her, Mama. I don't *like* her," I said, and then felt slightly bad that the words had finally come out of me. It wasn't nice to speak badly about anybody's mother, but I knew it was even worse to be saying it about my own grandmother. "She cusses all the time and always gives her opinion when nobody wants to hear it. Her teeth are always loose and the gas—it's nonstop. Her way of being a grandmother is scary."

Instead of scolding me, Mama nodded weakly. "If I'd understood what she'd gone through, maybe I wouldn't have run off with your daddy the way I did."

"She made you run off, though, didn't she, Mama?"

"Oh, no," said Mama. "Love made me run. And I ran—I flew! Your daddy and I couldn't stay here and have the love we'd found. I'd been dropped into Damascus from a cloistered world. The people here didn't like it, didn't trust me. I was awkward, shy, and had the nerve to talk like white people. The children mocked me. Even the adults rolled their eyes at me.

"After your daddy was in that accident, he didn't belong either.

284 RACHEL ELIZA GRIFFITHS

He'd shattered the way these people wanted to see him and the saintly Kindred family. He didn't want to sacrifice his life before he had a chance to live it. They couldn't stand the thought of him being anything but a hero, and it's hard for heroes to breathe. They nearly hanged him with all that talk of Legacy. Because sometimes you can go too far with that kind of thing. It makes you depend on the past and the future in a way that makes you forget how you need to be right now."

"But it wasn't his fault."

"Fault? Oh, that had nothing to do with it. It rarely ever does in a tragedy. Where you find a tragedy, you will not find justice. Though the people here might say different; and they could very well be right. These are good people. Wise people. They only let your daddy and me go because they knew we'd come back."

"But we're here because Ruby's father killed himself and they'd blame us and—"

"And I'm dying, Cinthy. We're here because I'm dying."

· · ·

THE NEXT DAY AFTER SUNSET, which I didn't like to admit I'd come to enjoy, I crept inside from where I'd been sitting on my grandmother's swing. The house was too quiet. Like Mama, my grandmother always had a radio on somewhere in the house. Carefully, I removed my sandals and crept up the tilted, crooked staircase. I was afraid that Mama had passed away. I was often afraid Mama had passed away, which made me skittish and transformed the lush landscape around me into a sort of horrorscape.

At the top of the stairs, I sighed with relief. I could hear their voices—Mama's soft and Ginny's brassy—in the bedroom. The door was ajar.

"Cinthy is a good girl, Mama," said my mother. "She has her ways, but when you get to know her, how deeply she feels the world, you'll understand. She's intelligent like her father. And sensitive, the way I was. Remember?"

"Oh, I remember," said Ginny. "You cried about everything."

"I had good reason to cry," said my mother. "After all that I went through. I was alone all of my childhood. I don't want Cinthy to go through that. I've let go of our past—yours and mine, Mama—but I need to know that I can trust you with *her* life."

"You speaking like I'm going take her out to the woodshed or something," said Ginny. "Shit, I'm a decent woman. I've made amends for the wrong I did and didn't hold my breath waiting for the world to make their amends for doing me wrong. Nobody apologized to me, for those years in that cell. Only thing I was guilty of was needing to be loved."

"I love you," said Mama.

"Jolene, I know all what I done."

"I want Cinthy to feel *wanted*," my mother was saying. "I don't know when Ezra will get here, but at least I know she's in good hands, hands that are like my own. When she comes, you'll need to love them both.

"Mama, I don't know how long I have. I don't want to leave this world. But I'm in so much pain. I want to be with my husband. I want to tell him, when I cross, that our girls were left standing inside a strong love."

"Don't worry about a thing, baby," said Ginny. "Your baby girl is so much like you. It'll be like me seeing you grow all them years I was locked up. And the other one? Don't you keep worrying over Ezra. Easy to see right away that she's strong. She takes after me."

"It was hard on me, letting her go with Caesar and Irene. But I knew that they could protect her, help her, in ways I've never done. In my dreams, I'm standing on the platform of a train station, watching the trains go by, and she's waving at me from a window. I can tell she's smiling, but she's going too fast for me to see her eyes. I have to believe," said Mama, "that my baby is safe. It's the only way that I can die. I have to use these last days to focus on the young girl down-stairs who'll have to grow up with a grief she shouldn't have to bear."

"World be like that," said Ginny. "Jesus, the world is a grief, a wrong, a miracle."

"The world is those things and so much more," said my mother. "I wouldn't have loved it any less, even with the suffering."

"Your head is so hot. Let me get you a cool cloth," said Ginny. "You've spoken too much, worrying your heart."

"Oh, I have peace," said my mother. I could hear her voice brighten. She called out to me. "Cinthy? Is that you? I hear you tip-toeing on the other side of the door, smelling like outside. Come in here with your grandmother and me, please."

I went into my mother's room. Ginny sat on the side of the bed where Mama lay under the quilt like a wisp. She lifted one hand for me to take while she slipped the other into my grandmother's palm.

"Mama, I'm giving her in trust to you now," she said, her voice dropping as she smiled tearfully into my eyes. I saw that my grand-mother's hands were shaking, but she turned to me. I wanted to run from their sad smiles, but I knew that it would hurt Mama too much. "Mama, my baby needs you. *But I will always be her mother*."

Without speaking, my grandmother stood and extended her arms to me.

. . .

LATER THAT EVENING, AFTER GINNY had bathed my mother, combed her hair, and put her to bed, I caught her wiping tears away from her eyes. When she realized I was watching her, she told me to come and join her in the kitchen. The kitchen wasn't very large, but our feelings filled the room and made it feel as though we'd been pushed inside a stuffy closet.

"Thirsty," I murmured, a little embarrassed for us both. Seeing her tears made my own eyes sting. I pushed my fingers against a pimple on my cheek.

"I don't like people creeping up on me in my own house," she said. "I'm not used to having . . . I'm not used to having family. Haven't had no family around me since your mama ran off. Guess I deserved that. Payback, you know?"

"You're my grandmother," I said. "Why do I have to call you Ginny?"

Carefully pulling off the wig she'd worn at the factory where she worked a part-time evening shift, she sighed deeply. It was a bob of black, wispy feathers, streaked with auburn highlights, like something that I'd seen on Dorothy Dandridge or Diahann Carroll in the movie magazines my sister and Lindy had once enjoyed.

"Girl, you might as well go on and call me whatever you want if it'll help you get used to the idea that you and me got a lot of time ahead together." Shaking her head and raking her scalp with her fingernails, she sighed hard. There was a fuzzy, silvery labyrinth of cornrows flat against her skull. "Lord, don't tell me nothing 'bout living or dying no more. I just don't want to know *nothing*. All I do is think about rest."

"Why don't you use some of the money we brought with us? Then you could just make your pies. They're very nice pies," I said tentatively, remembering how I'd come into my parents' bedroom as we'd packed to leave our house in Salt Point and seen Mama snatching stacks of bills from a hole in the floor of their closet, beneath my father's suits. *He never put it all in the bank,* she'd tried to explain to me while she beckoned for me to help her. *We couldn't trust them to be fair.* I remembered how heavy the money had felt in my hands, like I was picking up pieces of my father's dreams.

Ginny glanced at me. Then she smiled. "Glad you thinking about bills and savings, Cinthy, but honey I paid this house off years ago. Living don't cost me much no more. Not far as the bank or the tax man would be interested in knowing.

"If all I could do was bake pies, I'd bake too many. Nobody would want them. They'd go to waste for sure. And I know about the money, baby. Jolene told me. I told her I'd keep it in a savings account for you

and your sister. You may not want to stay in this place for too long. I
hope you don't. Jolene says you could be in college already, smart as
you are."

I watched Ginny pour herself a glass of iced tea. She sipped it,
glancing at me. She was almost shy. "I got me a smart grandbaby,"
she said after a long time.

"And I have a grandmother," I said, smiling a little. "A grandmother who cusses and uses bad language in front of me when she
shouldn't."

"You ought to try thinking of me as your family," she said, shrugging. "Cussing ain't cruel and who says I got to be nice in a world
such as this. I'm soft in my own house. Don't see no reason to change
what's kept me safe." Pushing her wig down into her scuffed patent leather purse, which she carried around everywhere, even at
home, she zipped it inside. A few stray strands stuck out like feathers through the zipper's teeth.

"Take your bath and see if you can get some rest, honey," she
said. "Maybe I'll teach you how to make a cobbler. You like cobbler?"

My eyes filled with tears as I smiled a real smile.

"Yes, ma'am," I said. "Mama used to make it for us. She used to
sing the whole time."

Ginny closed her eyes, leaning against the counter. "Praise that
child," she said, lowering her head. "Praise God for giving her to me.
Lord knows I didn't deserve her."

Ginny stood up at her full height in the sky-colored kitchen. Her
sweat had dried. In the sigh of evening, her skin carried the scent of
chickens, dust, and grit.

"Best thing a woman can learn to do," my grandmother said, "is
to feed herself some sweetness so she ain't got to wait on nobody
else to give her something she already has. You keep that in mind,
little sister. Far as I can tell, you're a Kindred *and* an Abbott. That's a
combination the world won't see again."

I turned away from Ginny's voice and walked out of the house to
the porch.

In the deepening twilight, a constellation of fireflies transmitted soft lime and yellow lights. Their pulsing floated in front of me like a portal to another world. There had to be hundreds of them, shining as they wrapped the farmhouse with light. I could hear the frogs and insects just beyond.

The more I tried not to think about Ezra, the more I saw her. Using the fireflies like connective dots, I assembled the shape of her face floating just there in front of me. I could hear her voice in my head. I felt her smile go through my skin, and it was both bright and awful because I missed her so much. I was angry that she wasn't with us, but I was beginning to understand how we all had been forced to change ourselves to survive.

I looked through the fireflies at the lush kudzu, which reminded me of Ezra's hair and how she'd always taken care with my hair. I could feel her fingers pressing oil into my braids, her fingertips circling the tips of my ears, and how she'd use her hands to turn my face to hers so that we became mirrors. Swaying, I tried to think of my life without Ezra, no Daddy, no Mama. The ache surged through my entire body.

"Magic, ain't they?" said my grandmother, pressing her hand against my shoulder.

Swallowing, I nodded as Ezra's shadow face vanished before my eyes. "We have them at home, back in Salt Point. But not like this."

"Did you catch them? You and your sister?"

"Yes, ma'am," I said. "We used to make earrings. Use them for nail polish. We would put them in jars."

"We don't catch them 'round here," said Ginny. "We let 'em be. We just enjoy them little lights they share. Don't let me catch you making nothing out of 'em. You too old for that. Let 'em fly and glow like nature wants."

"I won't touch them," I said, tears filling my eyes. For once, I didn't feel like I could float away and that nobody would care. A strong sensation, which I realized I'd never had in Salt Point, went across my face like a breath. Perhaps I did belong here.

"They don't live long, those lightning bugs," said my grandmother. "That glow in they butts is all about attraction. They got about two months to get it on before they die. Old folks say the female ones will eat the males. Not all the time but enough to make things interesting. The female will use her light to trick the male into thinking he's getting himself something sweet when it turns out that she's actually just hungry. Ain't that something? Animals can be a trip. They got to survive. Just like us."

"Yes, ma'am," I said.

"With this strong storm coming, they'll take cover soon," said Ginny. "Do you like storms? Because the rain is perfect here. Hm, I had to run all over the world just to find myself running back here 'cause I missed these storms so bad. When they locked me up, called it putting me into confinement, I spent a lot of time remembering these storms. In that dark cell, lightning flashed across the walls and the sounds of them iron doors opening and closing all around me was a little bit like thunder. God was missing from the hearts of the guards who beat me, starved me, did worse. In my cell there were no trees. I'd pretend, the way I did as a girl, about helping Noah get that ark together. I had to keep myself strong, keep my mind from blacking out. They'd left me in there with next to nothing to eat, nothing but rags to wear. They was ready to make me an animal. But that didn't happen. The more they thought they was hurting me, the more I moved around the world inside my head.

"I remembered them good-looking boys that once drove me down a straight road to nowhere 'til I barely recognized my own voice. My good times left me broke and high. The only thing I could sing when I got done with myself was about being a junkie. At first, the music I sang was about never begging nobody but myself to love me. I didn't like to sing nothing about needing a man and his mess. I liked singing about love and I didn't know—I didn't know—when I took off from here in a rush that I was running away from a pure love I'd made myself.

"Tried to find the boy who was Jolene's father but realized I didn't know who he was, where he came from; and back then I always had my legs up. They was fine, strong legs, by the way. Hm. I know you can't barely see that no more, but back in the day people would pass around a hat just so I'd show these legs off.

"I got so confused after a while. Got mixed up, got strung out. Got into the kind of trouble that I sang about looking for—then it was real. It was real as the time I served. Hard time. I ain't trying to scare you by talking to you this way, but I guess that if Jolene's forgiven me, I need to ask you to forgive me too. In our families we can pass hurt, same as we can pass new life. Baby, I don't want no more hurt passed to you."

"Grandmother," I said, nearly whispering it. My voice vanished inside the showers of her words. She pointed at stars, named birds I could not see. I thought of how Daddy had shown me how to recognize the world, how it could be spoken yet untouchable in its mystery. With each word my grandmother spoke I felt lighter, stronger, better. She trusted me the way Ezra had trusted me.

Ginny's voice went on, surfacing from her memories and their solitude.

"See, baby, you can smell the dirt, the rain's ready—goodness, we haven't had near enough rain yet this summer. If we'll get a good soaking tonight, maybe my poor tomatoes will survive."

28

WHEN I CAME UPSTAIRS, I DECIDED TO GO TO MAMA'S ROOM INSTEAD OF the little closet down the hall where Ginny had set up a cot for me. I wouldn't be able to listen to the rain if I slept in there. Already, I could feel the electricity in the air. The lightning and bald scream of thunder was something I craved, knowing I was safe inside my grandmother's sturdy farmhouse.

Pulling a thin nightgown over my head, I crept past Ginny's room, though there was no need for me to tiptoe. Her snoring rivaled a parliament of elephants.

At the end of the hall, there was a window. When lightning flashed it cast everything in a sudden light that then vanished sharply. Instead of being fearful, I smiled. There'd been a few storms in June, but Ginny and Mama had claimed that the July storms were something to see.

I went to the edge of the hallway to stand at the window, waiting for the next moment of lightning. I let my eyes adjust so that I could look down at my grandmother's front yard to the space where the oak trees wreathed a path that led out to the main road.

I was surprised to see what looked like a man on a horse there in the middle of the opening between the trees. He wore a hat that looked very old, from another time, but when he tilted his head back as if to meet my eyes, I waved immediately, because it was my father. I'd never seen him on a horse, and this one was quite large, with strange, humanlike eyes. For some reason, I knew not to call out. So I pressed my hand against the glass as the lightning traced it in rapid bursts. I wondered if my father had come from heaven or if he was a ghost, his body fully restored as it had arrived in this world at birth. Then I realized he couldn't be my father, because he was holding the reins to his horse with two hands. In my mind, I heard children crying and the sound of rushing water, louder than the rain that thundered on my grandmother's roof. When I looked again there was nothing. Wrapping my arms around my body, I felt unbearably lonely, afraid to walk into a future whose air felt too sad and shaky to let me breathe.

Pushing away my thoughts, I slipped into Mama's room, startled to hear her voice greet me.

"Hi, baby girl."

"Hi, Mama," I said. "I wanted to hear the storm. And it's too hot where she has me sleeping. Can I listen to it in here with you?"

"Of course, baby," she said. Her voice was tired, but I could tell that she was happy I'd come to her.

"Open the window a little bit, won't you? When you hear that sweet rain touching all her crazy bottles, you'll feel like you're sitting inside a symphony."

"Did you used to listen to the rain all the time when you were a girl?"

"Oh yes," said Mama. "When I knew a good rain was coming, I treated it like a friend. I'd be so excited!"

"Did Daddy like it?"

"Yes, in his way," said Mama. She paused. Her voice picked up again thoughtfully. "When we first moved to Salt Point, I'd open the windows wide when it stormed. I'd sit on the porch or stand out in the yard so I could feel it on my skin. Your father would appreciate the downpours for the way the world stopped. He liked the rain for his reading."

"Were we scared of storms when we were little girls?"

"Come over here," she said, moving just a little under the quilt. "See how the breeze has made it so cool. You can smell what's alive in the garden. You can feel the river too.

"Long ago, though anybody would say I couldn't possibly remember, I was born on a rainy day in a bed like this. Not this bed but something with feathers in it. I can actually remember how the air felt on me, how it smelled. I can remember my mother's voice speaking. It was a proud voice. Still is."

"Yes, she sure is proud," I said. "But what about Ezra and me, Mama? When we were little?"

"You would sleep through storms in Salt Point or you'd keep yourself busy around the house," she said. "But Ezra . . . Ezra would ask me if she could go outside, even when the lightning was close."

I curled against Mama. Her voice grew distant under the rumbling world beyond the window. "Did you ever wish you had a sister?"

"Oh, I don't know," said Mama in a wistful voice. "Everything I wished for I've received. I have my daughters. I've done my best with how the world has done me. Who says that anymore? In another world, we'd be sisters, you and me. In another time, you might be my mother. I'd be your daughter. In the next life, it wouldn't matter to me what I was, long as I'd get to call you mine."

"Mama," I said.

"You'll always have me," she said. "Because we love each other. In every world, this love will be the same."

"The earth always has rain," I said, yawning.

"Yes, you understand enough," said Mama. I could hear her smiling.

. . .

IN THE MORNING, OAKS WAVED beyond the window. Bands of scalloped light stenciled the periwinkle walls of my mother's bedroom. The air blowing over us lifted the sheer curtains as though the gauzy panels breathed with the wistfulness of something having passed. In the wake of hard rain, the sun was shiny. The birdsong was bold.

Like every Saturday morning since we'd arrived, there was the scent of strong coffee brewing. I listened to my grandmother's humming, down in the kitchen, not unlike the birds in the rinsed-blue air.

Without touching Mama, who was still sleeping, I moved a little so that more of the breeze could touch the skin on the top of my toes. The tinkling of wind chimes wafted up pleasantly. I remembered the riot of fireflies the evening before, the flotilla of stars above them twinkling, and how the natural world could always pull me away from the thinking part of my mind.

This was surely a river day. It was likely the storm had made the waters rise. I would try to stay outdoors, away from the thoughts that kept me up at night. A simple day beside the backwards river with a book and all the world surging around me would be enough. When I returned from visiting the river, I might walk back the long way to make sure there were flowers on Daddy's headstone. Maybe later Mama would want her hair brushed out. We could sit on the swing and wait for the floating fireflies. I knew Mama would love them.

Ginny was on the stairs, and by her breathing, I could tell that she was carrying a breakfast tray, which she often did for Mama on Saturday mornings. She was already speaking as she opened the door.

"Jolene, I can't believe you and this child slept through that storm last night! Tell me that wasn't the devil rattling his nasty teeth on my clean roof. I been up early. Got to have Mr. Davis and his grandson over here. Some of the shingles fallen, and my little myrtle over by the shed has been ripped up off its roots. Lot of broken glass out front too. Don't see why that storm had to go and do that. My jars wasn't hurting nobody.

"I swear this storm's not going to stop me today. Shit. What a mess. Like I don't already have one hundred things to do on a Saturday."

I pushed the covers back, swinging my legs over the bed. I didn't want Ginny's fussing to disturb Mama, who hadn't stirred.

"Didn't I tell you not to get in the bed with her?" said my grandmother, glaring at me in my thin gown. She set down the tray. "Who opened that window?"

"Mama. She asked me to," I said, wincing at the sharpness of her voice.

"Did you know what your mama was asking you to do? Didn't you know what she wanted, asking you to do that? You don't understand rain?" There was spit in the corners of my grandmother's crazy, unpainted lips.

I went around the bed, protectively, to Mama's side. When I pulled her hand, there was no resistance, no word from her. I could feel a little warmth but not much. I pressed my fingers at her pulse and listened with closed eyes. I said her name in my mind. *Mama?* Touching her shoulder, I noted the early breeze gentling some of the loose curls that had come undone from her thick bun of hair. The vein in her neck that I'd watched for months, like a clock, was quiet.

"Jolene?"

Ginny pushed past me. The room filled with Shalimar, whipped eggs, Nu Nile, cane sugar. My grandmother's throat whined as she drew the quilt away from Mama's face and used her fingertips to smooth her dark curls.

"Jolene?"

My grandmother's tears rolled down into her open lips as she sank on her knees against the bed. Her mouth was open, trying to draw the air out of her body. Before she could let herself do that in front of me, Ginny closed her mouth, swallowing her scream. She shook her cornrowed head, vulnerable in a way that filled me with terrible understanding. Then she buried her face in the nubby ivory chenille bedspread. Although it was only minutes, I felt as if Ginny and I were frozen inside years before either of us could move.

Mama's eyes were half-opened, abandoned.

"Jolene *knew*," said Ginny, pushing herself upright. "Not a clock in the world can hold your hand when it's your time." Her body heaved as the floorboards beneath her moaned. She crawled up the side of the bed, gathering Mama's silence against her. "Sweet Jesus, I made a pretty girl. Didn't I make a beauty? She won't have to ask this world for nothing never again."

Then my grandmother motioned for me to come by her side and close my mother's dead eyes. She guided my fingers to my mother's face. I touched the tender skin of my mother's sockets. The shock that she would not blink, would not turn her eyes to me in question, filled my mouth.

"She won't have to beg this life for one more thing. Not one more thing," sobbed Ginny. "And neither will I, have mercy. Who knew in this life that Jolene's peace could break my heart?"

. . .

HOURS LATER, MY GRIEF TURNED into something firm and inflexible. I was no longer interested in listening to, or obeying, anything that my grandmother said to me. If I allowed myself to open, to listen, I could lose the trace of my mother's voice, which I clung to while I was raging and spinning inside.

When I said she wasn't my mother and couldn't *make* me take a shower, Ginny peered through her red eyes at me, shaking her head. "You laid up next to death all night, you're going to wash yourself. And if you're selfish enough to make Jolene's death about you," she said, "then you can't be the daughter Jolene said you was."

"I'm afraid of going up there," I said.

Ginny held the stained, yellow plastic receiver of the telephone in her hand. Attached to it was about a yard of dirty, corkscrewed plastic that she could stretch as far away as the porch, if she decided she wanted to sit and talk there.

"She said you'd help me," said Ginny. "Look, I got to make these calls. Ain't much time for you to be 'fraid of nothing no more. You fighting me on the basics. You held your mama up in life, you got to hold her up at her crossing."

"Yes, ma'am," I said, feeling guilty that I was angry at her. I couldn't admit that I was angry with Mama too, for leaving me with this woman.

"We got us an understanding?"

But I was already backing out of her kitchen, away from her hoarse voice. My foot was on the step leading upstairs when I heard the grandfather clock bellowing in the good parlor. Pivoting in rage, I ran into the room, with its plastic-covered sofas and the artificial irises arranged in cheap crystal vases on the windowsills. I opened the door of the clock to stop its voice.

Ginny had followed me. She overtook me, gripping my fingers.

"No, Hyacinth, that ain't going to help nothing. That's *time*. That ain't yours. You can't stop living. You can't stop time or living 'cause they hurt your feelings. Time and feelings be damned. You got to live."

. . .

POWDERED AND DRESSED, I SAT outside on the porch. My clothes were soaked in sweat and nerves. It was dusk. Time poured like syrup. I folded my arms across my chest, using my stiff legs to push against the floor.

"Mr. Randall and his grandson coming over soon to take your mama," said Ginny, appearing behind the screen door. "Ain't you hot sitting there like that? This is country heat. I would've thought the storm would cool things down but, Jesus, it feels worse."

Turning from her voice, I stared at the low hills that repeated and repeated their green and yellow curves until they touched the deepening horizon.

"I have to go out for an hour with all these pie orders," said Ginny. "Put those pies I left on the counter in my car and roll the windows down so they don't melt. I can't lose no money. I'll need it for flowers and a little something to give Louise for singing at your mama's service. Louise don't never ask nobody directly, but everybody knows how much it costs to have an angel sing."

"An angel like my mother?" I asked. "How much did it cost her when you left her alone, left her worse than trash?"

"Only reason I'm not smacking your whole face is 'cause I see my daughter's eyes looking back at me," she said. "This is not just about some grief in you. What is wrong?"

"Will you take me somewhere and leave me with strangers?" I asked quietly. "Just tell me."

"I ain't leaving you nowhere," said Ginny, stepping outside. Her voice broke against duets of katydids. "Mercy, I want to sit. So *bad*. But I can't, not yet. If I sit down, the Lord knows I might not get *up*."

"Yes," I said in agreement. Because I couldn't tell whether it was easier to stand up or fall down, I didn't say anything else.

"It was my girlfriend Ernestine who took your mama over to white folks' charity," said Ginny. "I can't blame her for what's been done. I didn't do your mama right by what I did, but nobody on this earth is going to shame me about my baby girl. Not in this world or the next. Me and your mama came to our peace. Praise God.

"Now you better come, and come quickly, to your own senses, thinking you going to sass me on *my* porch. You're a good girl. I can't begin to imagine what it would feel like losing my mama and daddy like you have. Little sister, I know the word *sorry* don't begin to cut it. But you need to know that this damn world ain't trying to apologize for itself neither.

"Back in the day, Black folks got lost all the time. Went missing. Whole families burned together in fires, in chains. They drowned in oceans. They caught diseases or some white people's massacre pushed they bones and they names into one black hole. Sometimes miracles happened, but most of the time there'd just be a question mark. Be a wound. Be an unmarked grave. Wouldn't be nothing to be done about it but to move on. Least you got me. You sitting here with the nerve to act like I'm nothing. You ain't going to act that way. My baby raised you better."

Staring at the bony caps of my knees, I let my arms go soft and gripped the edge of the flecked wooden swing.

"I'm sorry for being disrespectful to you, I—"

"Don't be sorry," said Ginny. "But don't do it again, you hear me? Abbotts don't traffic in no kind of shame, no kind of spite. Abbotts keep close company with they souls. If you live in your soul, live near it as close as you can, you can live through just about anything. Sooner you try living that way, sooner you'll arrive at a way to go on suffering and smiling like the rest of us."

29

SOME OF THE WOMEN WHO ARRIVED AT GINNY'S SAID THAT MAMA would be *put back* while others said *called back,* and what I came away thinking was that none of the women said a word about death.

To be called back was to return home.

To be called back meant that Mama belonged to a home beyond the one she'd made on earth, had made for our family all those years in the village of Salt Point.

To be called back meant that someone else, maybe God, had a voice.

To be called back meant Mama had been listening her whole life for that voice to remind her that her time in the world was a temporary home.

The women—Miss Lyrae, Mrs. Porter, Miss Tina Lee—had arrived in a beat-up truck. When they got out of it, I saw that they were all wearing white. The dust lifted beneath their feet as they paused to take in the piles of shattered blue glass Ginny and I had swept up so that anybody who came up to the house wouldn't go away injured.

When Ginny came out to greet the women, she was wearing white. What a backwards place. Why didn't they wear black? Did it have to do with the heat?

The women walked through the darkening of Ginny's oaks to our porch. Their eyes were wet and dark. Their skin glowed against the white fabric. Quietly, I watched how they embraced my grandmother. A lavender breeze filled me, mixed with notes of herbs, lemons, memory, and homemade soap.

"Oh, honey," said Mrs. Porter, lifting her voice to my grandmother's greeting. "I'm so sorry. I know your heart is broken."

"Where is she?"

"Up in the front room."

"Where's her baby?"

"Behind you, Lyrae."

Miss Lyrae spun around and came to me. I couldn't back up in the corner of the porch without falling over the swing. She pulled me into her arms tightly. "Cinthy? You've joined a difficult club, baby, a very difficult club. My mama died ten years ago from a heart attack. I still can't seem to accept it half the time. Her presence is around just the same—loving me—just like your own mama will be near you." She drew back to hold my face between her hands. "Have mercy, what a pretty girl. You come by whenever you feel like it. You could be my daughter. I lost both of my babies years ago."

"How?" I said, looking into her eyes.

"By not letting them tell me who they really were. I was too busy wanting them to be who I thought they should be. They got their own lives now, and those lives don't include me. I respect their decisions, but I regret all of it. The way I made my peace with them was to let them go. But peace don't happen once. It's something you got to do all the time, like breathing." The woman let go of me. I couldn't help but feel as though she'd carried some piece of my heart away with her. Miss Lyrae returned to the other women, who were stroking Ginny's arms and face. Their voices were soothing.

"We're going to prepare her for Mr. Randall. Then we'll have to go and open the church," said Miss Tina Lee. "Do you want to come upstairs for the washing?"

Shaking my head, I frowned. Mama wouldn't have wanted three

strangers, much less her own mother, touching her body so intimately.

"Am I going to have to worry about you?" Ginny's head was wrapped with ivory material. Some of her pancake foundation had dripped, melting from her face onto the white blouse she was wearing, and left a thin mud stain.

"You have to be washed again too," she said. "I didn't forget."

"I already showered, ma'am. I don't want a bath."

"Didn't you sleep in that bed with your mama? *In the deathbed?*" Mrs. Porter's voice was unyielding brass. *"In the deathbed?"*

"Little sister, I'm going to draw the water," said Miss Lyrae, eyeing me. "And when I call for you, Sweet God in Heaven, you best be ready to be the daughter your mama raised."

Miss Lyrae scrubbed me herself. The bristles pulled my flesh in circles against my bones. Already, my skin carried the scent of difficult, motherless memory. The sensation made me want to scream, sigh. Cry. The entire time, Miss Lyrae was singing.

"Don't speak an evil word with this water on you," she said. "This is listening water. This is hearing water. This is water healed from the river. This water will pull the grief out of you before I pour it back into the river from where I drew it. In the river the grief will clean itself and find joy in its reunion when it flows back into the ocean."

When I stepped out of the tub, exhausted from my resistance to the entire world, I held my arms out shyly as she dried me with a fabric that felt like satin and burlap at once.

"Kneel," she said, and I knelt on my grandmother's hand-sewn rug while she poured oil into my hair and used her fingertips to work it into my scalp, where its minty scent made my entire head tingle. Her hands touching my hair made me remember Ezra. I'd have to wait for Mr. Caesar to phone to tell him about Mama. My stomach crumpled inside as I realized that I wouldn't get to hear Ezra's voice, to tell her myself. Who would hold her while she cried? I was slightly consoled by the thought of Miss Irene comforting her. Our parents were dead within months of each other and now Ezra and I had no way of knowing when we would be together again. How could I accept this?

Miss Lyrae dressed me in white clothes and wrapped my head with matching fabric. She guided me into Mama's bedroom, where the shadows of the other women stretched to the tops of the walls, folding across the ceiling. My grandmother wept quietly. There were candles everywhere, and the smell of burning sage pulled my senses inside its clarity. The women's scents and mysteries filled the room, so that it was hard for me to breathe while they sang "One Morning Soon." One of them touched the lids of my eyes and told me I must look from within.

"Open your hands, Cinthy," said Miss Lyrae. "Close your eyes."

Then she placed what felt like heavy flowers in my palms. The petals were soft and warm. In my dark vision, Mama's face glowed as I memorized the shape of her lips, lips that had always held a smile whenever I needed her. I heard Mama's voice so clearly that tears stung my eyes: *You are my mercy.*

Miss Lyrae told me to keep my eyes closed so that I could see Mama's peace in the place where it would live in me. "Learn how to reach that place," Miss Lyrae said, her voice seeming to float above me as she spoke. "You are holding your mother's heart."

· · ·

MY MOTHER LOOKS LIKE SPRING. They have covered her in flowers as though she has already been spread in a field. She rests on a bower of green-and-blue fabric. They have placed a thin gold crucifix at her throat. Her hair has been combed out and curls just past her shoulders. From the pocket of my white dress, I remove Daddy's gold-rimmed spectacles, my eyes so full of tears that I hold my father's glasses away from me so that I don't get them dirty. I touch one of the fine metal tips that once fit around his ear, remembering how carefully and lovingly he adjusted them so that he could see. I want Mama to have a part of him and for him to be with her, as they would now always be in death. I slide Daddy's glasses under a little space I see beneath her folded hands. It is like she is holding him against her breast. I take out the small seashell Ernest had given Ezra. I'd stolen this from my sister's desk before we were all forced to leave our home. I tuck it under a fold of Mama's finger. The women catch me as my knees give out from under my body.

Kiss your mother's face, the women say.

Remember her beauty, the women say.

Cry for her, they say. *Look at how she is shining,* they say. *That is the sunlight in the Promised Land. Joy will be her burden and her wings.*

30

MR. RANDALL WAS INSIDE WITH GINNY, DISCUSSING THE DETAILS FOR carrying Mama's body out of the farmhouse. I frowned as much as I could at Mr. Randall's grandson, who ignored me as he tore into the plate of barbecue on his lap.

Miss Lyrae, Mrs. Porter, and Miss Tina Lee had already left for Hinder Me Not. Miss Tina Lee had said I was welcome to come with them, but I mumbled something about staying with my grandmother. Inside, Ginny's and Mr. Randall's voices carried small talk easily between the cicadas. I knew that when Mr. Randall's grandson finished his plate of barbecue, and Mr. Randall finished his fried chicken, they'd go upstairs and lift the pallet bearing Mama's body, strewn with flowers, above their heads. As I glared at the covered truck and Mr. Randall's grandson, whose name I refused to ask, a frustration welled up under my lavender-drenched skin like a bruise.

"Like the country, youngin? You used to it yet?"

His voice rang out, sweet and male, his head still bowed over the food. I wanted him to look up and see me rolling my eyes, but he was too polite to do so. When I didn't reply, he kept on talking and chewing. "Sorry about your mama. That's real hard. Since I was little,

I been working with my paw-paw, helping to carry folks' mamas and grandmas and aunties out of they houses. Family business and all, but the way I see it, we all family 'round here."

"I don't know anybody," I said.

"Your grandmama in there," he said, glancing up at me like I wasn't making any sense. "Man, I miss mine. I miss mines every day. Nothing better than a grandmama, for sure."

"I barely know her."

"Don't matter," he said, pushing food into his mouth.

I kissed my teeth hard.

He shook his head before he swallowed. "You know how lucky you is to still have her? To be having them pies she be making? Shoot, everybody like Miss Virginia 'cause she don't take no shit off nobody."

"So you mean to tell me that you'd be fine with spending your whole life here carrying dead people out of their homes?"

Shrugging, he licked the tips of his fingers. "How old are you?"

I folded my arms across my chest.

"Right," he said. "You don't know shit, plus you got a few years of required living here in Damascus before you can take off for the moon. Maybe by then you won't want to, if you gave it a chance. This a pretty place."

"I'm just not used to it."

"That's okay," he said, his voice softening as though we were sharing a secret. "But if you can just let yourself love it a little, I think you'd like it. This where you and your people from. That's something right there."

He placed his plate down respectfully next to his feet on the step. His polished Sunday shoes looked too rigid for the ease of his body. "Man, a piece of pie would sure be nice," he said, smiling.

"Do you want some?"

"Ain't no room," he said, patting his stomach. His gentle eyes took me in. "You look real nice in that fabric. Your face is beautiful."

"I don't usually walk around like this," I said, flushing at his directness. "I mean they made me wear this stuff."

"They call me Will," he said, pulling his body straight and squaring his shoulders.

"Cinthy."

"Yeah, I know," he said, smacking his hands together before he drew a pair of immaculate white gloves out of the pocket of his pressed pants. "Cinthy, you going to need to have some friends 'round here. You going to need at least one friend, so it might as well be me."

Then he went into the house, as if on cue, as if there were a chime that only he and his grandfather could hear. His young shadow met his grandfather's silhouette at the bottom of the steps before they went up the stairs.

Ginny appeared in the door. She pushed open the screen and came out to me. She didn't say anything, but she was shaking.

There were a few fireflies. I tried to focus on them.

When I looked at the door again, they were coming out, speaking quietly now and then to each other. *Easy now, yeah? Slow down, son. Yeah, Paw-Paw, I got her. Move it on that side a bit, son. My arms is sore today. Yessir. Easy like I showed you, yeah? This gal light as a feather. Poor thing. Pull it up that way; don't drop none of them flowers, son. Not a one. Lift your shoulders like me. See that, boy? Yessir, but I can't see too much in the dark. The dark don't got nothing to do with this, son. Told you before that this is all about respecting a life.*

They carried Mama down the steps solemnly, slowing so that we could look at her.

"Jesus," said Ginny, clutching my arm.

In that early starshine, I stared down at Mama's veiled shadow. Lifting my eyes to Will's face, I was startled by the tears streaming down his strong, brown cheeks.

"Church open?" said Mr. Randall.

"Lyrae, Tina Lee," whispered my grandmother. "They all over there."

Then my breath drew itself inside me like a bit of dark glass. Without speaking, I wrapped my arms around my grandmother.

"All right then, Ginny," he said, nodding. "A real pretty gal going home. A fine woman, truly. Remember they don't never leave us. God's got her."

My mother's silent head trembled a little between his arms.

"Out of my home and into the Lord's house my daughter goes to that great table," said Ginny. "We can't leave the dead alone and they can't leave us. They can't leave us."

"Amen," said Mr. Randall. Then he said something to Will, who pivoted automatically in the direction that he needed to, so that it wouldn't be awkward to lift Mama's body into the clean bed of the truck.

Pulling down a metal ledge of the truck, they loaded Mama into the back. Will lifted the ledge and locked it. The sound was so normal I was horrified. They'd loaded my mother's body inside there like she was furniture. It made me remember how Mr. Caesar had driven up to our home in Salt Point with my daddy's burned body in the back. They'd driven Daddy away in a truck too. The noise of the car door in Salt Point and the click of the truck's safety lock here in Damascus collided violently in me.

I ran to the back of the truck and began to pound on it with my fist. The fabric fell away from my head. Under a growing canopy of fireflies, I tore up handfuls of grass. Clawed dirt. Shuffling painfully towards me, Ginny tried to throw her heavy arms around me. Sweat beaded my throat, twisting around my neck as I thrashed. I threw my cries into the dust. The taillights of the truck flickered red, and, worried that I'd knock my grandmother down, I sank down in the dust.

Across the gravel of my grandmother's yard, Mama's flesh was carried out of our lives.

In the dust of my people, the steel of my life strikes the flint of my memory.

Here is the glowing shirt my father once wore over his bones, and

the education that fit around his ribs like armor. I remember his patience, and how he taught me to take my time with every test, every
story. I am my father's patience. Here is Mama escaping through
the window, her suffering dissolving in the low yellow moonlight
of the world while faraway stars blaze like oceans. I am the light in
the bones beneath the sea, rising to meet the sky; I remember what
those bones believed. The songs inside shells, the children who became coral, pearls, and anchors.

Do you see how the hard land glittered around the foundation of
the house my mother and my father built for me? Do you remember
the blood? I am Theodore, Alma, Calliope. Do you see how my great-
grandparents kissed those schoolchildren they could not save from
their dream? Do you remember our blood?

There is a memory so old it has known better than to trust us
with its full face.

I am in the blood of that, the flare of firelight my great-grandfather
admired before the white men shot him through his eyes. I am the
eternity he cradled in his arms as he crossed. I am the smoke curling
from the earth where indigo headstones wait for justice and sublime,
undisturbed rest. I am but one voice—and there are countless dark
women who live in the rivers, ashes, moons, and oceans. I remember when they rolled my name against the stars until I expanded. I
remember what I was before flesh—the blood of unafraid loving, of
love and its afterlife.

And somewhere with her flashing eyes and her fist raised like a
black nova against the horizon, my sister is making her way to our
people.

Do you know how long our blood will stain this history? She is
protected by our fathers, our heroes, our mothers, our power. She is
a force of new remembering. And she will return for me.

Ginny's clear voice suddenly rose beneath the oaks. There was
a song we'd lived, a song we both knew. And it would go on, rolling
along the score of our black bones. Joining my raw voice to my grandmother's, I stretched out my hand and it brushed Ezra's face in the

night. I heard her singing too, her lungs pushing her voice across the evening sky to me.

Sing where blood yields.

I stood up now, singing our names back into an old song that burned as clean as the heart of a man who'd given us his word, his life and blood. His history would carry me in its arms across the river one day. My family had known, had believed, that I was strong enough to remember who I was and the power through which I had arrived.

Surrounded by incandescent ancestors, I would praise what it took to sing, to have the laughter and the nerve to devour love's bittersweet feast.

Acknowledgments

The love of my mother and father is the spine by which I am formed and breathe.

Mom, you taught me how to love by your example. I am letting the world see.

Dad, your sincere attention, care, and support continue to guide me when I feel afraid.

I'll never forget the power you each have placed inside the belief of living by one's word and actions. The language I have learned as a daughter and a woman comes from the love you gave to each other and to our family. I love you both forever.

This book exists because of the wisdom and wonder of the village of communities that raised me:

My family—

Mom (1952–2014), Dad, Chris and Leigh-Anne, CJ, Michele, Adam and Jeff, Melissa and Eumir, Peggy Manel, Jacqueline Deneen, Ellen, Deborah, Carolyn, Arthur, Darren, Harvey, Elyse, Kandasi, Wanetta, Pinky, Michelle. And all of the cousins on every side! Uncle Ronald: I grieve your early departure from this world but I know that the love you gave this family means that you are with us always. Aunt Stephanie, Beloved Godmother: Your laughter, your trust, and the music of your brass bangles are my talismans. I'll always hear your last words. Thank you for showing me how to be bold and to laugh with my entire mouth.

Melissa: The sisters who live in this story would not exist without my love for you. The way you shine keeps my heart on the dance floor.

Kamilah Aisha Moon: Rise, rest in love, my sister. I did not get to place this book or story in your soft hands but know that we are always holding hands, ever joined in our solidarity and poetry. Forever you will be Stevie Wonder–lovely to me. Your sudden farewell has changed me forever. *girl, girl, girlgirlgirl*. Meet me on that porch at eighty anyway, the way we'd planned, and tell me what you've seen wherever you are, sweet star.

The lives and powers of my elders—James Baldwin, Lucille Clifton, Audre Lorde, Toni Morrison—sing their truths, joys, and visions in the language they forged from the flesh of their words and lives. When I thought of surrender, they listened to my tears until I could stand up.

Walter Mosley—may I never forget the kindness, humor, and encouragement of our friendship. Thank you for reminding me of craft. Thank you for your genius, for your reading, and reading, and reading, and reading of my pages. Those early drafts would have never moved and leapt without your clear eyes and voice.

Sheldon Itzkowitz, PhD, ABPP, and Garrett Deckel, MD, PhD—your counsel and support kept my heart and head grounded in the name of resilience and possibility. Dr. Itzkowitz: The house will always greet you as part of our family. Your care has shown me how to trust the truth of the stories I have lived. Thank you.

There are many individuals and organizations that have welcomed and supported me over the years. I would like to thank the following individuals here for professional and/or emotional support: Chris Abani, Jeffery Renard Allen, Sarah Arvio, Paul Auster, Jill Bialosky, Nicholas Boggs, Mahogany L. Browne, Marie Brown, Margaret Busby, Christian Campbell, Jan Castro, Rachel Cobb, Edwidge Danticat, Toi Derricotte, Kiran Desai, Natalie Diaz, K.A. Dilday, Barbara Dimitratos, Cornelius Eady, Morgan Entrekin, Danielle Evans, James Fenton, Nikky Finney, Nick Flynn, Suzanne Gardinier, Aracelis Girmay, Angela Guerra, David Haynes, Rufus Scott Heath, Siri Hustvedt, Marcus Jackson, Mitchell Jackson, Marlon James, Riis Laurentiis, Canisia Lubrin, Valeria Luiselli, Nina Angela Mercer, Dante Micheaux, Ella Montclare, John Murillo, Steven and Annie Pleshette Murphy, Darryl Pinckney, Maya Pindyck, Iain Haley Pollock, Katie Raissian, Nicole Sealey, Taryn Simon, Oberon Sinclair, Safiya Sinclair, Tracy K. Smith, Suphala, Cheryl Boyce Taylor, Nafissa Thompson-Spires, Margaret Porter Troupe, Quincy Troupe, Sally Van Doren, Jenisha Watts, Phillip B. Williams, and L. Lamar Wilson.

Versions of what would (finally) become this book took place with the support of these institutions: Cave Canem Foundation, Kimbilio, the Robert Rauschenberg Foundation, the Civitella Ranieri Foundation, and Yaddo.

One of my great fortunes in this journey has been to have the faith of two incredible editors, Robin Desser and Caitlin McKenna. Robin: You said *Yes*. You recognized me right away in that immediate and necessary way that is crucial for a debut author. Your insight and voice carried us through an electric passage of ideas and imagination. For this alchemy, I have such love and respect for you. Caitlin: The gift of having you as my editor is indescribable. Your questions, your clarity, your warmth and wonder are the flare I carry to this finish line. I am filled with appreciation and beyond elated. I truly can't say *Thank you* enough. I must praise the Random House team too: Tangela Mitchell, Rachel Rokicki, Clio Seraphim, Noa Shapiro. I am also delighted to praise the brilliance and kindness of my editor Dr. Yvonne Battle-Felton, and my publisher Jocasta Hamilton, and the entire John Murray Press team in the United Kingdom.

My agent and friend, Jin Auh, took me on in 2017. Her incredible faith and encouragement have been great gifts. Her care, respect, and brilliance gave me the ability to see something greater than I ever would have believed. Jin, what a beautiful journey we are on! I want a fuller word than *gratitude* for how I feel about you. One day I will find it. Thank you always. I would also like to express my thanks to the entire Wylie Agency, and across the sea: Jennifer Bernstein and Tracy Bohan.

Salman, let our love show this impossible world that nothing is impossible. I love you with every heart and story that has ever lived in me and every story that is to come. Salman—my joy, my home, my joy, my dream, and my miracle—*Always*.

About the Author

RACHEL ELIZA GRIFFITHS is an artist, poet, and novelist. *Seeing the Body* (W. W. Norton, 2020) was selected as the winner of the 2021 Hurston/Wright Foundation Legacy Award in poetry, was the winner of the 2021 Paterson Poetry Prize, and was nominated for a 2020 NAACP Image Award. She is the recipient of fellowships including Cave Canem Foundation, Kimbilio, and the Robert Rauschenberg Foundation, and was selected as the 2020 Stella Adler Poet-in-Residence. Griffiths is also the image designer for the libretto *Castor & Patience,* written by Tracy K. Smith and composed by Gregory Spears, which premiered at the Cincinnati Opera. Her work has been published in *The New York Times, The New Yorker, The Paris Review*, and *The Georgia Review*.

rachelelizagriffiths.com

About the Type

This book was set in Fairfield, the first typeface from the hand of the distinguished American artist and engraver Rudolph Ruzicka (1883–1978). Ruzicka was born in Bohemia (in the present-day Czech Republic) and came to America in 1894. He set up his own shop, devoted to wood engraving and printing, in New York in 1913 after a varied career working as a wood engraver, in photoengraving and banknote printing plants, and as an art director and freelance artist. He designed and illustrated many books, and was the creator of a considerable list of individual prints—wood engravings, line engravings on copper, and aquatints.